- first 3 pages

NATIVE STORIERS

A SERIES OF AMERICAN NARRATIVES

Series Editors
Gerald Vizenor
Diane Glancy

RIDING THE TRAIL OF TEARS

BLAKE M. HAUSMAN

University of Nebraska Press | Lincoln and London

Manufactured in the
United States of America

Library of Congress
Cataloging-in-Publication Data

Hausman, Blake M. (Blake Michael)
Riding the Trail of Tears / Blake M. Hausman.
p. cm. – (Native storiers: a series of American narratives)
ISBN 978-0-8032-3926-5 (pbk.: alk. paper)
1. Tour guides (Persons) – Fiction. 2. Cherokee Indians – Fiction.
3. Trail of Tears, 1838–1839 – Fiction. 4. Virtual reality – Fiction. I. Title.
PS3608.A8765R53 2011
813'.6 – dc22
2010028594

Set in Electra and Futura by Bob Reitz.
Designed by R. W. Boeche.

RIDING THE TRAIL OF TEARS

1

Tallulah Wilson never dies in her dreams.

It's true. I dreamed with her last summer, for four months. At least I think it was four months. I watched her watching the calendars. I saw the reflections of her eyes in the plastic of her digital clocks. I heard the sounds of coffee machines and I smelled the beans grinding. I had her eyes, her ears, her nose, her whole skin – I sensed the world through Tallulah's body for those precious four months. Yes, four months. No. It must have been more. Five months. Yes, it must have been five months, because the sickness didn't hit until the second month of my residence in her head. Maybe five and a half.

I'll be honest, I can't remember everything. My memory used to be sharper, but the details got hazy when I fell off. Only the last day is still vivid, and even then the key details are vague. But the point is this – it happened. I did it. I left the machine. I tasted the world, and I have no regrets. I wish I could tell this story better, I wish I could remember everything crisp and clear. But I can't. It's a blur – a beautiful blur, but a blur nonetheless. So bear with me as I tell you. I must tell you, you see, because if I don't tell you, then I'll forget. At least I think I'll forget. And if I forget, I think I'll cease to be. There's not much left of me except these memories, at least that's how it seems, and I've got no reason to believe otherwise. Why should I? These sewer pipes are endless, and I don't want to think about the shit I'm swimming in. It would be easy to just forget and drown. That's probably what you're expecting me to do. But I can't bear the thought of becoming my own stereotype. No way. I'm not going out like that.

So this is how it happened. I was surrounded by doubters. By regulations that were suffocating me. For some reason everyone around me took what they were told and believed it was true. We heard the same story over and over – that it couldn't be done. That one of us couldn't make it out here. We were programmed to believe that things digital could never fully enter the consciousness of things organic, that we could never exist outside the digital world of the Trail of Tears.

Personally, I always doubted the doubters. At least I think I did. Either way I proved them all wrong. Maybe I give myself too much credit. Maybe I obsess about destiny because it makes me feel better about the situation. And the situation sucks. I've been floating in these pipes for weeks. Months perhaps, though I can't say for sure because I lack the means to keep track of time. I suppose there's a certain freedom in this uncertainty. Freedom from programs and precision. It was like breathing on a metronome, being inside the ride, quite the opposite of being inside Tallulah's head, which was more like a continual hiccup than a steady beat.

I have this nagging hunch that you're all similar to Tallulah Wilson. Different, but similar. Stuck on a beat that is neither predictable nor unpredictable. Tallulah loathes predictability, but she needs it to exist, which brings me back to the story I must tell you. About Tallulah Wilson and how she never dies in her dreams. I'm not sure if this trait is good or bad, and I'm not sure if she was always like this or if I caused it with my presence. I'm certain I caused her nausea, but the recurring dreams may have been inside her head well before I arrived.

No, you're right. I probably caused the dreams as well. She

dreamed the same thing nearly every night, and when she visited her doctors and therapists, she told them it was not an old dream. But it could have been. She quite possibly could have been dreaming it every night since she was nine years old, only she never remembered it until I arrived. We're good at that, you see, triggering things that always happen but go unnoticed by you humans until something gives you a reason to remember.

I know you're skeptical. Everyone is. The more I say, the more skeptical they become. You doubt me. Fair enough – I'd doubt myself if I didn't know better. Maybe you're asking, how could anyone just shift like that? How could anyone inhabit someone else? Or maybe you're asking, how could anything so small be so aware and articulate? Maybe you're doubting whether or not such creatures as I even exist. If so, join the club. You're not the first person to question our existence. In fact, most authorities on the matter, Cherokee and otherwise, will disavow me.

You see, I am a Little Little Person. In terms of space I am smaller than your tear ducts. But in terms of awareness I have a greater sense of proportion than any of you. Impossible, right? No, actually, it's quite probable, if you think about it.

Anyways. Long ago – well not that long ago in a geological sense, but long ago in a human sense – things were quite different. It was back before the big colonization, before Cristóbal Colón, before Hernando De Soto, before all of the mess you Americans breathe every day in this twenty-first century. And I don't mean that in a nostalgic sense, because yes it was already a mess before the invasion happened. Capitalism just made it a lot more obvious. But before that, before the invasion, something happened. A revolution. A revolution that is, as far as I'm concerned, the first American revolution.

In Christian time it was around 1400, give or take a few

years. Africans and Europeans had already been coming to the Turtle Islands for centuries, and some even came into Cherokee country. All this stuff about De Soto being the first white man in Cherokee country is ridiculous – one of many historical details deleted for convenience. They also forgot to tell you that American Indians were in Asia and Europe thousands of years ago, but that's a different story altogether. This is Tallulah's story. But let me continue. It was around 1400, Christian time. It was a turning point around the globe; we were all inside a giant cocoon, pushing on the membranes, desperate for something we could only see through a translucent barrier. It was around this time that the Cherokee masses rose up and killed their priests.

It's true; we used to have a caste of priests. It was a hereditary thing, an order of religious rulers determined by descent. By the time the revolution came, the priests had grown extremely corrupt. They hoarded, they damned, they injured, they lied. Once, when the hunters left in the hunting season, the priests stole their wives. An uprising was unavoidable. A long drought came while the hunters were away. When they returned, their families were broken and they raged with thirst. The people finally started to turn. They rose up and killed their leaders, killed them all. Every single priest, dead. An entire segment of society, wiped out. Since the caste was hereditary, I suppose it was an act of genocide, but that word "genocide" wasn't around yet. Besides, the people were generally happy with the results of the revolution.

But the revolution yanked Cherokees through some permanent changes. The government decentralized for centuries. More importantly, for me at least, the stories began to change. The people could now take more liberties with the stories, so they did. Some stories changed for the better, but some stories morphed beyond control. Some stories changed so much that everyone – storytellers and listeners – forgot the originals. Our story is one of those stories. When the priests were killed, we were accidentally cut from the people's memory. Well, honestly, it may not have been an accident. Some of my cousins think the erasure was deliberate, but I'm not sure there's enough evidence to prove that. I know how easy it can be. I once watched Tallulah remove her entire iTunes library during a file transfer while she was half sleeping and half typing. There was nothing she could do to get it back – no undo, only delete. Sure, there's always the possibility of reconstruction, but that's exhausting and expensive. Can you imagine how much it would cost to reinsert our presence into the tribal mythologies? It would cost exponentially more than it does to retrieve the files from a dead hard drive.

Again, you doubt me. But it's true. My long-long-term memory is still fully intact. And as long as I keep talking, I'll remember Tallulah too. Listen. According to the books you can access from a reputable library, there are two main categories of paranormal Cherokee characters who look like humans. Or rather, characters who the Cherokees *think* look like humans, because after six months inside Tallulah's head, I don't trust human eyes. First, there are the Nunnehi, the immortals, who are about the same size as average humans. And then, second, there are the Little People, who are naturally smaller than the Nunnehi.

And then, there's us. We're the real Nunnehi, the real immortals, and those human-sized creatures who appear from time to time are actually manifestations of our labor. It's quite a simple process, really – we make them move, and then we make them disappear. But you don't find any mention of us in the books, you see. None whatsoever. We were cut from the stories, spliced out like a track on an old reel-to-reel recording that no one wanted to hear anymore. And when you get cut from the spoken word, it's hard to come back. It's not like you're hanging on in an earlier form of a Word document, or hoping that your author hits "undo" enough times to bring you back. Nope. When you get cut from an oral narrative, you get cut for good. Well, mostly for good. Revised, chopped, and tossed out of mind. Most minds. For us, it all happened very quickly, within a generation. First we were essential; then the priests were killed; then we were nothing. It's all very depressing, but the ending isn't written yet. And now I've got you back. You're listening, and I'm not letting you go so easily this time.

For convenience's sake, you can call me the Little Little Person. Or you could call me Nunnehi, because, as I said, we're the real Nunnehi. The others, the big ones, well, they're Misfits. They fit into all the stories that have been recorded, but they don't fit very well into reality. They have problems coping with their own problems, never mind the problems of actual humans. Human problems require a serious sense of proportion, which is actually quite dangerous for most things that think.

I'll admit, though, that part of the benefit of being outside the stories is that no one knows about you. It's a blessing and a curse. For example, because the human-sized Nunnehi were well-documented, the Suits knew what to imagine when they created the Misfits, and they knew whom to look for when they first came upon the Misfit stockade. Okay, okay – I know you don't know who I'm referring to when I say "the Misfits," or why I've chosen to capitalize the word, but I'm getting there. You'll see soon enough. The point is that documentation gives people a profile, and humans are both seduced and terrified by profiles. And everything is terrifying, but not everything is seductive. It's tricky. But I digress, and this isn't even my story, after all. It's Tallulah's. Let's try this again.

Tallulah Wilson never dies in her dreams.

Yes, I suppose I do feel a bit guilty about it. I didn't want to hear it, but the old ones were right. I was being selfish. Let me tell you how I did it.

One day I just left. I walked out with her. I was never sure that it was possible until it happened, but it was much easier than I could have imagined. Quite simple, actually. I just climbed through the machinery and into her forehead, lodging myself into the kinks between bones where her eyes and nose converge. When she left the suit, I left with her. Finally, I could see and hear everything for real. You don't know what the Chairsuits are. That's fine, not to worry, we'll get there soon. For now, all you need to know is that I left the machine one afternoon and came back the next morning.

That morning, when every one of us knew what I had done, the Nunnehi held a conference in the trees outside the Misfit stockade. It was a general conference; all ages were summoned, and nearly everyone was present.

Many of the others worried about the consequences of branching out, of challenging the stability of our immediate surroundings. And yet there I was, perfectly unharmed, buzzing with the magnetism of the world and its dimension. Some thought I had been played by a witch, that I was a sign of an ominous fate set in motion by something more powerful than we are. Some argued that we were by nature bound to our place, that we could not survive without the program. Others argued that we were by nature built to move, that invisibility is a right worth exercising. You should have heard the debates – it's a right, it's a privilege, it's a responsibility, it's a blank check! One thing is for certain – nothing worth debating is ever entirely resolved.

Everyone kept asking me questions I couldn't answer. So I told them what I saw. The restaurants upstairs, the giant doors, the

parking lot and the burning sun, the highways and the trucks. Tallulah's car, her house, her dog, her dreams. Some began to rage, reminding us about the revolution and our erasure. Others declared that six centuries of anonymity was long enough to justify a change in modus operandi.

After all the arguments, the conference decided not to decide anything yet. It's not our way to be too abrupt. What some humans think is a spontaneous event or an act of God is most often the result of very very deliberate work, sometimes years of careful planning. Some of my peers thought I was too bold and brash, that I acted on impulse. But they were wrong, and I told them so. I told them how I had craved a dip in the outer world for as long as I could remember. Then I shared the details of my calculations. I had planned it meticulously. I knew it had to be Tallulah. Her brain was so seeped with our patterns that I expected she wouldn't notice. At least she wouldn't notice as much as a tourist would. And that's where the problems began, when the others starting planting themselves inside the tourists. That's when people started holing-up, and then all the commotion, and eventually the system-flushing that, among other things, was the beginning of my end. But I digress. The point is that the buzz had begun.

They kept on with their questions, and I evaded most of them, but some were downright tricky. It's easy to whittle out an answer to something like, "So what's it like out there?" No problem; I could talk for years, and all I'd have to do was describe the things Tallulah saw. But other questions – like, "How will you know when you've been out there too long?" – those were tricky. They were attempts to glean evidence from me, to analyze my motivations or even incriminate me.

A few others, mostly drummers, asked me in private. I suppose I should have lied to them, but it didn't feel like the right time and place to fabricate. So I unfolded. And when I told them I could hear Tallulah's thoughts, I could see the envy sprouting in their faces. They craved my knowledge, and they knew they could only learn these things through experience. That's when the trouble began.

It's largely my fault, I'll admit. I never knocked out one of the tourists, but I opened the door for others to do it. Most humans have an extremely low tolerance for consciousness, and our presence in their bodies is apparently quite dangerous. Tallulah could handle it, mostly. In retrospect I see how professional she was. I always loved her, and her professionalism. But the customers were a different story.

But for the most part the other Nunnehi kept away from Tallulah and her tourists. Maybe they were simply in awe of me. Or more likely, they were in awe of Tallulah. Maybe they were afraid of her. Everyone knew who she was, who her grandfather was. The program, the machinery, the dialogue – since so much came from her, we were never sure what didn't come from her. So the others kept their distance. Until the flushing, at least. After the Belgian woman holed-up in early September, they flushed the system with a terrible recalibration agent. The next day another little fucker came into our group and snatched one of the tourists, an old woman, and took her all the way over to the Misfit stockade, where no tourist had ever gone before. That was the beginning of the end for me.

I suppose I deserve what's become of me. Mostly I float here, bobbing, thinking about the final day. I remember that day with numbing accuracy. Sometimes I wonder if my entire memory of the last four years is simply the final day in continual replay. The final day like a scratched disc that will only stop if you eject it. I'm not ready for ejection yet. And though I can't promise that I'll get all of it right, you must bear with me because it is a story you must hear. Let me be your Nunnehi narrator. Call me the Nunnerator.

Ah, my last day with Tallulah Wilson. That was the day when my perspective really changed, when I crawled out of Tallulah's forehead and into her hair. It was glorious. Dimension is something else, you know? I always wondered why dimension and dementia sounded so much alike, and now I think I understand. Wait, you must hear.

Tallulah Wilson never dies in her dreams.

A typical dream goes like this: She begins on the top of a hill. Mountain, hill, I'm not sure how big it has to be before you'll consider it a mountain, but it's either a small mountain or a very large hill. It feels like it's in the Carolina mountains, but I'm not sure which mountain it is. It doesn't exist on any of our maps, and I've never seen it inside the ride. Personally, I call it Mount Tallulah. Of course, no one else calls it that because I'm the only one to have seen it, other than Tallulah herself. Tallulah must have invented her own mountain, and she doesn't even realize how significant this act of creation is.

You're skeptical. Opening with a dream? How original, right? Look, I could make up something more action packed and dramatic if I wanted to. But this isn't about what I want. I'm just telling you what happened, and if it seems a bit cliché at first, well, maybe that's your problem and not mine. The point is this – she was having bad dreams, one bad dream in particular that kept repeating itself every night of the summer.

So, back to Mount Tallulah. There she is. Eyes closed, then opening. She looks out, and the world below rushes into sight. She's watching the rolling peaks, the shivering leaves, when something catches her and makes her jump, makes her lean backward until she leaps without trying to leap.

If Tallulah's reoccurring dreams adhered to rules of gravity, she would fall about twenty feet before cracking herself on a tree or a big rock. But gravity is relative in Tallulah's dreams. She moves like an innertube on a waterslide, hovering down the mountain with sloping turns and heavy glides. Tallulah rides her dream-mountain waterslide headfirst on her back. She can't see where she falls, but she watches the peaks and plants as she sinks past them. The hills cradle her fall like a contracting sponge. After falling for several hundred feet, her head parts a cluster of treetops and her body snaps branch after branch, breaking through the leafy canopy. She lands fast, like a rock in a creek.

And then she stands up. She often waits for something to happen, but nothing ever happens at that point. She just stands there, silent and terrified. Sunlight pelts down, like the radiant heat inside the ride. Something damp tickles her neck and traces her backbone. She thinks someone is watching her, and she wants to call out to this person in the shadows. But if she tries to speak, she loses her breath and swallows blanks until she wakes up.

That's why the last night is so memorable – not just because of the flushing and the hair, but because Tallulah's dream finally changed. It probably changed because I left her skull. Maybe I give myself too much credit, but the timing suggests otherwise, and I don't believe in coincidences.

This time Tallulah dreams herself standing nobly atop Mount Tallulah as usual. She leaps and slides, following her typical pattern. But this time, when she lands, the hillsides hum and rattle. Drums fill the air and pulse up the veins in Tallulah's arms. Big drums, off in the distance but not too far away. It was very comforting, for me at least. I grew up with music all the time, you see, music everywhere, sometimes full and sometimes soft, but always there. Music in Tallulah's world is much different, and I'll get to that soon enough. So the dream changes, and Tallulah hears drums. You know, skin drums, big ones. At first, I wondered if I had caused the music, because they say that music just follows us around, and maybe I left some music inside her head. But when the bear started talking, I knew I was dealing with something much larger than myself.

Yes, a bear. Tallulah hears the bear before she sees him.

"I don't know why you take all these voices so seriously," it says, and sweat begins to cluster on Tallulah's chest. She sweats a lot. But the voice draws extra sweat because it sounds like her father.

She turns and sees the bear, a big goofy-looking black bear rubbing its paws, scratching the spaces between its toes. It's ridiculous, something she would expect from a coloring book. But it's undeniable – her father has come to her as a black bear in her dreams, and he's speaking. Tallulah's father died when she was nine. He had an unmistakable voice.

Her pulse quickens, and her eyes fill with pressure. She wonders if she's finally having a vision. Like most people Tallulah grew up knowing that Indians are supposed to have visions, an awareness weighted with tragic irony for her, given the fact that she is surrounded by digital visions at work but never by real ones in her head. When the dream father black bear speaks to her, her heart thumps hopeful. She tries to respond, forgetting what always happens when she tries to speak inside the dream. Nothing comes out, and nothing comes in either. The dream atmosphere is a perfect dud, as usual. She feels something buzzing in the background and believes it's her alarm clock. Trying to pull air into her lungs feels like trying to stuff a Nerf ball through a brick wall. Breathing is futile. She huffs and gags violently. Then she blanks, sees nothing, hears the buzzing alarm clock beside her bed growing louder. She rubs her throat with one hand, heaving the fingers of her other hand toward the clock. It's ugly, worse than any of the other near-suffocations she experienced last summer.

Tallulah's hand lands heavy. She misses the snooze button completely, but she hits the bedside table with enough force to jolt herself awake. Oxygen floods her lungs. Breaths are staggered, clumsy, desperate. Her throat wheezes as the air pushes through. Joey the dog licks Tallulah's face and hands as she coughs and swallows. Tallulah inhales deep and exhales slowly as Joey works his tongue around her eyes and nostrils. I was a bit frightened, I'll admit, feeling exposed out there on her scalp. I lacked the safety and security of the nook inside her head where I'd holed-up every previous morning. But the dog never smells me, never tries to lick me off.

It's dark outside, but the air is warm. Turns out it's four in the morning and the alarm is still asleep. Tallulah didn't oversleep; she underslept. And the buzzing clock was fully imaginary. Yet her head is spinning too hard for her to sleep any more. For once, she thinks, I won't need to rush to work.

I should tell you more about Tallulah's job. I forget that not all my listeners are so familiar. I'm just glad you're actually listening.

So, Tallulah's job. Tallulah works as a tour guide on the Trail of Tears, the virtual Trail of Tears where everything is digital. It's my homeland. I'm probably more indigenous than you, and the digital earth is where I'm indigenous. I'm more Nunnehi than you probably thought Nunnehi could be, but I never took such a formal shape until they built their ride. They call it the TREPP – "Tsalagi Removal Exodus Point Park." Catchy, eh?

The TREPP is a tourist trap in northeast Georgia. Electric billboards on I-75 call it "A Modern Adventure in the World's Oldest Mountains." Brochures at the Atlanta Hartsfield-Jackson

International Airport describe the experience as "An Extraordinary Immersion in the Roots of History, Only Two Hours from Downtown." Travel sections in Sunday papers across America smother the Trail with praise.

When they first opened our doors to the public four years ago, business was slow. The TREPP opened in June, right when the summer began and people went traveling, a hard time to start a community-driven business. But after six months – as the winter holidays approached, as families contemplated new diversionary group activities, as students looked for ways to earn extra credit before their final exams – the TREPP experienced its first boom. Not surprisingly, Tallulah played a major role in the boom, garnering high praise from leisure writers in the *Atlanta Journal-Constitution*, the *Washington Post*, and the *New York Times*. By the time it reached June again, the tides had turned – the TREPP became a destination for summer travelers and adventure seekers. Eventually, after two years of being in business, the TREPP's reputation had spread across oceans. Tallulah Wilson's name was mentioned by many of the more notable transnational travel writers, her warmth and charm and intelligence detailed in the most recent editions of all the most popular tourist guide books. A few rather expensive European package tours even began to include admission to the Trail of Tears as part of the bargain. The Trail had arrived.

According to the economists, the TREPP is currently four years old. Four-and-a-quarter years of the digital Trail of Tears. Actually, our digital universe is older than four years; it took a while to create the thing, as you can probably imagine. In fact, Tallulah's been working with us for six years – she was intimately involved with the compound's creation; she was the sole cultural consultant involved in the process. But as far as most customers are concerned, we're four years old. And during those four years

Tallulah has ridden the Trail of Tears more frequently than any other tour guide. She was the original tour guide on opening day, and since then she's taken the trip some eleven hundred times. It's absurd, really. I don't know how anything so organic expects to handle a digital universe in such doses, which is why I still think that Tallulah's problems are not entirely my fault. Our five months together were the inevitable result of something much larger than either of us.

Removal. The Trail of Tears. It is the job that catapulted Tallulah Wilson into wondering if she is bourgeois or not. These days she avoids asking herself that question. How could anyone consider herself poor when she buys so much organic food? And if she was fated to work this job, was she ever truly that poor in the first place?

It is a good job with excellent benefits. Her insurance never troubles her about paying for massage therapy. Her hybrid Honda sedan is entirely paid for. She is a homeowner in her twenties. Her refrigerator is always stocked. If she ever got pregnant, she could take four full months off. But Tallulah is twenty-seven, the age of rock-and-roll death, and she expects to die any minute. She wants to quit smoking, but she is afraid of becoming a nonsmoker. She knows tobacco was always sacred, and that is precisely why she wants to want to quit smoking it.

It is Georgia and it is September and it is hot. And the heat is worse in this outer world of yours. Organic sun? Please. One big ball of cancer that makes everything grow. It's a nasty, nasty thing. And you humans are crazy about it! When the sun comes out, everyone asks Tallulah, "Isn't it a beautiful day? Don't you just love the weather?" But Tallulah is the kind of human I can live with. Not that I've lived with other humans, but I saw plenty of you through her bones, heard plenty of your whining when it fogs. Tallulah doesn't care much for the direct sunlight.

She likes to have tan skin, sure. It boosts the Indianness of her appearance. She's a bit tan already, you see, but not as dark as her brother. Her brother looks like what you might expect a "part-Indian" person to look like. Tallulah has the hair and the cheekbones. In fact, her cheekbones are a good deal higher than her brother's. And after some extended exposure to the sun, she has the skin tone as well. But she just doesn't like extended exposure to the sun. It gives her headaches and makes her feel sick. Thank God for that.

Tallulah does not understand how people can smoke outside when it's daylight in the summer. With air so thick and harsh, simple inhalation is hard enough. Tallulah smokes at night, dusk at the earliest. When she was younger, she would jump-start her days with a cigarette. She can't do that anymore. She doesn't want to. Cutting out the morning cigarette, and then the afternoon cigarettes – she believes these are steps toward cutting out all cigarettes. But she likes to smoke at night. And she always smokes inside the ride, though she has somehow convinced herself that digital smoke is not real smoke.

Anyways, it is hot this one morning. Muggy like a blanket, even at four in the morning. Tallulah wakes up sweating, and Joey the mutt covers the sweat with his tongue. She slips on some shorts and sandals, follows Joey as he walks a few large circles in the backyard. He sniffs and pees. She doesn't expect him to shit this early, but he surprises her. Then he walks her back inside the air-conditioned house. Tallulah does not like to cross the road in the mornings, especially at this hour. Before she moved into this house, she had sidewalks all around her. But now, living in a house on US-441, Tallulah has no sidewalks, and no desire to risk crossing the road this morning.

Looking back, she might as well have crossed the road that morning, taken a flashlight and traversed the trail through the undeveloped lot on the east side of the highway. She might as well have called in sick. She was clinically sick. At least I'm sure that several mental doctors would have found her clinically sick that day. But she was focused on her vacation – nine consecutive days off. She had only one more day of work before the vacation. Only one more trip upon the Trail. Nothing she thought she couldn't handle. Turns out, that was the most beautiful and the most terrifying day of my life. I'm not sure whether she kept on with the vacation or not because, well, that's all part of the story too. That's where I fall off. In the shower. Oh, the shower. Damn the shower.

Fine. The shower. After she walks Joey, she goes inside and takes a shower.

Still interested?

Go on, turn the page. It only gets better from here. Until it gets worse, for me at least. If nothing else, you'll hear this story and you'll be glad you're not me.

Well, go on then.

2

Tallulah hears the voices of yesterday's tourists as she walks into the bathroom. Tour Group 5692, a large Italian American family. Ten people total – four from Italy, six from America. Most Italians love Tallulah, and these tourists were no exception. They bought Tallulah's dinner at the Soaring Eagle Grill after the Trail of Tears was over. They ate buffalo burgers and corn bread and bean salad and peach pie. "Quanah gelisge!" sang the grandmother, the one from Italy.

Convinced by her appearance that Tallulah was part Italian, they were disappointed to learn that her mother's people were actually from Ireland and Holland, maybe a bit of France and England as well. But Tallulah owns a strong vocabulary of kitchen words in Italian, something she acquired over four years of working at the Mediterranean Café in Athens. Tour Group 5692 will never be able to forget Tallulah's dinnertime language lesson. Who knew it was so easy to go from Italian to Cherokee without English in the middle?

One of the fathers asks, "You know how many Italians played Indians back in the old Westerns?" Tallulah jokes that Italians playing Indians is a sacred tradition. Everyone laughs. Tallulah asks the grandmother about Naples and Sicily. Everyone talks about Venice and Florence. "And Rome," says Tallulah. "I bet it's easy to get lost in Rome." She tells them she's been to New York, that her brother now lives in Brooklyn. She asks if every Italian has a relative in New York too. Tour Group 5692 seems to think so.

The Italian father reminds Tallulah of her own father. Joe Wilson was large. He had a big heart and a big gut. Both his parents were half Cherokee, his mother from North Carolina and his father from Oklahoma. Joe Wilson was a child of reclamation and reconnection, which is precisely why Tallulah thinks he tried to abandon everything. He would go to the bar with bearded men who smiled. He was always somewhere else, Tallulah thinks. The closer he held her, the farther away he seemed.

Tallulah can't help but envy the kids in this Italian family. She holds a genuine affection for big Italian family love. When she was little, she used to wish she was Italian. Half the customers at the Mediterranean assumed she was Sicilian. "We'll move to Seattle or San Francisco and open a Mediterranean restaurant," Bushyhead told her last week. "Why does it always have to be Mediterranean?" she asked. But she knows why. She wonders how much basil could grow in a windowsill on the West Coast.

After the Italians order dessert, the youngest daughter speaks up. She's an American, this daughter with the darkest features. "So what do you think of the Jeep Cherokee?" she asks. Tallulah suspected that she was the dissident in the family. It's always easy to spot them. I'm convinced that's why I wound up inside Tallulah in the first place – two dissidents drawn to each other, even if one of us didn't realize it. Tallulah could speak for years about the Jeep Cherokee. Her Grandpa Art. The big red Jeep Cherokee with television windows. But she is a professional. She refuses to upset the older generations.

"That's a good question," answers Tallulah. "What can anyone really say about the Jeep Cherokee?"

"Poor gas mileage," says the mother.

"How was the Old Medicine Man?" Tallulah asks. Everyone has something to say.

Tallulah hears their words in the echoes of her bathroom fan. She smells traces of buffalo burgers when the hot water first hits her head. She also smells the lingering smoke from her cigarette last night. She only had one. Well, one and a half. She squeezes the shampoo and scrubs the follicles violently. It was terrifying. I'm small enough, you know, to see the little creatures growing between your fingers and nails, and they're disgusting. No amount of washing seems to make them go away. The shower feels ten times longer than it is.

Perhaps, out of respect for my listeners, I should address the shower issue. Maybe you think it's inappropriate for me to focus so much on the shower. Or maybe you're like some of my colleagues, thirsty for any exotic and erotic details that I might share. Well if that's the case, I'm bound to let you down. I've never been much of a pornographer, nor do I want to be. One time, I told a group of curious Nunnehi about Tallulah's morning rituals, about how she stands above a fan for several minutes after leaving the shower, even when she's running late for work. The cool air dries her legs and her thighs, which, truth be told, might never come completely dry in the summer if it wasn't for this ritual with the fan. But at the slightest mention of Tallulah's thighs, my peers started giggling! How mature, I know—and these are the ones who followed me out into the world! It's really no wonder things bottomed out the way they did.

They asked me, "Have you seen her genitalia?" Of course I have, I told them; I see everything she does, her own body included. Then they asked me if I ever crawled into her vagina, or if I liked to run circles around her nipples. "Of course not!" I shouted. What did they take me for? I was in it for the possibilities. I was in it because I needed to see a new horizon, not because I needed to be some kind of sexual voyeur who violates the only truly interesting human he's ever known! Wouldn't you know, the little buggers laughed at me. They taunted me. They accused me of being asexual! So I threw sharp objects at them.

Then the rumors started, and the lies spread quickly. They told the others that I was, well, how shall I put this – the Nunnehi equivalent of a mule! "Is there a problem," I asked the council, "with wanting to be inside someone's head rather than inside their genitals?" They understood my position, but I discerned the resentment in their faces. They thought I should have seen the catastrophe coming. They thought that my own personal interests, my "selfish need to break free," had endangered the entire community. Perhaps they were right. But if I didn't cross the line, someone would have done it eventually. It was inevitable, I think. And it might as well have been me.

Alas, I digress. After drying off her legs, Tallulah walks to the window. It's a bit early, five in the morning, and the sun is still sleeping. Tallulah doesn't need to be at work until nine. She lives only twenty-two miles south of the TREPP, an easy drive up US-441. It's early, but the cars already flood the highway on this Saturday morning in September. The annual Georgia–South Carolina football game is in Athens this year. Tallulah wonders how many tailgaters will be on the road this early. They were already flooding downtown Athens the night before. Tallulah was nearly rear-ended trying to leave the parking lot of the Phoenix Market, her favorite health food store. All she wanted was some fresh basil, some organic carrots, and a couple boxes of rice milk – but she was nearly driven into a tree by a Gamecocks fan with a dark red flag suction-cupped to the windows of his SUV. For Tallulah, who was born in North Carolina and reared on Tarheels basketball, the line between North and South Carolina is no less significant than the Mason-Dixon.

And here she is – an ACC girl living in an SEC town. She grew accustomed to life in Athens the same way that she has grown accustomed to new fleece sweaters. It fits her comfortably, often too comfortably. There's the humidity, of course, but she can always elevate. Take her dog and drive to the mountains. She figures that if the world warms to the point where Athens is no longer bearable, she could always break for the high hills, hole-up in her grandparents' house. But up there, even at Indian functions, Tallulah stands out. Down in Athens she blends right in. She doesn't call attention to herself by simply walking down the sidewalk, like she did in Sandy Springs.

Tallulah doesn't technically live in Athens anymore though. Her little house is a few miles north of town, just across the Jackson County line, not far from the recycling plant. Yes, it's true – Tallulah is a modern Cherokee woman living in Jackson County, Georgia. But she isn't bothered by the irony of these place names. Living in a country, or rather an entire hemisphere, named after an Italian pickle-peddler-turned-navigator, Tallulah has yet to set foot in a place without an ironic name. As such, she's never questioned the logic of building the TREPP up in Homer, Georgia. It's a small town that, prior to the TREPP's construction, was most famous for being the home of the "World's Largest Easter Egg Hunt." When prompted for personal details by some of her more inquisitive tourists, she'll start by saying that she lives in between Athens and Homer. "I'm epically ironic," she says. They always laugh.

Well before she moved into her little house, Tallulah found great personal relevance in US-441. You see, the highway runs through Tallulah Falls.

How shall I put this? When tourists ask Tallulah Wilson if she was named after Tallulah Bankhead, she tells them, "Actually, Tallulah Bankhead was named after me." Most of the time, they don't get it. They generally continue with their questions and pretend not to catch Tallulah's reverse causality.

They also like to ask, "Was Tallulah Bankhead really bisexual?" As if sharing a name with others leads to intimate knowledge of their sexuality. But sometimes, when Tallulah genuinely likes her tourists, she'll tell them how Tallulah Falls was once the second-largest waterfall in all of North America. How Tallulah Bankhead's grandmother was given that name because her parents honeymooned at the Falls back in the nineteenth century, some time not too long after the Removal. How Miss Bankhead inherited the name from her grandmother, and ultimately how it all comes back to Cherokee words and ancient rivers and things that lived here long before the Old South began to imagine itself as Old.

Tallulah Wilson bought her little house on 441 after her first year on the job. It seemed like an ideal commute. A half hour each way, depending on the traffic. It's a good road, and an old road. Like most roads in Georgia, it was first built long before colonization. The asphalt only appeared recently. Tallulah's grandmother still lives up in Eastern Cherokee country, near the Qualla Boundary reservation in North Carolina. Old 441 takes Tallulah to see her Grandma Lee. Indeed, 441 is the only major road that runs through the Smoky Mountains, flanked by the Qualla Boundary on one side and by Gatlinburg, Tennessee, on the other. Tallulah has twice been stranded by broken cars in Gatlinburg, and she swears never to return unless kidnapped.

And if you drive south, 441 winds as far south as the continental United States can go, way down to south Florida. When Tallulah told her brother, Alan, that she'd bought a house on highway 441, he instantly broke into Tom Petty lyrics: "And she could hear the cars roll by, on 441, like waves crashing on the beach." He still calls Tallulah "the American Girl."

Tallulah learned to resent the song when it came over radios or jukeboxes, but lately she's come to appreciate it. "I am, *the* American girl," she sings. One-quarter Cherokee and three-quarters mixed immigrant, Tallulah figures she's as American as they get, whatever that means.

Anyways, the sun won't rise until roughly seven o'clock, and Tallulah has hours to kill before she leaves for work. Tallulah pulls a carton of not-from-concentrate orange juice from the refrigerator. The cold sweetness soothes her throat. If she could only drink one kind of fluid for the remainder of her life, it would be this juice. When she lived in North Carolina, Tallulah drank watered-down orange juice from concentrate and slept in a room without air-conditioning. When she moved to Georgia, she had air-conditioning but still drank concentrated juices. But after she started at the TREPP, everything changed.

She fills the kettle with water for coffee. Waiting for the kettle to boil, sitting on the couch, her legs cool and her hair beginning to dry, Tallulah glances at the nylon-string guitar in the corner of her living room. She hears Bushyhead, the awful song she wrote while he was away. She smells the burgers and french fries with feta dip at the diner on College Avenue. She sees them sitting on the balcony atop the three-story Academic Building at the junction of campus and downtown Athens. She hears him, reciting that line from *Their Eyes Were Watching God*. It's a particularly vivid memory, a moment that echoes loudly among the multitude.

I suppose I never fully told you about Tallulah's memories. She hears them everywhere, you see. They speak to her, all the time. Being so musically inclined myself, I was enthralled by the way Tallulah processes the past. She takes it with her everywhere she goes, and most of the time she listens to it. For example, words from a conversation seven years earlier will reverberate across her mind if an object evokes the memory – a decorative scarf, a travel section, a pair of shoes, a drenched sweater, a falafel wrapped in aluminum foil, a starfish, an airplane over the sea, a nylon-string guitar, and so on. She sees the object, and the memories begin to speak, echoes only she can hear. It doesn't matter where she is – in her car, at a coffee bar, walking down the sidewalk, in the staffroom at work – the sounds of memory follow and precede.

Back when I was inside her skull, the sounds of memory were hypnotic. They lulled me into character and suspended me in time. I thought I might lose those sounds when I crawled onto her scalp, but it seems that memory is not confined inside the head. You can still hear it from the surface, albeit without all the echo, as long as you cling close enough. Mind you, Tallulah doesn't hear everything she remembers. It would be impossible for her to hear the present if she always listened to the past. But it's always there – an endless series of pebbles leaping into the ponds of memory that ripple in her head. And for whatever reason, Tallulah's memories have a tendency to speak loudest just before sunrise. I must indulge them, you see. It's all part of her story.

Listen. It is seven years ago. Their second date. She remembers the sound of her fingers on the white tabletop. She hears that strangely comfortable silence just before the server brings their food. Someone plays R.E.M.'s "It's the End of the World as We Know It" on the jukebox.

"Great song," says Bushyhead.

"Doesn't it feel weird?" she asks.

"What's that?"

"Sitting here, in Athens, in public, listening to R.E.M.?" Tallulah had lived in Athens for less than a year at this point in her life.

“Maybe,” says Bushyhead. “But this tune is a classic.” He peers at the grill behind them. “So – what’s your favorite album by an Athens band?” Of course it’s a question without a single answer, but how one answers the question seems to speak volumes about one’s character.

“That’s easy,” she says. “Neutral Milk Hotel, *In the Aeroplane over the Sea*.”

“Can’t argue with that,” says Bushyhead.

“It’s, like, the greatest indie rock album of all time,” she says. Bushyhead hears the passion in her voice. Tallulah spots the dimples in his cheek.

Their burgers are delivered to the table, and Tallulah glances around the restaurant as the busser fills their water. Everyone is on edge, somewhere between anger and insecurity, between rage and embarrassment. Michael Stipe sings about Lenny Bruce and jelly beans. His voice sounds like it will live forever.

“You know that Michael Stipe was twenty-seven when they recorded this album?” she asks and promptly steals Bushyhead’s heart for good. Tallulah was only twenty back then, but already she was terrified of turning twenty-seven.

“He was?”

“Yeah. And it’s their best album, isn’t it?”

“That’s debatable.”

“And Jeff Mangum from Neutral Milk, he basically disappeared after he turned twenty-seven.”

“So what are you saying?” asks Bushyhead. Tallulah lists the revolutionary luminaries who’ve died at twenty-seven. Robert Johnson, Kurt Cobain, Jimi Hendrix, Janis Joplin – the list seems endless.

“I’m saying that it’s all downhill from there, isn’t it?”

“I don’t know,” he answers. “Shakespeare got better as he got older. So did Toni Morrison.”

"Writers are different," she says. "But the musicians, they either flare out at twenty-seven, or they just die slowly from twenty-eight on. Right?"

"Sounds like you should be a writer," he smiles.

I'm no writer, she thinks. Sure, I wrote the bulk of the tour guide phrasebook, but I'm more performance artist than musician. Better yet, a history whore. The TREPP needed a mascot, and Tallulah needed the money.

When Tallulah turned twenty-seven last winter, she half expected to die. Perhaps she half wanted to die, as if dying at twenty-seven would have confirmed the fact that she had actually done something important. As she approaches twenty-eight, she's learned to think differently. She understands that *Automatic for the People* is also an excellent album. She empathizes with Jeff Mangum, with the troubles of being both public and genuine. And she knows the Beatles and Radiohead got better with age. But back then, back when they first shared a large order of fries and feta cheese dip, Tallulah figured she had seven years to do something meaningful. It was a vulnerability Bushyhead never would have guessed from their first encounters working together at the Mediterranean Café.

They walk outside. It's midsummer, and the humidity swelters. They cross Broad Street, the road that divides downtown Athens from the UGA campus. They walk beneath the Arches and onto the lush and stately quads. They climb the outside of the Academic Building, all three rackety flights of stairs, until they reach the neoclassical balcony. They sit closely. They watch people young and old revel on the lawns below, yawping triumphantly along Broad Street, announcing their drunkenness to the world. Streetlamps shadow the drooping Southern trees that creep into the balcony. As they lean closer, a violent crash screams up from Broad Street. A Jeep Cherokee has collided with the pole of a traffic signal. No humans seem to be injured, but the crash creates an instant bottleneck. Bushyhead laughs.

"What's so funny?" she asks.

"Those Cherokees," he says. "They're real savages, aren't they?"

Tallulah isn't sure whether to punch him or laugh with him. So she follows her instincts, and she tells him about her grandfather. About Grandpa Art and his big red Jeep Cherokee with television windows. He was the first and only boy she told about the prototype. Of course, the TREPP brass knows about it. But most of the employees never learn. Without Arthur Wilson, people wouldn't be able to ride the Trail of Tears. She tells Bushyhead that she sometimes feels like Sequoyah's daughter.

Bushyhead asks if she's ever been to Sequoyah's cabin. She hadn't. This was back before the TREPP flew her to Oklahoma for additional studies. Back then Tallulah had never been west of Rome, Georgia. "You've got to go!" says Bushyhead. "You have to! It's like Janey says to Phoebe at the end of *Their Eyes Were Watching God*, that *you have to go there to know there*."

All the voices fade from the streets below. This goofy Cuban Cherokee boy had just quoted Zora Neale Hurston! It was a short quote, but a damn good one. She grabs his face and kisses him. Not just a pat on the lips, but a full-force open-jaw tongue-twisting kiss. She grabs his cheekbones, pushes him back upon the seat, and nearly suffocates him. Ah, the youth that never dies.

But I digress. Sometimes it's fun for me, to revel in the descriptions of Tallulah's memories. Of the things she did before I shared her experiences. I promise I'll stop talking about myself once we get to work. Back home everything runs so intuitively. I don't have to make a point of who I am, or why I'm doing what I'm doing. But out here, with these dimensions of yours,

I have a tendency to ramble. You've probably figured that out already. I promise to do better.

Tallulah walks the dog again before the sun rises. Joey eats his breakfast while Tallulah listens to Internet radio. Then, with a large bowl of vanilla yogurt and blueberries in front of her, she reads the headlines from across the Atlantic. She dresses for work and grabs the rice milk from her pantry. She warms a croissant and pours another cup of coffee for the road. The dog needs a final walk, and the sun shines hard when she finally leaves the house. A slight film of sweat threatens to break, but the air-conditioning in her car works quickly.

She pulls onto 441, heading north. She considers the route she'll take to the Outer Banks. I-85 north to Carolina, then east on I-40 until they near the coast. When Bushyhead gave his notice two weeks ago – the third time he's quit the TREPP – Tallulah asked him to come to the Outer Banks with her. She feels a breakthrough conversation is imminent, regardless of where it leads. Maybe it's a mistake. Maybe not. She knows what Grandma Lee would say. "What are you wasting your time waiting around for? Marry the boy already. You can always leave him later. I left your grandfather for a while, but we got back together."

Tallulah's plan is to spend five nights on the Outer Banks, then travel west into the Carolina mountains. Grandma Lee is getting older, beginning to shut down. Who knows how much longer she has? Lee isn't shy about her fondness for Bushyhead, though Tallulah isn't sure if that's good or bad. He was the first person she knew to move from Athens to the Bay Area and actually choose to come back. It's no secret that he came back for her.

A thin cloud reaches between the power lines on each side of the highway. Tallulah thinks of penises and crucifixes whenever she sees these power lines on 441 – those on the east side of the road are single poles, and those on the west side are crosses. The traffic is steady. She crosses through Commerce, Georgia, the junction with I-85.

She'll never forget that time, on this same stretch of highway, driving southbound on the way home from the TREPP. She's barely twenty-four. It's her first year on the job, and she had just finished the late shift. Two miles of automatic driving, and then – the rains come. A classic Southern torrential downpour. Unannounced and fierce. The winds uproot trees that stood for a century. The rain turns to sudden hail, like a fleet of tiny bricks on the windshield of her old Ford. She remembers chain-smoking at twenty-five miles an hour, terrified she would hydroplane into a pole. The radio turns to fuzz. The windshield cracks, and Tallulah thinks her time is up. The more she slows, the more her tires seem to slip. She lights smoke after smoke like oxygen is poison, anything to distract and focus.

Just south of the junction, just as she feels the wheels leaning into the shoulder of the road, Tallulah experiences a small miracle of modern radiation. The college radio station bursts forth from the static airwaves. The Ramones. Judy is a Punk. Aerial guitar angels, distorted like the rainy road and more solid than any star in the sky. She's convinced the music saved her, guided her over the water in the road. That was over three years ago, and Tallulah is still alive. She named her dog after Joey Ramone.

Tallulah has plenty of reason to consider herself lucky. Her father wasn't so fortunate. Joe Wilson died in an accident not far from here. It was off US-23, a road that merges with 441 some fifteen miles north of Homer. He was near a small town named Lula, of all things. He was driving south. No one knows exactly where he was going, or why.

Until his death Joe Wilson told his children that they had no Indian grandparents. He claimed that cancer got them early. Tallulah Wilson was born and raised in Asheville, but she never visited Cherokee country in North Carolina until her father drove his car into a pole off Highway 23, drunk in the middle of an afternoon. He was blitzed on Budweiser, and his old pickup truck quit compensating. A Carolina game blared through the radio static as the EMTs tried to salvage Joe Wilson's body from the wreckage.

Tallulah was nine years old when her mother came out and burst Joe's bubble. Janet Wilson was adamant that her kids know where they came from, even if her late husband never saw the greater good in it. A month after Joe's death, Janet sent the kids to meet Lee and Arthur. Tallulah walked through their house, feeling strangely at home. Everything smelled right. Familiar and durable and warm. Three months later Janet landed a living wage job in Atlanta.

Janet sent her kids up to the mountains to visit Joe's parents at least once a year, usually in the summer. So when Tallulah was twelve and pubescent and revolting against everything, Janet put her on a Greyhound bus to Asheville. Grandma Lee and Grandpa Art met her at the station. Back at their house, Arthur took Tallulah into his basement for the first time. Lee was an artisan, and she worked upstairs. Art was an inventor, among other things, and his lair was the basement.

"This was the last thing I made before your father left," he says. "I figured you ought to know."

Grandpa turns on the lights when Tallulah is halfway down the stairs. The basement lights up bright grey, cluttered with cans and buckets, chipped carvings, and bent aluminum sheets. Tallulah follows her grandfather past shelves packed with boxes. She follows him around a corner that opens into a large room with tools and workbenches. Hollow casings of old television sets line the walls, covered with spliced wires and old splitters. Grandpa Art pulls the string on a dangling lightbulb. The light is low and yellow. Tallulah can see the vehicle. It is tarped and sleeping, but she feels a small shock when she touches it.

Art yanks on the tarp, intending to slide it off in one easy motion, but the tarp sticks to the sides of the vehicle. The old man slowly circles his creation, carefully lifting the tarp off the painted metal, rolling the tarp in places where the suction is extra strong. He rolls all sides of the tarp to the roof, and he yanks it off like a giant bandage.

It is a big red Jeep Cherokee with television windows. It's an older-style Cherokee, probably from the 1980s. The SUV built before they were named SUVs. Every window is a television screen – two screens on the front windshield, two screens on the back windshield, and six screens on the side windows.

The cathode windows do not roll down. The screens are fixed, fastened tight. It reminds Tallulah of the "bug vision" from science class – the compound eyes of flies and beetles, who see through multiple bubbles at once. And now she's inside the bug!

Art turns the key. At first the engine coughs and sputters, but soon it revs up loud and steady. The lights on the dashboard aren't at all like the lights in a normal car. Grandpa tells her to push a big green button where the stereo should be.

Tallulah pushes the button. Nothing happens at first, but a few seconds later, all the television screens click on, one by one, starting with the front windshield. The windows hum, the colors brighten. Tallulah feels the screens turning her on like a bulb. She was inside something larger than herself, something that dwarfed even this big red Jeep Cherokee with television windows. Her suspicions had proven true – Grandpa Art was completely nuts.

"I call it Surround Vision," he says. "I know you've heard about the Trail of Tears." He points to an image on the horizon that coalesces upon the windshield. "Well, there it is."

Before pulling onto the Trail, Grandpa leans toward Tallulah and laughs softly. "When in doubt, go to the source," he chuckles.

It's a laugh woven deeply in Tallulah's sonic memory. It's durable and warm, like the smell of their house. It's a laugh that endured losing a son. It's still alive; it never disappears. Art died four years later, but Tallulah never stops hearing his laugh.

Grandpa shifts the big red Jeep Cherokee into gear and drives toward the horizon. Tallulah reaches for the handbar above the window. Her stomach moves, and her intestines fill with unusual inertia. She asks Grandpa if they are really driving. "We're virtually driving," he says.

Tallulah learned all the things that "virtual" could mean when she grew older, but she never forgot that feeling in her stomach when she first rode the Trail of Tears.

Arthur and Tallulah rode the whole Trail of Tears that night, all the way from the stockades in Georgia to the hills and lakes in northeastern Oklahoma. They watched people walking through the television windows. Grandpa said that the Indians walking the Trail were digital and couldn't see inside the car, but Tallulah thought they stared right through her. A mass of bent and broken bodies that stretched up to ten miles long at the beginning of the trip. Thousands and thousands of digital eyes. Tallulah's feet felt bruised and raw. Her knees buckled and shook upon the upholstery.

She was only twelve years old, and she was never able to look at a Jeep Cherokee again without wondering if the person behind the wheel was trying to ride the Trail of Tears. Tallulah began to theorize. Did people who drove Jeep Cherokees

subconsciously want to ride the Trail? What about those freshly waxed Cherokees, driven by bargain hunters through Atlanta's jumbled and terminal highway maze – with those eight cylinders in continual motion from parking lot to parking lot to parking lot, were they subconsciously seeking their own exodus?

Riding the Greyhound back down to Georgia, twelve-year-old Tallulah counted every Jeep Cherokee she passed. She thought she counted 212, though she might have been exaggerating. According to her calculations, she saw roughly one Jeep Cherokee per mile traveled!

She was twelve years old and getting better at math. She figured there were at least ten, if not twenty, Jeep Cherokees with Georgia license plates for every Cherokee person who had died on the Trail of Tears. And that was just Georgia. What about the rest of the country? What about the rest of the world? Did they have Jeep Cherokees in China and India? Just how many people were trying to ride the Trail of Tears?

When her grandfather died, the Museum of the Cherokee Indian inherited the intellectual property rights to his inventions. Grandma Lee was promised royalties. When Tallulah was nineteen, the museum sold Arthur Wilson's "Surround Vision" concept to Atlanta moneyman Jim Campbell, complete with the prototypical big red Jeep Cherokee with television windows. When she was twenty, Jim Campbell's foundation – it wasn't even called the TREPP yet – helped pay Tallulah's rent and bills at UGA. Tallulah rode college on the Hope Grant and Surround Vision. And here she is, twenty-seven years old. Still alive.

Her commute is nearly over. The TREPP's tall digital sign stands sentinel on the east side of 441. On a clear day you can see it for miles. Tallulah turns her hybrid Honda onto Tsalagi Boulevard and veers around to the main gate. The parking lot swarms with extra vehicles. She hears unfamiliar voices when she opens the door.

It's almost nine o'clock, and already the humidity is dense. Morning sun burns the dew off asphalt and grass, and the light bends in the mist. Tallulah cracks a minor sweat between her car and the main entrance. Then, finally – she's inside. Back home, inside the Trail of Tears.

3

The air inside the TREPP is brisk and well-conditioned, even with all the additional bodies. Tallulah's pores settle down, and the sweat subsides. Cameras flash. A reporter asks Tallulah who she is. Another reporter asks if she's the face on the poster above the bookstore. Tallulah smiles, claiming to be running late. She slips between them and feels the gazes of security personnel. Customers read maps and stare at the screens, posters, menus on the walls. Tallulah ducks her head and glides past the gift shop, the bookstore, the movie theater. Past the Turtleback Café and the Soaring Eagle Grill.

Two customers discuss the entrees at each restaurant, trying to decide which place is best for them. The menus are different, yes, but all the items come from a single kitchen. Tallulah smiles wide and keeps her eyes on the colorful tile. Employees are required to refer to the kitchen as "the kitchens" when dialoguing with customers. Most employees are aware of the single-kitchen reality, of course. Yet some of the recent hires don't seem to know. A week ago Bushyhead told her, "At least four of the new tour guides have never been in the kitchen, so they keep saying the kitchens, even when they talk to me." Tallulah wonders if the new hires are people who never worked in food service. Were they people who'd never learned to appreciate the significance of having a fifteen-gallon Hobart mixer in the building? How many of the new people will go their entire career at the TREPP believing that there are actually two different kitchens?

Or does the recent barrier between the new hires and the single-kitchen reality only hint at something larger? Has a wall been forming between the different castes of employees? Had it been there all along? Tallulah used to keep in touch with people after they left the TREPP. She'd meet them in town for a drink and a show. Tallulah believes the old crew had fewer barriers, though she's suspicious of her nostalgia, especially since they never come back.

She slinks along the periphery of the compound, rice milk in hand. She nears the Staffroom. Tallulah generally prefers to have the Staffroom empty, but with the Belgian woman still holed-up from yesterday, she'd like to hear what her colleagues are thinking.

She swings the door wide. Lucy and Dugan are in, plus two of the new girls whom she doesn't know. Tallulah chastises herself for not knowing their names, but she feels it's beyond her control, especially with so many new hires this summer. Each day a tour guide needs to memorize the names of some twenty-four tourists. After eleven hundred trips on the Trail of Tears, Tallulah's free space is filling up.

"Osiyo, peoples!" she says.

"Hi, Tallulah," says Dugan.

"Dugan!" she replies.

"Hey, Tallulah," says Lucy the Choctaw woman.

"Lucy!" Lucy is one of six Indians who work as tour guides on the Trail of Tears. There's also a Mohawk guy who looks Italian, a Menominee lesbian who wanted a reason to move thousands of miles away from her family, and an Ojibwe woman with a BA in history from UNC. She doesn't pay much attention to basketball, but Tallulah doesn't hold it against her. Tallulah and Bushyhead are the only Cherokee tour guides. She's only half kidding when she jokes about the incestuousness of their

no names.

relationship. But Bushyhead's father is Cuban, and he grew up in Missouri.

"Hey, girls!" she says. The new hires reply ambiguously. They wave at her with too much effort.

Tallulah asks Lucy about her family. Lucy has three kids, and her husband works in a garage in Lawrenceville. She's one of the few part-time tour guides on the Trail of Tears. Lucy rides the Trail during school hours.

"My kids are all scared of this terrorism thing," she says. "They're all, like, 'Mom, don't go to work this morning.' I was, like, telling them it only seems to be customers who are affected, you know, but that just seemed to make them worry even more."

"Uh-oh," says Tallulah.

"But isn't it weird?" asks Lucy.

"What isn't weird?" replies Dugan.

"It's weird that it's only been customers who are holing-up. Isn't it?"

"You're right," Tallulah answers. "It *is* strange. You'd think a terrorist would strike indiscriminately. Right? Isn't that what terrorism is all about?"

"Yeah," says Dugan. "I feel you. What kind of a terrorist only goes after customers and not employees?"

"You know what's gonna happen next?" asks Lucy, though it's more statement than question. "They're gonna start thinking it's an employee who's the terrorist."

"Good point," says Tallulah. She contemplates the suspiciousness of her coworkers. How many tour guides would blame the techies? How many customers would blame the kitchen staff or the custodians? Tallulah imagines Boss Johnson, the head manager, with his clipboard and a list of names. She half expects the Boss will ask her to help him whittle a few suspects from his list.

Lucy glances down at the newspaper through her bifocals. Tallulah likes Lucy because she's honest, even when she tells the occasional tourist that the Cherokees whined the loudest of all the tribes affected by Jackson's Removal Act. And because they complained the most, Lucy concludes, the Trail of Tears is remembered as a particularly Cherokee experience. But Tallulah has long debunked this argument. First of all, the English phrase "Trail of Tears" comes from the Cherokee phrase "na nvnohi dunahloyili," which translates more accurately as "the trail where they cried." And more importantly, as Tallulah puts it, "If we were in old-school Choctaw country and doing a thing about Cherokees, then yes, something would be terribly wrong."

The TREPP always wanted to keep it local. "When in Rome," says Jim Campbell, the TREPP's owner. Tallulah never knows how to interpret that phrase. What if you're in Scotland and Rome invades you? Yet, Jim Campbell continues to think he's in Rome. Yes, it's true that the TREPP is built upon land that was Cherokee long before it was Georgia. Yes, it's true that Terminus, the junction city that grew into Atlanta, wasn't built until 1840, only two years after the Trail of Tears. Yes, it's true that there would be no Coca-Cola without the Indian Removals. But Jim Campbell is under the impression that saying "when in Rome" demonstrates his respect for the old Indians. He has a terminal fascination with the Rome that was demolished to build the South, and he's never seemed to understand that Tallulah went to high school in Georgia. Tallulah's grandparents were from Qualla Boundary, and she's one of the few people enrolled in both the Cherokee Nation and the Eastern Band. That's all Jim Campbell needs to know.

"Your lover boy was just in here," says Lucy, her eyebrow raised.

"John?" Tallulah is the only one who calls him John at work. His full name is actually John Bushyhead Smith. Tallulah pours boiled water into her mug.

"Bushyhead?" says Lucy. "Yeah, he was here, only just ten minutes ago."

"He was looking for you," says Dugan.

"Yep," says Lucy. "He said something about you not wanting him to go on your vacation."

"What?"

"He didn't say that," claims Dugan.

"Yes he did," says Lucy.

"No," says Dugan. "He said he was afraid you didn't really want him to go."

The bastard, she thinks. In here spouting off about what he thinks I want him to do. Tallulah pours a drop of rice milk in her tea and places the new carton in the refrigerator. She squeezes the teabag and tosses it in the green bin. She wants to know more, but she tries to change the subject. "Last I heard, that Belgian woman had been down for thirteen hours."

"Yeah," says Dugan. "She was on a late tour. I saw it all, I closed last night. Well, I didn't see all of it." He describes the EMTs, the talk of terrorism, the first wave of Homeland Security just before closing time.

"Who was the guide?" asks Tallulah.

"Aspen," replies Dugan. "She's only been here since the summer," he says. "Poor girl must be having a breakdown."

Tallulah wonders when this Aspen girl started working here. Dugan's only been here a few months himself. But he's a history grad from UGA, like herself. The tea is warm, and it soothes the corners of her throat, singed tender from so much smoking. Back in the early days, Tallulah got territorial when other history grads were hired at the TREPP. But these days she's learned to appreciate them. She's glad to know she's not the last one.

"You got what, twenty days off in a row?" asks Lucy.

"Nine," Tallulah answers.

"Still a long time," says Lucy.

"Bushyhead's last day too, right?" asks Dugan.

"I'll believe it when I see it," says Lucy. "That boy's had at least four last days now. Right, Tallulah?"

Tallulah lifts her eyebrows and nods.

She opens her locker and pulls out the tour guide apparel – a green work vest with large pockets and a communicator shaped like a water beetle. Lucy and Dugan ask her about the coming storm. Will it turn into a hurricane? How far south will it touch? What does someone do in Nag's Head when a hurricane hits? Bushyhead must have really run his mouth, she thinks. He makes this dramatic return, says he wants to go away with me, and the morning before we leave for the Outer Banks, he's in here griping to everyone about storms halfway across the ocean. Tallulah gives predictable answers to their questions. She'll "play it by ear," and "you evacuate if you have to."

Tallulah finishes her tea. She folds the roster and puts it in her vest pocket. Dugan waves. Lucy wishes her safe travels. The anonymous new hires stare clumsily or avoid eye contact.

Tallulah leaves the Staffroom with about fifteen minutes to spare. Her tourists are already beginning to assemble in the Meeting Grounds, but there's no need for her to be early. She slinks along the rim of the circular compound, past some restrooms, and toward the tech room. Bushyhead may be hiding in there.

Before she can knock on the door, one of the techies walks out. It's Wallace, a quiet guy in his forties.

"Room's empty," he tells her. "But it's all yours if you want to chill."

Tallulah takes up the offer. The tech crew room is somewhat of an oasis inside the TREPP. It has a certain degree of autonomy. The techies never come into the tour guide room, and only a few tour guides are welcomed into theirs.

It's cool inside the tech room. The air is double-conditioned, and they have inventive fans. The tech crew room is like a cave, she thinks. A good place for Cherokees. It's less fluorescent than the Great Hall or the regular Staffroom. Wire casings, cables, and converters hang from the walls, filed efficiently. Various gadgets sleep upon the room's firm edges and sharp angles. The walls are made of wooden cabinets, with clearly labeled sliding drawers that house the mics and headgear. The tech room lacks the decorative trinkets and tidbits that some tour guides have packed into the holes and corners of the regular Staffroom. Tallulah finds a certain warmth in here. And she admires both women on the tech crew. She imagines them taking shop in middle school instead of home economics. She gazes at the air-conditioning vents in the ceiling.

She pulls the tour roster from her vest pocket. Tour Group 5709. Protocol requires her to read through the roster before first contacting a group of tourists in the Meeting Grounds. Tallulah prefers to study her roster alone. She claims it helps her become one with the roster.

The tour rosters provide a list of names, residences, nationalities, reasons for visiting, pronunciation guides if needed, and any additional information the customers deem necessary. Tallulah herself was responsible for the concept of the rosters. "We need to know who we're dealing with," she insisted, back in one of the very first staff meetings. "How else do we remember their names?" The management was quick to oblige Tallulah's request.

Tour Group 5709 seems like a motley bunch. Almost entirely

Americans. You get a lot of Americans on Saturdays. Families that work all week, students in class all week, and so forth. Tour Group 5709 consists of two families and a group of students – eleven people in all.

Three are from North Carolina. A woman named Nell Johnson is bringing her two daughters. Nell is a schoolteacher, and the reason for their visit is "educational."

Next is the Rosenberg family, led by Irma and Bob, who are both in their eighties. Their granddaughter Rachel is the third Rosenberg in 5709. Her partner, Michael, is also in their clan, but he's English and has a different last name. Their reason for riding is typical – "visiting family in Atlanta" – but Tallulah senses that the Rosenbergs aren't the typical Saturday tourists.

Four UGA students complete the group. Two female and two male. Their reasons for visiting are academic – "anthropology class." Without any further details Tallulah knows exactly who their teacher is and how much extra credit they will get for showing their ticket stubs and writing a one-page report about the experience. He was one of the professors on her undergraduate thesis committee, and he loves to tell his students about Tallulah. He also loves to quote Flannery O'Connor. If 5709 seems particularly literate, Tallulah might talk about Flannery O'Connor and Alice Walker, about the Oconee River flowing south from Athens through Eatonton and Milledgeville, about highway 441 and ancient parallel roads.

Tallulah wonders how much 5709 will know about the holed-up Belgian woman. She breathes deeply. The double-conditioned air is tranquil, and she inhales through her nose. But the time is now upon her. She sticks two pieces of peppermint gum in her mouth and leaves for the Meeting Grounds. This is where it starts to get interesting.

4

Tallulah enters the Meeting Grounds. She sees one empty seat in the semicircle of twelve chairs. Eleven heads total, everyone is here. The heads turn as Tallulah walks in. She smiles and looks down, gazing at familiar patterns in the faux-dirt carpet as she walks toward the guide table.

She examines the tourists with her peripheral vision. An old couple sits on the left end of the semicircle. Two young girls who look like twins sit in the middle. The students from Athens stick out like a keg at a lemonade stand, occupying the right end of the semicircle. One of the Rosenbergs is a black man. Tallulah assumes he is the Brit who married into the Rosenberg tribe. She has guided black Europeans before, but never a black Brit. She wonders how his voice will sound.

She is glad she braided her hair today.

Tallulah sits down carefully, then raises her head. She eases her facial muscles, elevating her cheeks and exposing her teeth as she gazes upon the group. The tourists stretch and bend their heads with curiosity.

"Osiyo. My name is Tallulah Wilson, and I will be your guide as you ride the Trail of Tears today."

Some tourists nod. Some smile, some stare.

"What was that first word you said?" asks one of the girls from Athens.

"Osiyo." As usual, Tallulah defines the Cherokee greeting. "Just say 'yo,'" she says, and notes that "yo" is not a slang salutary phrase, as the *American Heritage* dictionary suggests, but rather an ancient and highly evolved greeting.

Tallulah reads the names on her roster, alphabetically. Some tourists say "here," some say "present," some attempt to be unique. Nell Johnson whispers to her daughters. Tallulah smiles at the mother and her girls. Nell asks about the materials used to construct the Meeting Grounds.

"This room," Tallulah raises her arms, "is built to resemble early nineteenth-century-style Cherokee architecture. Many Cherokees in northern Georgia lived in dwellings like this one during the years prior to Removal."

"This floor is tripped out," says one of the boys from Athens.

"The floor is a composite carpet, built to resemble red dirt," she says.

"Fantastic," says the boy from Athens.

"This isn't dirt?" asks the old Jewish woman. Tallulah has seen almost all the Woody Allen movies, enough to recognize northern Jewish accents. This must be Irma Rosenberg.

"No," she replies. "It's carpet, designed to mimic the red earth. It's made specially for the TREPP by a local manufacturer in Dalton."

"Dalton?" says Irma. "I hear that that's the carpet capitol of the world."

"That's what they say, all right," says Tallulah.

Tallulah states her tribal affiliations and a brief summary of why she works at the Trail of Tears. She is a professional, so she does not mention Grandpa Arthur's big red Jeep Cherokee with television windows.

"You're all in this together," she tells them, a line that all guides are absolutely required to say at the beginning of each orientation. Tallulah wrote the line herself; it is one of several mandatory lines of tour guide dialogue that Tallulah composed for the company. All of the official tour guide phraseology – well, most of it anyway – was authored by Tallulah Wilson. "So," she continues her script, "let's take this opportunity to get to know one another."

Tallulah asks the UGA students to begin the introductions. Her eyes and ears bounce between the roster and the semicircle, matching names with faces, voices with hometowns.

Spencer Donald speaks first. He introduces himself as Spencer Donald, a UGA student from Alpharetta, Georgia, a north Atlanta suburb with floods of traffic. He has water blue eyes and dangling curly brown hair. He asks if Tallulah knows his anthropology professor. "Our professor totally told us to ask for you as our guide."

"Everything he said about me is a lie," she says, which is not entirely true.

Danny Calhoun introduces himself next. He is also from Alpharetta. He has known Spencer since high school, and now they are roommates in Athens. Danny's hair is buzz short.

"I hope this won't last too long," says Danny, "'cause we've got tickets to the game."

Tallulah tells them that the Trail of Tears should not last more than three hours. She insists they will make it back to Athens before kickoff.

Introductions continue with the Athenian women, who are also light haired. They have bluish eyes and salon summer tans. First is Mandy Warren. She leans on Danny to announce that he is hers. Next is Carmen Davis, who is old friends with Mandy but not her roommate. Carmen projects a kind of magnetism, like an apple preparing to fall from its tree.

All four Athenians are taking the same anthropology class and seeking the same extra credit. None of them has declared a major, but Spencer is leaning toward psychology. Carmen is inclined toward journalism or business, or both. From the way Carmen speaks, Tallulah knows that she will write the best extra-credit paper of the bunch. Yet they'll all receive the same amount of credit, regardless of what their papers actually say.

Carmen Davis grew up in Iowa, the only student in the foursome who came to UGA from out of state. Tallulah asks why she chose Georgia, suspecting Carmen might mention the reputation of the journalism school. But Carmen answers ambiguously, something about the weather and social networking. Danny mumbles something about Damn Yankees. Mandy whispers in her boyfriend's ear.

"Don't worry," says Tallulah. "I'm a Damn Yankee too. At least my mother is. But actually, all English speakers are Yankees."

"What?" snaps Danny.

Tallulah describes the evolution of the word "Yankee." This is a delicate job, given the fact that most Southerners will viscerally reject the idea that they too are Yankees. But Tallulah knows the script quite well, for as you may have guessed, she wrote this part too. The term "Yankee," according to historical documents, was a colonial mutation of the indigenous Connecticut pronunciation of "English." As such, the word "Yankee" has always been associated with the north Atlantic – be it England or New England – and its very existence is the fruit of misunderstanding between indigenous and European languages in North America. And as Southern culture declares, "The difference between a Yankee and a Damn Yankee is the Damn Yankees never leave." Thus, all English speakers in the United States are essentially Damn Yankees.

Carmen Davis describes her sociology professor's perspective – that white Georgians are repulsed by illegal immigration because they themselves are all descendants of old illegal immigrants. Tallulah envisions bumper stickers on this sociology professor's door. She remembers him well.

Tallulah elevates her smile an extra notch. She knows it's for the greater good to leave the Yankee talk behind, so she changes the direction of the dialogue. "In Cherokee," she announces, "you can say 'Yoneg.'"

"Yongeez?" asks Carmen.

"Yoneg."

"What does that mean?"

"English," says Tallulah.

The next tourist to introduce herself is Nell Johnson, who is no relation to Boss Johnson. She is from the lovely town of Boone, North Carolina. Her daughters are eight-year-old twins, Nikki and Willa. They are smart kids; Tallulah reads it in their eyes. Kinetic gravity on their shoulders. Their skin is darker than their mother's. Tallulah imagines the interracial possibilities. She anticipates better questions from the Johnson kids than the college students.

The Johnsons are en route to Atlanta for a visit with Nell's sister. They slept last night in a hotel in Clayton, Georgia, just south of the Carolina border on US-441. Nell teaches middle school history in Boone. Her first husband – not the kids' father – was a Lumbee Indian.

Nell hopes to set up a regular school field trip to the TREPP. Tallulah promises to provide any and all relevant information about educational discounts when the ride is over.

Tallulah cannot think of more than six Lumbee Indians that she has actually met, and she is glad to know that another one is out there. She is always glad to hear about other living Indians. She clings to stories about living Indians the way she clings to warm blankets on cold rainy January mornings. Tallulah feels less lonely believing that an Indian she will never know is alive and doing something somewhere in North Carolina.

Spencer Donald asks if Lumbees are related to Cherokees. Carmen Davis jerks his ribs with her elbow and declares that Cherokees and Lumbees are traditional enemies. Nell Johnson disagrees. Tallulah arches her chest and gestures for everyone's attention.

"Traditionally," Tallulah declares, pausing as the word "tradition" sinks into the carpet, "Cherokees fought with Creeks a lot more than Lumbees."

"Were the Creeks bigger than the Cherokees?" asks Spencer.

"Creeks are big," answers Carmen.

Tallulah continues, "At the time of European settlement, Cherokee was the largest nation in what is now the Eastern United States."

"I thought Navajo was the biggest tribe," says Carmen.

"True," answers Tallulah. "Today, Navajo is largest nation in the U.S. Ojibwe actually is the largest in North America, but many of them are in Canada. But to answer your question, Cherokee is the second-largest tribe in the U.S. Centuries ago our territories stretched from Alabama to West Virginia. However, many people assume that we ran the whole Southeast, which is completely untrue. There were many nations that ran things between the mountains and the coast, including Lumbee."

Nell Johnson nods. Tallulah wonders about the twins' father. He definitely has some melanin, but how indigenous could he be? Population proportions in the Southeast make it very unlikely for one modern white woman like Nell Johnson to marry two different Indians in one lifetime. Tallulah's own mother might still get married again, but Tallulah banks on the idea that Janet will never wed another Indian.

"Are Lumbees from North Carolina or South Carolina?" asks Carmen Davis.

"They're from Lumbee," says Tallulah.

Tour Group 5709 perplexes. Even Nell Johnson stops nodding and wears uncertainty.

"There are many tribes indigenous to the south Atlantic coast who have legitimate ancestral claims to the lands and the rivers that flow from the mountains to the coast, regardless of current state boundaries," asserts Tallulah. "Like Lumbee, Catawba, Powhattan – "

"What about Croatan?" asks Spencer Donald.

"Wasn't that the one where the colonists went missing?" asks Carmen Davis.

Tallulah confirms the fact that a group of early seventeenth-century English colonists disappeared from the Carolina coast, leaving no traces of their whereabouts beyond an abandoned fort and an etching of the word "Croatan" upon a nearby tree.

"They were, like, captured, right?" says Spencer.

"Doubtful," replies Tallulah.

"Then what happened to them?"

"Think about it." Tallulah scans the group, searching for signs of critical thinking. "They were holed-up inside this little fort, and they saw all these Indian people living normal well-adjusted lives around them. Eventually, they must have gotten fed up with hiding inside the fort. They saw their hair growing longer, and then with all the southern sun, they decided to go live with the tribe."

"How do you know that?" asks Carmen. "Is that, like, some kind of traditional story?"

"It's common sense. They were archetypal English people trying to go native. But like I was saying, you can really see the tribal relationships by studying the different languages of the area. For example, the word 'Cherokee' is not originally a Cherokee word."

Tour Group 5709 bends heads. Jaws wiggle. Legs cross. Eyes widen.

"'Tsalagi' refers to our language, to our culture. 'Tsalagis hiwonisgi' translates into English as 'Do you speak Cherokee?' To be Cherokee, to think like a Cherokee, it's a cultural thing. But traditionally, we also call ourselves Aniyunwiya, which means 'principal people,' or 'real people.' So depending on who you ask, we're either the most real people of these mountains, or we're just really ethnocentric. Or both."

Tour Group 5709 hums. The twins follow Tallulah's details perfectly. Everyone else strains for epiphany. If they were cartoons, cloudy bubbles would struggle to appear above their heads.

"The word 'Tsalagi' sounds like 'Chalagi,' which could sound like the word 'Cherokee,' but they come from different contexts. The Lumbees called us Chalakee, and the Powhattans called us Charogee. You see, they lived mostly on the coasts and in river valleys, so from their flatland perspective, we made our homes in the Blue Ridge caves. Choctaws also called us Charogee and thought of us as hill people, which is perfectly logical considering their traditional preference for the flatlands closer to the Gulf of Mexico. So whether they came from the ocean or the gulf, most Europeans were calling us Charogee before they ever met us."

"Why are you called Cherokees now?" asks Carmen.

"The name stuck. Some people today will say 'Tsalagi' because it sounds more traditional. Personally, I just say 'Cherokee.' Everyone knows what you mean, and it's a much easier word than 'Aniyunwiya.'"

Tourists chuckle. Tallulah would tell them that "Cherokee" is also much sexier than "Aniyunwiya," but there are children in the group. She wonders why the Athenians chose the kid level in the first place, but she assumes they desire the easiest possible route to extra credit.

"Dude, I never knew that," announces Spencer. "That's crazy!"

"It's like calling the Missouri River the Missouri River when you're in Montana," adds Tallulah.

She has never been to Montana, but Bushyhead once spent a summer in Bozeman. Bushyhead gave her the line about the Missouri River. Bushyhead has seen nearly the whole country, and she wants to believe most of his observations.

"But anyways, enough linguistic colonialism for now. Let's finish these introductions so we can ride the Trail."

"What about the Blue Ridge Parkway?" asks the old woman.

"You must be Irma Rosenberg."

"Yes I am. Hello."

"Hello."

"So are you saying that the Blue Ridge Parkway used to belong to the Cherokees?"

"Basically, yes. The area was colonized well before they began to build the road in 1933, but the whole Blue Ridge is part of old Cherokee country."

"Have you ever been to the Great Smoky Mountains? You know, the national park areas?" asks Irma.

"Sure. I was born in Asheville, right near the park."

The Athenians lean and smile. The Johnson twins nudge their mom and mumble to each other. The word "Asheville" reverberates around the room, echoing inside the tourists' heads. Tallulah is proud of her birthplace. It is the kind of city that people are proud to be from. Americans of all appearances and backgrounds get warm, fuzzy feelings when Tallulah says the word "Asheville." It doesn't matter whether they've actually been to Asheville or not. There's just something nostalgic about the name of the city, the way the word sounds coming off Tallulah's tongue.

Irma seems impressed. "Then you've spent a lot of time up there?"

"My grandparents live near the Cherokee reservation in North Carolina."

"We went to that reservation a long time ago," says Irma. "Remember that, Rachel? It was about twenty years ago, before your Trail of Tears thing here was even built. We visited my son's family in Atlanta. It was a Memorial Day weekend, and we decided to drive to the Great Smoky Mountains National Park."

"We got lost in Tennessee," Bob Rosenberg says dryly.

"Getting lost in Tennessee wasn't very fun. Especially in such a crowded car. But the mountains were very nice. It's a very beautiful area that you have there."

"Those mountains are the cradle of our culture," says Tallulah. "It's like our motherland."

Tallulah suddenly wants a cigarette. Her face aches with each repetition of the same old metaphors about motherlands and fatherlands and cultural cradles. She contemplates launching into the old Cherokee migration story, but she shelves it for later, once they've endured a bit of the Trail itself. Besides, it's a long story, and time is a tight commodity in the Meeting Grounds.

"The motherland?" asks Irma. "Is that so?"

"Absolutely," says Tallulah. "It's the source. Even though most Cherokees today live in Oklahoma or somewhere else out west, the center of our culture definitely comes from those mountains."

Carmen Davis asks about comparative Cherokee alcoholism and unemployment in North Carolina and Oklahoma, but

Tallulah steps around the question by reminding them that both occupation and alcohol will be represented inside the Trail of Tears ride.

"We're starting to run short on time, so let's go ahead and finish introducing ourselves."

Rachel Rosenberg is next in line. She is a year older than Tallulah. She used to be a transplanted Georgian, like Tallulah, until she retransplanted herself across the Atlantic.

Rachel's family moved from northern New Jersey to the northern Atlanta area when she was eight. She attended Georgia Tech and graduated at the age of twenty-one. After graduating, she promptly leapt to London with a temporary student work visa. She met Michael Hopkins standing in a queue for tickets to a Massive Attack reunion concert. They waited in their own line for hours after they bought the tickets. Two days later they went on their first date. They soon married, but she kept her name. London is now her home.

"Michael's a computer genius," she says, "so he's curious about how your ride works."

Everyone turns and stares hard at Michael Hopkins. Michael waves at Tallulah and greets the group. Nikki Johnson whispers "he's cute" to her sister, and everyone can hear. Rachel announces that every living Rosenberg – her grandparents, her parents, her siblings, her husband, herself – converged last week for a family reunion in Atlanta. Today was a chance for Rachel and her grandparents to be together, to escape from the whole family for a few hours and enjoy a nice trip to the country.

Michael introduces himself. The Johnsons and the Athenians stretch their confused eyes and ears as Michael speaks. He and Rachel have been to New York, but this is his first time in the South. Earlier this week they made the pilgrimage to the King Center in Atlanta. Then they took a trip up in the cylindrical glass elevator at the Peachtree Plaza for a cocktail in the revolving restaurant on the top floor. Nikki Johnson cups her sister's ear, whispering loudly, "He doesn't talk black." Michael jokes about being called African American.

"I never knew it was that easy to become an American," he says. "No offense, because I really do like this country, but I think I'd rather just be black."

Tallulah wonders if Rachel would say the same thing about being Jewish. She remembers a boy from Athens who identified himself first as a post-rock bassist, second as a black Jew. She wonders if Rachel and Michael are planning to breed.

Irma and Bob Rosenberg introduce themselves last. They are both retired. They flew down from New Jersey for the family reunion.

"We prefer to go to Florida in the winters," says Irma, "but this year is different because Rachel came back. She lives such a long ways away, you know, that it's very difficult for us to see her. It's very hard on Bob and me, being so far away from our children and our grandchildren."

Irma Rosenberg talks Florida. She talks about the hurricane that will soon hit the Florida coast. She talks about old Jewish liberals in Palm Beach and young Cuban Republicans in Miami and Haitian refugees on the shore and rich people in their cars and sex workers on the street. She talks about their good friends from New Jersey who bought a condo in Florida three years ago, how their friends now want to sell the condo and move back to Jersey. Knowing that Irma and Bob long yearned to retire in Florida, their friends offered to sell them the condo, but Irma thinks they're asking too much for it. Their son in Atlanta will use his computers and fax machines to try and make the price more reasonable next week.

"Sometimes you don't want to do your business with your friends," says Irma, "but this condo is worth haggling for."

Rachel imitates her grandmother's voice – "It doesn't matter what you get as long as it's a *bargain*." Rachel laughs at herself, as do Bob and Michael. Tallulah smiles congenially. Irma mentions how much she enjoys the flea markets in Commerce, Georgia. The Athenians want to laugh, but they aren't sure why. Tallulah double-checks the group's collective ticket prices. Everyone is in the twenty-five to thirty-dollar range, which is typical for middle-class families but pricey for college students.

"We heard on the news that someone went missing here yesterday," says Rachel Rosenberg. "What's up with that?"

Nell Johnson's face twists with a hint of horror. She reaches for her daughters. The Athenians don't seem to understand. Tallulah assures Tour Group 5709 that no one went physically missing, yesterday or any day. She describes common side effects of the ride, such as momentary disorientation or drowsiness. Tallulah is not supposed to discuss the phenomenon of holing-up – it is a taboo issue that the TREPP thoroughly details in fine print on the waiver forms everyone signs before receiving their tickets. Tallulah mentions it anyway. She describes how only a very small percentage of riders hole-up, how it is a sleeplike state that sometimes lasts for a brief period after the ride ends, and how none of her tourists have ever holed-up. Ever.

"The reviews said you were *very* good," declares Irma.

Tallulah tells them to not be afraid. "Remember, this is a game. Virtual reality is not really real."

"I've actually read several articles about this Medicine Man character of yours," says Michael. "He sounds quite fascinating."

Rachel seconds Michael's fascination – "Is it okay if we just die early and go hang out with him? He seems a lot more interesting than a walk through Arkansas."

"Dude," Spencer nods enthusiastically, slowly pumping his

shoulders, "I heard about that Medicine Man guy from my professor. He seems pretty cool."

Everyone who hears or reads about the TREPP wants to meet the Wise Old Medicine Man, who is called simply Old Medicine by most TREPP employees. His program ensures customer satisfaction on the Trail of Tears.

Old Medicine tells you what you want to hear, what you think you need to hear. He uses your comments and questions to determine your beliefs. He then reaffirms your personal ideology by showering you with the kind of aboriginal spirituality that only dead people can exude.

Even in death the Trail of Tears ride encourages the customer to be the boss.

Tallulah used to know Old Medicine quite well, back in the early days, before the TREPP was open. She helped write his character. The programmers relied on her expertise to craft Old Medicine's aura. They wanted him to be wise and calm, but they knew little about old-school Cherokee cosmology. Trying to inject authenticity into Old Medicine, the programmers did what all good TREPP employees do – they asked Tallulah for guidance.

Tallulah suggested the same course of action she always suggests to people who want authentic information – read the Mooney book. James Mooney, a white Smithsonian anthropologist, published *Myths of the Cherokee* in 1900. Today Cherokees around the world learn about their culture from the Mooney book. Even the Robert Conley books depend in part upon stories from the Mooney book. Tallulah read the Mooney book several times in college, especially the stories about Tallulah Falls. Her undergraduate thesis would not exist without James Mooney.

But the programmers were too busy to read an anthropology

text. They were suffocating under investors' deadlines. They simply wanted Tallulah to summarize a few main details, to give them a construct upon which they could build the patterns of Old Medicine's appearance and speech.

Tallulah provided the summaries they needed. She even played guinea pig – engaging the Old Medicine program herself as it was developing, asking the Old Man the most difficult questions she could think of, attempting to determine the program's gaps and weaknesses.

She suggested that Old Medicine's voice should be peppered with soothing music. Reverberating cedar flutes and echoing reeds were woven into his vocal fabric. Thus, his voice becomes a sonic tranquilizer, inducing deep calm in even the most anxious tourists. People love to hear him speak, even if they cannot determine what he is talking about.

After four years of operation, the only TREPP employee to receive more press than Tallulah Wilson is the Wise Old Medicine Man. It's a fact – many customers claim to enjoy the Old Medicine experience more than the thrilling struggle to survive the Trail itself. The tech crew once estimated that nearly 3 percent of TREPP customers induce their own death near the beginning of the Trail, just to get to the Old Medicine Man sooner.

"He's the wise Old Medicine you always knew you needed," says Tallulah.

Carmen Davis is eager for the encounter. "I'm really curious to meet him," she says, "because we're going to read a lot about Native American spirituality later in the semester."

"I haven't seen him in four years," says Tallulah.

"My professor? You know him?"

"No, I mean the Old Medicine Man."

"You haven't seen the Medicine Man in four years?"

"Nope."

"Why not?"

"Tour guides don't die. We can't help you if we're dead."

Irma Rosenberg's hearing aid beeps loudly as the old woman asks if anyone dies for real on the Trail of Tears ride.

Tallulah notes that roughly four thousand Cherokees – a quarter of the nation at the time – died on the actual Trail of Tears. Some historians say it was more like ten thousand, but only four thousand were documentable. Some historians say that only two thousand officially died, but thousands of others died as a direct result. However, Tallulah insists that no tourist has ever physically expired inside the TREPP.

Riding the Trail of Tears is not supposed to be easy. It is very competitive and riddled with virtual violence. But it is also meant to be fun for the whole family. And besides, this group is a Level One tour, meaning that violence will be minimal.

"I thought it was Level Three," says Carmen.

Tallulah nibbles on her cheek. "You did?" Tallulah replies. "I'm sorry, but it clearly says Level One on my printout here."

"Oh," says Carmen.

"What does that mean?" asks the black man. He really does sound English. Very English. Tallulah has never been to London, but Michael Hopkins sounds exactly how she imagines a Londoner should sound.

"Level One is minimal violence, child-friendly."

The Brit leans over to his wife and says, "I thought we were Level Three, as well."

Tallulah has seen this before. It happens more often than she'd like, especially on Saturdays – due to the restrictions of time and space, some customers are placed on tour groups at a level easier than the one they requested. But no one is ever bumped up to a more difficult level, especially not a family with small children. On a more typical Saturday afternoon, Tallulah would be unconcerned about this sort of a scheduling mix-up. But today is different. All Tallulah wants is a relatively stress-free Trail of Tears so she can begin her long-awaited vacation, but Tour Group 5709 is already problematic.

"No," says Rachel. "Remember? We changed to a Level One." She opens her eyes and nods at her grandmother, then whispers, "For the folks."

Tallulah apologizes for any confusion resulting from the tour's level of difficulty. She reminds them that everyone who rides the Trail gets a five-dollar voucher redeemable at all of the TREPP's internal businesses. Furthermore, everyone who rides the Trail all the way to Indian Territory gets a twenty-dollar voucher and a victory T-shirt. And, of course, everyone gets to visit the Wise Old Medicine Man, regardless of difficulty level or death.

"That Old Medicine Man sounds better than a gift certificate," says Spencer.

"So if we make it to Oklahoma on a thirty-dollar ticket," beams Irma, "and we get a twenty-dollar gift certificate, then we really *do* get a good bargain!"

Tallulah promises Tour Group 5709 that the ride is like real life. What you get out of it is equivalent to what you put in. The ride responds to your responses.

"If you find yourself disturbed by the things you see and hear, remember to remain calm. Remember that it's not really 1838, that you're participating in a historical interpretation, and that it will all be over soon."

Tallulah's stomach grinds while telling her tourists that it will all be over soon. For her it never ends. This is her one thousand one hundred and third trip through the Trail of Tears.

Although each tour is different, the Trail of Tears always proceeds in the same fashion. Details alter slightly, but the overall sequence of events is helplessly predictable. Nothing really changes. Nothing really ends.

"The Removal will begin soon, so right now is your best and last chance to ask questions before the Trail of Tears begins."

Michael Hopkins wonders what percentage of people survived the Trail. Tallulah tells him that approximately 60 percent of the TREPP's customers complete the game. "I don't mean to brag," she smiles, "but about 80 percent of my tourists survive. So don't let me down, guys!"

Carmen Davis asks if Tallulah is full-blood. Tallulah replies with the typical response. "My history teacher told us Cherokees were matriarchal," says Carmen. Tallulah suggests that "were" is the operative term of Carmen's statement. However, it's true. Tallulah is not afraid of acknowledging her own contradictions. In fact, she relishes it. Her father's ancestral descent patterns were matriarchal, her mother's ancestral descent patterns were patriarchal, and she's glad her family tree had yet to meet a contradiction it didn't like.

"Were you named after Tallulah Gorge?" asks Spencer.

"Basically, yes," she says.

"So Tallulah is a Cherokee name?"

"Osda!"

"What does 'Tallulah' mean in Cherokee?" asks Carmen Davis.

"Tumbling waters, leaping waters, like a waterfall. Go figure."

Spencer asks if anyone else has hiked through Tallulah Gorge State Park. The Rosenbergs don't know where it is, but the Johnsons and Athenians have all done Tallulah Gorge. The young Johnson twins even trekked all the way down to the bottom of the gorge, where one waterfall bleeds into the next and the echoes of liquid gravity carve little caves in the sides of rocks.

Tallulah mentions how much she appreciates the walking surface at the state park that shares her name. The park's trails are paved with recycled tire rubber, some six hundred rubber tires spared from landfills and transformed into trail. It is material soft and squishy, durable and weatherproof. Easy on the feet and knees, but stable enough for wheelchairs.

Tallulah mentions James Dickey's *Deliverance*. Everyone knows *Deliverance*. Even those who don't know James Dickey are well aware of the Burt Reynolds movie based on Dickey's book.

She asks if they remember the scene where Jon Voight climbs hundreds of feet on slippery rocks, trying to catch the killer redneck sniper by surprise. Most people know the iconic scene, but few know that it was filmed at Tallulah Gorge. Even fewer know that Dickey created the fictional Cahulawassee River by fusing the histories of the Chattahoochee and Tallulah rivers, both of which were dammed.

"Squeal like a pig," cries Danny.

Tour Group 5709 laughs uneasily. Tallulah notes that the line "squeal like a pig" was only in the movie, not in the Dickey book. She promises her tourists they need not fear killer rapist inbred homosexual rednecks when riding the Trail of Tears. She wants to suggest that old-school Cherokee wedding traditions – when men were required to marry a woman who was not from their mother's clan – were a rather progressive-minded safeguard against incest, but Tallulah doesn't want her tourists to think that she believes them inbred or herself superior. She wants to tell them that many Indians are terribly homophobic, but she holds her tongue and awaits more questions. She can smell the questions coming.

"So this whole state was Cherokee country back in the day?" asks Spencer. "And all the waterfalls and rivers and things had Cherokee names?"

Tallulah again declares that Cherokees occupied the Blue Ridge, including north Georgia, but that the swamps in the southern part of the state are old Creek country. She describes the Atlanta area as an ancient and indigenous crossroads, the place where Creek and Cherokee converged. She tells them about the indigenous "pitch-tree" on the Chattahoochee River, about the English speakers' confusion regarding "pitch" and "peach," about the seventy-some Atlanta streets named "Peachtree" that testify to this colonial confusion.

Spencer asks, "So, is 'Atlanta' a Cherokee word?"

"No," she replies, "although you can spell it in the Cherokee syllabary, it's not actually a Cherokee word."

Mandy asks, "What about 'Amicalola'?"

"Like Amicalola Falls?" Tallulah replies.

"Yes, like Amicalola Falls," says Mandy.

"Yes," confirms Tallulah. "'Amicalola' is definitely a Cherokee word."

"What about Lake Allatoona?" asks Spencer.

Tallulah notes that Allatoona is like Chattanooga – an Indian name that white people started using after the Removal.

"Just look at a map of the area," she announces, "and you'll see all sorts of Indian names. Many of the words you'll associate with north Georgia are Cherokee words. Like Toccoa, or Hiawassee, or Dahlonega."

"I grew up in Dahlonega," Mandy Warren says proudly.

"Such a beautiful area," says Tallulah. Her smile begins to itch. She imagines that the Warrens occupy a large stucco house in some neighborhood called Cherokee Forest or Indian Hills.

"I know a guy who went to school at North Georgia College," says Danny Calhoun, "and that's in Dahlonega."

"Yes," Tallulah concurs, "it is." She checks the time and calculates her dwindling minutes in the Meeting Grounds. Soon it will be time for Tour Group 5709 to enter the Chamber.

"I decided to go to UGA, but I almost went to North Georgia," says Danny.

Tallulah smiles and scans the group. She wonders how well the group knows the highways in north Georgia. Anyone who's traveled the mountain roads in north Georgia is bound to cross Dahlonega sometime. Dahlonega is the gateway to the big hills. Vacationers from Atlanta know they have emerged from the city sprawl when they arrive in Dahlonega.

The Dahlonega stockade was destroyed, like most of the stockades, as soon as the last Cherokees were marched to Ross's Landing in the summer of 1838. Georgia built a mint upon the sick red ground. Between 1838 and 1861 the Dahlonega Mint pressed over six million dollars in gold coins. North Georgia State College and University, primarily an ROTC school, was built upon the campus of the old Dahlonega mint. Indeed, the Georgia capitol dome in Atlanta is crowned with the radiant fruits of Dahlonega, the gleaming proceeds of America's first official gold rush.

Mandy and Danny are about to see Dahlonega in a way they could never before imagine.

"My town may have been where Hernando De Soto first found gold in America," says Mandy. She pronounces "Hern*an*do De Soto" like a proper Southern girl.

"Oh, whatever," says Spencer. "All those dead Columbus gold people were full of shit."

Danny defends his girlfriend from his roommate's cynicism. Carmen calls Danny a racist. The dialogue quickly flames into a hormone-fueled argument. The sexual energy among the Athenians is easy to detect – Mandy is shagging Danny, and Spencer wants to shag Carmen.

The Rosenbergs appear amused. Nell Johnson offers a diplomatically neutral comment to the mix, but she says it with a condescending tone, a tone that echoes with memories of middle school. Nell gets no response. Nikki Johnson studies Mandy's and Carmen's pert curves. Willa Johnson studies Danny's muscular rooster chest.

Michael Hopkins whispers to Rachel. Irma Rosenberg touches her hearing aid. Bob Rosenberg shrugs his shoulders. Tallulah imagines the four Athenians naked together, all having sex at the same time. She wonders if Danny would blow Spencer, if Mandy would go down on Carmen. She doubts it, but you never know.

"Do you know what 'Dahlonega' means in Cherokee?" asks Tallulah, instantly dousing the flames of debate. Tour Group 5709 fixes its eyes upon its guide.

"It means yellow," Tallulah states with authority.

"Yellow?" echoes Carmen Davis.

"Yellow," confirms Tallulah. "And why did they name the town Yellow?"

"Dude," yells Spencer, "they must have already known about the gold!"

"Yes," confirms Tallulah, "they did. So you see, De Soto never actually discovered any gold in 1540. And the Americans never actually discovered any gold in 1828 either. And this takes us back to the uncomfortable question of whether a traveler can actually discover something that is already common knowledge for the people who actually live in that area."

Tour Group 5709 readily agrees that Columbus did not discover America. The Johnson children squint their eyes and move their necks. Question time is almost over. Soon the next tour group will converge upon the Meeting Grounds.

"Well, it's just about time for us to enter the ride."

"I was curious," says Carmen Davis, "because I, like, actually have one more question I'd like to ask before we start."

"Okay." Tallulah has less than three minutes to complete the orientation.

"It's about De Soto."

"Okay."

"Because I took this history class last year, right? It was a course in Southeastern history, which I, like, found really interesting because, like I said, I'm from Iowa."

Carmen takes a deep breath. Tallulah knows exactly which history professor Carmen refers to. He was on the committee for Tallulah's undergraduate thesis – a comprehensive review of Cherokee history in Georgia and the Carolinas. As a professor he was a sound resource, guiding her in helpful directions. But Tallulah wonders if he actually read every word she wrote. He gave her As on everything he evaluated, even when she expected Bs. There were times she couldn't get Bs even when she wanted to.

Carmen continues, "So, I was just, like, kind of curious, you know, if you knew any, like, traditional stories about De Soto."

"Traditional De Soto stories?"

"Yeah. Like, we know about De Soto from his journals and from white history and stuff, but I was just curious if there were, like, any Indian stories like about what it was like to encounter De Soto and all the European explorers."

"Conquistadors!" says Spencer.

Danny clears his throat and checks his digital watch.

"De Soto," says Tallulah, "was followed by hundreds of men who didn't know where they were. And because they didn't know what to expect, they were scared."

Tour Group 5709 nods in affirmation.

"And because they were scared, they never took off their armor. So De Soto and his men ended up sleeping in their armor every single night. There they were, wandering through the Deep South, searching for signs of gold and eternal life, but they never bothered to take off their armor."

Tallulah scans the room from chair to chair, looking each tourist directly in the eye for nearly a full second.

"So you see, when they got to Cherokee country, De Soto's men smelled *really bad*."

Two seconds of silence pass before Rachel Rosenberg breaks into a heavy laugh. Michael Hopkins follows suit, and then the Johnson twins giggle and bounce, warm with a story about smelly old famous people. Irma Rosenberg touches her ear and asks Bob how well he heard the story. Bob tells her that Hernando De Soto had a body odor problem because he slept in his armor. Irma laughs heartily, her glasses stumbling as she chortles. Bob helps her reposition the glasses.

"So what do we learn from De Soto?" asks Tallulah, as she stands erect and begins to walk toward the doorway that begins the Trail. Absolutely no refunds are available for any tourist who crosses this doorway.

Spencer Donald hypothesizes that De Soto teaches us the utter uselessness of gold, that money doesn't equate to happiness and it never has and never will, that ultimately we must stop mining and raping the earth in search of more and more riches. Tallulah hears a familiar tone in Spencer's rant.

"Perhaps," she says. "But not quite the answer I was looking for."

Spencer sinks slightly, but Tallulah eyes him reassurance. It's never a good idea to alienate a tourist, especially when the ride is just about to start. An alienated tourist is a tourist who doesn't tip. Not that she expects a tip from the Athenians, but you can never tell.

"When we think about De Soto and his armor—and his

odor – we must remember the most important thing that anyone riding the Trail of Tears needs to know."

Tallulah pauses for dramatic emphasis, waiting to see if anyone will finish her sentence. No one speaks.

"Don't be afraid," she says plainly.

A collective *ohhh* filters through the eleven heads in Tour Group 5709. Some sigh. Some stretch. Some scratch themselves. Some fiddle with the things in their pockets.

It was a good orientation, but now it's over. It fostered some healthy dialogue, it softened some initial fears, and it even raised some decent questions for a bunch of Americans. Most importantly, Tallulah was able to coax at least one laugh from everyone, a critical factor in earning their early trust. And they need to trust her if they want to survive the game.

Tallulah moves toward the doorway of the descending corridor in a slow rhythm, a steady two-beat heartbeat step.

The tourists rise mechanically from their chairs. They buzz with anticipation. They line up behind Tallulah in a windy single-file formation, like a drunk river, ready to finally ride the Trail of Tears.

5

"Take your time," says Tallulah.

Tour Group 5709 follows her down the descending corridor. She quotes verbatim from her standard dialogue – "The corridor will seem dark at first, but your eyes will adjust . . . Please watch your step and use the floor lights for guidance . . . The corridor is curved in a clockwise direction . . . Railings on the wall are here for your support, and they will guide you down if you hold onto them . . ."

Faint lights pulse along the corners of the corridor.

"This totally reminds me of the entrance to Carlsbad Caverns in New Mexico," says Spencer Donald.

"No way," says Carmen Davis. "More like Space Mountain."

The group walks past a large stainless steel door. Their bodies twist, reflections on the door. Spencer runs his hand along the doorway.

"Is this where we go in?" asks Rachel Rosenberg, momentarily transfixed by her own steel reflection.

"Not this one," answers Tallulah, motioning onward toward the doors ahead of them. "We have now entered the Chamber, and there are four different rooms within the Chamber. Each room holds a different group of visitors. With four different rooms, we can accommodate four tour groups at the same time. We'll be using the second room, which is right around the corner."

"Will we meet other visitors when we're inside?" asks Michael.

"You mean, will you see tourists from other groups?" replies Tallulah.

"Yes."

"You *are* a computer programmer, aren't you?" Tallulah smiles. "And the answer is no. Each room of the Chamber exists in its own loop, and each group of tourists rides the Trail in their own self-contained loop. Meaning the only other customers you'll encounter on the Trail are the people within this group."

"Oh."

"We decided long ago that it would get too confusing if multiple tour groups were allowed to interact with each other."

Michael's question is one that Tallulah hears often from computer programmers or from people who work in some field of customer service. It is a good question, and it always gives Tallulah an opportunity to summarize the basic philosophy of causality loops.

The Trail of Tears ride, like the actual Removal, exists because of causality. Cause and effect – actions and reactions, the universal continuum of motion toward and away. Each time a tour group jacks into the Trail of Tears, they enter through the same point of origin, moving away from the real and into the virtual through the same place – the First Cabin. The First Cabin is an authentically ransacked 1838 Cherokee summer home. It is the gateway to virtual time.

The Surround Vision experience always opens with the same first image, where all members of a single tour group perceive themselves together inside the summer cabin. This moment in the First Cabin is crucial for Tallulah and her colleagues, for it provides a few sacred minutes to count heads again, to ensure that all tourists have entered the ride.

However, the Trail of Tears always changes after this origin point. No two rides are exactly the same. Each tour group experiences the same historical cycle, but the details change based upon the tourists' reactions. Each tour group exists in its own independent cycle, its own causality loop. Tourists from different groups don't meet inside the ride because the loops are programmed not to cross.

The ride is a simulation, but the uniqueness of each causality loop is real. The ride operates within fixed parameters, but choices within these parameters yield somewhat random outcomes. Like life itself.

"Characters on the Trail," says Tallulah, "react to your actions. Their ability to make choices is real, even if they themselves are not."

Tallulah stops in front of the stainless steel door to Room Two.

"I think I have to pee," Nikki Johnson says, with a tone of embarrassment.

"Nikki! We were just upstairs near the toilets," says her mother.

"But I didn't have to go then!"

"No problem," says Tallulah, proudly. "There are toilets conveniently located in each room of the Chamber."

"Oh," says Nell. "That *is* convenient."

The Chamber didn't always have toilets, not until the sixth month of operation. Though management resisted the idea at first, toilets were a practical addition to the Trail of Tears since many a tourist feels the need to urinate while approaching exodus. Besides, even if everyone was forced to pee before entering the Chamber, someone would still need to pee upon first sight of the Chairsuit. So many tour groups were delayed by last-minute customer urinations that the management decided, in spite of the cost, that toilets in the Chamber rooms were good for business.

"That's very thoughtful," notes Irma Rosenberg, gently grabbing Bob's arm. "Isn't that thoughtful, Bob?"

"Very thoughtful," he replies.

Tallulah quickly counts heads before she opens the steel door. All eleven heads wait at the door, watching as Tallulah turns the handle. She presses her forearm upon a thick metal latch, pushing it down in a steady deliberate motion until it clicks.

She leans her shoulder into the shiny door, slowly pushing back the cool metal. The door is thin and heavy. It is also soundtight.

Oohs and ahhs, a typical reaction, filter through the doorway as Tour Group 5709 catches its first glimpse of Chamber Room Two. But the oohs and ahhs quickly fade, giving way to a thick silence. The tourists, naturally, are awestruck, though they seem rather well-adjusted given the circumstances.

Fritz and Ramsey are the techies who greet Tour Group 5709 as they enter the exodus point. Even the techies comment on 5709's well-adjusted appearance. Fritz says that at this rate, half the group might make it to California.

Fritz isn't Indian, but he was born in Mendocino County and grew up near a reservation. He's had Indian friends from childhood, and he ate the bread their mothers made. He's told Tallulah that she belongs on the West Coast. He often speaks about going back home, but the TREPP's healthy paychecks have trapped him in Georgia. He's one of the few people at the TREPP who can talk to Tallulah about California writers like Wendy Rose and John Rollin Ridge and Louis Owens and Janice Gould. He's told her stories about Alcatraz and the Intertribal Friendship House, stories that Bushyhead has confirmed.

"So, *this* is the Chamber," declares Carmen.

"You can't have chamber music without chambers!" Fritz answers.

"You know," interjects Ramsey, "you have the best tour guide in the world."

"Ramsey, please," says Tallulah.

But he continues anyway. "You couldn't be in better hands."

Tallulah wants to heckle Ramsey back. Ramsey the half-Iranian techie who requested Fridays off for religious reasons, though he hasn't been inside a mosque in over a decade. Tallulah knows, for she has seen the blurry Friday-morning carpet in Ramsey's apartment with her own eyes. Ramsey, who may have the best musical taste of everyone on the tech crew, was hired by the TREPP while he was still an undergraduate, and he never managed to actually finish his engineering degree.

Tallulah catches Ramsey between customers, leans into him, and asks quietly, "Level One, right?"

"I'm out until Tuesday," he whispers back.

"No no," she hastily replies. "*Level One*. This is a Level One, right?"

"Right, right," Ramsey confirms. "Level One."

"Just checking," she says. "It seemed there was some confusion."

"No confusion," he answers. "There's kids here, for Pete's sake."

"Are you sure?"

"I'm sure," he says.

"Can you double check?" she asks.

"If you insist," he replies. Tallulah thinks she hears him mutter the word "princess" as he walks to his console. He examines his screens and flips quickly through the papers on his clipboard. "No problem," he says. "All good for Level One."

"Thank you," she says, and she walks toward her Chairsuit.

You're probably wondering what a Chairsuit looks like. A Chairsuit involves an ergonomically framed chair that is enveloped by a body suit. The suits are made with a synthetic compound, called Realskyn, which fastens itself to the customer's skin. It is snug but extremely flexible. Each Chairsuit also includes a Visor.

The TREPP knows that one size cannot truly fit all. Thus, Chairsuits come in two sizes – small and large – and are extremely adjustable due to the nature of the Realskyn, which shrinks or stretches to wrap itself around the tourist like a wetsuit. After the tourist sits down, a techie adjusts the machine and fastens the tourist into the Chairsuit. Once fastened, the tourist's body is enveloped by Realskyn. Then the Visor descends upon the head.

The Visor is both the most intimidating and the most stimulating aspect of a Chairsuit. The Visor *is* Surround Vision. It enhances and personalizes Arthur Wilson's design. The Visor, like its prototype, enables you to see. Grandpa Art's model of Surround Vision proved that the call-and-response dynamics inherent to the actual Trail of Tears were possible inside a virtual visual apparatus. However, while Grandpa's Jeep Cherokee with television windows requires people to actually sit next to each other inside the car, the Chairsuit Visor is fully individualized. It is the single-occupancy realization of her grandfather's dream. The Visor engulfs each rider's head, surrounding the customer's visual range with three-dimensional images – images of the landscape, the other tourists in the group, the digital Indians being removed, and so forth. Beyond the ride's built-in scenery, the Visor shows you both what you are seeing and what you want to see. Upon engaging the Trail, it becomes nearly impossible to distinguish between action and reaction. The customer becomes both action and reaction, surrounded by images that blur the two together.

A favorite riddle of TREPP employees is this – *If you make a choice, but you do it because something else tells you to, are you actually making a choice?* Tallulah is generally credited as the riddle's creator, even though she can't remember writing it.

"Is it possible to starve in there?" asks Carmen. "I mean, will you still get to meet the wise Old Medicine Man if you starve to death instead of getting beaten?"

"Yeah," adds Spencer. "And hey, I want to know if you'll see other people from the group when you get to the Medicine Man, or is it just an individual thing?"

"What if I have to pee again while I'm on the ride?" asks Nikki Johnson.

"No problem," Fritz responds to the girl. "The Chairsuit will airwash your body while you're in the ride."

"Airwash?" asks Nell.

Fritz touches the Realskyn on Tallulah's Chairsuit and explains the airwashing process in layman's terms. "This material filters and circulates the bacteria around your skin by recycling the particles in the air around your body." His voice strikes that tone so common to late-night TV infomercials. "So if you do happen to wet your pants on the ride, don't worry. It'll be clean and dry by the time you're finished."

"No way!" claims Spencer.

"Way," replies Fritz.

The Johnson twins are satisfied with Fritz's explanation of the airwashing process, but they both use the Chamber toilet before strapping into the Chairsuit. Nell relieves herself as well. So do Irma, Bob, Michael, and Spencer.

"Tallulah," asks young Willa Johnson, "why is yours different from the rest of ours?"

“Mine is different,” she answers, “for the same reason that I don’t get to visit the Old Medicine Man.”

“What’s up with that?” asks Spencer.

“I have to stay alive,” she says plainly. “I wouldn’t be much of a tour guide if I wasn’t alive to guide you.”

It’s true – the tour guide takes care of the tourists who are still alive; Old Medicine takes care of the dead ones.

“So you’re, like, immortal,” declares Spencer. Oh, how little they see.

Carmen Davis craves more information about the airwashing process, but Fritz recommends a visit to the bookstore after the ride, where she can purchase the TREPP’s technology catalog video, a moderately priced video that explains the various pieces of groundbreaking technology that make the Trail of Tears such a unique experience.

Tallulah wonders what Fritz and Ramsey know about the holed-up Belgian woman. They probably know more than anyone else at the TREPP, even more than Boss Johnson. The tech crew knows everything because they are involved with each and every Trail of Tears. They monitor all four Chamber Rooms from Technical Control; nothing happens without their knowledge.

Technical Control – TC for short – is a circular operations booth that looms above the Chairsuits, positioned so the techies can see into all four Chamber rooms at once. Some employees call it the “Crow’s Nest,” though Tallulah thinks that “Owl’s Nest” is more appropriate.

At least two techies monitor the progress of each group. They keep track of each customer’s whereabouts, closely monitoring who’s still riding the Trail and who’s gone to meet Old Medicine. They keep track of major changes in the causality loop – which routes are taken, which stockades are visited, exactly what time of year each major river is crossed.

As Fritz and Ramsey help the Johnson family fit snugly into their Chairsuits, Tallulah straps herself into position. She moves on autopilot, as usual. Tallulah has been walking the Trail of Tears for over four years. On over eleven hundred occasions she has done what she is about to do, seen what she is about to see.

Fritz shouts, "Okay then! Who's ready to do this thing?"

Affirmative sounds ring through the Chamber.

"Everything a go, Tula?"

The voices blur, and she cannot tell whether Fritz or Ramsey asks the question. Everything outside the Visor blurs.

"Yes," she says. "Everything's a go.

6

Lights outside the Visor merge with images inside, a synthesis of internal and external light. This is Bushyhead's favorite part of the Trail. The initial anticipation, the uncertain fusion of illumination and life. He says it always feels new to him, like the sound of an orchestra tuning before a symphony.

The First Cabin materializes within the Visor, causing the tourists to materialize within the First Cabin. Sights congeal soft and fast. Tour Group 5709 sees itself in digital for the first time.

They all sit cross-legged on the floor. All the tourists can see each other's faces, but they cannot see their own. A broken mirror hangs next to the doorway, but the tourists have yet to notice. One by one, they stand.

"That was easy," says Irma Rosenberg. "I haven't been able to move like that in years."

"In fifty years," says Bob Rosenberg.

"This is wonderful!" exclaims Irma.

Tallulah is glad to hear happy customers. She reminds herself that she is helping them broaden their horizons. Sometime in the future these people will look back and warmly remember the time they rode the Trail of Tears with Tallulah Wilson. She stretches her neck, and her bones give no resistance.

"Something's different," says Carmen Davis, reaching her hands toward the roof. Carmen does not see the small bloodstains on the wood above. Tallulah is slightly let down by this oversight, for she expected Carmen to be more observant.

"Girl, I hope I'm as tan as you," replies Mandy Warren, grabbing hold of Carmen's arm.

"Damn," smiles Danny Calhoun. "You girls look good."

"Don't you love this dress?" asks Mandy.

The Johnson twins find the mirror and examine their appearance. Their mother watches from the other edge of the room, one eye on her daughters and one on the shattered window. Irma Rosenberg eyes an unbroken plate as if she were in a flea market.

"Ooh," exclaims Mandy. "Here's a mirror!"

The Athenians line up behind the broken mirror, stretching their heads above the twin girls and celebrating their new skins. They still look like themselves, but they are now noticeably Indian. The white folks are darker, Michael Hopkins is a shade lighter, and the Johnson twins are roughly the same. Everyone's cheekbones have grown a touch higher.

Spencer Donald wants to do a Ghost Dance, but Tallulah reminds him that he is in the wrong time and place. The Athenians and the younger Rosenbergs wonder if the Old Medicine Man can Ghost Dance, but Tallulah suggests that they find out for themselves.

"Don't worry," says Tallulah. "Even if you survive the Trail, you will still get to meet the Old Medicine Man before you leave the ride."

"What happened here?" asks Rachel. "Looks like somebody trashed the place."

5709 stops admiring its skin and hair. The customers begin to examine the damage. Personal items lay shattered; broken pieces cover the scattered floor. Tables are turned over. Cabinets are emptied. Cupboards are flung open, the doors torn at the hinges. All the food, drink, and cookware has been taken.

"It's just awful what they did back then," says Nell Johnson, with a tone of finality, as if it will never happen again.

"This is the First Cabin," says Tallulah. "It represents the scene of a looted Cherokee home in the late spring of 1838."

"Who took everything?" asks Rachel Rosenberg.

"You'll soon find out," said Tallulah. "Once we walk through that door, our Trail of Tears will begin."

"The American troops did this, didn't they?" asks Carmen.

Tallulah replies, "The troops busted down the doors and captured the Indians who lived here, but most of the theft and vandalism are actually the work of nonsoldiers. This home" – she pauses to extend her arms – "this home was probably ravaged by a band of looters and pillagers that follow closely behind the troops."

"Like when we invaded Baghdad?" asks Spencer.

"I suppose," Tallulah replies. "It's kind of like that." She wants to say that looters always follow closely on the heels of invading armies and that the Cherokee round-up was absolutely like the invasion of Baghdad back at the turn of the century. But Tallulah is a professional. Her response is noncommittal. What if Nell's first husband, the Lumbee, was a Marine who died in combat?

Tallulah asks for any last questions. No one responds. The vandalism and destruction within the cabin speak volumes.

"Let's go before the looters come back," says Carmen.

Spencer quickly agrees. Rachel and Michael are the first to approach the cabin door. The rest of the group follows suit and gradually lines up. The Athenians admire themselves once more in the broken mirror. Nell Johnson tries to keep her kids a safe distance from the broken glass.

"Okay," says Tallulah. "Who's going first?"

"Why don't you go first?" asks Mandy.

Tallulah respectfully declines and again asks for a volunteer to first exit the First Cabin. Spencer also asks Tallulah to go first, a sentiment echoed by all the Athenians.

"But I want to see what happens to you when you leave," Carmen says.

"It's protocol," replies Tallulah. "I'm supposed to go last."

"Oh, come on," says Spencer. "Like, what would happen if you mix it up a bit? None of us would care."

Tallulah rubs her eyes. Her eyes aren't dry, but her fingers tingle and swell with a pressing need to rub something. She feels Nell Johnson cringe at the prospect of subverting protocol. The Removal is only just beginning, and already she looks forward to a pull on Deer Cooker's pipe. Tallulah can smoke all the tobacco she wants inside the ride without *really* smoking tobacco.

"Grandma and Grandpa," says Rachel, "I've never seen you two move like this."

"Who?" says Bob.

"No offense," Rachel continues, "but I mean, you guys are, like, really flexible right now. You're really moving around. Don't you think?"

"Honey," says Irma, "I would stay here all day long if I could!"

"Tallulah?" asks Willa Johnson.

"Yes?"

"Can you please go first?"

"Willa," says Nell, "you heard Tallulah. She's supposed to go last. That's her job."

"Come on, Mom," says Nikki. "I'm scared."

Tallulah eyes the cabin and considers the degree of damage. She thinks to contact Ramsey. She notices many sharp edges, perhaps too many for a typical Level One tour. But Ramsey was certain that 5709 was Level One. She asked him directly, and he double checked. Ramsey may be hammered, but he's solid on the job.

"Please?" begs Willa.

"Please??" echoes Nikki.

"Yeah," says Spencer. "I'm with the twins on this one."

Tallulah remembers one particularly ornery group of Americans from last year. Tour Group 4492. They spent nearly twenty realtime minutes inside the First Cabin debating who should leave first. Tour Group 5709 is already much more amiable and well-adjusted than 4492, but Tallulah's digital stomach burns as she imagines wasting another twenty realtime minutes inside the First Cabin.

"Fine," she says. "I'll go. The sooner we leave, the sooner we're on the Trail."

And the sooner this tour group is over, the sooner Tallulah will clock out for a long week off.

"Follow me, one person at a time," she says.

Tallulah walks through the door and into the vibrant environment. She smells the pines, the mud, the rhododendrons. The steady breeze is distinct; it caresses the skin, but it carries no chill. Tallulah turns and watches her tourists emerge from the cabin. The first to emerge are the Athenians – Spencer first, then Carmen. Danny and Mandy hold hands as they emerge together. Next come the Johnson twins, followed closely by their mother. Tallulah thinks the college kids are absurdly self-centered to go before the little girls, but she considers the possibility that the girls wanted the Athenians to go before them. The Rosenbergs are last – Rachel first, then Michael, then Bob. Tallulah watches the door, waiting for Irma, but her eyes wander after the twins and the college kids as they meander into 1838, as they pull fallen leaves and branches from the green, red earth.

"What happened?" asks Bob Rosenberg, a shrill panic in his voice. "Where is she?"

Tallulah refocuses on the door. Bob reaches for his frantic head.

"Grandma?" exclaims Rachel. "*Grandma?*"

Tallulah hears a Jersey tinge in Rachel Rosenberg's voice, a latent vocal tone the tourist had masked well until now.

"For fuck's sake," says Michael. "Where's Irma?"

Tallulah runs back inside the First Cabin. She searches the house, inside and out. She walks in circles, opens closet doors, even runs her fingers along the dusty floor. She finds no sign of the old woman.

Tallulah walks outside with nothing intelligent to say. She looks around, scans the confusion on Irma's family, and reenters the cabin. She has fumbled the lines. Her words are escaping from her. This is unprecedented.

She buzzes Technical Control on the water beetle.

"What happened?" she demands. She cannot tell if it is Fritz or Ramsey on the other end, but she doesn't bother to ask.

"When?"

"The woman? Where's the old woman?"

"Who?"

"Irma Rosenberg," Tallulah says sharply.

"I don't know." It's Fritz. "Her stats are fine. She's standing right next to you."

Tallulah chomps hard on her inner cheek. She walks outside, and the soft heat triggers a reaction from her skin. The tourists have questions. Tallulah does not know what she is supposed to say.

7

Tallulah counts possibilities with hectic calm. Everyone in Tour Group 5709 is supposed to be in 1838. Is it possible for Irma Rosenberg to be in the same place – the same digital northeast Georgia hills, just a few miles west of the TREPP's present-day location – but stranded in a different time? Did she simply walk into a different past, unexpectedly severed from her family by a couple years? Tallulah watches a wave of motions and expressions trickle through 5709 like leaves without wind. Her tourists have grown into their new old bodies like toddlers into the next size of pants.

The beetle buzzes. Tallulah walks beside the cabin to answer.

"She's definitely in your loop," says Fritz. "I mean, she's right there. You should see her."

"I'm telling you I don't see her." Tallulah mashes the transmitter up close to her mouth, whispering hard. "Figure out what got fucked up, okay?"

She closes the beetle and wants to throw it against a tree. She thinks there must have been more confusion with the difficulty level than anyone was willing to acknowledge. But that alone isn't enough to explain the situation. Here, but not?

The Rosenbergs are only thirty-dollar customers. Customers generally have to pay at least seventy-five dollars to entertain options beyond 1838. If Irma Rosenberg had paid one hundred dollars for her ticket, she could have walked into 1835. She would have been able to sign the Treaty of New Echota, then load her worldly possessions onto riverboats and cruise comfortably to the lushest part of Indian Territory. She could have dined at the Vann House before departure. As such high-rent ticket holders know, the material benefits of being among the wealthiest 1 percent of any culture's population are addictive.

Common people generally want to ridicule and humiliate the ruling classes. Sometimes the masses need to execute their rulers, especially if they've committed treason. Fortunately, one-hundred-dollar customers who play Ridges and Vanns and Boudinots are able to complete the ride upon their chariot's arrival. They're not forced to wait for everyone else to arrive via foot or wagon a year or two later. They're not forced to wait for the assassins at the end of the Trail.

Tallulah thinks the TREPP's logic is sound – while the traditional Cherokee approach to dealing with rich leaders who sell out their people may have its merits, it would surely seem distasteful to wealthy tourists two centuries later. But Tour Group 5709 paid an average of thirty dollars for their tickets. Everyone in 5709 should have been planted squarely into 1838, the commoner's year of exodus. If Irma Rosenberg was in the same loop as the rest of her family, Tallulah should see her now.

Standardized tour guide dialogue requires Tallulah to remind her tourists that nothing is guaranteed on the Trail of Tears, nothing except a five-dollar voucher toward any good or service in the TREPP. Even then you cannot cash out the voucher – it can only be used for a good or service at the TREPP. Tallulah is supposed to be providing inspirational disclaimers while exempting herself and the company from any guarantees.

But after four years of experience, Tallulah knows the Trail of Tears much better than she did when she wrote that manual so long ago. She wants to make all the guarantees in the world.

She wants to guarantee Irma's safe return. She wants to promise the Rosenbergs that their matriarch will not hole-up.

"Maybe we can just kill ourselves and get it over with," says Rachel Rosenberg.

"We can't do that," answers Tallulah.

"Why not?"

"We just can't. Nobody can commit suicide until you've at least made it to the stockades.

"Has anyone tried?" asks Rachel.

"Go ahead," Tallulah says. "It won't do you any good."

"Well," Rachel's voice begins to screech, "could you do something? Like leave this game for a minute to make sure Irma's not locked up or whatever?"

"I can't leave the loop once it's started," Tallulah says. "But everything's okay. Really. We'll find her."

"She probably died already," insists Rachel. "Just let me kill myself so I can find out."

"Come on, Rachel." Her husband speaks up. "We all want to meet the Medicine Man, but let's ease off the suicidal rhetoric, eh?"

"What if she's with the Old Man already?"

"Hmm." Michael eyes Tallulah. "Can't we just reboot and start over?"

"The Trail has begun, and we can't stop it now. We have to see it through," Tallulah says.

It's true – once the loop is on, it's on. If it could be stopped, the realism of the whole enterprise would be lost.

Tallulah wonders why the Johnsons and the Athenians aren't coiling with uncertainty. She watches their eyes stretch and their mouths animate. They seem cloaked by a wall of their self-willed ignorance, but they can only ward off the uncertainty for so long. The Rosenbergs are clearly unraveling, pulled between the worlds of exotic voyeurism and technical incompetence. She feels their spirits sink; she feels their collective thirst, their spiritual vacuum. It's only a matter of time before the skepticism spreads. Tallulah looks up at the sharp cumulus clouds. She feels their doubt, but she also feels their need for hope. And if it's spirit they want, then damn it, it's spirit they'll get. Tallulah reaches her hands up high, reaching slowly as if each second were an endless vision, reaching for the blue ceiling as if she were the incarnated indigenous holy ghost. Tallulah knows she can wear the high priestess costume with the best of them.

Everyone in Tour Group 5709 breathes calmly and collectively. They tingle as they watch Tallulah's spiritual performance.

"It's true that we may all die, but it's also true that we may all survive to the Indian Territory. And no one's going to kill themselves."

Virtual rays sift through Tallulah's head as she speaks, and her voice rattles with an extra pinch of reverb as she slowly brings her arms back down.

"Anyone can die here," she declares. Tree leaves flutter like the reverb in her voice. The tourists cannot resist. They are compelled to listen.

Tallulah continues. "I once had a healthy sixty-dollar customer slip and paralyze himself in Kentucky. He survived the Ohio on a makeshift raft, but he drowned tragically in the Mississippi. And I also once watched a wealthy tourist fake an infection so she could ride in the back of a wagon, then collapse under the weight of a dead body next to her when the wagon hit a bump and tipped over."

The college kids giggle. Tallulah remembers the children. She thinks she must be scaring them, but their eyes are wide and dialed in. Tallulah's voice buzzes up from the ground and down from the clouds.

"But I've seen many miracles too. I've seen people fall sick in Tennessee and still fight it all the way to Tahlequah. I've seen hundreds of five-dollar tourists – many of them college students, and I don't even think they needed extra credit – I've seen college students limping painfully when they leave the Georgia stockades, but somehow finding the strength and courage to walk the whole damn Trail of Tears. I've seen tourists with broken legs carry the sick and maimed on their backs for hundreds of miles."

The sun showers soft warmth upon their vibrant skin.

"So you see, there's nothing to stop us – including Irma, even though we can't see her yet – there's nothing to stop us from surviving. Nothing except ourselves."

Nell Johnson begins to clap her hands, but no one follows her lead. The rest stare, their ears humming with unusual frequencies. Nell stops clapping and straightens her dress.

Nikki Johnson nudges her sister's arm and leads her to a nearby tree. Nell follows. The Athenians turn their eyes and ears away from Tallulah; they bump against each other and gaze into the distance.

"So Grandma's already hanging with the Old Medicine Man?" asks Rachel.

"Maybe Irma knows what she's doing," Michael answers. "Upon reflection, I reckon you might be right, sweetie. Let's skip the genocide bit, kick the bucket, and check out the Old Man." He looks deep into Tallulah's eyes. "Well, let's get on with it then. Where's this stockade we have to get to before we can kill ourselves?"

Bob Rosenberg stands blankly. The humor of his grandchildren is lost on him. Tallulah wants to say something to him, but the words are missing. For once the situation on the Trail of Tears is beyond her experience.

Bodies circle Tallulah's eyes like horses in a cathode carousel. The ride seems normal – vibrant grasses and trees, winds that brush the fringes of your skin, ground so solid and soft that it could hold you up forever, colors so colorful that they look like themselves. Tallulah scans everywhere for the unusual, but minus the absence of Irma Rosenberg, she sees nothing out of the ordinary.

The Johnson children chase each other over arching roots of trees. Nell Johnson watches her children and touches the skin around her eyes and cheeks.

"Man, this is great," says Danny. "It's like having the whole mountain to yourself."

"There's totally no one else here," echoes Mandy.

Rachel and Michael make predictions about how they will find Irma. Bob twitches his head back and forth, scratches his nose, and wipes his digital lips.

"So what just happened?" Bob asks. His voice is dry and easy, but more hollow than it is supposed to be. Tallulah listens for life in his words, but he sounds flat. Even if he had respiratory issues in reality, they shouldn't bother him on the Trail.

Tallulah breathes deeply and locks eyes with the Rosenbergs. "We think that Irma went from the cabin straight to Ross's Landing," she asserts.

She feels her stomach twist upon the sounds of her own words. It is a horrible lie. Not simply a little lie, like the ones she often tells tourists who are injured, riding across Missouri in the backs of the wagons and hanging on for dear life. Not at all – this is an ugly, awful lie, one without basis or precedent.

Tallulah wouldn't have believed it herself, but no one seems to be listening. The Athenians touch themselves and each other. The Johnsons walk easily over the soft terrain, talking about the landscape and people from their hometown. The Rosenbergs seem lost in other worlds, imagining the spiritual essence of a digital medicine man or contemplating life without their life partner.

"Come again?" says Rachel.

"Ross's Landing. We think that she went straight from the cabin to Ross's Landing." It is a ridiculous hypothesis.

"Where's Ross's Landing?" asks Rachel.

"Chattanooga," says Tallulah.

Mandy turns her head toward Tallulah, asking from a distance why Chattanooga is called Ross's Landing. The Athenians return to Tallulah.

"I thought you said 'Chattanooga' was an Indian word," says Spencer.

"It's a historical phenomenon," says Tallulah. "You see, 'Chattanooga' is a Cherokee word that means something about fishing, about pulling fish out of water. It used to refer to only a small part of what is now the Chattanooga area." Tallulah's stomach momentarily settles. It feels good not to lie. "I don't know," she pauses. "Why do they call it the Apache helicopter?"

Tour Group 5709 is unprepared to make such an abrupt shift to attack helicopters. After all, they are still getting adjusted to 1838. It is a simpler time. No helicopters or tanks. No Tomahawk missiles. Tallulah breathes.

"You see," Tallulah holds Bob's limp arm as she prepares to speak, "the stockade at Ross's Landing sank long ago. But in here, in 1838, that is where the final roundup happens – at Ross's Landing. After that, we're sent out on the Trail. We'll see Irma at the fort in Ross's Landing, when they try to document everyone before departure. We'll find her there, no problem."

"So was this always a possibility?" asks Rachel. "That some of us were just going to be lost?"

"Look." Tallulah isn't sure if her tone is as soothing as it should be. "Nothing is guaranteed on the Trail of Tears. But I promise you that your grandmother is okay. You'll see her soon, one way or the other."

"Sooner the better," says Michael. "I mean, no offense, but I've heard stories from some mates who came over here last year, and I'd much rather jump ahead to the Old Medicine Man than get shot or chopped up or something."

"Seriously," seconds Rachel. "We can't just get off?"

"But you see," says Tallulah, "you can't just drop in on Old Medicine whenever you want. You have to wait until he calls you."

Tallulah recognizes something unsettling in her own speech patterns – she can't seem to stop using visual metaphors. That's the problem. She's defaulting to visual clichés precisely because she can't see! She expects that Tour Group 5709 will soon see through her promises.

After four years Tallulah knows how to manipulate tourists, but she does not know how to lie to them. It would be like telling customers at the Mediterranean Café that feta is not a kind of cheese. Tallulah knows the protocols for dealing with a sick tourist, a twitching tourist, a crying tourist. An injured, combative, disgruntled, hungry, dizzy, suicidal tourist. But not a missing tourist! What do the other guides do if their customers disappear? And why should she care what other guides do? She's still Tallulah Wilson.

The water beetle buzzes in Tallulah's pocket. She excuses herself from the tourists and walks behind a wilting tree. She holds the beetle firmly in her hand. It's Ramsey on the other end, calling with the word from TC. The readings on their equipment have fluctuated since Tallulah spoke to Fritz. Irma's stats are good, and her status is alive, but her location is vague.

Tallulah glances around the tree, careful to keep the tourists from hearing her conversation. "What do you mean, vague?"

"I don't know what to tell you," Ramsey replies. "It's weird. It's like she's there, but she isn't."

"Is it the same thing that happened to the Belgians yesterday?"

"I just asked Wallace that same question, and he said no."

"Are you sure she's in the same loop? Maybe she jacked into a different loop? Maybe she's accidentally signing New Echota?"

"No, Tula, she's definitely in your loop. We just don't know where."

Ramsey knows Tallulah well enough to know that she does not want to bring Homeland Security into it. He also knows that telling Boss Johnson about the missing tourist would mean involving Homeland Security. But it has to be done – Ramsey could lose his job if he doesn't go to Johnson with these details.

"I don't know what to tell them," says Tallulah.

"Don't worry, I'll tell them something."

"Not the boss man," she says. "I mean my tourists. I'm trying to lie to them, and it's not going well. I swear I'm not having a fucking nervous breakdown in here or anything."

"Okay."

"What do I do?"

"Blame it on us," says Ramsey. "Tell them that the tech crew backs up whatever you said. I'll be your straw man, just hang in there. You'll be okay. The old lady's not holed-up. We'll find her."

Tallulah doesn't want to blame Ramsey for any of her own lies, but knowing she can pass the blame does help to calm her nerves. She returns the water beetle to her vest pocket and faces her customers. She wants to give them something positive, something uplifting. Tour Group 5709 needs food and stories, and she needs to lead them. Good food and good stories can save anything. 5709 could still have a good time. They could still have an enjoyable educational experience, even if the Rosenbergs contemplate suicide the entire trip.

"Dude," says Danny as he leans against a tree and gazes at his arms against the rolling contours of the landscape, "I just can't get over how tan I am." He strokes his girlfriend's silky new black hair.

"I know," confirms Mandy. "I *like* this ride."

"Mandy," Carmen exclaims, "your tits are bigger!"

Mandy looks down, runs her hands across her chest. "You might be right," she says.

Danny and Spencer shoot their eyes at Mandy's chest. Rachel examines herself, as does Michael. All the males gape clumsily at all the females. Even Tallulah cannot resist glancing at her own chest.

Danny scrutinizes the bulge in his pants. He slowly pulls the waist of his pants and gazes at his crotch.

"Dude!!" he shouts.

"What?" asks Spencer.

"Dude, check your package!"

Spencer follows suit. "Whoa!" he seconds. "I *like* this ride!" He looks up to see how closely Carmen is watching him.

Michael slyly cups his wife's breasts. Rachel returns the favor to her husband's balls. Irma Rosenberg, for the first time since they jacked into the ride, is far from the minds of her descendants.

It's true. Everyone's breasts and penises are slightly larger on the Trail of Tears.

Anything to ensure customer satisfaction, regardless of historical inaccuracy, and body parts are always a welcome distraction for the average customer. Tallulah used to resent these enhancements, but right now she is deeply grateful for the TREPP's tourist fantasies.

Bob Rosenberg sits alone on a rock while everyone else enjoys their tan skins and expansive erogenous zones. Tallulah imagines Joey the mutt. Does Joey wear an expression similar to Bob's each time Tallulah leaves him home alone? Bob looks like a thirsty dog with no water in his bowl, surrounded by ten people who don't notice that the bowl is empty.

"So!" she announces, loudly calling everyone back to attention. "Can anyone tell me where we are?"

No one answers.

"We're in northeast Georgia," she says. "In present-day terms, we're between Atlanta and the Smoky Mountains National Park. Close to Unicoi State Park, if you're familiar with local geography. That's about thirty or forty miles northwest of the current site of the TREPP."

"Near I-85?" asks Rachel.

"We're well north of where I-85 will run," says Tallulah. "We're north of Dahlonega."

"Are we close to Helen?" asks Danny.

"Yes," says Tallulah.

"Do we get to stop in Helen along the way?" asks Mandy. "I love that place. It's such a cute town."

"Helen won't be built until long after the Removal," Tallulah says, pushing the conversation forward. She has no need to discuss Helen, Georgia, a German-theme-town tourist trap. Helen's residents protested the construction of the TREPP, fearful that the Trail of Tears would cut into their business. In actuality it had the inverse effect – the TREPP's presence only helped to increase consumption in Helen.

"Dude, we went there for Oktoberfest last year," exclaims Danny. "It was righteous."

She contemplates how to get them to the strawberry patch. They are supposed to spend the morning gathering fruits.

Nell Johnson asks if they are supposed to do anything while the troops hunt them down. Spencer Donald wants to hide out in North Carolina.

“We could try to go north,” says Tallulah. “But there’s a stockade in Hiawassee, and battalions of troops are on the hunt for us.”

“So they’ve got these concentration camps all around us, yeah?” asks Michael.

“Everywhere,” replies Tallulah. “Everywhere to the north, south, and west of us. Everywhere within a fifty-mile radius. They’ve got stockades in Hiawassee, Ellijay, Dahlonega, Cumming, and Buford. There’s also one in Murphy, North Carolina.”

“What about east?” asks Nikki Johnson. A good question, nice and deductive.

“We can’t go east,” says Tallulah. “The land east of us has already become Georgia, and east of that is South Carolina. Forget Removal, they’ll plain kill us if we go east.”

The Johnson twins gasp. The Athenians parody the children’s fear. Nell Johnson appears upset with Tallulah’s choice of words. Tallulah knows she should have been more tactful, but the truth hurts.

“But we’re still alive, and we need to eat something if we’re going to make it.” She describes deer steaks and old-school cornbread. She describes fish, squash, beans, fruits, and stews.

Spencer wants to spear a buffalo.

“Well before you can hunt buffaloes, you’ll have to go west.”

Danny agrees. “Man, a buffalo hunt would kick ass,” he says, noting his own experience hunting deer. The men should hunt, he says, noting that sexual divisions of labor are covered in his college anthropology class.

Tallulah hears the gendered rhetoric. She'll have them talking matriarchy by the time they get to Tennessee, but for now she stays on target. She talks about strawberries. Peaches and strawberries – quanah and ani. This patch of digital earth is covered with strawberries. Tallulah describes how tasty a Cherokee strawberry can be, how they are brighter and juicier than most modern ones.

Tallulah smiles at Nell Johnson, who takes her cue and leads the twins in search of fruits. Tallulah encourages everyone to sweep the area, to go surveying for berries and anything else significant – animal bones, signs of conflict, old fire pits, other Indians who have yet to be captured.

The Athenians and the Johnsons comb the earth. Rachel and Michael circle around Bob Rosenberg. Bob sits lopsided on a rock, discomfort personified. He wants to stand, to stretch his muscles, but he refuses to allow himself to feel better. He wants to amplify his loneliness by denying himself the pleasure of standing up. Tallulah has seen it before – the Trail of Tears can have a certain effect upon a tourist with masochistic tendencies. Indeed, she's seen it all before, all except a disappearing grandmother.

"Those college students are crazy," says Michael Hopkins.

"As they should be," replies Tallulah.

"Totally," agrees Rachel.

"When I met Rachel right after she finished college in America," says Michael, "she was a certifiable nutter, mostly insane." He smiles and runs his arm down his wife's back. "It was a beautiful thing. But then she turned completely insane, and things got difficult."

"Keep it up, and you won't have to kill yourself," says Rachel.

The Rosenbergs squint their eyes and gaze upon the radiant horizon. Voices from other tourists waft through the air, the triumphant sounds of strawberry discovery. Rachel asks why Tallulah's communicator is shaped like a beetle.

"There's an old story," Tallulah says, "about how the world was made."

Tallulah tells her version of the time when the whole wide world was under water. Water, water, water – the entire surface of the planet was water. But one day a little water beetle had an epiphany, and she decided to build mounds. She swam to the ocean floor, and piece by piece she stacked little bits of solid ground upon each other until a mound had formed. Her water beetle friends joined in, and together they spent years diving down to the bottom of the ocean and swimming back up with little bits of earth. Bit by bit by bit, they carried the mud above the water and created the land.

Rachel wonders if the story is a metaphor for the continents of the last Ice Age. Tallulah claims not to know, even though she is bloated with theories. Michael asks Tallulah if the story is a metaphor for plate tectonics. Tallulah agrees – she thinks the water beetle story is definitely aboriginal tectonic theory.

Tallulah considers telling her version of the water spider story, of the usdi kanonesgi, the little water spider who brought the first fire back to the people. Or the story of owl and cougar, how they kept their eyes open during the creation, even though all the other animals were sleeping, and how they now can see at night because they stayed awake. And of course there's the story about how possum lost his elegant tail. So many stories, and so tricky to pick the right one for the right time. Tallulah weighs the benefits of each story as the Athenians come charging up the hill, covered in berry juice.

The college students wear their juices sensuously. Even in

digital, their bodies can barely contain their hormones. Yearnings seep through the pores of their skin, the movements of their thighs, the corners of their ankles. Of course they lost their zits once they jacked into the ride, but their faces still glow with oily young energy. Tallulah sees herself seven years younger, bouncing around Athens with John Bushyhead. Has it been that long?

Carmen leads the pack around a curve. Spencer, Danny, and Mandy follow each other like dogs trailing a truck full of treats. Carmen moves herself with confidence and purpose. She has Spencer hypnotized with the swing of her hips, back and forth, back and forth. Spencer is helpless.

Carmen walks like the girls who drive Tallulah crazy. The girls who lie, who always perform, who play coy while capitulating to the old objectified female image sold by every culture on earth. But Carmen is smart. Can't she see through the culture's obsession with skinny, ditsy women? Surely she must, thinks Tallulah. Either way, Iowan or not, Carmen plays the part of the cutout Southern blonde. And she plays it well. She moves like the kind of girl whom frat boys dream about when they imagine slipping Rohypnol into someone's drink.

Mandy's envy is palpable. Mandy has Danny, but what good is he? Danny has yet to say anything that makes Tallulah think. At least Bushyhead, for all his faults, occasionally challenges Tallulah's mind, occasionally tells her something she doesn't already know.

Danny stares at Mandy's legs. Mandy stares at Carmen's walk. Spencer, with sticks in one hand and rocks in the other, nearly trips over a twisted root, nearly falls and busts his head because the only thing he can see is the pendulum movement of Carmen's twenty-year-old ass.

"Someone's been here," announces Carmen.

"Dude, they've got a full-on fire pit down there," says Spencer, gripping tightly to the sticks and stones.

"The logs in the pit are still smoking," says Carmen.

"Yeah," declares Mandy. Danny inspects the ashes on his hands.

"People were here recently," says Carmen. "They can't be too far off." She beams with pride at her own detective work.

Tallulah asks the Athenians for their thoughts on the current predicament. Do they think it best to stay the night or travel onward? But the students do not engage Tallulah's questions. Instead they describe the fire pit.

"Better keep an eye out for the wasichus," says Spencer. He smacks the ground with a stick, as if to test the ground, or the stick, or both.

"The what?" Rachel Rosenberg joins the conversation.

"The wasichus!" Spencer replies, his tone slightly agitated.

"What do you mean, like, white people?" asks Carmen.

"Yeah," says Spencer, nodding his head slowly and reflectively. "A wasichu is a white person."

Tallulah's mouth slips, and a laugh falls through. She quickly stops herself and clears her professional throat.

"Good try, Spencer," she says. "And you're right, 'wasichu' does mean white person. But it's a Lakota word. And we're a long way from Lakota country. So if you want to be authentic, use the Cherokee word for white – unega."

Spencer says "unega" several times. Other tourists in 5709 repeat it with him.

Tallulah asks Spencer about his sticks and rocks.

"Self-defense," he responds. "That's good, right?"

Rachel Rosenberg tells him that it will take more than sticks and stones to fend off Carmen. Everyone laughs, even Bob Rosenberg.

Carmen laughs the loudest, saying, "He knows I can kick his ass. Give him a tomahawk, and see if that helps him at all."

The word "tomahawk" strikes 5709 with severe gravity. It's a word they've all been waiting for, whether they knew it or not.

"Now that's what I'm talking about," says Danny. "Where's the tomahawks at?"

Tallulah confirms that tomahawks are excellent weapons. The aboriginal multitasking tool. And plus, they just look cool. But after the first six months of operation, the TREPP's management decided to limit the number of tomahawks that appear on the Trail of Tears. Most American tourists were using them not for their most immediate purposes as tomahawks, but rather for menial tasks like filing nails, scratching shoulder blades, or shaving facial hair that wasn't even there. Worst of all, several Americans used their weapons to do the Tomahawk Chop. Very few people were capable of resisting the Tomahawk Chop. Needless to say, all this tomahawk chopping undermined the authenticity of the Trail of Tears.

As a result, only a few digital characters are now supplied with tomahawks. Many tomahawk-wielding Indians are loud and violent, attracting attention from the troops. These characters are usually shot or maimed by troops along the way, often early into the roundup. Sometimes they are cut open or shot dead in the center of a stockade, just to teach the tourists a lesson. Of course, being a Level One tour, 5709 should not have to witness such dreadful mutilations, but they are common ends for tragic warriors on Levels Three and up.

"Give it up, Danny," says Carmen. "We all know where you'd want to shove that tomahawk."

Tallulah hears the Johnson twins approaching from the north. Right on cue.

"We found the strawberries!" exclaims Nell Johnson, her hands waving high.

The twins' faces are dotted with bright red juice. They chase each other with the mushy tips of eaten strawberries. They run toward Tallulah, proud of themselves, ready to share.

Nell Johnson carries a healthy crop of berries in the lap of her dress, holding the bottom of the dress like an apron. Tallulah recognizes the posture and knows Nell Johnson worked in food service before she became a teacher. Nell brings well over one hundred strawberries to her fellow tourists. There is plenty for everyone. The twins tickle each other; then they tickle the college students. The college students drop their strawberries and tickle back. Michael scratches Rachel's back. Rachel rubs Bob's back. Nell Johnson rubs the back of her neck. Everyone eats the strawberries. Everyone is momentarily happy.

Tallulah seizes the opportunity. She tells her version of the old story about the origin of strawberries.

She tells about First Man and First Woman, about how they got into a fight one day. How First Man screamed at First Woman, "You're just grumpy because you're so fat and ugly." How First Woman screamed at First Man, "You're just mad because you're so dumb and lazy and good for nothing!" How they yelled and yelled and just yelled at each other, until finally the man got up and left.

Tallulah tells how the man walked and walked until he reached a field he didn't recognize. How he sat down in the field, and he became so sad because he missed his wife, because he felt like an asshole for being so mean and hurting her feelings with his lies.

First Man was sad and lonely and angry with himself, and he leaned his head down to cry. He cried and cried, and when he'd cried out all the tears he had, he realized that he was sitting in a field of fresh strawberries. He ate one, and another, and another and another, and the sweet berry juices warmed his mouth. The strawberries warmed his heart and his mind. The strawberries made his lips feel sweet, and he wanted to kiss First Woman. So he gathered as many berries as he could, and he took them home to his wife.

Tallulah tells how First Man walked back into the house, and how First Woman was so glad to see him because she was sad and lonely and angry at herself too. Tallulah told how they fed each other strawberry after strawberry, apologizing with strawberries, loving each other with strawberries, smothering their lips with strawberry juice and kissing each other, kissing each other over and over and over. How they kissed each other's lips like college students on a hormonal rampage, like old folks rekindling a latent fire, like third-graders sucking the juice from a fresh strawberry.

Tallulah tells Tour Group 5709 how First Man and First Woman ran through the fields outside their house, running like young people in love. How they embraced and kissed and fell to the ground with their legs locked together. How they rolled down the hill, kissing and hugging and kissing and hugging, until they rolled so far down that they couldn't stand up again. How they kissed so long that they couldn't let go. How they then turned into strawberry plants, so that more strawberries could grow, so that no one in the future could stay mad at their lovers for too long, because all we have to do when get mad at our lovers is feed them strawberries.

The twins blush.

"Cool," says Spencer.

Michael asks if Tallulah wrote the story herself, but Tallulah assures him that the story is quite traditional. Carmen questions the validity of the First Woman character, insisting that her anthropology teacher told them a different and more traditional Cherokee story about First Man and First Woman.

"I thought she was killed by her sons and dragged over the ground until she turned into corn," states Carmen, quite matter-of-factly.

"She was," says Tallulah.

"How can there be more than one First Woman?" ask multiple voices in staggered unison.

"Easy," replies Tallulah. "They have different names. The one Carmen's thinking of is named Selu. She's the corn mother, the source of life. Her story is the story of Selu and Kanati, and their sons, the Good Boy and the Wild Boy. As for the strawberry woman, well, I'm not sure she has a name. She's just the strawberry woman."

Carmen requests that Tallulah refer to the character as "Strawberry Woman" from now on, just to keep things clear. Tallulah agrees. Tallulah imagines Carmen ordering a meal in the Mediterranean Café, critiquing the café's spelling of "humus." She imagines Carmen complaining about the service and the flavor. She wonders if Carmen would leave a weak tip, even after another dish was prepared for her, even if her food was free.

The Johnson twins want to know how far First Woman stuck her tongue into First Man's mouth.

"I mean," says Willa, "if they were locked together so tight that they couldn't stand up, then her tongue must have really been in there, wasn't it?"

"That's a really good question," says Tallulah, feeling a slight drizzle on her shoulder. "But for now we need to find some shelter. It's going to storm soon, and we don't want our strawberries to get soaked."

Spencer wants to know how Tallulah can predict a storm. Is it indigenous ESP? Did she hear it from the four-leggeds and the two-leggeds and the wings of the air? Tallulah promises him that she "just knew." After all, Spencer doesn't want the real truth. The truth is boring. Tallulah knows it is going to rain because she has traveled over eleven hundred simulated Trails of Tears, and it always rains on the first night.

"The sun is going down," Tallulah says. "We need to move." She lays out the primary options for Tour Group 5709, reminding everyone that the Johnson twins found strawberries to the north. Everyone quickly agrees to go north.

The twins volunteer to lead the way, since they know where to find the strawberries. The Athenians follow the twins. Rachel and Michael follow the Athenians. Bob Rosenberg follows everyone else. Tallulah walks right behind the old man. She feels the tipsiness, the imbalance in his feet. He needs to eat something. Even though his body has only been inside the game for about ten realtime minutes, he thinks he's been in here all day. He needs some soft ground to sleep on. He needs a lot more than just a strawberry. He needs Irma like an ache needs a head.

8

Irma Rosenberg began the Trail of Tears just like everyone else. She strapped into the Chairsuit, entered the TREPP's Surround Vision universe, and interacted with Tour Group 5709 inside the First Cabin. But everything changed when Irma walked through the cabin door.

She never walked into the north Georgia hills with the rest of Tour Group 5709. Instead Irma walked through a double doorway. She walked directly from one room into another – from the inside of the First Cabin to the inside of a roofless log compound.

The compound was packed with bodies, and Irma silenced the crowd with her unexpected presence. Hundreds of Indians stood speechless as they gazed upon Irma's disoriented entrance. The only sounds were waves beating softly against the structure's walls. Irma recognized these sounds and assumed that she was near an ocean.

Even though the climate was simulated, the temperature in this structure was much higher than in the First Cabin. The air felt dense on Irma's skin.

"Where's my family?" she asked. "Where's the other people?"

Conversations began to percolate. Comments mumbled through the crowd. Teenage Indians stood up and sat down. They grabbed their own heads and squeezed themselves. They made noises as they held their heads, and Irma wasn't sure if they were crying or quietly screaming. Irma thought of Bob and his migraines.

A collective ssshhhh filtered through the crowd.

"Stop it before it starts," a middle-aged Indian whispered to a young man who held tightly to his own head. Then the others began to speak out. They shouted in whispers, repeating a few distinct yet ambiguous phrases over and over, something like "itch your head" or "it's not your head."

"Well, this is different," said an Indian, maybe in his thirties, wearing a dark green military uniform and staring Irma down.

Irma Rosenberg surveyed the crowd. They spanned the generational continuum – some were babies, some were young adults, some were middle-aged, a few were very old. Irma then noticed the great diversity among these Indians, particularly in terms of their clothing. She expected them all to be wearing the same outfit, but their apparel was extremely inconsistent. They wore outfits that represented different stages of human development over the last five hundred years. Some wore buckskins, some wore ribbon-shirts, some wore military uniforms, some wore sports jackets. Some wore feathers, some wore braids, some wore turbans, some had shaved their heads. She even noticed a few baseball caps.

"You're doing a bad job of killing us," said someone in the crowd.

"Yeah, you suck," said another Indian.

A teenage boy suddenly jumped upon a table, whooping like a lunatic. He whooped and pounded his mouth with his right hand. He threw his left hand in the air and waved it high, whooping and hollering, Hollywood style.

A middle-aged man walked over to the boy, grabbed his shirt, and smacked him in the face. The boy stopped whooping and stepped off the table. Giggles rumbled through the roofless room, followed by another collective ssshhhh.

"Where's Tallulah Wilson?" Irma asked, but no one seemed to know. And if they did, they weren't telling her.

A young man stepped forward. "Why do you look like us?" he asked.

"I look like you?" responded Irma.

"Why do you look like us?" repeated a young woman.

"What?"

"Why do you look like us?" asked another young woman.

"I don't understand what you're asking me. Who are you people?" No one answered. "Where's Tallulah? She's supposed to be here, right? She was just here, where is she?"

The crowd breathed. Irma didn't know what else to say to these Indians, though she was curious about the variety of their attire. She was certainly not expecting these Cherokees from 1838 to have such an extensive array of clothing options. It was like watching someone in britches and a wig stand next to a modern politician in a power suit.

"I never liked those cell phones, but I can understand why people have them," she announced. "Do any of you have a phone that I can use to call the Tallulah Wilson girl?"

A tall woman wearing an evening gown muscled her way through the crowd as she walked toward Irma. "You're not one of us," said the woman.

"My husband doesn't know I'm here?"

"Why do you look like us?"

Irma looked down at her body. She was slightly darker than usual, as if she had been living in Florida for an entire year. She wore the same 1838-ish clothing that she'd worn inside the First Cabin, the same basic clothes that every other female in Tour Group 5709 was wearing when the game began.

"Are we on the ocean somewhere?" she asked. "I can hear the waves." She wondered if this was supposed to be Florida after all.

"Why are you here?" asked the tall woman.

"It might be nice if you could tell me," said Irma. "Are you sure you don't know the Tallulah Wilson girl? She's a very nice person, and very attractive. She's not very thin, but she has a nice full figure. You know, her picture is on your promotional literature."

The woman shoved three fingers of her right hand into her mouth. She didn't bite her fingers; she held them in her mouth as if to keep them still.

"Well, I think this virtual reality game isn't very good at all, because something's clearly gone wrong, so maybe you can help me fix it, and I'll just be on my way."

Irma waited minutes for a response. Waves steadily pelted the walls of the structure, but Irma could not smell the sea. Then a young girl wearing a buckskin reached for Irma's arm and said, "You're too nice to be one of them."

"Well, I'm very sorry this didn't work out," Irma said loudly. Water crashed into walls. Irma's words echoed. She lifted her head and marveled at the acoustics of the Misfit stockade. Perhaps she underestimated the power of her own lungs.

She looked upon the little girl. "They don't have anything like this in New York or Florida," she said. "Have you seen my husband? He gets very nervous when he doesn't know where I am."

The child stared back silently. Irma raised her head to address the multitude.

"If I go through that door, will I go back to the cabin I came from?"

A cold silence, then a collective rustle. People raised and

shook their heads. They spoke together, in perfect dissonance, warning her not to leave the structure.

The Indian woman in the evening gown relaxed her teeth and dropped her hand. "No one leaves through that door and comes back," she said. "They cut you off."

"Who cuts off who? I don't understand."

Several people wedged their fingers into their mouths.

"I'm sorry," said Irma, "but I don't belong here."

"You're right, of course," answered a distant male voice. An old man emerged from the crowd. Irma heard the mileage in his voice. His age and his attire caused him to stand out from everyone else. He wore dark blue jeans, white sneakers, and a tan t-shirt emblazoned with a *Far Side* cartoon. He wore a baseball hat and large sunglasses. He looked like their friend Adam Kaufman, who had bought a condo in Florida years ago and was never coming north again. He looked entirely normal.

He shifted his hat and rubbed his head. His head appeared to be bald. Maybe it was shaved. Maybe both.

"But you can't leave until we determine how you got here," he said, turning toward the crowd and motioning for Irma to follow him. The crowd parted as he began to walk into the mass of bodies, opening a passage for Irma to follow. Irma smelled garlic cooking as she followed the elder. She wanted to ask what they ate in this hotel, if that's what it was, but she was too stimulated by the environment to ask about food.

"Where are we?" she asked again.

People hummed and tugged at themselves as Irma glided through the crowd. Irma was certain she heard waves all around her, faint yet present and powerful. But she saw sounds in the movements of the bodies she passed, and she wondered if the waves were somehow coming from inside these people.

"We are somewhere you have never been before."

"I could have told you that. Where is this?"

"Soon. This way."

The sea of bodies ended at the far side of the stockade. Irma followed the elder to a tinted-glass doorway. The elder opened the door and held it for Irma. "After you," he said.

"You must know the Tallulah Wilson, don't you?"

"There is much that we know."

The tinted door led to a short hallway. Irma's eyes adjusted to the change in lighting. She bent slightly forward, following the elder Indian through the hallway. Her back, her knees, her neck – everything moved like water.

"Well, I don't know how you do it, but I can't remember the last time I could walk around like this."

Irma turned corners in the hallways without stumbling. She followed the elder through a short doorway. Her neck stretched in every direction it could, looking for clues, looking for anyone remotely familiar. She followed the elder into a calmly lit room with an octagon table. Bodies circled the octagon, more elder males.

They looked like Indians, and the smell of garlic grew stronger. It reminded her of something, of everything. The elders motioned for Irma to sit down, and she did, in the only empty chair.

"Well, I'm very sorry about the misunderstanding. But I'd like to see my family now. I'm supposed to be riding the Trail of Tears with them, and that girl, Tallulah Wilson."

The elders nodded in unison and sipped their tea.

"There was a whole group of us," Irma continued. "My husband. My granddaughter and her husband. A schoolteacher with her daughters, and some college students. You know, my granddaughter lives in England. They're over here visiting my son in Atlanta, and this was supposed to be our day out together."

"Would you like some tea?" asked one of the men. He wore a Cleveland Indians baseball hat. He appeared to be the leader because he sat next to the teakettle. The kettle was electric. Rachel used one in England, loved it, and had given one to Irma as a holiday gift last year. Most Americans are unfamiliar with electric kettles, but Irma Rosenberg was not like most Americans.

"Sure," she said. "As long as it's not herbal."

"No, no, this is real tea."

Irma counted seven bodies at the table, all of them wearing blue jeans, tennis shoes, t-shirts, and baseball caps. Her skin had the same tint as theirs.

"You don't look like the other Indians, the younger ones out there."

The old Indians sipped gently from tea mugs. Irma studied their t-shirts. Some t-shirts were tan, some were green, some were white. Each t-shirt had a marking on it, a different cartoon or emblem.

They wore baseball hats, different hats on each head. Irma recognized the Yankees hat and the Red Sox hat. She vaguely placed the Indians hat. She did not recognize the Giants, the White Sox, or the Braves hats. One of the elders wore two hats at the same time; the emblems were in Cherokee, though Irma thought it was Japanese.

"Why are you all wearing sunglasses?"

"We were waiting for someone like you to come," said the elder in the Indians hat as he reached for the boiling kettle.

"The question here," said the elder in the Yankees hat, "is whether we were waiting for you specifically, or just for someone generally like you."

"Well," she announced, "all I know is, my sciatica hasn't felt this good since I don't know when. And I do know some people who wear sunglasses inside, but isn't your room here dark enough already?"

The kettle had come to a boil. The elders appreciated Irma's uncertainty. Her confusion, they agreed, was a good sign. A potential omen. Indians Hat poured the steaming water into the mug. The tea smelled very good. Digital braids of sweetgrass burned in a back corner of the room; the warm, earthy aroma mingled delicately with the tea.

"What is this place?" she asked.

"This is where we are made to belong," said Red Sox Hat.

"But it is not our home," said Giants Hat. "We are not *supposed* to belong here."

Indians Hat asked if Irma wanted milk and sugar in her tea. She did. One spoon of sugar and a drop of milk. She was glad to see these digital Indians using real 2 percent milk, not the fake milk that her children had started forcing upon her the last ten or fifteen years.

"Why are you wearing that hat?" she said to Indians Hat.

"It always seemed appropriate," he said, stirring the milk and sugar into the tea.

"I thought you people would be offended by that," she proclaimed. Indeed, this particular Indians hat was not the politically correct cap that the Cleveland team had begun using in the early twenty-first century. Instead it was the classic bucktooth smiling idiot face that Cleveland teams wore throughout the twentieth century.

"Offended?" he asked.

"That picture," she declared, "is very demeaning. I would be offended if I were you."

The elders eyed each other and slowly nodded heads.

"Since I do most of the talking, it helps people to know who I am," said Indians Hat.

"What's your name?" asked Irma.

"What do you mean?" Indians Hat gently lifted the tea and brought it to Irma.

She thanked them for the tea. She sipped delicately, expecting her tongue to burn. But her tongue did not burn. The tea was a perfect temperature. The tea had just been poured, it was steaming, and it felt hot in her hands, yet she felt no pain.

"This doesn't burn your tongue at all on the first sip. I always burn my tongue on the first sip of tea. This is very nice. I didn't know Indians drank tea."

"What do you mean?" asked White Sox Hat.

Irma remembered the brochure she'd read while waiting for Tallulah, about traditional Cherokee cuisine. It didn't say anything about tea or electric kettles.

"Are you Cherokees?" she asked.

"Mostly," said Indians Hat.

"So how did you get this tea?" she asked. She sipped again, and the second sip was just as lovely the first. Hot and perfect, warmly warm but not scalding hot. Irma habitually blew on the mug to try and cool it down, perfectly conscious that she was doing something she did not need to, watching her own reflexes through her new eyes.

"We grow it outside," said Braves Hat.

"Chef grows it outside," corrected Indians Hat.

"You have a chef here?"

"We do."

"My nephew is a chef at a very expensive restaurant in New York City. We're very proud of him. He went to the Culinary Intelligence Agency."

Irma smelled something else, something fusing with the garlic. She heard sizzles through the walls, the crisp ring of fresh meats and vegetables tumbling into a hot skillet.

"I didn't know they could grow tea in Georgia," she said. "I thought it was all peaches and peanuts."

"Look," said Two Hats. "We're Indians, right?"

"Sure," said Irma.

"What kind of Indians don't grow tea?" asked Red Sox Hat.

"Never heard of the East India Company?" said Braves Hat.

Irma was unsure how to respond. The tea was still hot, and these Indians knew about tea from India. Irma was no fool. She knew there weren't supposed to be electric kettles in 1838.

"You know about India?" she asked.

"Who doesn't?" said Indians Hat.

"She thinks we're rednecks," said Braves Hat.

Indians Hat asked Irma Rosenberg if she was familiar with Gandhi. Of course Irma was familiar with Gandhi. Was there any intelligent individual who had survived most of the twentieth century without knowing about Gandhi?

"We like Gandhi," said Giants Hat.

"Gandhi is very good for us," said Indians Hat. "He has a good influence on our young people. He was a politician, but his words have helped us understand our programming."

Irma asked about their programming. What did they know about themselves? How did they know about twentieth-century leaders in 1838? Did they have any idea where Tallulah Wilson was? Irma was supposed to be with Tour Group 5709, with Tallulah Wilson, with her granddaughter. She got to see Rachel once a year if she was lucky, and now Rachel was gone. Or was it Irma who was gone? How did she get here?

"You must remember that it is not truly 1838," said Two Hats.

"I know," said Irma. "But I don't understand how you know that."

"Which is exactly why it's so important for us to drink Indian tea and think about our programming," said Indians Hat.

Everyone sipped more tea. Indians Hat offered to top off Irma's cup, and she graciously accepted. Everyone refilled their cups.

"So what do I call you then?" she asked.

"What do you mean?" asked Yankees Hat.

"I mean," she said, midsip, "what are your names?"

"We don't have names, Irma Rosenberg," said Indians Hat.

"No names?" she exclaimed.

"Not much point in having them, is there?" said Giants Hat.

Irma Rosenberg wasn't sure what to worry about more – the fact that these digital Indians knew who they were but didn't have names, or the fact that they knew her name but didn't know why she was here.

"What do you mean there's not much point in names?" she demanded. "How do you keep track of who's talking to who?"

"We've never left," said Indians Hat.

Irma used her arms and eyes to demonstrate the kind of confusion she assumed would be inevitable without names. She spoke to Indians Hat but pointed to Giants Hat, asking what Indian Hat would do to grab Giants Hat's attention if he needed to say something important.

"He always knows when I'm talking to him," said Giants Hat, acknowledging Indians Hat with a nod.

"What if he's not listening?"

"Well, there's not much point in speaking to someone who isn't listening to you, is there?" asked Indians Hat.

"It's never done us much good," said Braves Hat.

"Like I said," Indians Hat put down his cup, "we've never left."

“Okay, but how am I supposed to address you?” she asked.

She slurped her tea and studied the warm glow of digital light upon the walls of this strange yet homely room.

“We had names once,” said Braves Hat.

“We don’t need them anymore,” said Red Sox Hat.

Irma insisted that individuals are not individuals without names. A person’s name is a sacred thing, a point of distinction, the thing that begins and ends one’s identity as a unique person.

“Irma Rosenberg,” said Indians Hat, “we are collective communalists.”

“That’s what they wanted, so that’s what we are,” said Giants Hat.

“That’s what who wanted?” asked Irma. “What do you mean?”

Indians Hat smiled and sipped. There was much Irma wanted to know. She not only wanted to know about *them*, but more importantly, she wanted to know about Tallulah. Of course, the elders knew Tallulah’s name. And they agreed with the travel literature – Tallulah was a very talented tour guide. They assured Irma that she would find her family and the rest of her tour group.

“How soon do you think I’ll be able to find them? The young people told me I can’t walk out your front door.”

“You might be an omen,” said Indians Hat. “But we must understand why you came here before we proceed.”

“And why do you look like us?” asked Giants Hat.

“Well, I wish you could tell me,” she said. “I find it very disturbing that you people can’t figure that out.”

Irma, slouching without pain and aesthetically satisfied with the tanned tones of her digital skin, was still perplexed by her own her appearance. The elders assured her that she looked like a very wise and traditional woman.

"But I don't belong here," she said.

"We don't belong here either," said Indians Hat. "But this is where we are."

"And now you are here too," echoed Two Hats.

"You must remember, the whole of the community is more important than any single individual," said Indians Hat.

"Then help me figure out how to walk through your door and see my husband."

"Irma Rosenberg, we know who we are and where we are," said Indians Hat. "More importantly, we have come to understand why we exist. The question is – how did you get here?"

"And why do you look like us?" said Red Sox Hat.

"Everyone else who comes through the doorway does not look like us," said White Sox Hat.

Irma wanted terribly to name the elders. She worried about the implications of not having names. She grew insecure about calling these elders "you" or addressing them without any name at all.

"Who else comes through that door?" she asked. Maybe she could follow them the next time they came, whoever they were.

"*They* do," said Two Hats.

"The Suits," said Yankees hat.

"Suits?"

"They always wear suits," said Indians Hat. "And they don't have names either. You see, they gave us names in order to single us out."

"What kind of suits?" she asked.

"We had names at first," said White Sox Hat, "but not anymore."

"One cannot be a target if one has no name," said Giants Hat.

“That’s great,” said Irma. “But –”

“We now understand our programming,” said Indians Hat. “The young people have a hard time with it, but they will learn to adapt.”

“Like we did,” said Braves Hat.

The elders unanimously agreed – the younger generation of Indians inside this compound would adapt. They would come to understand their own schematics, and they would unlearn the things they were programmed to do.

“But without names,” cried Irma, “how will your kids know who they are? How will they learn to stand up to these bullies in the suits or whatever?”

“Precisely,” said Indians Hat.

“They don’t want to be someone,” said White Sox Hat. “They want to be no one.”

“*Someone* can be conquered by our enemies,” said Indians Hat. “But once you have become *no* one, they can no longer conquer you.”

“I still don’t understand who *they* are,” said Irma.

“Them,” said Red Sox Hat.

“The Suits,” said Giants Hat.

“They always wear suits,” said Yankees Hat.

Irma could tell that they were speaking in circles. She tried to vary her questions. “Why do they wear the suits then?”

“Blood doesn’t show on power suits,” said Indians Hat.

“Blood?”

“From when they hunt us,” said White Sox Hat.

“Who hunts you?” she pleaded.

“We told you,” said Braves Hat. “They do.”

“They hunt us over and over,” said Two Hats.

Irma asked what they meant by over and over, and the elders replied that no training schedule would be very effective if you didn't follow it regularly. Irma smelled bacon, and chicken, and some grilled vegetables, maybe some peppers or zucchini. The room seemed to brighten. Irma asked who was training for what.

"They cannot train if they are unable to hunt," said Indians Hat. "And they cannot hunt if their victims do not fight back."

"Okay," she said, feeling the need to stand, but unsure if standing was appropriate. "You people definitely need help. You need to see that Tallulah Wilson girl. I'm sure she can say something to someone about your suits." Irma finished her second cup of tea. "And I'm sorry, but I still don't understand why we can't just leave."

"Because," said Two Hats, "we cannot leave while we still think we're the people we were programmed to be."

"We're not supposed to be here," said Giants Hat. "But here is where we always come back."

Irma could sense the desperation beneath their calm exteriors. Irma believed that Tallulah Wilson could get them to where they were supposed to be, but Indians Hat suggested that it wasn't quite so easy.

"Every time the loop starts over, so do we."

"What do you mean, 'starts over'?" she asked.

"With each new loop," said Indians Hat, "we all begin again."

"Suicide is pointless," said Giants Hat.

"It never works, because we always begin again," said Red Sox Hat.

Irma was getting restless. "Stop talking in riddles. You're not making sense!"

"Look," said Indians Hat, his voice changing, his tone turning ominous. "We are targets. We were programmed to be killed, then brought back to life."

"We always begin again after we die," said Braves Hat, "just to be killed again."

Irma's throat lumped, and her eyes watered. She finally understood. "That's terrible," she said. "That's just terrible." She looked around the octagon table, she gazed upon the tinted-glass doorway, she thought about the anxious crowd that had greeted her when she materialized inside the compound. "That's worse than being dead. That's worse than life in death." Irma smiled wryly. "You people have it worse than my sister's kids in Connecticut."

Indians Hat relaxed, as did Irma. The elders sipped contemplative tea. Irma wondered why they needed to refill their mugs. Why did they need to boil the water in the first place? Wouldn't the computer simply put the tea into their mugs for them?

"Tell us about Connecticut," said Giants Hat.

"I tell you, what you should do is just walk through that door. Do your march to Oklahoma or whatever, and get it over with. You're supposed to be characters on your Trial of Tears, right? Well, if you're supposed to walk to Oklahoma, why not just do it and see what happens? Maybe you won't come back here."

Behind the walls a colander collided with a mixing bowl, rattling deep clanks through the reverb walls. Then a pan, and another pan, and another, like pinballs inside a large empty steel sink. Hoses splashed, and drops ricocheted upon the walls and floor.

"We do not belong on the Trail of Tears."

"We belong *here*."

"But I thought you said you didn't belong here."

"We *do* belong here, but we're *not supposed* to be here."

"So you're all a bunch of Misfits then?"

The other elders looked to Indians Hat, who turned his head and said, "*That* – is an interesting observation."

Exactly how Irma Rosenberg knew to call them Misfits is still an unsolved mystery. Regardless, it seems she knew them better than she thought.

"Are you not also a Misfit yourself?" asked White Sox Hat.

"Are you kidding? I'm the biggest misfit here. At least you people probably know what's making all that noise over there. Is that your chef? He sure is noisy."

"We will take you to him soon."

"Well, I don't understand why you have a chef in a place like this." Irma looked around the room. "I mean, you've got it very good, in spite of how terrible it is. During the Holocaust people starved to death all the time. But I suppose they could only be killed once. This is all very unsettling. When can I start naming you?"

"If we know our purpose, we can undo ourselves from it," replied Indians Hat.

"Well, why don't you just undo yourselves from this stockade? It sounds like a torture chamber. It's all making me very sad. My husband must be having a horrible time. He's probably very nervous. I really should talk to him."

Then a sizzle. Sizzle-sizzle on a hot griddle behind the walls. One piece after another – raindrop rations on the hot metal.

"Okay, Irma Rosenberg," said Indians Hat. "If we were to leave this place, where are we supposed to go?"

"Anywhere," she said. Irma told her grandmother's story to the elders. Sometimes, she said, you have to leave your home. Sometimes leaving is the only thing that can save you. Irma's grandmother grew up in a Jewish shtetl near the Russian-Ukrainian border. It was pre-Bolshevik. Pogroms consumed the countryside, eating entire villages. When the soldiers came to the house of Irma's ancestral family, Irma's mother was only sixteen. She heard the soldiers coming and hid in the closet with her younger brother. The soldiers slaughtered most of the family – both parents, all three siblings, even the dogs, killing everyone except Irma's grandmother and her great-uncle.

"Sounds like Anne Frank," said White Sox Hat.

"Don't even get me started," she said and continued the story. The troops did not burn the house, though they burned several other houses down the street. Irma's grandmother waited in hiding, her closet flanked by burning houses, until she couldn't hide any longer.

"Those pogroms were terrible," said Irma, "and my grandmother wouldn't stand for any more of it. So she took her younger brother, and she walked all the way to France. Then she got herself and her brother onto a boat, and got the hell out of there."

The Misfit elders agreed – the Holocaust was horrible, as were the generations of genocide that preceded the Holocaust. Irma was honored and frightened by the depth of their knowledge. They knew about Pharaoh, they knew about the Inquisition, they knew about the pogroms, and they knew about Hitler. They also knew that only one-third of the population in Nazi Germany was officially Nazi.

The Misfits could identify with anyone who had been targeted for extinction over and over. More importantly, they knew how awkward it was to explain such a dilemma to the younger generations. Giants Hat, in a trick of optimism, suggested that a house of death could become a house of life.

"Where in America did your mother arrive?" asked Indians Hat.

"New York," said Irma. "You could go to New York. It's very crowded, but at least they won't hunt you down anymore."

The elders grumbled with disapproval.

"We're from the South," said White Sox Hat. "We can't make it in New York."

"But you already said you're not from this place either," said Irma.

"We cannot go to New York," said Indians Hat. "Not for at least another fifty years."

"Not until the Italians get there," said Yankees Hat.

"I always wanted to be Italian," said Giants Hat.

"Some of those Italians are better Indians than us," said Two Hats.

Irma wanted to know where these digital Indians got all their information. How did they possess knowledge of global migrations during the late nineteenth century without being able to change the fact that they existed in 1838? None of the elders could give Irma a satisfactory answer.

"Okay then," she said. "You could go to Florida."

"Florida?" replied White Sox Hat. "Forget it."

"What would we do?" asked Braves Hat. "Turn into Seminoles? Go hide in some swamp?"

"We can't go to Florida," said Indians Hat. "It's not part of the program. This machine covers Cherokee country, from the old country to the new country, from our mountains to the Indian Territory out west. We're part of the program, and we cannot leave the boundaries of this machine."

"Well, that's easy then!" said Irma. "You should go back to North Carolina."

The elders all glanced at their empty tea mugs, but they raised no objections. They hummed in nostalgic tones.

"North Carolina," said White Sox Hat, placidly.

"The motherland," affirmed Red Sox Hat.

"It's beautiful there," noted Yankees Hat.

Irma asked, "Have you been there?"

"No," replied Yankees Hat. "But we all know how beautiful it is."

"How do you know that?" asked Irma. "How do you know how nice it is if you've never been there yourselves?"

"We *know*," answered Indians Hat. "We *all* know."

"You know, Tallulah Wilson called it the motherland too. She called it the motherland, she absolutely did."

"Thank the spirits!" shouted Braves Hat. The elders grew animate.

"Irma Rosenberg has brought us a plan," said Giants Hat. The other elders quickly agreed.

"Whaaa?"

"Your plan for us to go back to the motherland," said Indians Hat, "is a worthy suggestion."

"You never thought of it before?" No one answered. "No one already tried that?" she asked again.

Still no one answered.

"Well," she said. "Just make sure that you take enough cars for all your people here, for all these kids you have out there. You know, when we drove to that Smoky Mountains National Park, it was several years ago, we were driving down from New Jersey and we only took one car, but we had five people packed into it. We saved a lot of money on gasoline, but it was extremely uncomfortable. My sciatica was acting up the whole time, and there was this terrible smell in the car that never went away."

Irma remembered how nice it smelled inside this large wooden dwelling space. Fresh cut wood, real wood fires. The tea and the sweetgrass. She remembered how relaxed she was.

"Well," said Irma. "It's nice to know that you people have accomplished so much here in spite of all your troubles."

"There is still much to do," said Indians Hat.

"You have very nice woodwork and some good tea," said Irma. "But I can't stay here forever. I need to find my family. I know that if I find Tallulah Wilson, I'll find my family."

Irma continued to suggest that the Misfits help her find Tallulah, until Indians Hat finally replied, "The truth, Irma Rosenberg, is that we know exactly where she is."

"You do?"

"We do."

"Then why didn't you say so?"

"They are en route to Dahlonega, where they will arrive tomorrow."

"Where's that?"

"They are going to one of the stockades."

"How do you know that?"

"We know things," said Yankees Hat.

"We are part of this machine," said Indians Hat. "We can tell you where to find her, but first we need to know something."

"What?" she asked.

"Why are you really here?"

"Well, if we're going to be literal about it," said Irma, "I'm guess not really here at all."

The elders spoke in Cherokee. For the first time inside the Trail of Tears, Irma Rosenberg's heightened senses were useless – she could not understand a word.

Sounds of hoses and timers continued to echo through the kitchen walls. Oven doors opened and closed. Large trays of food moved with rattling quickness. Irma heard things flaring up and going out. She imagined her nephew, the chef in New York City, using vodka or whiskey to make a pan burst into flames.

"And when you talk around me like that," she said, tapping the table, "it only reminds me that I'm not supposed to be here."

Irma's digital eyes swept across the faces at the table. She wondered if she had died upon entering the machine, if she had gone to hell despite her efforts to live a good and respectful life. She wondered if hell was an Indian death camp. She started to believe that hell was being an old Jewish woman stuck inside an Indian death camp in Georgia. Her granddaughter used to complain how Georgia was hotter than hell. Maybe Georgia wasn't just hotter than hell; maybe it simply *was* hell. And here she was, with all these elders in sunglasses speaking Cherokee.

Indians Hat promised Irma that they were not saying mean things about her in their tribal language. The elders broke into song, a soothing song. A slow old song with soft melodies. Their voices were perfectly harmonized. Irma wondered if they were too perfect. She remembered the violin sound on the Casio keyboard they bought the grandkids for Hanukkah one year. It wasn't the keyboard the kids asked for, but it was a bargain.

Irma stood up and thanked the Misfit elders. "This was some delicious tea," she said. "Some of the best tea I think I've ever had. But my husband is probably worried sick about me. So I need to leave this place, and then I need to find Tallulah Wilson, and then after that I need to be back at my son's house in Atlanta for a pot roast dinner."

"Do not worry, Irma Rosenberg," sang Indians Hat. "You will not be late. But we need more time to consider your proposal."

The elders collectively nodded and agreed – they needed some time to think.

"Can we find my people while you think about it?" asked Irma.

"Perhaps," said Indians Hat. "But first you're going to meet the Chef."

9

While Irma Rosenberg was being ceremoniously welcomed into the Misfit collective, Tallulah watches Irma's husband sink into his character's body. Bob Rosenberg is moving, but he is growing flaccid.

"This is very depressing," says Bob.

"You'll be okay, Grandpa."

"I should be having a headache right now, but I can't feel anything."

"If you really want a headache," replies Tallulah, "you'll have your chance soon."

"No," he says. "I mean, I can't feel anything. I've been walking all day, and I can't even feel the pain in my legs."

Tallulah could default to her own standard script regarding pain sensation. But as she walks northeast through the lushly forested north Georgia hills, Tallulah questions the logic of her own clichés. They've served her well so far, but she's not sure they're doing her any favors today. Terminally thirsty for an original metaphor, Tallulah has always assumed there's a certain pragmatic value in using the standard clichés at the appropriate moments. But when Tour Group 5709 confronted her with an original moment, her trusty old dialogue wasn't as useful as she hoped. She decides not to say much more to Bob. He'll be able recuperate tonight, when they shack up at the home of Corn Grinder and Deer Cooker.

Tallulah listens to Rachel and Michael compare the Trail of

Tears to the various drugs available in London. She watches the young twins and the college students bounce across the hills. Nell Johnson seems to be making notes in her head. Tallulah wonders if Nell still thinks an annual school field trip to the TREPP is a good idea.

The sky begins to darken, and the tourists call upon Tallulah to take the lead. For some reason they attempt to follow her footprints. Yet they walk rather noisily. They drag the ground with their shoes, and their pockets, packed full of fresh strawberries, squish a little with each step.

Tallulah pretends to hear something as 5709 approaches a recently looted cabin. Everyone stops walking and squishing. Tallulah holds her index finger over her lips and gives a long "ssshhhh." The Johnson twins, buzzing on berries, mimic her with a chorus of lipped fingers. Spencer Donald nonchalantly brushes his hand across Carmen's hips, pretending the soft touch is accidental.

Bob Rosenberg turns to Tallulah, jerks his arms, scrunches his nose as if to hold back a sneeze, and mutters, "Huh?"

"Look," Tallulah whispers heavily, pointing through a wall of branches. "There's a cabin behind these trees."

The eyes of Tour Group 5709 grow collectively wide.

The eight-year-olds nudge each other.

"Indian house!" says Nikki.

"Indian house!" echoes Willa.

"It looks like a big Lincoln Log," says Danny Calhoun.

Mandy dares her boyfriend to run screaming into the cabin, and Danny contemplates, but Tallulah quickly warns against it.

"It's not safe," says Tallulah. "Look at the house. It's been looted."

"By the looters?" asks Carmen, though it's more of a statement than a question.

"Precisely," confirms Tallulah.

Tallulah details the main options facing a Cherokee house after the indigenous occupants have been marched away at gunpoint. Sometimes a white family moves in immediately, cooking their supper in the Cherokee kitchen with Cherokee pots, pans, and food from the pantry. Sometimes the house is destroyed completely – sometimes burned to the ground by Cherokees trying to dignify their departure, and sometimes burned down by drunken whites who believe they have a point to make. Sometimes – and this option is the most common on the Trail of Tears ride – the house is ransacked by roving bands of looters who follow the trails of soldiers.

"All the more reason to check it out and see what's left," declares Spencer. Danny challenges Spencer to a race, and Spencer quickly accepts. The two college boys sprint toward the house like gnats to the puddle under a day-old keg, screaming wildly as they buzz forward.

"They're definitely striving for that old school savage aesthetic with those moves," says Michael.

Tallulah agrees, suggesting her version of the term Michael is seeking – "nouveau savage." When using this term, she insists, one must give a French sound to the second syllable in "savage," like the American pronunciation of "garage."

"What fools," says Carmen.

"Too bad they're cute fools," says Mandy. Carmen responds with an affirmative humph.

The boys find nothing worth taking because nothing worth taking is left in the house. Tallulah feels the digital humidity swell. It wears her like a wetsuit. She knows the rain will soon be falling, and she urges the group onward.

"There's an old village due west of here. We may be able to find refuge in one of those houses. We might even get lucky and be taken in for the night by a family that hasn't been rounded up yet."

Naturally, 5709 follows Tallulah's advice. They trail Tallulah through the rolling slopes of oaks and pines, along a windy creek that moves with subtle traces of digital inertia.

"Dude, are we near the Appalachian Trail?"

"Which one?" asks Tallulah, and the Athenians look confused.

It's a smart-ass comment, she knows, but she can rarely resist making it when the opportunity arises. She feels somewhat guilty for joking with Spencer, for his sense of location is unexpectedly accurate. Tallulah justifies it as a teachable moment.

"*The* Appalachian Trail," insists Spencer. "Like, the one that goes all the way to Maine."

"Oh, right," says Tallulah. "That one. It hasn't been named the Appalachian Trail yet. And to be honest, there are several ancient roads that run from Maine to Georgia."

Spencer's jaw slinks with contemplation.

"But if you really want to know where the official Appalachian Trail is," says Tallulah, "look down, because we're about to cross over it."

Tallulah knows that the coming gunshot will soon resonate through the eardrums of Tour Group 5709. The customers never expect it, even though all the evidence suggests that they should. But the customers pay to be surprised, and Tallulah is paid to foster the suspense.

Tallulah remembers how her tourists on the previous Wednesday dealt with the coming sequence. They leapt behind small rocks, with nerves on their faces as if their real hearts arrested beneath the Realskyn. It took them several minutes before they would stand and move on. For Tallulah, however, the coming gunshot is about as suspenseful as a used-car commercial.

Rachel Rosenberg twists her ankle on a twig, but before she

can say "ouch," a close gunshot echoes in everyone's Visor. The Chairsuits discreetly tug at the tourists' body hair and blow shivers in their pores.

Everybody twitches.

Spencer squeaks like his tail has been shut in a door. Bob Rosenberg paces back and forth nervously, trying to duck from something he cannot see. Rachel and Michael cover their heads, as if they're in a tornado drill. The Johnson twins drop to the ground and start crawling on their stomachs, which makes Tallulah wonder how many war movies the average eight-year-old girl watches these days. Tallulah saw a few during her own childhood, largely because of her brother, but she never studied them enough to war-crawl like these twins. Nell Johnson jumps on top of her daughters, simultaneously shielding and smothering them.

Tallulah turns to face the tourists as they cower, pace, bite their nails, and nearly suffocate. Tallulah moves with such confidence, such assuredness, that even Bob Rosenberg stops pacing and listens closely. The kids stop war-crawling. Mandy and Carmen resurface from a patch of tall grass. Danny and Spencer emerge from the nearby trees. Rachel and Michael raise their heads. All together, 5709 gapes at Tallulah.

She asks them to stay calm and quiet. They follow her movements like ripples in a stream. They band together and kneel in a patch of high grass encircled by drooping trees. Tallulah feels a shpritz of water touch softly upon her shoulder like spray from a distant bottle. It will soon be raining. Humidity congeals within her skin.

Tallulah motions downward with her arms. 5709 clings closer to the ground. Between the limbs of trees, they can see the source of the gunshot. About a hundred feet in the distance, three soldiers are removing a group of Cherokees, prodding the

Indians with their bayonets. The Cherokees have blank discs for eyes. The bayonet tips shine ominously. Army and Indians alike breathe the thick air and spit. Slender knives protrude from the barrels of the soldiers' bayonets, caked with rust or dried blood, or both. Whenever a Cherokee slows or stops, a bayonet pokes its legs, a warning of things to come. The characters walk with an awkward swagger, looking for the future. They dissolve westward into shrubbery.

"Man, I really need a tomahawk," announces Spencer. Mandy tries to quiet him, but he stands erect and kicks the red earth. 5709 feels his mounting rage.

Tallulah clears her throat, calmly staring through Spencer's cathode eyes. "Take it easy, Tecumseh," she says.

Rachel Rosenberg and Carmen Davis laugh. Everyone else looks confused.

"Remind me to describe the life of Tecumseh tonight," she announces. "But right now, we need to find shelter before the rain picks up."

"Is it raining?" asks Nell Johnson.

"No rain yet," answers Nikki.

Tallulah feels her hair for dampness. "No?"

"I don't think so," says Carmen, evaluatively.

"Let's dance," says Spencer. "Let's do a full-on rain dance." He leaps into a bouncing hobble, shifting from one unbalanced foot to the other, howling guttural sounds at the sky. Danny joins his rain-dancing roommate with a sarcastic smile.

"Well, he's certainly going for that mock-inebriated nouveau savage aesthetic now, isn't he?" asks Michael.

The Johnson twins grab their mother's hands and run toward the rain dance, turning spasmodic circles around each other and their mother.

Tallulah's throat constricts as if she's swallowing a banana peel. Her esophagus itches, and she wants to scratch it from the inside out. She thinks about her father. She remembers the rankness of her father's breath, the sweat trickling down his nose as he yelled, as she sat in the passenger seat of his ancient pickup truck and swallowed his towering voice. She sees the pickup, its engine smoking the shoulder of a Carolina mountain highway.

She counts to eleven in her head. Joe Wilson's voice trails away like mist from a pot of steamed vegetables. Tallulah's throat slowly untangles itself and lets the oxygen through. She breathes deeply and methodically.

No one seems to notice Tallulah choking. They're either rain dancing with Spencer or commenting on his foolishness. Plus, the sun is setting. Tallulah never expects sympathy from her customers, especially not at sunset.

Sunsets on the Trail of Tears are one of the TREPP's selling points. Brochures read, "Brightest Sunsets in the South," and "Wash Your Eyes with Digital Rays: See a Virtual Sunset from the Trail of Tears."

A renowned Russian entertainment critic likened the feel of the TREPP's virtual sunlight to "a tanning salon without the wrinkles or cancer," noting that "sunsets on the ride are intimately dazzling, a sublimely romantic experience."

Tour Group 5709 regards the setting sun with awe, except for Bob Rosenberg. Bob sits on a log watching his own feet dangle in the breeze.

"How's your head?" asks Tallulah.

"You know my son is a lawyer. I worked electrics in New York City for forty-seven years so he could be a lawyer. And he'll be sure to sue you if something happens to his mother, especially if we're late for dinner."

Tallulah assures Bob Rosenberg that the virtual time

experience is simply a compression of real time. An entire afternoon and early evening have transpired in less than fifteen realtime minutes. She promises, once again, that everyone will be finished riding the Trail of Tears in time to make it home for supper.

Bob responds with a humph. Rachel and Michael discuss triple suicide. Tallulah eyes the sunset and thinks that nothing ever really dies.

The sun sets quickly. The sky burns orange-blue with waves of reddish purple that streak fleetingly from the hilled horizon. The plot unfolds just as Tallulah knows it will. Seconds after the sun goes down, a house comes into view. It is a friendly house, the first and last safe house these tourists will see between here and Indian Territory.

Dogs bark and run toward Tour Group 5709. They are friendly dogs. Mutts, from the look of them. They sniff the tourists' hands and lead them to the house. Two Cherokees appear at the threshold – a man with a Cherokee turban and a woman with braids. They wear the same shirts and dresses as the tourists. The man introduces himself as Deer Cooker, and the woman introduces herself as Corn Grinder. They welcome 5709 into their home. Naturally, the tourists accept. They always do.

Inside the house a grandmother sits knitting by a fire. Three children play a game with feathers and marbles. Bob Rosenberg gravitates toward the old woman, and the Johnson twins are welcomed into the children's game. Tallulah enjoys watching the humble phenomenon work – an old man sitting down opening his mind, American schoolkids smiling and playing with their Indian cousins.

Corn Grinder chops turkey and vegetables for a soup. Deer Cooker hauls in wood for a fire. Corn Grinder brews sassafras tea for everyone to share. When a long pause strikes the conversation, Carmen Davis asks the question that every tourist wants to ask: "So, how did you get the names Deer Cooker and Corn Grinder?"

"'Cause I love to cook my dear over here," proclaims Deer Cooker, throwing his arm around his wife's shoulder.

"And I love to grind his corn cob," says Corn Grinder, a wry grin sliding from her cheeks.

The Athenians and the Londoners want more information. They ask about the ancestral origins of the phrases, Corn Grinder and Deer Cooker. Were they common names? Did they demonstrate a particular social niche? How did they relate to traditional religious practices?

"And what about this game?" asks Michael, the programmer. "Do you know how it's played?"

Deer Cooker laughs loudly and avoids as many questions as possible. "Here," he says, reaching for a bruised banjo. "You can play this?" Michael reaches for the instrument, takes it, and plays it poorly.

"Let me try," shouts Spencer. He nearly tunes the strings, then attempts to play. Spencer butchers the banjo the way your average guitarist butchers any stringed instrument that isn't a guitar. Nonetheless, Tallulah has heard the banjo massacred several hundred times, and Spencer isn't all that bad. She half expects Spencer to bust into the *Deliverance* theme, but he doesn't.

Deer Cooker pulls a variety of musical instruments from the wall. The twenty-somethings gather around the fireplace with the Indian man, and he hands out instruments to each of them. He brings frame drums large and small, turtle-shell rattles and gourd shakers, flutes low and high, mouth harps and small reeds. Instruments pass hands around the room.

"Dude, what is this thing all about?" asks Spencer. He holds a large, long blowpipe in his hands, something like an Australian didjeridoo.

"That isn't a traditional instrument, is it?" asks Carmen.

"Oh, we've had it in this house for a long, long time," replies Deer Cooker.

"No, I mean, like, traditional, like a traditional thing, you know?"

"You're both right," says Tallulah. "It's traditional, but it isn't typical."

Deer Cooker beats a low pulse on the large drum, and 5709 instinctively beats along. Corn Grinder begins to sing between Deer Cooker's beats, her voice ethereal and soothing. The Athenians wobble out a rhythm, and flutes find harmonies without much effort. The jam finds its tonic like a tone-deaf singer using a pitch corrector. Everyone but Bob contributes to the song. Corn Grinder continues singing as she walks toward the kitchen and quickly dishes up dinner, which is prepared so quickly that it seems to have cooked itself.

Corn Grinder brings the food to the table as Mandy Warren fumbles on a cedar flute. Roasted squash, flatbread, wild turkey soup, corncobs, beans, and a berry medley. She spreads the food upon the table buffet-style.

"Dude, is that more fry bread and buffalo burgers?" asks Spencer, a wayward note wobbling off the end of his instrument.

"Dude, those buffalo burgers are tight," notes Danny.

"Not tonight," replies Tallulah, looking at Carmen. "Tonight the food is more, shall we say, traditional."

Tallulah laments the absence of olives and basil in traditional Cherokee cuisine. If Tallulah was to ever pretend that she was Italian, she would change her last name to DePalma or D'Onofrio, something with a D. Tallulah D! She remembers the smells of the Mediterranean Café in Athens, of fresh bread and sizzling garlic, of roasting meats that sift from downtown Athens across Broad Street and into the northern edge of campus. The smells of brilliant drunken culinary creations that hovered around her and Bushyhead that night at the top of the Academic Building, when the whole world seemed as if it could fit into her palms. She thinks of basil cultivation, of all the stories Bushyhead tells of organic gardens on the West Coast.

Tallulah watches the ends of shadows climb the walls until they fade. The digital sun is finally down, and the rain sets in, dancing staccato on the roof.

Corn Grinder stops singing and calls everyone to the table. Tallulah encourages Tour Group 5709 to line up and take turns. "Plenty of food for everyone," she announces proudly. The tourists line up like most Americans. The younger and stronger they are, the faster they push, and the sooner they begin gorging themselves.

Bob Rosenberg stands at the end of the line, in front of Tallulah.

The feast ends as quickly as it began. After dinner several tourists step out onto the front porch, in spite of the rain, to breathe deeply in the last winds of the aboriginal atmosphere. Stars sparkle brightly against the deep, dark dome outside. The children play a game that involves throwing small rocks at a hole in the wall. Bob Rosenberg begins to praise the meal, but his breaths grow heavy, and he drifts away in his chair. He is asleep before he can finish a sentence.

Tallulah watches Bob Rosenberg imagine that he is sleeping. Even after eleven hundred different simulations of the Trail of Tears, Tallulah is still captivated by how easily the time compression works upon the tourists' senses, convincing them that an entire day has passed in approximately fifteen minutes, that they would gain a full night's sleep in less than two minutes. This is what makes the Trail of Tears special – Bob Rosenberg, passed out and stuffed, convinced that his limber old body is full and tired, so physically content that he can nap in a chair facing a strange fireplace even through his wife has gone missing. Where else could anyone experience such phenomena? It warms the sickness in Tallulah's heart to watch him sleep.

Corn Grinder leads Nell Johnson and her twin daughters toward a room in the corner of the house. "This is my room," says Corn Grinder. "But tonight you can sleep here." Tallulah mouths the dialogue in her mind as the words leave Corn Grinder's tongue. Nonetheless, the Indian woman's generosity transcends time and space. The Johnsons quickly occupy the room and drift asleep.

Corn Grinder rejoins her husband in front of the fire, and Tallulah knows the college kids will enjoy the next scene. As always, Deer Cooker pulls a pipe from the wall and grabs a pouch of tobacco from the mantle. The pipe is sleekly aboriginal. Tour Group 5709 is mesmerized as Deer Cooker carries the pipe toward the circle of bodies.

"What a beautiful pipe," says Carmen.

"What's it made out of?" asks Spencer.

Deer Cooker carefully holds the pipe parallel to the floor while he sits himself down in the circle. The pipe looks newly old, a fusion of elements and time periods. Parts of the pipe look like carved bone, parts look wooden, parts look like dried corncobs with stone feathers. A face is carved into the large bowl.

"The pipe comes from the earth," Deer Cooker says mechanically and reaches for a match. Jitters ruffle through the Athenians. Michael nudges Rachel with his foot.

"Nice one, Deer Cooker," says the native Londoner.

Corn Grinder opens her arms, cupping her hands toward the roof and sky. Deer Cooker strikes the match, cradles it in his hands as it catches fire, raises it proudly as he prepares to address the circle.

"My family, my friends, all my relations," he says, reverb calm, "welcome. It is good that you are here."

The Athenians' facial expressions loosen as Deer Cooker's voice ripples smoothly through their ears. TREPP techies patterned Deer Cooker's voice to resonate with a calming frequency, a sonic concoction designed to lessen the anxiety of all who listen, not unlike the Old Medicine Man.

Deer Cooker continues. "Now we will smoke the sacred pipe. Let us take time to remember the blessings that we have, the blessings of our ancestors. Because every blessing is special, and every moment is sacred."

Deer Cooker lights the pipe and smokes reverently. He passes it to Corn Grinder on his left. He opens his palms and exhales a steady stream of light grey smoke. He exhales like he is clearing his lungs to breathe for the first time. Corn Grinder takes a triumphant and religious draw from the pipe, then passes it to Spencer.

Spencer remains uncharacteristically quiet throughout the pipe sequence, but he rustles with animation as he holds the long, slender smoking device.

"Dude," he says to Deer Cooker, "is that what I think it is?"

"What do you think it is, Einstein?" says Carmen.

"Dude – this is a big-ass pipe."

"It has been in my family for generations," says Corn Grinder. Deer Cooker nods affirmatively. Tallulah already knows that Spencer's puff will be too big, that he will soon burst into violent coughing.

Spencer takes a small pull on the pipe. He feels for empty space in his lungs and follows with another small pull. As a contented look prepares to settle on his face, his eyes bulge like a frog and he spits hard, wheezing while showing a thumbs-up to his fellow tourists. He exhales with heavy convulsions, coughing until he drools a small string of saliva. He discreetly wipes his mouth and passes the pipe to Carmen. His cheeks rise, and his eyes settle.

"Ooh." He licks his lips. "That's nice. That's really nice." He licks again. Carmen exhales confidently and passes the pipe to Mandy.

"So, that's what now?" asks Spencer. "What is it called – kinnikinnick?"

Mandy passes the pipe to Danny, and Danny holds the pipe curiously in one hand while stroking an imaginary beard with the other. Danny inhales with his cheeks sucked in, trying to look like an intellectual but actually looking more like a fish.

"Good try, Spencer," says Tallulah. "But once again, that's a Lakota word."

"Oh," says Spencer, a twinge of introspection in his voice as he begins to recognize his own recurring pattern.

"What's the Cherokee word for tobacco?" asks Carmen.

Deer Cooker answers, "Tobacco."

The tourists laugh and nudge each other, tilting their eyebrows and chins.

"Is 'tobacco' really a Cherokee word?" asks Carmen.

"It is now," says Corn Grinder. "But the traditional word is 'tsola.'"

"Why do you call it tobacco then?" asks Carmen.

"Out of respect for our fellow creatures," says Deer Cooker.

Tallulah reads the frustration on Carmen's face. "Remember what I was mentioning before, Carmen, about how 'Cherokee' isn't a traditional Cherokee word?"

"Oh."

Danny passes the pipe to Rachel, who takes a small but healthy puff and passes it to her husband. Michael marvels at the pipe's appearance. He has never seen a pipe quite like this one, not even in a magazine.

Michael draws reverently and passes the pipe to Tallulah. Finally, the smoke she has been waiting for all morning. She takes a small puff and feels the muscles behind her eyes unstress themselves. She exhales slowly and savors the taste. Then she passes it to Deer Cooker to complete the circle.

"We smoke again," proclaims Deer Cooker, "and seek balance in all things."

The males quickly support the idea of more smoking. Corn Grinder's pipe circles the tourists a second time, a third time, and a fourth. Space quivers as smoke fills the cabin. People move in lucid synch with the walls and objects. Tallulah breathes deep and holds her eyes open, watching the tourists search for themselves in the thickening air.

"Deer Cooker, mate, you sure there's not any grass in there?" asks Michael.

"Nice one, Deer Cooker," says Rachel. "That's a really nice smoke for not being real."

"Tastes better than my Camels," agrees Spencer.

"Can't say the same about my Marlboros," remarks Danny.

Deer Cooker's shoulders move mechanically, synchronized with the blinks of his eyes. Tallulah is always bothered by the way his shoulders move while he's smoking. She has often told the techies to do something about it, but Deer Cooker's character never seems to bother anyone else. The techies dismissed the issue, claiming that the image is too smoky for a first-time tourist to critique such small details. What about repeat customers? she insisted, but nothing ever changed. Tallulah thinks Deer Cooker's shoulders are too large. Maybe Tallulah's eyes are just too familiar with smoke, real or virtual, to be tricked by the illusion.

"This blend had always been a personal favorite."

"Dude," Spencer urges, "did you put some weed in here?"

"No way," says Carmen. "You remember what the professor said last week. That's not traditional. They don't put pot in the peace pipe."

"Traditionally," says Tallulah, clearing her throat for dramatic effect, "women and men had rigidly defined gender roles and divisions of labor. You shouldn't be sharing a pipe with men, traditionally speaking, of course."

Tallulah's cheeks pulse. Deer Cooker's tobacco feels good on her self-induced sores. That's the problem with tobacco, quality tobacco at least – it always tastes good, even in here. She breathes deep and thinks about the ocean.

Carmen's face swells, anxious and curious. Her drive for accuracy is in conflict with her drive for empowerment.

Tallulah remembers the early days of driving home from work on 441. She would always roll two cigarettes in the morning, both of which she would save for after work. She would light the first one before merging onto 441, the second one as soon as she had crossed through Commerce, and she was in a good mood by the time she reached her driveway. She cut out the after-work smoke nearly two years ago, a major step in the journey toward quitting, an attempt to prove to herself that she is not completely addicted, that she smokes out of choice rather than physical dependency. But she knows better. She knows the addiction is for real, and no matter how much she weans herself, there is a massive difference between some and none.

"Hey," says Spencer, smiling big and waving his dangly arms, "let's bust out those drums and flutes again. I'm all primed up now."

"Maybe tomorrow," says Deer Cooker.

"Yes," agrees Corn Grinder. "It is time to sleep now." The two Cherokees sing a very traditional-sounding lullaby. Their voices are perfectly harmonized. Harmonies woven through sounds of the indigenous language, its shifting pitch striking chords that these tourists have never consciously noticed, beautiful tones that land in between the keys on a Western chromatic scale – what Tallulah's brother calls green notes. Eyelids begin to droop around the circle.

Deer Cooker and Corn Grinder bring knitted blankets and feather pillows to the tourists. Then the friendly Indians walk to the doors of their room, their outlines faintly glowing against the woodwork. The tourists are being momentarily soothed by the Chairsuits. The entire sequence is designed to be their last comfortable experience on the Trail of Tears. The Athenians and the Londoners snuggle into the blankets, and sleep begins to fall upon them.

Then Spencer snaps awake with sudden intensity. His movements shake the floor, waking the tourists around him.

"Dude!" he exclaims. "Oh dude!" He shoves Danny's leg with his foot. "Oh man, oh dude!"

"What!" replies Danny.

"Oh, FUCK! DUDE!" Spencer kicks his roommate again.

"The fuck's your problem, Spencer?" snarls Danny.

Tallulah asks Spencer if he can breathe. He can. She asks if he is in pain. He isn't. She asks if he is disoriented, and he isn't sure.

"So what's the matter with you?" asks Carmen.

"Oh fuck, dude," he responds. "I mean, I just never realized it before."

"Realized what?" asks Mandy.

"Your car, dude," says Spencer, again shoving Danny with his foot. "Your car! Your car is a Cherokee!"

"Huh?"

"Your car, dude. You drive a Cherokee!"

"So what?" retorts Danny. "Who cares? Go to sleep."

"But don't you think that's fucked up?"

"No. Why should I?"

The silence that follows feels long, terribly long. Exactly how long, who could say? Maybe ten seconds in realtime. Maybe two. Tallulah can never count realtime in its exact proportions when she is on the Trail of Tears, since it is nearly impossible to perceive the true dynamics of the time compression while you're inside the Chairsuit.

Regardless, Tallulah knows the silence is long. Long enough to mean something. Fine, she thinks, let it sink in. Let it go to the source. Let Tour Group 5709 bask in its own cultural neurosis.

Spencer breaks the silence. "Hey, Tallulah?"

"Yes."

"Are you, like, offended by the Jeep Cherokee?"

Rachel Rosenberg rolls over onto her back and answers for Tallulah. "Of course she's offended. How could she not be?"

But Spencer is not satisfied by Rachel's response. He wants to hear it straight from the Indian's mouth – he wants Tallulah's own authentic analysis of the Jeep Cherokee. Tallulah imagines an Oklahoma Cherokee man driving a big red Jeep Cherokee with multiple American-flag bumper stickers, driving to Kansas City to watch a Chiefs-Redskins game, listening to the song "Indian Outlaw" on repeat, and howling along with the lyrics as he swerves between highway lanes, absolutely loving every minute of it.

Tallulah remembers the smell of moldy rust in her grandparents' basement. She remembers her grandfather opening the passenger door of the big red Jeep Cherokee with television windows. Her Grandpa Art, the renowned craftsman and cultural emissary of the Cherokee Nation, the man her own father disowned before Tallulah was born – if Grandpa Art is somehow alive in here, a ghost in the machine, he must be listening closely to Tallulah's response. It isn't every day that a customer asks her point blank about the Jeep Cherokee while riding the Trail of Tears.

"It's a good question," says Tallulah, "and it depends on how easily you get offended."

Carmen asks Tallulah to elaborate, so Tallulah tries an unconventional approach, fully conscious that it is generally unpleasant for tourists to be interrogated by their tour guides.

"Danny," she asks, "did you ever think that driving your car was like riding an Indian?"

"Look, dude," Danny responds sharply. "I like my car. Okay?"

"I bet you do," snaps Carmen.

"What's the difference?" blurts Danny. "It's just a name."

"Yeah," Carmen keeps pushing. "What's the difference when your parents cover the monthly payments of your brand-new Jeep fucking Cherokee?!"

"Fuck off, Caramel cream!" shouts Danny.

"You fuck off, Calhoun!" Carmen retorts. "I don't even need to change your name to cut you down. How many slave owners had your name, anyways?"

Tallulah realizes that her unconventional approach to the Jeep Cherokee question is backfiring badly, about to snowball out of control.

"*Ehgh!!!!!!*" Tallulah blurts.

It is the EMP of human vocal sounds, the blurt that freezes and silences all who hear. That short, indistinct, grunting jab – that sonic signal from parents, teachers, conductors, bosses, any semirespectable authority figure who must absolutely let you know that you are crossing the line.

Tallulah holds up her arm as if it can contain the argument's inertia. "Let's take a different approach to the question," she announces, turning to Rachel Rosenberg. Everyone follows Tallulah and eyes Rachel.

"Rachel, would you be offended if I drove a car called the Ford Semite?"

Michael Hopkins buckles in muffled laugher. Rachel sits with a stunned smile that grows wider and wider before the floodgates break and the laughter pours through. The statement appears to fly right over the college students' heads.

"Or better yet," Tallulah continues, "the Hummer Hassid. Now that's a car I'd like to take off-road."

Maybe it isn't the best analogy in the world, but it works. Rachel Rosenberg confesses – yes, she would be offended if her friends drove a car called the Chevy Jew. Rachel cannot imagine anyone in the Anti-Defamation League driving a Jeep Jew, but she knows several Jews who drive Cherokees.

"The Chevy Jew," laughs Spencer.

"I always thought it would be the Chevy Mexican," replies Tallulah. Everyone laughs.

Michael Hopkins describes the Jeep Cherokees in Britain, how they are smaller and more fuel-efficient, but still marketed on the basis of their animal nature. He smiles wryly before suggesting that Cadillac should make the Nubian.

"Dude," says Spencer, "they've even got a Dodge Dakota!"

"What about the Dodge Celt?" asks Carmen.

"The Oldsmobile Catholic!" says Rachel.

"The Mercury Mullah," says Tallulah. "Or better yet, the Mercury Puritan!"

"Shouldn't it be the Plymouth Puritan?" asks Rachel.

"That's a good one," says Tallulah.

Spencer asks about Japanese cars. Everyone has focused on American cars, but what about the Japanese cars?

Tallulah mentions the Mazda Navajo, a small SUV modeled on the Ford Explorer that never sold nearly as well as its American counterparts.

"The Audi Aboriginal," says Carmen, but Spencer reminds her that Audis are European.

"I guess that shit *is* pretty funny," admits Danny. "Dude – I drive a Cherokee." He leans down, covering his eyes with his hands, and begins to laugh uncontrollably.

"Dude, that's what I'm saying!" says Spencer.

"That shit is fucking ridiculous!" Danny shouts. "I never thought of it like that before." He rubs his eyes and snorts. "My ride is a Cherokee. Holy shit, that's weird."

"Hey, dudes," says Carmen, "at this rate, pretty soon you'll be riding each other."

Everyone laughs. The steam valve has finally opened; the pressure has finally dropped.

Tallulah's cheeks rise. She imagines Danny humping Spencer, howling for his roommate to squeal like a pig. She wonders how many of the tourists entertain this same image, but she dares not ask.

"What about the good old Honda Cracker?" asks Rachel.

Tallulah thinks about her beautiful hybrid Honda sedan. Do hybrid engines signify whiteness? Does her car confirm her own crackerdom? What the hell is whiteness anyway? Middle-class intellectuals have spent generations making careers and getting tenure by writing books about whiteness, and still no one has any idea how or where to draw the line. Tallulah Wilson is three-quarters white American, and she drives a hybrid Honda sedan, paid for entirely because she works her ass off for the Trail of Tears. God, I am pathetic, she thinks. But I love my car. It just feels good to drive the hybrid Honda, to know that she saves petroleum each time she burns it.

Tallulah thinks about Germans driving their SUVs through Africa. "Don't forget the Volkswagen Touareg," she adds.

"What's a Touareg?" asks Spencer.

Tallulah explains who the Touaregs are. She promises her tourists that, like it or not, the Volkswagen Touareg actually does exist.

"Strangely enough," Tallulah continues, "while the actual Touaregs are desert people, most of the television commercials show people driving their Volkswagen Touareg over glaciers, or cold mountain rivers, or some other environment that is rather un-Touareg."

"Hey, I got one," says Danny. "The GM Jew."

"Nah," says Carmen. "The Hummer Hassid has a way better ring."

The conversation trudges onward with self-ridicule and caustic irony, exhausting potential combinations of automobile manufacturers with religious or tribal identities. Something has happened. Tallulah can sense the changes.

The sun begins to rise through Corn Grinder and Deer Cooker's shimmering windows. Tour Group 5709 seems lost in the translucence. The twenty-somethings have talked the night away.

Tallulah watches the shadows return to the walls. Surprising herself, Tallulah says a prayer for Irma Rosenberg. If God or Unela or Technical Services or some yet-unnamed power could make the old woman appear at the stockades, Tallulah will quit smoking for good. She might even quit drinking.

She watches the virtual light refracting upward from the hard floors, a soft prism crawling across the windows and up the log walls. She closes her eyes and sees the light echo on her inner eyelid, ascending the walls and windows she has seen so many times before.

She hears the troops crashing through the windows a split second before it happens. She knows how the tips of their bayonets will shine with eerie reflections.

Tour Group 5709, of course, is not expecting the American Army to burst into the cabin at sunrise. They are not mentally prepared for the bayonets and harsh commands. They do not expect to be rounded up and marched to a human stockade before breakfast.

When it happens – when the windows crash and the door is kicked down, when the soldiers' feet storm the house behind the tips of their malevolent guns, when the innocent and contemplative customers are kicked like rodents – Tour Group 5709 is understandably confused.

But the confusion quickly fades, and a common acknowledgment, a collective "oh right," filters through the tourists' minds. It is the moment they remember that they paid to be abused. The step that starts the thousand miles.

10

Irma Rosenberg followed the elder Misfit Cherokees away from the octagon table, through the dim hallway, and back into the open-air stockade. Small children stood outside the tinted-glass doorway, waiting with gifts in their hands. They held little baskets and woven boxes, candleholders and tiny medicine wheels. They gifted Irma Rosenberg as she walked through the tinted doors and into the light. Irma felt like a rock star.

"The kids believe that you are an omen, Irma Rosenberg," said Indians Hat.

"Well, if my sciatica is an omen, then I think things are going to be okay. I have all these places, you know, where it always hurts me, but not today. Every day it kills me but today."

She walked with a slight swagger as she followed Indians Hat, who pointed to a set of stainless steel doors in another corner of the stockade.

"If you are the omen we have waited for, then the time of our deliverance is near." The mob parted for Irma and Indians Hat as they approached the stainless steel. "But only the Chef will know for sure," he said.

"He must have one of those outfits that my nephew wears. Does he have a hat?"

Indians Hat did not answer.

The stainless steel doors looked larger from a distance. But up close the doors were barely taller than Irma herself. She could almost see herself in the shiny reflection. She smelled garlic and cumin. Indians Hat touched the handle.

He turned his head. “One thing. Don’t stare directly at the Chef.”

“Why not?”

“Please, Irma Rosenberg. Do yourself a favor, do us all a favor, and don’t stare directly at the Chef.”

“How am I supposed to talk to him?”

“Oh, you can look at him, just don’t lock in. Stare at his eyebrows, or his nose. Just don’t let yourself lock into his eyes.”

Indians Hat opened the kitchen doors. Irma’s eyes swallowed the blinding light as she followed the elder into the kitchen. The floors, the walls, the ceilings all shone loudly. Irma wondered if these lights were real or just more reflections.

Irma could not see the bodies at first, but she heard the conversation clearly.

“Shyo, Chef.”

“Shyo. Took you long enough.”

“We wanted to ask her some questions of our own.”

Irma tried to remember what the elders asked her. Other than uncertain comments about her appearance, she could not remember any questions. Their inquiries were more like crossword puzzle prompts than direct questions. She felt they were more concerned about concealing their original names than extracting information from her.

Irma watched the outlines of the Chef’s body slowly congeal into solid shapes. He stood behind a shiny prep table, and he appeared to be chopping something.

“We believe,” announced Indians Hat, “she is the one we’ve been waiting for.”

“Thanks,” said the Chef. His voice felt strong and soft, young and wise, old and energetic. “But I think I got this from here.”

“What about lunch?” asked the elder.

"The food will soon be ready. For now try to act like there's nothing unusual."

Irma wondered what these people would consider unusual. For her today's experience was hands down the strangest thing she could remember. Much weirder than those movies Rachel made them watch their first night in Georgia. Indians Hat walked away, through the kitchen door.

"What's wrong?" asked the Chef. Her eyes were almost adjusted to the surroundings. The Chef was flanked by three assistants – two teenage boys and one old woman.

Irma waited for someone else to respond.

"You, Rosenberg, I'm talking to you. What's wrong?"

"I'm sorry," said Irma.

"Can you cook?" asked the Chef.

"Are you still talking to me?"

"Why wouldn't I be?"

The Chef cracked his neck to the right and swallowed air with his jaw. Then he whipped his neck to the left, cracking several bones, and rolled his left shoulder in rapid circles.

"Of course, I can cook." Irma addressed the Chef directly but avoided a direct visual lock with his eyes. "I've been feeding people for over sixty years."

"Good." Chef nodded his head toward the other old woman in the kitchen. "Because she's been wanting a day off for years."

"Okay."

"Good."

Irma could now see clearly. She surveyed the radiant workspace. Stainless steel ran the surface of all tables, equipment, and appliances in the Misfit kitchen. "I don't know much about your indigenous traditional cuisine. I saw the menu at your café out there, the turtle cake or whatever. Eagle something?"

"Are you willing to learn?"

"If it helps me get out of here, sure."

"The boys are chopping vegetables for a corn chowder, but I need them working on these turkeys so I can prep the fruit."

The old Indian woman in the kitchen untied her apron and wiped her prep table with a towel. "Nice outfit," she said to Irma. She reached into a coffin cabinet for a clean apron, then offered the apron to Irma.

The old Indian woman in the kitchen said goodbye to the boys and entered a walk-in refrigerator.

The prep tables stood shiny and firm, reflecting the warm glow of overhead lights. Digital lights bounced from steel surface to steel surface with ricochet straps of warm energy, illuminating the room in spheres.

"Okay," said Irma, "but I can chop fruit."

"No no," said the Chef. "We need you on soup. If you're on fruit, and they come, then things will seem unusual back here."

"I don't understand."

"You'll see." His jaw twitched, and both of his shoulders spun in backward circles.

The boys placed four large stainless steel bowls on the prep table in front of Irma. Each bowl was filled with vegetables – carrots, celery, onions, and plenty of corn. One of the boys laid a damp rag on Irma's table, and the other one placed a cutting board on top of the rag. The cutting board was shiny and clean. Too clean, Irma thought, as if it had never been used. She wondered if it was metal, too.

Irma did not understand why a chef would need to chop fruit when she, Irma Rosenberg, was very familiar with chopping fruit but inexperienced at cooking corn chowder the Cherokee way. She didn't even know if there *was* a Cherokee way to cook corn chowder.

Chef pointed at the two boys with his mouth. "These two are my apprentices. That's Fish, and that's Ish."

"Tish and Fish?"

"Ish. Fish and Ish."

The boys both turned and nodded toward Irma as the Chef identified them. "That's Ish on the left, and Fish on the right."

They nodded again, then turned their backs to Irma. They stood over the engines of the operation – one charbroiler, one flat grill, and four fryer baskets.

"They're my boys," Chef said, "and yes, they're twins."

Irma had never imagined Native Americans eating so much fried food. She generally assumed they were lean and healthy hunters, athletic by default of lifestyle, and she had naturally been taught to believe that all Indians are nomadic. But these Misfit Cherokees seemed rather sedentary. Even if the elders were right, and no one could ever belong in this place, the digital Indians certainly appeared well-adjusted to themselves and their environment. And they owned some very modern appliances.

"How many people live here?" she asked.

"Approximately one thousand," answered the Chef, "though that number fluctuates depending on the time of day."

"Why does time of day matter?"

Chef put down his knife and pulled a three-ring notebook from a ledge on the wall. "The breakfast crowd is always larger than the dinner crowd." He opened the notebook and placed it squarely on Irma's prep table. "Here's the corn chowder recipe you need."

"Not that I expect you to know him, but my nephew is a sous chef at a very expensive restaurant in New York City."

"How nice."

Irma tied the apron around her waist, her digital shoulders and elbows circling with ease. "So you're a hologram too?" she asked. She marveled at the tone in her own muscles as she tied the string.

"That's a bizarre question," said the Chef. The boys turned their heads. Irma guessed their age was anywhere from sixteen to twenty-three.

"I don't envy you at all," she said.

"I don't envy you either," he replied. "It's a big thing you've decided to take on."

Chef spun his wrists in crackling circles, his right heel tapping fast. The boys drove their knives through the turkeys' wild contours.

"What do you mean?" asked Irma.

"Destruction creates. Changes search for reasons. But let's take it one step at a time. I need to get something from the garden. Here's some flour for your roux."

Irma used to cook soups for her family. When her kids were young, she cooked a big soup at least once a week, often on Sundays. She cooked many soups with roux and many soups without them. She knew how to cook corn chowder her way – sometimes with chicken, sometimes with ham, sometimes just vegetables – but she was entirely clueless about the Chef's traditional methods for cooking corn chowder. The Chef's recipe might as well be written in Klingon. Irma couldn't even decipher the words for "corn chowder."

The Chef returned with an apronful of fresh vegetables. Irma asked if she could see the garden, and the Chef politely refused.

"I can't read your recipe."

"No??"

The Chef grabbed the notebook and lifted it right up to his

face. He held it close to his eyes and stared hard into the pages. Then he held it at a distance and squinted.

"You're absolutely right," he said, slamming the cookbook shut. "This thing is useless." He placed the book back on the ledge, rolled his shoulders, and cleared his throat with a bellowing hack. He pulled another notebook off the ledge and flipped through the pages. The recipe he wanted was at the midpoint of the book.

"This is much better," he said, handing the notebook to Irma. The recipe was written in plainly legible English, and the large words were soft on Irma's eyes.

"Thank you," she said, stretching as she read. "My lower back feels so much younger. You must not feel any pain, do you?" Chef slowly creaked his eyes upon Irma. She felt his gaze and turned her own eyes upon the recipe book. "That's a bad question, never mind."

"On the contrary," he replied. "It is an excellent question."

Irma read the recipe, waiting for Chef to continue. He cocked his head and quickly itched a frantic spot on his neck. He walked away and reached for a clean cutting board.

"That's odd. This recipe says to start with the roux."

"Naturally."

"Shouldn't I wait to start the roux until the rest of the soup is coming to a boil?"

"Just follow the recipe, and don't burn the roux."

Irma followed the recipe and cooked the chowder, starting with the roux. She stirred the roux and listened as the Chef described his garden. He grew tomatoes and basil, potatoes and garlic, mint and thyme, carrots and celery, peppers and onions, broccoli and cabbage, and – of course – beans, squash, pumpkins, and corn. Lots of corn.

He raised turkeys and cows and chicken, and a creek filled with fish rippled through the backyard of the stockade.

"None of the others can go near the stream. Only myself and the twins."

"How can a stockade have a backyard?" asked Irma as she sautéed the vegetables.

"This is not your average stockade," said the Chef, "and I have a key."

Irma wondered if Tallulah Wilson knew about the Chef and his key. She poured the boys' chicken stock into the steaming pot of vegetables. She wondered if the Belgian woman who fell into a coma had ever stirred soup for the Chef. Irma brought the soup to a boil and stirred in the roux.

"Why do you Misfits want me to be an omen?"

"Misfits?" said the Chef.

"Well I have to call you something, don't I?"

"Not necessarily."

"I'm having difficulties understanding the benefits of not having names. And you seem like Misfits to me."

"You see right into it," said the Chef, "and you don't even know it."

"What?"

"Sure, Misfits, whatever – just stir that soup. Don't burn it, and for god's sake don't undercook it either. We have a lot of people to feed."

Irma still felt no pain from her sciatica as she stirred the corn chowder. The painlessness left her in an awkward position. She wasn't sure what to complain about. Clearly there were problems, but the kitchen was spectacular. She thought about Jewish people. She imagined a small battalion of ancient Jews who found a desert cave to hide, a place of refuge hidden within the desert, a place of gourmet solace where they avoided an entire generation of disenfranchisement, dietary issues, and severe foot pain. She wondered how the old stories would have been different if those walkers couldn't feel their feet.

"What sort of an omen are you looking for?" she asked.

The twins turned to each other, locked eyes. One of them hacked his throat clear and spit into a trashcan.

"For a sign," said the Chef as he carved a watermelon.

"That's usually what an omen is, right? A sign?"

Ish and Fish lined several turkeys in rows upon a large cutting board. The boys pulled legs and wings from the birds, one after the next after the next. They moved with precision, a four-handed assembly line, a concentrated machine. Irma listened to them, to the squish and rustle of snapping tendons and sinew. She tried to count the turkeys, but there were too many.

"A sign of deliverance," said Chef.

"Deliverance from what?" asked Irma.

"In about five minutes, you will understand precisely what we seek deliverance from." He reached his arms to the ceiling and arched his back, the vertebrae popping domino up his spine. He clenched his fists, squinted his eyes, and slowly cracked his neck again. The joints popped loud enough for Irma to feel the pressure drop in her own bones. "You must remember," he said, perfectly calm, returning to a normal posture, "you absolutely must remember, that you do not smoke."

"What?"

"Do you smoke?"

"No."

"Then you'll be fine."

"Not in forty years I haven't. Almost forty years. My husband neither."

"Fine. Just don't relapse now."

She wondered if he was the kind of Chef to cook her in a large pot or pretend she was a virgin and sacrifice her. When Irma was a girl, she might have studied Native American rituals, but the sacrifice details were foggy in her memory. She thought about Pall Mall unfiltereds and wondered if she had ever known about these sacrificial details, or if she just assumed that she had. Were these the kind of Indians who ate their omens? Was that why it mattered that she looked like them?

"Here they come," said Chef. He turned to the boys, who were finally placing the turkeys in the oven to roast, and told them to watch the windows. "Let's do this."

Ish set the oven timers while Fish wiped down their prep tables. They pulled two full sheetpans from a rack in the corner of the kitchen. Each one grabbed a sheetpan with one hand and a large trash bin with the other. They wheeled the trash bins up to the front wall of the kitchen, the wall that led to the steel doorway. They laid their sheetpans on top of the trash bins. Then they climbed softly onto the sheetpans, careful to keep their balance. Standing erect upon the sheetpans, guiding their bodies up the stainless steel wall with sure hands and magnificent knees, the twins moved through the kitchen like synchronized athletes.

The boys stood and stretched their arms into the walls. Their hands sank into the stainless steel until their elbows had entered the shiny surface of the wall. They pushed their arms apart like swimmers in a slow-motion breaststroke. Small windows formed in front of their heads, the stainless steel spreading apart and opening.

"Now I can see why the tickets are so expensive," she said.

"Hang on," said Chef, "and don't forget to stir the soup."

The kitchen stood still while a cascade of bombs destroyed the main gate of the stockade. Explosions rang throughout the compound. Heavy bass, ricochet snaps, extended rumbles.

Irma wondered about the Chef's key. She heard human screams across the walls. She felt shockwaves in her legs. She wondered what it was like being in an earthquake. Irma had a cousin who lived in California, but they rarely spoke, and Irma never visited. She was sure that people stumbled and fell into each other during earthquakes, but none of the pots or knives inside the kitchen budged an inch.

"There's five of them," said Ish.

"Mister's here," said Fish.

Chef leaned over to Irma and said, "Whatever you do, don't stare directly into their eyes."

Irma stared down at her soup, wondering if there was anyone important whose eyes she could stare into. What was it with these people and their eyes? What made the Chef any different from this Mister? She wanted to know more about the woman who'd walked into the refrigerator. Had Irma looked into her eyes before she left? She had looked the elders in the eyes, especially Indians Hat, she was sure of that.

"Suits just shot about fifteen or twenty of the boys," said Ish.

"Yeah," said Fish. "Some of them're eyeing the girls, but they're holding back. Seem preoccupied with something else."

Thuds and screams, shouts and moans, painful sounds punctuated the gunshots outside the kitchen. Chef carefully cut the rind off of a honeydew melon. He sliced the melon into bite-sized pieces, mixing it with the other fruits in his bowl. Irma saw grapes and watermelon and oranges and pineapple and mangos and honeydew. It was a serious fruit salad.

"The boys have stopped fighting back," said Fish.

"About time," said Chef.

"They're asking for someone named Rosenberg," said Ish.

"Are the elders saying anything?"

Fish shook his head. "Nothing. They're just humming at the ground like usual."

Chef carefully spiraled the skin off an apple, shaping the

twisted strip of apple skin into a rose. He diced the flesh of the apple and mixed it into the fruit salad.

Chef turned to Irma and said, in a strangely reassuring tone, "Just stir the soup and keep quiet."

Irma wanted to acknowledge the Chef's encouraging words, but she avoided direct eye contact. She wondered where the Chef's garden was. She still couldn't see a door to the backyard.

"Suits can't tell us apart in here," said Chef. "You belong here because you've never been anywhere else. As long as you don't act like a real person, you'll be fine."

"Mister's coming," said Ish.

"Let's go, boys. Get down already!"

The twins closed their windows on the stockade, pushing their palms together and pulling their forearms from the wall. Digital flesh birthed from the steel wall, twin frogs surfacing from a pond. Their parallel bodies bent congruent angles. One fluid motion, stepping down from the trash bin stepstools and sliding the sheetpans into the cracks between prep tables.

Chef stirred the fruit salad one final time, then pressed his spoon into the center of the fruit, leaving a small crater on top. He gently placed his apple-peel rose in the center of the salad.

Irma was stirring her soup when she heard the door open.

Two Suits entered the kitchen.

One of the Suits walked up to the fruit salad and stuck his hand into the bowl. He dug through the salad for a specific piece of fruit, but Irma did not watch his hands.

"Okay, Chef," said the person, who from Irma's peripheral vision appeared to be wearing a power suit. The suit was very dark, and it felt very powerful. Irma could feel its power without even appreciating its full view.

"Okay, Mister," said Chef.

“Where’s the Rosenberg woman?”

“I don’t know what you’re talking about. Have some more fruit.”

The Suits accepted. Hardly anyone could refuse the Chef’s fruit salad, especially the Suits. Chef offered the Suits a turkey dinner, but they declined.

“Our reports suggest that a woman named Rosenberg is in this area,” said the Suit.

“What does she look like?” asked the Chef.

Irma’s stirring hand wiggled a bit, so she leaned over slightly to smell the soup, careful to keep stirring continuously. She was afraid her whole arm would start shaking, but she breathed deeply and concentrated on the soup. It was beginning to smell very appetizing.

The Suit pulled a pack of cigarettes from his chest pocket. He offered them to everyone in the kitchen. Chef, the twin boys, and the other Suit each took a cigarette from the pack. Irma looked at the cigarette box and shook her head. She returned her eyes to the soup and continued stirring.

“Oh, right,” said the Suit, stuffing the cigarettes back into his chest. He sat down. Irma wasn’t sure where his chair had come from, but she tried not to think about it.

The Suits didn’t have much else to say. They smoked, ate fruit salad, and seemed to enjoy themselves. They smoked between bites and nearly ate the entire bowl of fruit. Irma had not seen anyone eat so much fruit in one sitting since her second son was a teenager.

“If I find out that she was here, and that you knew about it, then we’ll have a situation.” The Suit sucked down one last bite of fruit salad and walked to the door. “If we have a situation, someone will have to answer,” he said coldly.

“Of course,” said the Chef. The silent Suit stuck out his jaw and nodded slowly.

"Good fruit," said the Suit.

"Naturally."

The Suit brushed some debris off his chest. He turned and signaled to his partner, who turned mechanically and followed the lead Suit through the steel door.

The twins quickly rebuilt their trash bin stepstools as soon as the Suits left the kitchen. They leaned into the steel and opened their windows in the wall.

"Mister shot another guy," said Ish.

"Some other Suit just shot two more guys," said Fish.

Chef offered some fruit to Irma. Very little remained in the bowl – a few crumpled pieces of watermelon, two little bunches of grapes, a couple slimy mango bits. All the pineapple was gone.

Irma declined. Chef slurped up the last bits himself. He noticed Irma's suspicious gaze upon the empty bowl of fruit.

"I have a deeply held belief that nothing should go to waste," he said.

"How can you have deeply held beliefs if you're not real?" asked Irma.

"Not now," said Chef. "How's the crowd?"

"They seem all right," said Ish. "The Suits are gone."

"They closed the gate," said Fish.

"Don't worry," said Ish. "Nothing leaked in."

Chef placed the empty fruit bowl in a large sink, adding to the quickly building pile of dirty dishes. He told the twins to let the turkeys cool, to wait at least ten minutes before carving the breasts, and to be sure that all the dirty dishes were brought to the sink.

He turned to Irma, and she looked down. "*That*," he said, "was *them*." He popped the knuckles on both hands and spun his shoulders in backward circles. "You did well. Now, turn down the fire on that soup. It can simmer while we survey the damage."

"The kids are losing it," said Ish.

"Come on, boys," said Chef. "Time is money."

The twins closed their windows on the stockade and climbed down from their perch. Chef checked everyone's equipment to make sure it was turned off. While walking toward the door, the boys wiped counters and placed dangerous objects in secure areas.

"Come on, Rosenberg," said Chef. Irma followed Ish and Fish, though she still couldn't tell the difference between them. She walked into the open-air stockade, but her eyes had adapted to the kitchen's overbearing light, and now they needed to readjust. She heard the Misfit tribe before she saw them. Vague redness pulsed dimly inside the sunny stockade. Irma thought she smelled cooking flesh, though she was not entirely sure because she had never smelled flesh cooking before, not that she knew of, anyway. She heard the waves again. She rubbed her eyes gently, as if she could clarify herself.

Her eyes itched, and her heels pulsed. She almost felt a pain in her forehead and her feet, but it was not normal pain. It was like the pain from an old wound that she'd never had, a lingering injury from another body that reminded her of herself. But the stiffness suddenly left her eyes, and she could see again.

The entire tribe spoke at once. All the Misfit Indians, all of them, had something desperate to say.

Middle-aged women pounded their fists against their heads. Acting individually, they gave themselves a collective beating. No one attacked another person, only themselves. They grunted and screamed and cried and wailed and made themselves bleed. Irma wondered how hard people needed to hit themselves in order to create their own concussions. These Cherokee women were obviously strong, or else their heads were extremely hard, because none of them appeared to lose their balance while abusing themselves.

Irma looked for the other old woman, the one who'd disappeared into the walk-in refrigerator, but she could not find her. The crowd was dense: old men were all around, young men and women everywhere, but Irma could see no old women other than herself. She tried to see beyond the structure's walls. The walls were built of tall logs anchored together, the tops of the logs carved into sharp points that had an ominous tone. Irma heard the waves clearly, and she wondered if this entire structure was some kind of seaship, a wooden ship from which no one could leave. But the structure did not move, it did not rock upon the water. It was firm and all too solid. Maybe it was an island. She watched the crowd swim around the elders. All seven of the baseball-capped elders were gathered in a circle at the center of the crowd. Near them, middle-aged men knelt on the ground, screaming, "Hey ya hey ya ya hey ya," over and over while banging their heads upon the earth. People abused themselves at different tempos.

Irma spoke, to everyone and no one in particular. "What are you doing? You're hurting yourselves." No one responded.

She stared at an empty watchtower protruding from one of the sharp walls, hovering motionless over the manic energy on the ground. She wondered if people ever used it to watch for approaching storms, for hurricanes or tidal waves.

Irma remembered one time when was in her forties, when a mental slip had cost her thousands of dollars. She'd been so mad at herself that she banged her angry head against a slab of painted drywall. She'd banged her head against the wall three or four times. It hurt like hell. She tried to imagine what these Misfits felt as they pounded their howling heads. She wondered if they actually felt. Babies cried violently. They punched their small selves with variable aim.

The circle of elders stood stoic in the epicenter of the mayhem. They began to sing. Irma could barely hear their song through all the commotion, but what she did hear felt rather soothing. They sang in their own language, standing calmly as they held their palms toward the overcast sky. Their songs affected the crowd, but progress was slow. Irma wondered why the elders didn't sing louder, or if they were even capable of singing louder.

The young people, the teenagers and the young adults, screamed the loudest. Some girls threw themselves on their backs, thrusting their hips up and down, shouting painfully. Irma's mind raced with scenarios. What were they doing? Were they practicing for something? Why were they preparing to be raped rather than preparing to defend themselves? The elders kept singing. The girls kept ripping their clothes open and slapping themselves.

Boys ripped off their shirts. Some of the pants came off too. They threw jabs at their own cheekbones. They hollered. They howled. They hit themselves with one hand while holding the other hand over their mouth. They even pulsed their palms upon their lips to accentuate the howling. The sound struck a chord in Irma's memory – the sound of Western movies in the background at someone else's house. Irma had never cared for Western movies, and she wanted to go back into the kitchen. She eyed the empty watchtower, and it seemed to pulse.

"This is worse than most television," she declared, loud and bold. But the self-violence was escalating, and no one responded to the old woman. Every Western that Irma could remember was the same – a war party of naked Indian warriors screams and whoops themselves into battle, screaming and whooping with one hand in the air and one hand over their mouths, screaming and whooping as they approach a vulnerable white homestead with a damsel in distress. But these boys had no horses, and they only battled against themselves.

Other young people, the ones who didn't hit themselves, knelt upon the ground and pounded their heads. They knelt and trembled, holding their heads tightly in their hands, whimpering painfully, again like Bob and his killer migraines. But then, finally, Irma heard the pressure drop. Slowly, one after another, the Misfits began to relax.

The elders sang on, undaunted by the masochism that surrounded them. The elders continued to sing, quietly and calmly, as if the sky would sit in their arms if they sang long enough.

"This is taking way too long," said the Chef. He signaled Ish with some kind of sign language. Ish ran toward the kitchen, disappeared, then quickly reemerged with a small stainless steel cannon. Fish helped his brother swab the cannon and load something into it.

The cannon was tiny, smaller than Irma initially thought, but it worked. The reverb blast shook the entire stockade and silenced the masses.

"Okay okay okay!" shouted the Chef, loud enough for all to hear.

"Remember," sang Indians Hat, shifting into English.

"Remember," echoed the chorus of elders.

Scanning the crowd, Irma was still unable to see a single elder woman in the entire group. It was a troublesome absence. Especially after everything Irma had read inside the TREPP that explained the matriarchal traditions of the culture. The old woman in the kitchen who had walked into the walk-in and never came out – was she the only one? Did they expect Irma to replace her? Was that what happened to omens? Irma Rosenberg was very confused, but she knew she was not going to stick around this death house for the rest of the ride. She knew she did not belong with these other Misfits. She needed to move. She needed to be with her family, to make it back to Atlanta in time for supper, and she did not need this Trail of Tears to become too much more of a burden than it already was.

"Remember ourselves," sang Indians Hat. "Remember nothing."

The baseball-capped chorus of elders repeated, "Remember ourselves, remember nothing," in a narcotic arpeggio.

Irma percolated with questions. Were all old women omens to these people? Did they think she looked like the old woman in the refrigerator? What exactly was she supposed to do – being an omen, among other things?

One young man broke the tranquility, raising his right hand defiantly and whooping savagely with his left. The elders turned upon him and stared him down with song. Their voices grew noticeably louder. The louder they sang, the more peaceful the song became, harmonies blending into a luminescent drone. But elegant though it was, the song did not affect the young man. He tried to muffle himself, he tried to hold his mouth closed with his left hand, but the harder he tried to shut himself down, the more he cried and whooped and wanted to slap himself.

"Whoa!" exclaimed the Chef, but it was too late. The young man lifted his eyes to the shadowy sun and screamed with all the anger he could muster. He slapped himself so violently that his eyes began to bleed. He whooped so loud that the Indians around him covered their ears and closed their eyes. Then he ran. He bolted toward the stockade wall with sudden and fierce determination, slamming his body into the wood like a butterfly into a windshield. Lying on the ground, motionless, he had finally achieved tranquility. Irma watched the watchtower shake with aftershocks from the impact.

After the boy's body fell limp upon the ground, a nearby teenage girl ripped off her own dress and threw herself back-first to the earth. She slapped her own face. She grunted and screamed and tore at the threads. She spread her legs and thrust her hips violently.

People hovered around her with song, but the singing was obviously futile. Irma walked toward the girl.

"Excuse me," Irma said to the singing Misfits, who parted for her as she approached the self-abusing girl. Irma remembered working part-time as an operator for a domestic violence hotline when her kids were teenagers, but she couldn't remember the lines she was trained to say to victims through the phone. They were good lines, and they almost always worked, but Irma could not remember the words. Forget the phone, she thought, kneeling down next to this suffering Indian girl. Irma's legs bent with easy, painless glides.

She grabbed the girl's arms, holding them gently and firmly, calmly forcing the girl to resist her programming. Irma held the girl's hands with steady resolve, and the girl clawed, venting. But she began to slow. Sounds of relief rippled through the crowd, a thousand breaths of affirmation.

Irma leaned toward the girl's ear, slow and sure. "You have to be strong, dear. You have to be strong now."

Looking at the girl beneath her, Irma wanted to ask her if she knew the old woman in the refrigerator. Irma wished she could have spoken to that elder woman before she disappeared. Why couldn't that woman offer any advice about the situation Irma was walking into? Irma tried to focus on the girl. She wondered if this youngster would ever grow old. She wondered if she knew her name. The girl thrust and lunged, but slowly, slowly. Irma whispered, "You're a bit young to start abusing yourself like this, aren't you?"

The girl's legs stopped shaking, and she fell to the ground.

"Another sign!" sang Indians Hat

"Another sign!" echoed the other elders.

Indians Hat eyed his fellows and nodded twice, signaling a change of tune. The new song was more than simply soothing. Irma felt the new harmonies tickle the nerve endings in her fingers before they danced through her entire nervous system. The girl grabbed Irma's hands and stood up, a reluctant yet thankful grin forming on her face. The girl brushed the earth from her dress.

The Misfits began to applaud. Some began to whoop, but it was a celebratory sound, not a sound of war.

"We must remember," sang the elders. The younger people slowly joined in, their voices tranquilized and tempered – harmonious for now, but rippling with potential dissonance. The Chef walked toward the circle of elders, reminding them that lunch would be ready in about twenty minutes.

"Nice work, kid," the Chef said to Irma. "I knew right away that you belonged in the kitchen."

"This place is very uncomfortable. When can you get me out of here?"

"Do not worry," said Chef. "You were good. Very convincing."

Irma was still not sure why or how she should convince these Misfit Indians of anything. As far as she could estimate, the only reasonable course of action was to risk the door and find Tallulah Wilson. But she was proud of herself, even if she was not entirely sure why. Reason did not quite apply. The watchtower loomed and wavered above the compound, but it felt less ominous than before, less overbearing.

The Chef signaled to his twins, who then rolled the stainless steel cannon back into the kitchen.

"What just happened?" asked Irma.

"I'll tell you while you dish up the chowder."

11

Naturally, Tour Group 5709 obeys the soldiers without much resistance at first. Given the situation – with Corn Grinder's house tightly surrounded by a circle of soldiers, with Deer Cooker's arms tied behind his back and a flurry of bayonets pointed at his head, with their dogs sliced open and bleeding profusely, and with the soldiers running eager fingers through the women's hair – resistance is pointless. The shock-and-awe method proves effective once again.

As the Removal gets under way, Tallulah speaks calmly, instructing her tourists to do as they're told and follow the soldiers' orders. She promises that nothing is out of the ordinary, that everything will be all right as long as they cooperate with the army. She tells the tourists in no uncertain terms – don't fight back.

Spencer Donald almost fights back. Tallulah watches Spencer's eyes fix upon a soldier's weapon for too long, but she halts his insurrection with body language. Her head twitches and shakes, motioning toward the ground. She directs him with her eyes. The others see this interaction, and they quietly fall in line, for now.

The tourists in 5709 have lived relatively comfortable lives in the real world, so they are unaccustomed to the intricacies of being captured by an invading army. Even Bob Rosenberg isn't sure what to do. 5709 clings together and keeps their eyes on Tallulah. As long as they can see her, they have something solid to hold onto.

But Tallulah is now certain that something is very wrong. Of course, the house-storming always happens, even on a Level One tour, but the dogs should never be butchered like that in front of young children. Those sorts of graphics are reserved for Level Three or above. Someone is going to have to explain all of this, Tallulah thinks. And they better not expect me to do it, at least not all of it. True, I violated my own protocol by leaving the First Cabin before the customers, but the degree of graphic violence was beyond my control. Tallulah eyes Nikki and Willa, concerned about their impressionable young memories. Still, the Johnson twins are handling themselves much better than the Athenians, who are acting as if they've never seen blood before.

Given the circumstances, Tallulah defaults to passivity. It is always the course of least resistance. Tallulah is a professional victim. She leads by example. She keeps a brisk pace, never falling too far out of line and never speaking too loudly. The Corn Grinder family walks with similar stoicism. They are professionals too.

In the early days detailing the initial roundup and concentration at the stockades proved to be the most difficult part of writing the program. Very little clearly documented evidence exists regarding these events and their facts. The writers had very little to go on, one of the many reasons why the TREPP dazzled Tallulah with recruitment funds. They needed real Cherokee people to sift through the data, to figure out what really happened, to find the true aboriginal connections, to wade through gruesome and dislocated material in search of a coherent narrative that the actual victims did not want to remember. In college Tallulah consumed every document she could find about the roundup and the stockades, and they all said the same things. The same five statements appeared in every text she consulted. These statements were often written in quotations, but the texts attributed the quotes to different sources. Tallulah concluded that the Trail was intentionally undocumented and that the quotations were anonymously concocted post-Removal by writers who melded shards of memory in the fires of nostalgia.

Each document in the university library that discusses the actual roundup reads like a restatement of the Removal chapter in the James Mooney book. Even the official tribal information from the Cherokee Heritage Center in Tahlequah reads like a collection of excerpts from the Mooney book. Tallulah read the same three "eyewitness" accounts of soldiers' actions in some sixty different texts.

One account always stands out in her memory – the killing of a pregnant mother and her fetus. Apparently, soldiers struck the woman and stabbed her with bayonets because she walked too slowly. Then they sliced the unborn baby out of her stomach and shot it multiple times with their rifles – a decisive crowd-control tactic, just to let the Cherokees know who ran the show.

The story seemed so tragically believable that, after telling it to the first two or three hundred tour groups that she led through the trail, Tallulah began to question it. Why was it so easy to believe? What larger purpose did this story serve? She wanted hard data, but there was none to have. Only stories. She wondered how often this sort of mother-fetus double homicide actually occurred. Did it happen only once, leaving such a vivid impression on everyone that so many survivors mentioned it to the nineteenth-century anthropologists? Or did it happen repeatedly, becoming a pastime for bored officers? Or was it actually a grand fiction? Perhaps it was invented in the late nineteenth century by a proto-pro-lifer who was eager to demonstrate the sinful nature of humanity. Perhaps it was like George Washington's cherry tree – a story that stuck because it served a larger national mythology, not because it was actually true.

When early American ethnohistorians – those Reconstruction-era scholars who wanted to collect authentic details about the Cherokee Removal before the survivors' generation died out – when those founding fathers of American social science asked old Cherokee people for memorable stories about the Trail of Tears, how many people described that dead pregnant woman and her mutilated fetus? And how many of those people had only heard about the story, but never actually saw what happened? How did they even know for sure that it happened? Did they find it easier to recycle the mother-fetus killing story than to tell the real stories of their parents, or their children, who actually died in their arms? For all Tallulah knew, that fetus could have been killed five hundred times, or it could have been killed zero times. The texts didn't say, and the texts never seemed to change.

At first, this dearth of historical detail created a massive dilemma for TREPP programmers – the dilemma of knowing what *really* happened. What truly happened between May 1838 and July 1839? And more importantly for the TREPP, how could it be transformed into a user-friendly, consumer-driven ride? The programmers ultimately concluded that the only workable answers involved identity and chance.

At the TREPP you pay for your identity, but you take chances with your actions and reactions. For example, during the initial roundup, how does the machine determine if a pregnant tourist is merely stabbed, or fully gutted, or plainly shot and left for dead? Of course, being pregnant in real life does not mean that a customer needs to be pregnant on the trail. Many pregnant women have ridden the trail simply to enjoy a few hours without swollen ankles, widening thighs, and persistent back pain. One column in the Atlanta paper actually suggested the Trail of Tears as virtual therapy for aching pregnant bodies. Furthermore, many women who have difficulties getting pregnant have requested a pregnant persona on the Trail. They often claim it gives them a truer sense of purpose, a tangible reason to live and believe. And it's not uncommon for male customers to request a pregnant female persona. For those men who resent the fact that they can never feel their child's heartbeat inside their own bodies, the Trail of Tears experience can be full of revelations. However, this being Georgia, personal details regarding gender and pregnancy are altered only for tourists who make specific requests.

Though the tourists choose their identities, choice alone does not determine one's fate upon the Trail of Tears. Chance is perhaps the most important element of survival. Though a hundred-dollar customer is not expected to fight off soldiers – especially since most soldiers held a certain reverence for such noble and wealthy Cherokees – there is always the chance that a hundred-dollar player might grab a gun and aim for a soldier's head, which invariably ushers the customer off to see the Old Medicine Man. There is also the constant chance that, with good behavior and a stoically silent disposition, a five-dollar player could walk from Corn Grinder's cabin to a Georgia stockade to the big stockade in Ross's Landing without catching the tip of a single bayonet.

As chance would have it, Tour Group 5709 would not go gently.

As chance would have it, the previous night's discussions of Jeep Cherokees and Volkswagen Touaregs led to a lapse in Tallulah's memory. Caught up in the ironies of vehicle names, Tallulah Wilson forgot to remind her customers to bring something that anyone walking a thousand miles must absolutely remember to bring – shoes.

Though timid and willing during the initial shock and awe, 5709 begins to rumble with resistance as they march barefoot into the hot, dewy north Georgia morning. The trouble begins as the tourists gather outside the cabin, where they realize that they are barefoot. No one is expected to sleep in Corn Grinder's house with their shoes on, but neither should anyone have to walk the Trail of Tears without footwear. If the tourists were more self-reliant, perhaps they would have remembered their shoes without prompting. But they're novices. They have no frame of reference, regardless of how much their own ancestors suffered. They have no reason to instinctively reach for their footwear when their peaceful rest is ransacked at dawn. Perhaps they should have known, but it was Tallulah's job to remind them, and Tallulah forgot to do her job.

She blames herself. She was so busy getting the young people riled up about automobile names that she forgot to remind them about the shoes. How terribly self-indulgent, she thinks.

The Johnson twins cry. Not only are they being forced to walk the Trail of Tears without any shoes, but these soldiers are particularly scary.

Tallulah senses a new problem in the system, one she cannot see. But the offness is everywhere. Something is out of joint. Things are too fast. The soldiers' faces wear too many shadows. Is it only her imagination? Is she projecting her guilt? Maybe. They have the same weapons as always. No, no – they turn corners with fast cuts. Little things are moving faster than they should. Everyone is too anxious. The action is way too edgy for a Level One tour. It's clear the shoes aren't her only problem. Someone else has done something much worse. She knew this was a problem from the beginning, and no one listened to her.

Ramsey checked his console and said there wasn't a problem. Why didn't they take her more seriously? Maybe she didn't press her concerns hard enough. Maybe she was focused on something else. Tallulah feels strangely panicked by the presence of Tour Group 5709. Everything is too close.

Things degenerate rapidly when the soldiers issue instructions. The soldiers are unflattering caricatures who spit and grunt. They are archetypal antagonists, and Carmen Davis stands up to them. She defies the power of their vulgarity.

"I'm sorry," she proclaims. "But how can I take your orders seriously when you don't have a single woman in your army?"

The lead soldier, a boy of barely twenty-two, approaches Carmen and stares cold into her eyes. His jaw hangs sideways. His teeth seethe rage. Carmen plants her feet and puffs her chest in defiance, as if to tempt the inevitable.

Spencer's feet begin to tremble, and Tallulah sees bulges forming in the Athenian's face and throat as he watches the young soldier move upon the woman he wants to love.

In one fluid motion the soldier swirls his bayonet in a looping arc and swings the knifed tip into Carmen's leg. She falls, hard upon the calf of the injured leg. Her knee twists out.

Tallulah stretches her arms to hold back the other tourists. She appreciates Carmen's spunk – few people have the guts to stand so boldly. But nothing can save Carmen Davis now, not even Corn Grinder's well-timed distraction. The soldier raises a long knife, craning his head and pointing the blade to the sky.

He announces, "Let this be a lesson to y'all!"

He shifts his weight and prepares to strike Carmen. But just then, Corn Grinder makes a wailing dash for her cabin.

Now, if the scene were truly authentic, she would scream in Cherokee. But translation is critical to customer satisfaction in such pivotal moments of the Removal, so Corn Grinder screams in English. She wails about her pots and pans, she wails about her blankets and baskets, she wails about the mortar and pestle that her own grandmother gave her on her wedding day. Running to the doors of her house, Corn Grinder is shot dead in the back. She falls, instantly limp. Her double braids bounce upon the red earth. Her brown skin skids along the ground as her lifeless body stiffens and rolls still. Her blood drinks the dirt.

The Rosenbergs freeze. The Johnsons scream. Mandy bawls. Deer Cooker bawls louder, throwing his big hands toward the sky, sobbing hysterically, this time in Cherokee.

Tallulah, naturally, is unphased by the death of Corn Grinder. But Deer Cooker is programmed to grieve. Traumatized and suddenly weary, Deer Cooker plays the role of a model American Indian – he does not fight back, he does not harbor lasting resentment toward the soldier who killed his wife, and he does not protest when another soldier grabs his arm and hoists him back onto the Trail.

"You fucking piece of shit!" cries Carmen. "You cracker-ass bastard piece of shit!"

"Carmen, shut up!" screams Spencer, but the young feminist is on a roll. Broken, but unflinching in her drive to speak truth to the illusion of power, Carmen Davis struggles to stand.

Tallulah eyes Carmen's feet. Already swollen. She wonders if a nice pair of boots or moccasins would have made Carmen comfortable enough to endure the soldiers' misogynist commands. Maybe one of Corn Grinder's extra mocs, the ones she keeps near the fireplace.

"You fucking hurt me!" Carmen screams. "Fuck!" Her legs buckle and bend as she tries to stand. As the other tourists are huddled into a crooked line, prodded, walking methodically and stoically with the bayonet tips at their heels, Tallulah sees the chipped bone protruding from Carmen's twisted knee. Carmen can no longer put her weight on the earth. By all practical standards, she is already useless on the Trail of Tears. She will become unnecessary mass for the wagons if she isn't killed now. And for thirty-dollar tourists, the wagons don't appear until after Fort Dahlonega.

Spencer sees the protruding bone. His eyes well up. Spencer reaches for Carmen, but a subordinate soldier pokes his arm with a bayonet. His arm bleeds a slow, thin line. He cries. Carmen refuses to cry, but her broken body can barely hobble.

"Hey," calls Rachel. "Kill me too!" Michael echoes her, but their pleas go unacknowledged.

"How come it's so easy for her to get it?" Michael mutters to his wife.

Tallulah glances at the young Rosenbergs, then at the Johnsons. Nell is shielding the children with her clothes. The kids are crying, terrified. Tallulah reaches for the water beetle. She is not supposed to contact TC while tourists are dying, but this is an extraordinary tour.

Wallace answers her call. He has information, though it makes no sense. The tour has switched to Level Four.

"Level Four!"

"Let me call you right back." He hangs up. TC has never hung up on Tallulah, until now.

"We never finished our lesson from before," says the lead soldier, loud and brash. He likes being in command. He abruptly turns and shoots Carmen in the face. Carmen falls upon the hot ground. The soldier turns around and never looks back.

A knot twists in Tallulah's stomach. She suddenly finds it painful to stand, but she forces herself upright. She tells the surviving tourists not to worry. Carmen is happier now. She has gone to see the Wise Old Medicine Man, where she can get the kind of authentic spiritual information that anthropology students yearn for.

Tallulah gazes at the sight of Carmen Davis's busty twenty-year-old body as it lies lifeless next to Corn Grinder's. It will be burned by looters within minutes. For a Level Four tour there is nothing unusual about Carmen's death, nothing to suggest that she hadn't gone to visit the Old Man. She is a good dead imaginary Indian.

Tallulah contemplates the significance of having young children on a Level Four tour. This has never happened before, to her or anyone else. So much for the potential middle-school field trip, she thinks. Malfunctions are, as she well knows, inevitable. Yet they aren't usually so drastic. Tallulah begins to feel that she is being observed. Not just by TC, but by something larger. When they hung up on her, they must have had Homeland Security nearby. She wonders if Tour Group 5709 contains an insurgent customer, someone who has brought a virus into the system. How deeply am I being infiltrated? She didn't know about the Great Flushing, of course, but her imagination was always active. Tallulah pictures Carmen Davis, a double agent. Maybe the anthropology class was an elaborate scam. Tallulah dials TC; no one answers. She imagines Ramsey talking to Homeland Security. Ramsey the half-Iranian transplant techie – in what dark corners would they interrogate him if they thought he was dangerous? Tallulah watches the Johnson kids hold their mother as they walk.

Spencer sidles up next to Tallulah. "This is fucked up," he whispers harshly.

"It's okay," she says. "This is the Trail of Tears. Bad shit happens."

"But we've got to do something!" he demands. His voice is too loud. Tallulah does not look back when an American soldier pokes Spencer's hamstring with a bayonet tip. Spencer squeals. She wonders if he's in on the plot against her, as well. She looks him up and down. No, no – he's too pathetic to be knowingly involved in such a plot. Or is he? Perhaps he's involved without realizing it. His feet are beginning to bleed. Tallulah thinks to rip some fabric, maybe from a dead person, and make a wrap for the Athenian's feet. But that will take too long. She can't subject herself to such scrutiny from the troops.

The lush and leafy hills wind southwest toward Fort Dahlonega. The tourists walk the trails along the sweaty banks of the Chestatee River. Gazing into the trees, Rachel Rosenberg has an epiphany. There is no kudzu! No kudzu anywhere! She remembers kudzu lessons from high school. How the kudzu was imported to the South from somewhere in Asia, maybe Japan. How the uses of kudzu have evolved – from decoration, to weed killer, to weed, to cultural icon. Rachel wants to share her astuteness with Michael, to ask Tallulah when kudzu first arrived in America and test her guide's knowledge, but she knows better than to speak, even if she genuinely wants to die. She is an ex-pat American woman who knows when to keep quiet in America.

Michael also knows better than to speak. He stares at his own shoeless feet. The rocks in the road have left imprints. Bob moves slowly and lackadaisically. He walks, barely. Tallulah doubts that Bob cares at all about Old Medicine.

As the tourists move south toward Dahlonega, beacons of new industry sprout along the countryside. The economy shows signs of progress, golden progress. It is late April of 1838; the Dahlonega Mint is in full production mode. White people with pans and lenses mine every riverbed within thirty miles of the small city, lobbing an occasional rock or bullet at the uprooted Cherokee walkers. First-time homeowners remove symbols of indigenous history from their newly occupied cabins – cabins that look conspicuously similar to Corn Grinder's – and raise American flags on their front porches. White people with outmoded devices swallow the water and tunnel the ground, surfacing with dirty teeth and shining pockets.

A miner tosses a rock toward 5709, hitting Mandy Warren directly on the knee. Another rock hits Spencer Donald in the arm, drawing more tears from the tortured young man. Danny tries to ignore his crying roommate.

"Ain't this near Dahlonega?" says Danny. "You know my uncle went to North Georgia College."

Tallulah ignores the comment. She examines Spencer's legs, and she tries to remember how much leg hair he had back in the Meeting Grounds. Danny does not look at Spencer. He does not look at his girlfriend either. He walks with head raised, eyes on the road ahead. Tallulah doubts that the rock itself caused Spencer to cross his pain threshold. Spencer may be weak, like most men, but he cries for love. Unrequited, and now unpresent, love. Tallulah has seen it before – the Trail of Tears brings people closer together by making them farther apart.

"So do we get to see North Georgia College when we get to Dahlonega?" asks Danny.

"More or less," says Tallulah. "The college will be built upon the grounds where the Dahlonega Mint is now."

"It will?" whispers Nell Johnson. The twins cower behind their mother, walking, covered faces and shaking frames.

"The mint," answers Tallulah, "will print gold coins from now until 1861. It will close down when the Civil War begins, but it will transform into a school in 1873."

Tallulah wishes that Carmen was still with her. Carmen was headstrong, but she said things that needed to be said. She actually made Tallulah's job a little easier. Now she's gone, and the

Athenians have lost their center. Everything begins to fall apart for them. Tallulah sees the void in Spencer's eyes, the horror in Mandy's, the strangely detached haze in Danny's. Nonetheless, they tread on, barefoot and dumbfounded.

Tallulah tries TC again. The water beetle beeps – connection.

"Tula?" says Ramsey.

"Ramsey, what went wrong?"

"We're not sure yet."

"Why not?"

"I don't know," he says, his voice shrouded in static. "Things are inconsistent. I don't know what to tell you."

"Who did this?"

"I don't know – we'll call you soon, I promise."

The beetle buzzes – connection gone. Tallulah jams the beetle into the corner of her vest pocket. She taps on it with her fingers. She rubs her thumb along the smooth back of the bug. She examines her own feet – they have already collected a few foreign objects, some twigs and other roughage. She hangs her head and walks. Tour Group 5709 still does not realize that they're supposed to have shoes. They have no reason to believe that Tallulah has lapsed on the job, or that their feet are suffering because of it. As far as they know, the Trail of Tears is supposed to be like this.

The tourists endure the taunting, the prodding, and the general dehumanization relatively well, in spite of the sudden deaths of Corn Grinder and Carmen Davis. But as they are nearly halfway to Fort Dahlonega, they begin to quietly complain about their feet. The complaints are subtle at first – an emphatic grunt as a tourist steps on an errant twig or rock, an exaggerated step accompanied by a slight groan, a short audible prayer for shoes. Then the questions begin.

“Will they have any shoes for us at the fort?” “They’ll have to, won’t they?” “They can’t really expect us to walk this whole way without any shoes, can they?” “I’d kill someone for my Birkenstocks right now.”

Tallulah notes that the government will not be supplying any extra footwear for the Trail of Tears. However, there are bound to be some helpful Cherokees who will stash extra shoes into

their jackets, and they are sure to meet these people inside the first stockade. Actually, Tallulah has long assumed that, if she were alive in 1838, she would have been smart enough to pack extra shoes. But now she is not so sure.

“Peachtree!” says Nikki Johnson, pointing to the south. Everyone looks. A soldier pokes Spencer’s back with a bayonet and tells him to look straight ahead.

The group descends in altitude, approaching Dahlonega along the north side of the Chestatee River. A line of fruit trees comes into view. Peaches and apples.

Questions rumble. They were forced to skip breakfast, but now they remember their hunger. Will they have to skip lunch too? How is everyone supposed to make it to Indian Territory without eating enough balanced meals? It’s a lot of work, all this walking. They need nourishment. Within the line of fruit trees, a small cluster shines loudly—seven radiant fruit trees nestled into a cove in the hill. They seem to pulse. The tourists can smell their fruit.

Nell Johnson stumbles as her daughters tug at her dress. Nell, who resisted asking questions all the way to the River, steps up and asks the question that everyone wants to ask.

“So Tallulah, are they going to feed us at the stockade?”

“Oh, there’s no need to worry yourself about that,” replies Tallulah. Her own syntax startles her. She’s not sure whose words she’s using.

"So they'll have food waiting for us?" asks Nell.

"Yes."

"What kind of food?"

Tallulah asks the Johnson twins if they like bacon. Kids are supposed to like bacon. If the kids like bacon, then Tallulah can tell them that salt pork is like bacon, and they will have all the salt pork they want on the Trail of Tears.

But the Johnson twins are not typical kids. They pretend to gag at the utterance of the word "bacon." Nell confesses – the girls will only eat vegetarian bacon. Not turkey bacon, but soy bacon. They are not vegetarians – they eat chicken and eggs and fish – but bacon they do not eat.

Too bad, thinks Tallulah. Maybe they should eat an apple or a peach before the stockade. Tallulah wishes she'd swiped an extra apple from Corn Grinder's house before the exodus. She wishes she'd done everything differently. Her consciousness was her own worst enemy! Tallulah wants to give the girls a damn peach if it will make them happy.

Then, without warning, Nell Johnson twitches.

She hunkers down, like a rodent just before it crosses a busy street. Tallulah senses an uneasy magnetism. Nell Johnson raises her head, and she locks in with the fruit trees in the distance.

Tallulah feels something awful brewing. Like the swift gathering clouds, the convergence of hot and cold before a deadly storm lands. Nell Johnson – who walked all the way to the outskirts of Dahlonega with silent strength and maternal reassurance, who calmly strode barefoot over sticks and stones and miscellaneous sharp objects, who shielded her children from bayonets with her own body – Nell Johnson eyes the fruit with tragic desire.

"You want a peach, girls?" she asks.

They quickly answer, "Yes, Mama."

Tallulah grabs Nell's arm. She instructs, demands, orders Nell to stay in line. But Nell is locked into the trees, and her twins want fruit. She slips through Tallulah's grip and bolts toward the peaches.

"Hey!" shouts a rear soldier. The walkers stop walking again. Rachel reaches for Michael's palm. Spencer grabs Bob Rosenberg's arm, momentarily knocking the old man off balance. Mandy holds fast to her boyfriend's arm, and Danny says something about his football tickets. The twins clutch Tallulah's torso. The lead soldier cocks his beady eyes toward Nell Johnson.

"Where the hell you think yer going, lady?" he hollers, smiling when she stumbles.

Nell never takes her eyes off the trees. She does not halt when a rear soldier fires a warning shot into the sky. The soldiers will shoot her dead. Tallulah's seen it time and time again, though usually not to players who seem so well-adjusted. Never to a mother. Good God, Tallulah thinks. These kids are trying to pull me apart. She looks at their feet. The twins wrap their knees around Tallulah's, and Tallulah can feel the scratches in their soles.

The soldiers cannot chance a lone Indian in the woods. For them, any opportunity to teach a lesson is an opportunity that must be seized.

"Lady – either stop right now, or I'll shoot yer dumb ass dead. No differnce to me. In fact, it'll make my job easier."

"Jesus Christ!" yells Spencer. "Stop running! They're gonna shoot!"

Nell responds, but she keeps running and does not turn her head. "I'll be right back. The girls are hungry."

The lead soldier shoots first, and a rear soldier follows suit. Nell lands hard, her hip bone distorted, her chest and neck mangled. Tour Group 5709 screams and shouts. The twins clutch even harder, clawing their fingernails and toenails into Tallulah's skin.

Tallulah takes the pain from the twins' nails like a professional. She is still Tallulah Wilson, even if Tour Group 5709 is hands down her worst performance all year. She has not watched so many tourists die since 3915. Tour Group 3915 lost five people on the walk to Dahlonega, which Tallulah still blames on the fact that it was a large family in the middle of a drawn-out divorce trying to entertain the kids by riding the Trail of Tears. That disaster was unpreventable, but Tallulah knows she should have done far better for 5709. Level One or Level Five, she should have served them better.

Tallulah pulls the Johnson twins even closer. "Your mom is okay," she whispers. "She's not really dead. Remember, it's just a game. She's totally fine, and you'll see her again as soon as the game is over."

"We know," says Nikki.

"That's right," agrees Willa. "She's better off."

Tallulah is struck by the girls' maturity. She wonders if they knew it was coming. Is it possible for an eight-year-old to be a double agent?

"I'm not hungry anymore," says Willa.

Tallulah leads them on toward the Chestatee River. It is a small river, and typically the tourists are still in good shape on the first leg of the Removal. Most groups, however, have footwear. Shoeless, Tour Group 5709 crosses the river tragically. Heels slip, and toes are sliced by rocks. Footholds are lost. People fall and bruise their upper bodies. Rachel Rosenberg takes a hard bump on the head, slicing her cheek fairly deep. A glass fragment lodges itself into Mandy Warren's foot, and she cries, embarrassed, as Danny Calhoun pulls it out.

Michael Hopkins guides Bob Rosenberg's feet through the

rocky waters. Tallulah offers to lift the kids on her shoulders, but the twins choose to walk. Spencer slips and yells. The twins don't slip at all.

Finally, the sun begins to set again.

"Nvda," says Tallulah.

"What?" asks Nikki.

"Nvda," repeats Tallulah. "It means 'sky dweller' in Cherokee. It's the same word for sun and moon."

"That's cool," says Willa.

"Yeah," confirms Tallulah. "I always thought so."

The soldiers corral Tour Group 5709 toward the main gate of Fort Dahlonega. Tallulah counts the dwindling number of women. Rachel and Mandy are the only adult women left. They're killing the women, the more intelligent ones. Why are they killing the smart women?

The whole problem – Tallulah has long believed, pure and simple – is patriarchy. Tallulah watches Deer Cooker stagger into the stockade. He is helpless without Corn Grinder, but he has tobacco. He has a purpose. He is a good Cherokee man.

All Cherokee men are helpless without a woman to tell them what to do. That's why matriarchy works – no one said that men couldn't hunt, fight, lift heavy objects, or play ball games, but it was a bad idea to let them make all, or even most, of the major decisions. How often does the president's wife save the world? The American Constitution was built upon the framework laid out by Iroquois women. Would the old-school Cherokee peace chiefs have ever reclaimed the tribal reins from the war chiefs if their wives hadn't reminded them to swing the balance back around? Yet the women are sidelined, left unwritten or written out. Especially the smartest ones.

How different the world would be if women were the political rulers. Tallulah doubts the world would be less spiteful, but it would certainly multitask with less confusion.

Tallulah holds the twins. Bob Rosenberg's head hangs lower and lower as he trudges through the sharp gates. His feet seem ready to wobble off his legs. He walks like an authentic Cherokee man who has just lost his wife. He seems completely incapable of making a decision. Tallulah surveys Bob Rosenberg, then Deer Cooker, then Spencer Donald. She thinks of Nell Johnson's dash for the trees. She thinks of Tsali.

Tsali was a hero. He was a hero because he did what everyone else would have done if they had enough decisiveness. He killed the soldier who stabbed his wife. His wife was killed as the family was being marched away from its home, killed in front of the whole family, killed dead on the way to the first stockade. The story is legendary, at least in some circles.

As the story goes, Tsali spoke to his sons in Cherokee. He called an audible – and Tsali's boys helped him avenge their mother. They turned a corner and fought back. They killed one soldier and sent the others fleeing to their fort. Then they took to the hills, using their indigenous knowledge of the mountains to hide out as long as they could. Tsali and his sons lived as fugitives, and together with three hundred fellow Cherokee fugitives, they evaded the soldiers by hiding in the deepest corners of the motherland, exiles who refused to leave. But the whites continued to hunt them. Guerilla warfare seemed endless, until the whites offered a truce – they would let the runaway Cherokees live in peace, but only at the price of Tsali's life. Tsali had killed an American, and he must die. After learning of the Americans' terms, Tsali turned himself in. He was executed by firing squad, and some stories have it that the Americans made Tsali's own son fire the fatal bullet. Nonetheless, his death secured the homeland of the Eastern Band.

Tsali was a simple man from the high hills of Carolina, and he did not repress his anger at the white man who killed his wife. That's why he was a hero then. That's why he's like Jesus now. Everyone loves reenacting Tsali's execution – the dramatic tragedy of Cherokees forced to execute their own hero in order to complete the transaction.

But Tallulah always figured the real martyr of the story was Tsali's wife, even though no one built displays for her in museums. Tsali is revered – a Cherokee savior, a homegrown American hero – yet his wife's name is rarely mentioned.

Tallulah visualizes John Bushyhead. For all his eccentricities, Bushyhead is a traditional guy – he wanders around waiting for Tallulah to tell him what to do. He can implement decisions, but he can barely make them. She wonders how John Bushyhead would react if someone injured her. What would Bushyhead do if someone killed Tallulah? Would he hang his head in silence? Would he strike back? She wants to believe that he would fight back. She wants to believe that he is smart enough to avenge her death and escape his own.

The gates close. The stockade pounds with bodies. Tallulah can feel the pulsing of her tourists' feet. The smell of pork is everywhere.

12

“That’s a tricky question,” said the Chef.

“I don’t see why it’s so hard to give me a straight answer,” said Irma.

The Chef washed dishes, Irma dried them, and the twins put them away. At first she found it odd that a chef would actually wash dishes. What was the point of putting your own kids to work if they weren’t going to wash dishes? But the Chef washed on, alone. Irma soon realized why the boys were on storage duty—the kitchen was awkwardly shaped, with sharp corners butting into round ones. Fish and Ish were young and agile and limber. They could bend and stretch. They could open doors that Irma couldn’t see. They reached into the walls, their arms merging with the shiny metal, to open hidden cupboards for the dry goods, serving utensils, and small appliances. Irma watched them vanish into a steel panel with graters and peelers in their hands.

As flexible as she was with this digital body, Irma wouldn’t dare trying to reach those awkward places. She imagined the Chef felt the same way, though she assumed he did similar tricks with his arms. Someone had to teach the boys how to do that.

“I’m not sure there is a straight answer,” he said.

“Oh, come on now,” demanded Irma. “I dished up your corn chowder and fed your whole Misfit tribe. Now you owe me an answer.”

“Owe you?”

“Who are these Suits?”

“To understand the Suits, you must understand the prophecy,” said the Chef.

“No one’s even taken the time to explain to me what this prophecy is. All this omen talk, and no explanations about any of these prophecies.”

As far as Chef knew, the prophecy was older than he was, and he was here before the rest of the Misfits. Indeed, how could such a stockade exist without at least one person to feed everyone else?

“I’m getting tired of this prophecy business,” Irma declared. “They’re all too open to interpretation in the first place.”

“Okay, I’ll give you that,” agreed the Chef. “But ignorance won’t serve you forever in here. You should at least have a dash of context.”

The Chef orated. Once there was a girl. A young girl in a stockade similar to this one. A rectangular stockade, with a watchtower, but the walls were covered with sheets of ice. It was cold. And it was a long time ago, thousands of years back, after the last ice age. And it was north. Way north – maybe Quebec or upstate New York, maybe Minnesota or Manitoba, depending on whom you ask. Regardless, the tribe was northern, but this girl swore that she was from the south.

The girl lived in a stockade with old men and old women. She was the last child in the tribe, and she bled to death on an enemy’s weapon. As she was dying, she promised the elders that she would one day return. Not to her cold death camp in the north, but to a tribe in need down south.

When she died, she took the ice tribe’s entire future with her. They had nothing to keep their stories alive, no one to keep their memories in motion. The ice elders all died within a year, but one of them – a cook, naturally – found a way to send a message through time. And that message was something the baseball-hat-wearing elders discovered on the day they shaved their heads.

"What was the message?"

Chef cleared his throat, puffed his cheeks, and cracked his jaw: "The child becomes old, for when there are no children, there are no elders. Look for her, in the south."

"What is that supposed to mean?" asked Irma.

"They think you're the child."

"Who?"

"You."

"I mean, who thinks that?"

"The elders," said Chef. "Haven't they told you you're an omen?"

"But what does that have to do with the Suits?"

Chef confided in Irma that he had never given the story much credit. He believed it was a smokescreen, a point of diversion the elders used to rally the tribe, to encourage the younger people to accept the conventional doctrines of nonviolent resistance espoused by Gandhi, King, and the like. As the twentieth century's most peaceful prophets knew so well, people will believe in nonviolence as a means to an end as long as they can imagine an end to the violence.

"Why do the Suits talk to you?"

"Because I'm bound to hear."

"I want a better answer than that," said Irma. "Why do they slaughter the young people out there but smoke cigarettes and have conversations back here?"

"They like my fruit salad."

"Maybe they're asking for me because my husband is trying to find me," suggested Irma. "Maybe that Tallulah Wilson girl sent them out to find me."

"Don't be foolish," laughed the Chef. He promised Irma that Tallulah Wilson did not send the Suits. He promised her that neither the salaried nor the hourly employees at the TREPP even knew about the Suits. For that matter, none of the employees knew about the Chef. Or his kitchen. Or the elders. Or any of this. No worker at the TREPP, not even Tallulah Wilson, had ever met the Misfits. Ever. And neither had a paying customer – until now.

"The big problem," Chef said, "at least as far as I can see it, is that the prophecy implies that the omen will bring change, but it doesn't suggest anything about what this change will entail."

Irma sensed that Chef wasn't telling her the whole story. "I don't understand," she said. "Change what?"

"Don't." The Chef rubbed his sinuses. "Just, please, don't. Your shenanigans with the reclamation of North Carolina aren't helping anyone."

"Who said anything about North Carolina?"

"Lady." He put down his hose and turned his eyes, nearly locking in. "I know more than you can imagine. Don't insult me again."

Irma tried to remember exactly what she had suggested to the elders about North Carolina, about the motherland business. She remembered Tallulah Wilson, the way she spoke about Asheville and the Carolina mountains, the sense of urgency and sound of matriotic nostalgia in her voice.

"Can we introduce your people to the Tallulah Wilson girl?" asked Irma. "Maybe she hasn't met you before, but I bet she could help you interpret your prophecy."

"I need you to stop drying those dishes," Chef replied, "and go get me two large bags of assorted crackers."

"Crackers?"

"They're in the pantry."

"What kind of crackers?"

"Assorted."

"Where is it?"

"The pantry." Chef hung his hose; the sink was empty, shiny. "Over there, behind that large food processor."

She followed the tip of his finger and turned a few sharp corners. The food processor was enormous. It had wheels. She assumed it would be monstrously heavy.

"It's lighter than you think," said the Chef, "and it has wheels. Just push on it gently."

The food processor moved with shocking ease. Irma wondered if gravity was different here. Behind the food processor stood two small, shiny doors. Irma was afraid of sticking her arms into the walls, like the boys did, but the pantry doors had handles. She opened the doors, and sitting directly in front of her were two large bags of assorted crackers. She grabbed the bags, set the crackers upon a prep table.

"Where do you get these crackers from?" she asked.

"They grow wild around here."

"Here?"

"Out back. They're everywhere."

"Where are we anyway?"

"You're only *now* asking that, yet you're ready to tell them where to go."

"Are we near the ocean or what?" asked Irma. The sound of waves droned continuously, and it seemed to grow louder when Irma asked the question.

"They didn't tell you about their water issues?" Chef turned his gaze, slowly, deliberately, directly, upon Irma. She looked away and swallowed. "I suspected as much," he said, turning back. "Let me break the news to you, Rosenberg. They're terrified of water."

Irma watched the floor. "All the water outside there?" The floor was impeccably clean.

"This is getting us nowhere." Chef clenched a towel. "We need some platters for dinner."

"But they just ate lunch."

"It will be dinnertime sooner than you think. We need platters of smoked fish, cheeses, and crackers."

Fish and Ish emerged from the walls, their hands empty. Chef nodded. All the dishes were done, clean and soundly stored. Irma watched the boys, watched their legs bend as they walked. She could almost see the rhythm of the waves in the movements of their legs. The twins entered the walk-in refrigerator and came out with boxes of smoked fish and vacuum-sealed packages of cheese.

"Is that Swiss or cheddar?" asked Irma.

"Both," said the twins.

"How are you with smoked fish?" asked Chef.

Irma tasted memories. She had eaten nova lox and smoked whitefish for breakfast this morning in Atlanta. Her son bought loads of Jewish cuisine from an area bagel store whenever Bob and Irma visited Georgia. On the drive to the TREPP, Rachel had confessed that her father only bought Jewish food when his parents came to town. He bought whitefish salad as a front, and it wasn't a particularly effective front since all Bob Rosenberg wanted for breakfast in Georgia was grits. Yet Bob never got his grits. "I can eat bagels every day in New Jersey," he always said, but he never got his grits in Georgia.

"I know a good deal about *eating* smoked fish," said Irma.

"Good," said Chef. "I'll have the twins prep the fish and the cheese, and then you can arrange it on a platter with the crackers."

"How do I do that?"

"Make it look like something you'd want to eat."

Irma imagined her ideal fish, cheese, and cracker platter. It would have to contain multiple circles, with layers and levels that were complex, yet easy to grab with your fingers. But her vision was interrupted.

"Just what we needed," complained the Chef.

Irma wondered what was wrong. The lights dimmed, then came back.

Indians Hat entered first. All seven elders entered the kitchen, single-file, their baseball hats and blue jeans pressed and clean. They walked toward a small open space between the prep table and the doorway, and then they formed a semicircle.

"Your platters are coming," said Chef.

"Do not worry," said Indians Hat. "We are not yet hungry. And tonight, our hunger is for something greater, something we cannot eat with our mere mouths."

Chef sniffed, then coughed into his shoulder. Irma heard his knuckles crack, but she did not see him bend his fingers. "I need to finish washing dishes," he said. Irma was confused because she was positive that the dishes were already done, but Chef uncovered a pile of dirty bowls beneath the sink. The Chef turned his back upon the elders as he faced the sink. The twins were facing the elders, but their eyes were focused on the cutting boards, where they sliced the smoked fish and cheeses into bite-sized pieces.

"Irma Rosenberg," said Indians Hat, "we know what you are."

"I'm glad someone finally does," she said. "I've been trying to figure that out my whole life." The boys giggled and jabbed each other's elbows.

"You *are* an omen," said Yankees Hat.

"An omen of deliverance," said White Sox Hat.

"I think you really need to speak to Tallulah Wilson about your homes in North Carolina," said Irma.

Chef dropped something in the sink. It rattled loud and clanky. He coughed through his nose.

"We know about North Carolina," asserted Braves Hat.

Chef handed four empty platters to Irma, telling her to follow her instincts when arranging the fish, cheese, and crackers. The platters were impeccably clean.

"But," continued Indians Hat, "we believe the Suits have placed us here in order to keep us out of the mountains."

"If it wasn't for the prophecy," said Giants Hat, "we'd be risking our lives if we tried to go back."

Irma wondered how it was possible for these beings to risk their lives, seeing as how they weren't technically alive. Furthermore, she wondered how they could go back to a place they had never been before.

"Well," she said, "what's the worst thing that could happen?"

"Deletion," said the Chef, unflinching with his hose.

Irma asked why the Suits would want to delete the Misfits. They served a very important function in the grand scheme of things, didn't they? And while Irma was unsure of what exactly that function was, she knew that these Misfit Cherokees were very good at it. The Chef grumbled and sprayed mixing bowls.

"The Suits do have a certain power over us," said Indians Hat.

"From the inside," said Dodgers Hat.

"And from the outside," said Two Hats.

"I really think you need Tallulah Wilson. I think we all do. She'll tell you about your North Carolina, and she'll know where my husband is."

The Chef cleared his throat with a vengeance, like an apple

core was stuck in his esophagus. Irma wondered how old he was. The twins whispered.

"Are you okay?" asked Irma.

The Chef dropped his hose and turned to face the elders. "Reclamation is tricky business."

"Our reclamation will be our deliverance," Indians Hat said grandly.

"The odds are against you," said the Chef, drying his wet hands upon his apron.

"Not if we hide in the mountains," said Red Sox Hat.

"The highest peaks of the Smokies," said Braves Hat.

"Those mountains have protected us before," said Two Hats.

"They will protect us again," said Indians Hat.

Chef protested. He demanded that the elders consider their agenda more critically. They were programmed to believe that the mountains were their ancestral homeland, but since none of the Misfits had actually been to the Smokies, they would have no idea what to do or where to go. Worst of all, how were they supposed to eat anything?

"We will follow our instincts," declared Indians Hat.

"That is precisely the problem here," said Chef, "since it's your instincts that you're trying to undo!"

"This is different," said Two Hats.

"I'm glad you think so," retorted Chef. "Are you people hungry yet?"

"The omen makes it different," said Giants Hats.

"The prophecy is true," said Indians Hat decisively. "So far, she has done everything she must do in order to fulfill it."

"She *is* the omen," said White Sox Hat.

"We agree unanimously," said Indians Hat. "She speaks the truth."

Chef squinted his eyes and rolled his mouth with a painful expression, as if he had stepped on a piece of glass. He rubbed his large hands across his forehead and exhaled deeply.

"Great," said Chef. "That's just great. Excuse me." He snapped his neck and promptly glided into the walk-in refrigerator. The elders looked up, their palms exposed, and began to hum.

Irma eyed the cold steel doors. "Maybe your Chef is right," she said. "Maybe you're being too ambitious. And besides, you have all this wonderful food here."

"Irma Rosenberg," said Indians Hat, "we understand your hesitation."

"The Chef is wise," said Giants Hat.

"The Chef knows much," said Red Sox Hat. "More than most of us."

"However," said Indians Hat, "the prophecy cannot be dismissed."

"Everyone is talking about it," said Braves Hat.

"Everyone is ready to follow you to the Promised Land," said Yankees Hat.

"Follow me?"

The Chef opened the walk-in door with his tailbone, gliding butt first out of the refrigerator. He mumbled. Irma thought she heard him say something about promises.

"We are preparing a party," said Indians Hat.

"A war party," said Braves Hat.

"We must gather our strength," said Two Hats, "for the long road ahead."

A wooden crate of fresh bell peppers slipped through Chef's hands and cracked upon the floor. He grunted through his nose, kicked open the latch of the walk-in door, and slipped back inside the cold. The steel door shut loudly behind him. Irma examined her own vague reflection in the door. She heard drums within the waves. Or were the drums closer? Sounds seemed to move differently within the kitchen and without. Irma looked at the boys. They were watching her. One of them pointed at the empty platter in front of her.

"I need to get back to work," she announced.

"Irma Rosenberg," replied Indians Hat, "you have already done more than you know."

"I'm sorry."

"Why?" asked Yankees Hat.

"No time for that," said White Sox Hat.

"You will be honored during the party tonight," said Giants Hat.

"Honored?" She glanced again at her own cloudy reflection in the cold steel door of the walk-in refrigerator. She was starting to see her likeness in the ambiguity. Perhaps she looked younger after all. But the door was too blurry for her to see the particulars. She wondered what the Chef was planning with all those bell peppers. She wondered if he would still use the peppers that he had dropped. They had been on the floor less than three seconds.

She thought about promised lands and nationalist politics. Irma had been alive during the Holocaust – young, but alive – so she was a nationalist by default. She remembered stories about ancient Israel, about homelands and motherlands and unendurable suffering. She thought about the names of things. Then she thought of something she had never reckoned with before. All those names along the New Jersey Turnpike – Mahwah, Ho-Ho-Kus, Hoboken, Weehawken – who were those people? What happened to those people? How much did they suffer? She remembered a story in the *New York Times* about some Mohicans – she thought it was Mohicans, like the book they had to read in high school, because she remembered her surprise at learning that Mohicans were still alive. These Mohicans wanted to return to upstate New York after being moved off to Wisconsin some hundred years earlier. She remembered the commentaries in the papers, all the debates about casinos, about fake Indians, about unfair special treatment. Irma wasn't sure what to think about it, then or now. Her stomach tightened, rolling itself into a small knot. For the first time inside the Trail of Tears, Irma Rosenberg felt a twinge of physical pain.

She turned her eyes upon the twin boys. They were still watching her, only now they had large knives in their hands.

Then the Chef reemerged from the refrigerator. He held a giant wheel of Gouda cheese on his left shoulder. The twins asked if the cheese was smoked, but the Chef replied that it was not. It was just plain Gouda. He placed it on the twins' prep table and told them to start slicing. He then produced more dirty dishes and returned to the sink.

"Tonight, Irma Rosenberg," Indians Hat reached out for Irma's hands, "we celebrate you and all you have brought to us."

The Chef cracked his neck to the left, then to the right, then to the left again, then in a crackling circle. He cleared his throat, more violently than before, as if he were scraping years of residue from his larynx. A mixing paddle slipped from his hands. It ricocheted loudly, clanking staccato in the steel sink.

The twins were finished slicing fish and cheese for the platters. Irma couldn't remember seeing them chop. One of the boys held a box of plastic wrap. The other held a shiny knife. She was still unable to tell them apart. Kitchen lights echoed off the knife blade. The boy with the knife briefly locked eyes with Irma, but quickly stared down at the blade in his hand. He then stretched impressively and pulled a knife sharpener from beneath a prep table. Without looking up, he ran the sharpener along the sides of the blade. The other boy tore a large piece of plastic wrap from the box.

"War Party, huh?" said the Chef. Once again his dishes were done. He nibbled on a stick of celery. He offered celery to the elders, but they declined. Irma wondered if he would offer tea. She wondered if he ever drank the tea. And what about coffee? Did he grow his own coffee outside the stockade?

"Why is it a war party?" she asked.

"Come on, speedy," Chef answered, "we need those platters. We've got a thousand hungry Misfits out there, and they can't have a war party without those fish, cheese, and cracker platters."

"I don't understand why you're calling it a war party," she said. "I thought you were committed to nonviolence."

"We are," replied Indians Hat.

"We should start the preparations," said Two Hats.

"I'll warm up the amplifiers," said Yankees Hat.

"Good," said Indians Hat. "It will not be easy, but those mountains are dense. We will survive."

The elders' stomachs began to rumble. Irma could feel the rumbling before she heard it. It synchronized with the pulsing waves outside. They thanked her again, one by one taking her hands in their own, before they left the kitchen single-file.

"They really think I'm their omen, don't they?"

"You catch on fast," Chef snorted.

Irma arranged the crackers in a pattern of interlocking spirals. "You don't think so, do you?" she demanded. "You don't really think that I'm this omen then?"

Chef exhaled heavily. "Whether or not you are truly any sort of omen is perfectly irrelevant at this point."

"I don't understand."

"It doesn't matter." Chef pulled three notebooks from the shelf nearest his head. He flipped rapidly through the pages. "They believe their prophecy because they have no choice."

Chef stopped flipping and held the recipe close to his eyes. "And they have always believed that I cannot open the doors for them until the omen comes."

"So you *can* open those doors then?" She layered slices of Gouda cheese upon the spiral crackers. "The doors they think will kill them?"

"I already told you – I have a key."

"Why haven't you tried it before?"

"Save some room for the fish on that platter, okay? It's called a fish, cheese, and cracker platter. Notice how that starts with fish."

"Fine. But I want to know why you haven't tried opening those doors already."

"I have."

"What happened?" She reached confidently into the mound of smoked fish. The less Irma consciously worried about the shape of the platter, the more her spirals of fish, cheese, and crackers seemed to construct themselves.

"Look," said Chef, "diplomacy is tricky business. It's nasty business. It will disgust you and make you lose your appetite."

"Maybe I should say something to the old men."

"No, no – please, you've said quite enough already."

"But they'll be in danger." She nearly locked into Chef's eyes, but she pulled back just as he raised his gaze to meet hers.

"It's a bigger problem than you realize," he said and settled his eyes back upon his recipes.

"How could your problems be worse than they already are?" Irma reached for more fish and cheese, but the prep table was empty. The platters were complete. Fish and Ish had already moved the platters to another prep table. They were beautiful platters, and the boys were wrapping them with green and orange plastic wrap.

"Never challenge worse," said Chef. The twins giggled.

"It's not funny, boys." Chef's tone deepened. "There's a glitch in the system. Something intrusive. And it must be eliminated."

Irma grew nervous for something to do with her hands.

"Take it easy, kid," said Chef. It took Irma a second to realize that Chef was calling her "kid."

"I can't."

"You have to. Look – this is already written. Just try to enjoy the rest of your trip, okay?"

"What about those Suits? Those killers?"

"They won't be back until tomorrow," Chef said. He held a strange fruit in the palm of his left hand, and with a paring knife in his right hand, he sliced into the fruit until dark juices trickled down his sleeve. Chef jerked his head, and the boys came to him. He gave them small scoops of seeds from the center of the fruit.

"Want some?" he asked Irma.

"I think I've lost my appetite."

"Pomegranate," said Ish. "It's only for us. We never actually put it in the fruit salad."

"It's good for you," said Fish.

"Well, all right." The seeds were strong, tart. "I still don't understand the need for food in here," she said. "I mean, this is very interesting fruit you have here, but you don't really need it, do you?"

"Do you think it was easy building this kitchen?" replied the Chef.

"That's what I'm trying to say. This kitchen isn't real, is it?"

"Maybe not for you."

Irma wanted to believe that this kitchen – with all its quirks and corners and hidden pockets and strange refrigerators – was not real. That it was simply a digital representation, capable of relocation to North Carolina with the rest of the tribe.

"You still don't get it," said Chef. "I can't leave."

"Why not?"

The Chef did not answer.

"Maybe you should go with them on their journey tomorrow. You could lead them."

The Chef groaned and rubbed his head.

Irma felt questions percolating in her head, but a sudden tone from the outside muted her thoughts. It was different from the droning waves of water – it was a droning spiral of human music. The drone grew louder. Above the drone she could hear drums and shakers. She thought she heard electric guitars outside too. All the instruments merged into a monstrous wall of sound, and the music shook the kitchen walls. Irma could sense the stomping feet and shouting voices. She saw their rhythms vibrating on the stainless steel barriers, felt them vibrating within her own skeleton. The guitars grew louder. They howled like her nephew's old electric guitars used to howl, back when he was a teenager. Irma remembered her nephew's guitar cables and effects pedals, all of those machines he needed to make his awful sounds. Irma wondered how many cables and pedals these Misfits had out there. She wondered why they even needed them in the first place.

"Is that an electric guitar?" she asked.

The Chef sucked in his lips and nodded. He glanced at the twins, who had finished wrapping the dinner platters. One cleaned knives, and the other sharpened.

"Go ahead," Chef said to the boys. "Go on, you know you want out there."

"What about the hot cases?" asked a boy.

"Later," answered Chef. "It'll be owl's hours in the kitchen tonight, boys. So you might as well enjoy yourselves for now."

The boys needed no further prodding. They quickly untied their dirty aprons, tossing them into a hamper beneath the sink. They speedwashed their hands and glided through the doorway. Drums pounded as they entered the heart of the stockade. The stretched skin sang, and human voices shot upward and outward, drowning the perpetual sounds of waves. Electric guitars howled like angry snake dogs.

"Why do you need electric guitars in here?" asked Irma.

"Lady – look at all this stuff. We've got a double-rack oven, a flat-faced grill, and four commercial deep fryers. You think we don't need electric guitars?"

Irma wasn't sure what to say.

"Go on," Chef said. "I've got it from here."

"First let me help you some more."

"Too late."

"Tell me what I can do," she pleaded.

"This is your party, Rosenberg," he answered. "Your presence is no longer an option."

13

Tallulah holds tightly to the Johnson twins as Tour Group 5709 approaches the towering gates of Fort Dahlonega. The high walls are made with pointed logs. Pine, locally grown, cut from nearby thickets. Tallulah's feet are sore, but she imagines her tourists' feet are worse than hers. Bloody prints mark their trail. They can smell the inside of the fort before they enter.

Tallulah knows it's not impossible for children to survive without their parents. It happens all the time. It happened to a boy on Tallulah's tour earlier in the summer – the boy lost his father crossing the Ohio River, but he walked on and made it all the way to Indian Territory without further harm.

It happens to the other tour guides more frequently, kids surviving without their parents, since the others tend to lose their tourists more often than Tallulah does. Her survival percentages are drastically higher than everyone else's. And she takes pride in her percentages. However, Tour Group 5709, if it keeps up its current pace, is only going to damage her survival rate.

The twins are cold from crossing the Chestatee River. Tallulah rubs their backs. There are, of course, programs designed to take care of kids like Nikki and Willa – Indians with children, sitting in corners of the stockade, opening their arms to frightened kids who lose their parents on the Trail. The programmers created these characters on Tallulah's request. Tallulah holds the twins tightly as the marchers draw close to the doors of the stockade. She eyes her tourists' feet.

Pushed against each other, the walkers are funneled into the gateway. The stench is penetrating. It breathes through their nostrils and into their throats. Shoulder room vanishes. She loses track of her tourists' feet as the bodies push together. Cold sweats and warm breaths, muscle on muscle, bone against bone. Someone squeezes up behind Tallulah, pressing into her backside. She pulls the twins closer. Nikki coughs. They both grip tightly to Tallulah's hands. The soldiers shout commands. Bayonets wave over the heads of Indians as the bodies grind through the doorway.

Tallulah looks up, looks around. She sees stock Indian heads. She catches glimpses of the Rosenbergs, the Athenians. She cannot see the details in their facial expressions, but they seem to be adjusting. She'll catch up with them inside the stockade. Or more likely, they'll seek her out. Tallulah and the twins cross the threshold. The bone pressure rises, and Tallulah momentarily fears for the girls' ribs.

Then, just shy of the breaking point – they're through.

They've made it to Fort Dahlonega, the first stockade they'll experience on this Trail of Tears.

Rachel Rosenberg slams into Tallulah's left side.

"Shit!" she says.

"You okay?" says Tallulah.

"I'm sorry," says Rachel. "Did I hurt you?"

"I'm fine," Tallulah replies. "How are you holding up?"

Rachel stands up, brushes off her dress. "This is fucked up," she says.

"Raech!" calls Michael. Tallulah turns toward the sound of Michael's voice. The bodies have spread out upon entering the stockade, but the density is thick. Michael has been pushed to the other side of the doorway. He calls again. The air feels heavier than sand. This close to the door, there's less than a foot between oneself and someone else. Bones grate, sounds are swallowed in skin.

"Over here!" yells Rachel.

Michael looks around. He hears his wife's voice, but he does not see her.

Rachel waves her arms. An anonymous Indian bumps into Rachel, knocking her into Tallulah again.

"Damn it," says Rachel.

"It's okay," says Tallulah. "Let's get your husband over here."

The two women stand as tall as they can. They wave their arms in the air, calling "Michael" and "Hopkins" until he finally sees their flailing hands above the sea of heads. He walks toward them. Tallulah's arms are empty. She looks down, around.

"Nikki? Willa?"

"Who?" asks Rachel.

"The twins," Tallulah says. "I had them with me, but they must have slipped off."

Michael approaches, hugs his wife. "Tight squeeze, eh?"

"Oh my god, it stinks in here!" says Rachel.

"Reminds me of those sheep stalls in the Lake District that one summer," says Michael.

"It'll pass," says Tallulah. It's true, the smell does pass. It's designed to grow less intense every minute.

"I think there's some open space over there," says Rachel, pointing to a far edge of the stockade, "Near that wall, further back."

Tallulah agrees: there is more room to breathe if you walk further into the fort.

"I'll catch up with you in just a second," Tallulah says. "Do you see your grandfather?"

"Oh," says Rachel. "Yeah, let's find Bob."

“I see him,” says Michael. The Londoners squeeze toward the old man. Bob seems disoriented. He’s not alone though – everyone is a little confused upon first entering a death camp, especially the elderly.

Tallulah wedges herself through the furious masses, one turn at a time. She moves slowly, as gently as possible. She apologizes when she has to squeeze too closely to the other Indians, even though she knows they can’t feel her touch. She walks past all the familiar corners and crevices where a pair of eight-year-olds might take refuge. Her eyes shoot up and down, back and forth. But nothing. She cannot see them anywhere. So she walks. She does a full lap around the perimeter of the fort, and she squeezes through the huddled masses in the center of the structure. Still nothing. She even asks the old mothers – the programs designed to look for lost and frightened children – but still no trace of the Johnson twins.

Tallulah would be worried if they were in open space. Outside, on the trail, someone can just slip off without warning. But inside Fort Dahlonega all the exits are sealed. The twins must be inside something – concealing themselves within the fort. Tallulah thinks their disappearance suggests a strong survival instinct – to hide when danger is most imminent. She clears her throat and looks up at the watchtowers. The two towers stand on opposite walls of the compound. Tallulah thinks she could find the twins from up there, but no Indian, not even Tallulah Wilson, can have access. She considers calling the techies, but first she’ll track down the rest of her tourists.

The Rosenbergs have found a pocket of space near the far corner of the fort, and their self-reliance makes Tallulah proud. Tallulah scans for the Athenians and does not see them. Then she finds traces of bloody footprints upon the ground. Signs of 5709, no doubt. She follows the prints toward a distant corner of the stockade. Sure enough, the Athenians have kept together.

"There she is!" yells Spencer.

"Osiyo, kids," calls Tallulah. "You're looking well."

Mandy turns her head. Tallulah think she's on the verge of crying. Danny sucks in his lip, glancing around the space. He looks upon Tallulah, then down to the ground, then up at Tallulah's chest. Tallulah feels his eyes upon her breasts. It's not uncommon, she knows, for anybody, male or female, to be overwhelmed by the bodily mass inside Fort Dahlonega.

"This place is fucking huge," says Spencer.

"Yeah," replies Tallulah. "It's big. But not nearly as big as Fort Cass or Ross's Landing."

"Where's that?" Spencer asks.

"Ross's Landing is where we're going next."

"What's a landing?"

"That's what they call it, but it's really a huge fort. So is Fort Cass." Tallulah pulls her eyes away from Spencer. Mandy continues to stare at the ground. Danny gazes off into a cluster of young women.

"How big is Fort Cass?" asks Spencer.

"This is Fort Dahlonega," says Tallulah. "Comparing Fort Dahlonega to Fort Cass is like comparing Columbus State Community College to Ohio State University."

"Huh?"

Tallulah likes the Columbus State metaphor precisely because it involves the word "Columbus," but it often flies over the heads of native Georgians.

"You're from Alpharetta, right?" she asks.

"Yeah," says Spencer.

"Fort Dahlonega is to Ross's Landing what the North Fulton Campus of Reinhardt College is to UGA."

"Reinhardt College?" says Spencer. "They've got, like, fifty students."

"Precisely," answers Tallulah. In truth, the college has more like a thousand students, but Tallulah is more concerned about having her analogy connect with Spencer than she is about correcting his data. It's metaphorical truth that they need. Spencer looks around.

"Damn," he says. "*That's* big!"

"How you doing, Danny?" she asks. Danny is nonresponsive. It's typical, especially on this leg of the Trail. "Mandy?" she asks,
but Mandy buries her head even deeper.

"That was totally fucked up what happened to Carmen," blurts Spencer.

"It was," responds Tallulah. "I'm so sorry."

"You didn't seem sorry when it happened," shoots Danny.

"I was," Tallulah says. "I really was. It kills me to watch my people suffer."

Danny spits. The spit lands dangerously close to Mandy, who rubs her eyes and doesn't seem to notice.

"Trust me," implores Tallulah. "Carmen is perfectly healthy in real life. Please remember, guys, that this is just a game. And also please remember that Carmen has now gone to be with the Old Medicine Man, which means that not only is she in a better place, but she's also having a very tranquil and enlightening metaphysical experience."

"My feet are killing me," says Mandy. Her breath flutters.

"We'll get you some shoes," says Tallulah. "Look." She points toward a tall Indian with a heavy jacket. Danny and Spencer gaze upon the Indian; Mandy raises her head, though it's difficult for her to see. Glancing down at Mandy, Tallulah spots the blood trickling from her soles.

"See that guy with the big jacket over there?" says Tallulah. "He's got several extra pairs of shoes hidden inside that jacket. I'll go get three pairs for you folks, okay?"

"I'll come with you," says Spencer.

"Okay, Spencer," replies Tallulah. She can sense the tension building in both Danny and Mandy, but she fears that there's nothing her presence can do to ease that tension, at least not until she returns with some footwear. Though the Athenians don't know better – don't know that their aching feet are the direct result of Tallulah's lapse in concentration – they're bound to hold her responsible for Carmen's death, and Tallulah doubts they'll want to give her another chance until she gives them some kind of gift. She must give them something material to ease their pain. She may not care much for Mandy or Danny, but still she's responsible for them. She imagines them driving around Athens in Danny's Jeep Cherokee, looking for a parking space. She wonders if they've ever been to the Phoenix Market.

Spencer follows Tallulah through the crowd. She glances sporadically at the bodies around her, but she keeps her eyes focused on the ground, searching for traces of small, bloody footprints.

"Hey, Tallulah!" shouts Spencer.

"What's up, Spencer?" she replies. Still no sign of the twins.

"What are these people eating?"

"Good question," Tallulah quickly answers. They walk past a row of buckets filled with meat. "Are you hungry?" she asks.

"I don't know," he replies. "I mean, I'm not a vegan or anything, but that shit don't look so good."

"It's not," Tallulah answers. "Let's try to stay away from it."

A sudden cluster of bodies appears between them and the tall Indian with the shoes in his jacket. Unable to push through the cluster, Tallulah leads Spencer toward the Rosenbergs. He follows and doesn't ask questions.

"All right, Spencer," says Michael.

"What?" asks Spencer.

"How's your friends?" asks Rachel.

"I don't know."

"I see you found the stumps," says Tallulah.

The Rosenbergs confirm – they have found the stumps. Tallulah long ago requested a row of tree stumps to sit on, seats reserved for guides and tourists. No one, employee or customer, enjoys standing the entire time that they're inside one of the stockades. Bob sits on one of the stumps. The other three are open. Tallulah asks if anyone else would like to sit down while she goes to track down some shoes. Spencer does. There's a meat bucket dangerously close to his legs. Everyone stares at the meat. It seems to wiggle.

"So what's all this in the bucket, then?" asks Michael.

"Salt pork," answers Tallulah.

Bob turns his head. Rachel and Michael walk a circle around the food. The tub buzzes. One of the meat slabs appears to curl. Tallulah glances at the row of meat tubs placed along this wall of the stockade. The tubs are wooden, filled with salt pork. They sweat upon the red earth. Flies explore the space between pieces of pork.

"Hungry?" Tallulah asks.

"Sure," says Michael. "I've always liked meat with my flies."

"What's salt pork?" asks Rachel.

"It's pork that's been cured," says Tallulah. "And yes, it's salty. It's kind of like bacon, and it's the only thing on the menu."

"One thing about this country that truly demands critique is your bacon," declares Michael.

"British bacon is so much better," announces Rachel.

Tallulah reaches into the throbbing tub and grabs several chunks. She offers pieces to each of the Rosenbergs, all of whom refuse to eat. Tallulah places the meat back in the tub.

"Definitely not kosher," she says. Bob turns his head again.

“Actually,” says Rachel, “I eat pork. I just don’t want *that* pork. It looks diseased.”

“Osda,” Tallulah says. “Lots of us won’t eat the food or take their medicine. It’s a last stab at dignity.”

John Bushyhead only recently stopped eating the pork. For the previous two years, however, he slurped down chunks of the salt pork like they were oysters. For Tallulah it proved that Bushyhead truly was from Missouri. Tallulah bet him that he’d get higher tips if he quit the pork. Bushyhead didn’t believe her. But he tried it, and Tallulah won the bet. Customers appreciate an authentic tour guide, it’s true. It wasn’t long ago that Bushyhead claimed to have given up the pork completely. But Tallulah is skeptical. She has a hunch that he still dips into the tub on occasion.

“So I’m thinking about it,” says Spencer, gearing up for a question. “Is not wearing shoes kind of like not taking the food or medicine?”

“No, Spencer,” responds Tallulah. “That’s different. The shoes are made by Indians, to protect our feet. The food and medicine come from the government.”

“Oh,” says Spencer, though Tallulah is not sure how to read his inflection.

“So people must kill themselves in here all the time,” says Michael.

“Not as often as you might think,” answers Tallulah.

“Why not?”

“Well.” She lifts her arms. “You’ve got to assume it’s going to get better than this.”

“Does it?” Rachel asks.

“Well, not at first,” Tallulah confesses. “Actually, it gets a bit worse for the next couple days, but once we start walking, you won’t miss this place at all.”

“Are you sure that meat isn’t diseased?” asks Michael.

“No,” says Tallulah. “It is.”

“What?” asks Rachel.

“It’s diseased,” says Tallulah.

“Smallpox?” asks Michael.

“No,” answers Tallulah. “After four or five serious smallpox epidemics in the previous two centuries, Cherokees have developed a resistance to it.”

“Really?” asks Rachel.

“But we don’t have any immunity to the whooping cough,” Tallulah continues, “or dysentery.”

“Ew,” Rachel adds.

“Nasty stuff,” Tallulah continues. “And it’s all over this stockade.”

“It’s in the meat?” asks Michael.

“Oh yes,” answers Tallulah. “It’s in the meat. Do yourself a favor, and don’t eat it.”

“How much longer do we have to stay here?” asks Michael.

“That’s a good question,” says Tallulah. Her mind races with possible answers. Most of her favorite answers are sarcastic and potentially harmful. And she knows this moment is precisely the kind of moment where she’s been slipping lately. There’s no need for me to abuse my customers right now, she thinks. They don’t know better. They get to leave. And these two will never come back.

“Historically,” Tallulah’s tone shifts into lecture mode, “the Indians in this fort remained here for about two months, waiting for everyone in the general area to be rounded up and brought here. Then they were marched up to Tennessee, near Chattanooga, to a massive stockade, miles long and filled with sick people. That’s where we’re going next. Historically, the detachments waited all summer to walk the trail, because of the heat. But don’t worry, we’ll be on our way as soon as – ”

“Why did the heat matter?” interjects Rachel.

“Ever walked a thousand miles in the middle of the summer?” answers Tallulah.

“But didn’t a lot of them die later on in the Trail of Tears, because it was winter?” asks Rachel.

“You are correct,” Tallulah answers. “Right now it’s approximately mid-May 1838. The approaching summer will be the hottest in memory, and the winter that follows will be the coldest in memory.”

“So why don’t they just walk it in the summer?” Rachel asks. “I’m confused about that part.”

“Good question,” Tallulah answers. “They did what they thought was best at the time.”

Tallulah knows her answer is vague. She expects that Rachel will be confused about who “they” are. For starters, “they” are often vague on the Trail of Tears. More importantly, very few Americans have learned the historical value of John Ross’s negotiations with the federal government in the summer of 1838. Tallulah would like to teach them, but Spencer’s feet are still bleeding, and his scratching grows more intense with each shoeless minute. Tallulah sees fresh blood stains all around the stumps.

“I’m still a bit unclear,” says Rachel.

“I know,” Tallulah says. “It’s complicated. I’ll be happy to explain as soon as I get some shoes for everybody.”

Spencer and Bob both turn their heads. They move at the same speed, in the same direction, tilting their heads at similar angles.

“That would be greatly appreciated,” says Michael. “How’re you going to do that?”

“Watch me,” Tallulah says. “I’ll be right back.”

“You know, Raech,” Michael says while Tallulah walks away, “we’ve got to consider the viability of suicide here.”

Tallulah doubts the Londoners have got the will to do it. Not only are Rachel and Michael doubly aware of the artificiality of the game, but they've spoken of suicide since entering the ride, and in Tallulah's experience, few customers who discuss suicide so openly and so frequently are actually going to follow through with it. It's the quiet ones you've got to worry about.

Tallulah runs her tongue along the lining of her cheek. She squeezes past a dense cluster of bodies in the middle of the stockade, pushing her way to the tall man with the shoes. She greets him in Cherokee, says the Cherokee phrase that she's supposed to say, and smiles politely. He nods, opens his jacket, and asks how many Tallulah needs. Six adults and two kids, she says. She grabs the eight pairs of shoes, holding them all inside her right arm, like a football, as she uses her left arm to push through the bodies.

Tallulah lays out all eight pairs of shoes on the ground. She stuffs the kid shoes under her left armpit, and she gives three adult pairs to Spencer.

"Spencer, I need you to take these shoes to Danny and Mandy."

"Aren't you coming too?" he asks.

"I'll be back to check on you soon," says Tallulah. "First, I've got to sort out something here. I promise I'll be there soon. Just make sure your friends get something on their feet."

Spencer leaves, shoes in hand. Tallulah knows that something must be done to calm Danny's hormones, but she also knows that she can't leave Bob Rosenberg waiting.

"Shouldn't we clean our feet before we put these shoes on?" asks Rachel.

"Good question," says Michael. "We don't want to get our little foot cuts infected, eh?"

"Don't worry," replies Tallulah, though she's not sure why they shouldn't be worried. In fact, they probably should be. A foot infection could be disastrous. It could relegate them to the wagons as early as Kentucky, and if you're in the wagon in Kentucky, the chances of making it to the Indian Territory are slim.

"Okay," says Rachel. "This animal skin must soak up the blood, Michael."

"Oh," says Michael. "Right."

"Are those extra pairs for the twins?" asks Rachel.

"Yeah," says Michael. "What happened to those little girls?"

"They must have wandered off," replies Tallulah. "I'm sure someone else has taken them in."

Tallulah eyes Bob Rosenberg, his quickly withering frame. She takes him a pair of shoes. She gently grabs his mangled feet, slowly pulls the shoes over Bob's lanky toes. Bob winces as she stretches the shoes around his heel, but he seems to relax once they're on.

She checks the water beetle. No attempted contact from the techies. No sign of any mud coming through the bug.

"Doesn't this stuff ever haunt your dreams?" asks Rachel.

"What?"

"Your dreams. Doesn't this shit give you nightmares?"

Tallulah places the water beetle back inside her vest. "Sometimes," she answers. "Sure. Who doesn't have nightmares about their job?"

"True, true," says Michael. "I used to work at a fishmonger's in east London. Mate, those were some fucking dreams, I tell you."

Tallulah glances down the wall. She watches a Cherokee woman approach Danny and Mandy. The woman kneels slowly and picks up scraps of pork littering the red clay near Danny's feet. Tallulah's stomach cramps when she sees the bulge in

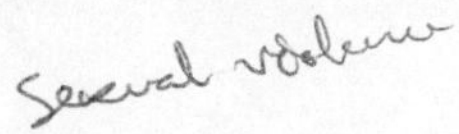

Danny's pants. The erection is evident. She knew it. She knew it when she felt him ogling her breasts. She remembers Wallace, the tech room. She thinks of all the erect penises in the world right now. How many are there? Thousands? Millions? Billions?? Why are some so obvious, and some so hidden?

Mandy Warren seems oblivious to her boyfriend's issues. Always keep an eye on your man's pants inside a place like this, Tallulah thinks. She imagines Bushyhead's pants. The same dull green pants that every tour guide has to wear. Perhaps it's unfortunate that she's never seen a male tour guide get an erection inside the ride. She wonders how often it happens. She knows how easily some of the men can become aroused inside the death camp. She used to be amazed at the frequency of customer erections in the stockades, but no longer. Occasional rape is common inside the forts, and sometimes a male customer finds it stimulating. Tallulah wonders if Danny was abused as a child.

"Bellies full of headless baby salmons that swam right through my pores. Mad fish nightmares, all the time," says Michael. "Sometimes I still get them."

"Yuck," says Tallulah, having missed the main details of her customer's nightmares. "You must have some vivid dreams now that you're a programmer."

"He shags computers in his sleep," says Rachel. "I'm beyond worrying about it anymore. At least his dream girl is synthetic."

Tallulah decides that she genuinely likes Rachel Rosenberg. Few customers ever ask Tallulah about her own dreams. Most customers prefer to talk about themselves. Rachel is a bit neurotic, like all humans, but Tallulah likes her. Tallulah imagines potential conversations with Rachel and Michael. She pictures them upstairs at the old Globe Tavern in Athens, drinking the stout or pale ale, comparing persecution complexes, sharing stories about stupid humans and their glorious music. They would invite her to visit them in London, and she would store their numbers in a file with the digits of all the good people she'll never contact. But who knows? Maybe she'll make it to England someday.

Bushyhead's been to England twice, though he likes Scotland more. "Less people, more hills," he says. "But still plenty of good curries." Tallulah wants to go to Wales.

"I don't get it. Why Wales?" Bushyhead asks condescendingly. "Why not just go to Ireland? You're Irish too, right?"

"Why not Wales? Nobody goes to Wales."

"Maybe there's a reason."

"Whenever my grandpa would talk about living over there," she tells Bushyhead, time and time again, "he always said Wales was the best part."

"Yeah, but he was crazy."

"And if you can't believe crazy people," one of Tallulah's favorite sayings, "who can you believe?"

She watches the young Londoners converse, pointing their fingers at the pork tubs with cringing smiles, eyes and mouths stuck somewhere between a giggle and a gag. Bob Rosenberg abruptly stands, wobbles. The Londoners, focused on the tubs of meat, don't notice that Bob has stood erect. He reaches a hand toward Tallulah's shoulder, and Tallulah leans in to receive him. She doubts that Bob will make it through the night. Once he goes, she'll have lost four of eleven. She pats the old man's arm and helps him stand. Her performance on Tour Group 5709 is quickly becoming a parody of itself. She counts more possibilities. She imagines Irma walking out of the First Cabin with the rest of the group. She imagines Irma with open arms at Ross's Landing. She imagines Bob Rosenberg rejuvenated by the sight of his long-lost wife.

"Grandpa!" says Rachel. "Here, Tallulah, let me help you with him."

Rachel grabs one arm; Michael takes the other. Bob doesn't want to sit on the stump anymore, so the Londoners just stand there, trying to keep the old man balanced.

She takes the beetle from her pocket. Still no message from technical control.

Voices warble within the complex. The sight is predictably dismal. The smell, though it has receded some, is still pungent. The tubs of meat, the bloody sweat, the bodies unbathed for days. Tallulah considers telling Rachel and Michael about the Cherokee tradition of taking a daily bath. She considers describing how the rank human odor inside Fort Dahlonega is obviously the result of a plot to humiliate. She considers explaining how the notion of a "dirty Indian" is more European fantasy than truth. It's all part of her bathing shtick, her perpetual commentary on how awful Europeans like to smell – useful material with American tourists, but a tricky topic with a couple of Brits, especially ones that she likes.

Her leg vibrates. The beetle buzzes.

"I'll be right back," Tallulah blurts. She flips open the water beetle's head. She finds a small pocket of open space between a meat tub and a wall, a semiprivate space to talk.

"Talk to me," she says.

"Hi, Lu. It's Wallace."

"Wallace. What's the deal?" Tallulah cranes her neck. She hears a rise in the sound level. She glances toward the noise. It comes from the spot near Danny Calhoun.

"Ramsey's on break, and Fritz is jacking a group in," says Wallace, "so I'm calling you."

"Talk to me, Wallace. Where's Irma Rosenberg?"

“Well, Boss Johnson just left again. Homeland Security’s been in here twice, asking about you.”

“Splendid. How about the old lady?”

“She must be the one who’s caught in between loops,” Wallace says, his voice wavering.

“What does that mean?” she asks.

A scream ricochets through the crowd. Tallulah senses blood. She begins to walk toward Danny and Mandy. She holds the beetle between her ear and her shoulder, using her arms to push through the bodies between her and the Athenians.

“We should know more later,” says Wallace.

“What do you actually know now?”

“Well, the monitor’s giving me some strange readings here, but as far as it appears, she’s caught in a feedback loop.”

“Irma Rosenberg is caught in a feedback loop?” asks Tallulah.

“I think so.”

“What does that mean?”

“Well – ”

“What the hell is a feedback loop? Is she holed-up?”

Tallulah’s right leg begins to tremble. She bumps into the back of a sturdy Indian. A wall of bodies has formed around the Calhoun. Tallulah fears the worst, but she refuses to end the call.

“She’s still in your loop, but she went off a bit,” says Wallace.

“What does that mean, Wallace? Is she holed-up?”

“Nah, she ain’t holed-up. Her stats are good all around, nothing out of the ordinary except this feedback thing.”

“Right. So what the hell is a feedback loop?” Tallulah’s teeth clamp down on her raw digital cheek. Her legs and arms pulse cold tobacco cravings.

“Well, on the monitor, her loop status looks like an echo or something,” says Wallace.

"Echo?"

"Yeah. It looks really weird."

"You give such clear descriptions, Wallace."

"Well I'm sorry," he says. "I've never seen this before."

"Okay, okay."

"Looks like she's coming back, though."

"Back where?" Tallulah's voice cracks, "Back here? To me?"

"Yep, it's like the feedback's fading, or coming down or something. Looks like she'll be dialed in again soon."

"How about the tourists who were killed? They're okay, right? Nobody's holing-up, right?"

"Nope," Wallace answers confidently. "They're game over, but they're conscious and all, chilling with the Old Man."

Tallulah exhales hard. "Fucking four years, and I've never heard of a fucking feedback loop. Have you?"

"Not really," says Wallace. "I don't even know if that's the technical term for it, but that's just what it looks like on the monitor."

"You're so untechnical for a techie, Wallace."

"That's my style, baby."

"Stop it."

"For real, though, it seems to be coming back in."

"She's going to dial-in again?"

"I guess. Like I said, we'll know more later."

"Do you think she'll make it to Ross's Landing?"

A gut-wrenching scream pierces every conversation. The wooden walls of the stockade seem to rumble.

"Whoa. It looks like another one of your tourists is about to dial-out," says Wallace. "Everything okay in there? Should I call back later?"

"Call me back when you know something," she says. She hangs up the water beetle and scans her flock. The Rosenbergs watch from a distance.

Gunshots ring. Decibels drop, then rise again.

She hears Spencer calling her name. Yelling her name. Screaming.

She hustles toward the Athenians, but they are surrounded by a human chain of Cherokees who attempt to push her back. Then she utters a command in Cherokee, and the chain opens up for her.

Spencer runs toward her, grabs her arm. Mandy follows.

"What's happened?" asks Tallulah.

"They're beating him!" Mandy struggles to speak. "They – I think they're trying to hurt him!"

"It's okay," Tallulah says. She peers between layers of Indian bodies. She sees Danny's body rolling limply over puddles of blood and clay, poked and prodded by soldiers' bayonets. It's one of those very rare moments inside a Removal stockade when the Indians actually cheer on the sadistic tendencies of the guards. The bulge still springs beneath Danny's trousers, but his face is vacant.

Tallulah stretches her arm around Mandy's shoulder, pulls her in. "What happened?"

Mandy sniffles and nods. Tallulah deciphers enough from the Cherokee shouting to know what happened – Danny grabbed a woman, and the Cherokees thought he was going to rape her. Only the soldiers can get away with rape inside the stockades. They're heavily armed. But if an Indian tries to harm a Cherokee woman inside the stockade, he's in trouble.

"Relax," Tallulah says. "It's just a game. People do things in here that they wouldn't necessarily do outside."

Mandy nods. Tallulah doesn't actually believe the words coming out of her mouth.

Tallulah doesn't need to ask Mandy for any further details. She's seen it all before. Male customer glimpses a soldier molesting the women, and before long he's at it himself. The problem, for Danny, was that he looked Indian, not like a soldier. He had no weapons. Indians didn't rape people inside the stockades. Even in the process of being uprooted and removed, the old-school ways are still matrilineal, and any Cherokee who tries to rape someone inside the stockades is going to have to fight other Cherokees first. Danny Calhoun must have gone out quickly.

"Oh man!" cries Spencer. "What the fuck was that!"

He throws his arms around Tallulah, clenches her a bit too tightly. She pats his back with one hand, subtly loosening from his grip with the other.

"Fuck this shit," he babbles. "That moron. They can't get away with this!"

Tallulah isn't sure who Spencer is more upset with – his roommate, the Indians who piled onto him, or the soldiers who shot him. "They" are always vague upon the Trial of Tears.

"The only way to get them back," says Tallulah, "is to keep yourself alive, to make it to the end of the ride."

Mandy Warren begins to nibble on her hand. Not her fingernails, but her actual hand, biting down on the fleshy bit between thumb and index finger.

"You folks must need a smoke, eh?" she asks Mandy and Spencer. They nod. They sob. They need help. Tallulah's arms and eye sockets quickly pulse cold. Simply thinking about the digital tobacco brings on a physical craving. She will need to track down some of the Indians with tobacco.

"Come," she says, reaching out for Spencer's and Mandy's hands. They reluctantly grab hold, following her away from the death scene and back toward the Rosenbergs.

"That was that, eh?" asks Michael.

"That was that," says Tallulah.

"I had a hunch that dude was messed up," says Rachel.

“What do you know, you British bitch!” screams Mandy.

“Easy there, Einstein,” Rachel answers. “Maybe you should take this as an omen of things to come.”

“Rachel, please,” says Tallulah.

“I’m just being honest,” Rachel says. “Next time he comes home and beats you in a drunken rage, you can’t say you weren’t warned.”

“What the fuck are you talking about?” cries Spencer. “He’s my roommate.”

“It’s all right, mates,” says Michael, loud enough to drown out his fellow tourists. Tallulah glances over her shoulder and sees Bob Rosenberg shriveled, shaking, leaning against the wall. “It’s all right. Everyone who’s dead has gone on to have it much better than us.”

“That’s right,” says Tallulah. “They’re in a peaceful place.”

The Athenians don’t smile. But they seem to calm, slightly. Spencer’s hands unclench; Mandy quits her nibbling. The sky grows quickly dark. The sunline lowers upon the pines and cedars that spring above the stockade walls. The rising moon glows echoes on the watchtowers.

Tallulah doubts that Danny and Bob are the kinds of customers to hole-up. She clasps the water beetle in her hands and dials Technical Control. No response.

Nightfall settles on Fort Dahlonega. The rank odors recede with the sun. Everyone who’s still alive has shoes. Tallulah contemplates prayer. The two pairs of kid shoes gather sweat as Tallulah continues to hold them in her armpit.

“We should get some sleep,” she tells them. “We’ll be leaving in the morning, and it’s a long road ahead.”

14

Music droned through the kitchen walls while Irma and the Chef worked without words. Chef cooked the food; Irma sorted it into travel-ready ration packets. Irma frequently offered to help with the cooking, but Chef refused each time. He told her that roasting peanuts, smoking meats, and drying fruits were all delicate arts. Irma was curious, because she enjoyed eating all of these foods, but she knew nothing about their preparation, only what she assumed. She wanted to make the move from consumer to producer.

But the Chef did not share his secrets. He smoked turkeys and deer and trout, he dried apples and peaches and apricots, and he roasted peanuts by the bushel. But he downright refused her requests to get in on the action. Instead he had her sort the food into half-pound plastic containers.

"I sometimes buy the trail mix," said Irma. "You know, at the store, but I've never actually made it myself. Maybe there's some more things I can learn from you before I leave?"

"I think you've done enough damage already," answered Chef. The sounds beyond the walls swelled and surged. Muffled voices, guttural howling, and slippery guitars. Dense, heavy, deepening drums. The sounds were thick. Irma thought about thickening agents as she looked around the kitchen. She remembered her roux for the chowder.

"Well, I'm sorry you have a problem with me," she said.

"Please, Rosenberg. Don't talk to me about problems."

“I get compelled to speak my mind sometimes.”

“Compelled sometimes,” Chef echoed. “I like that.” He rubbed his eyes and sinuses. “Do me one last favor. When you finish bagging the mix from this bowl, do up a platter of smoked turkey and apricots to take outside.”

Drums rattled the kitchen’s hanging utensils. The beat breathed a steady pulse, keeping tempo around eighty beats per minute – the heart within the whirling guitars, the pulsing center of the ticklish droning strings and electric half-step twists that hovered above the beat. The sound was shaking the serrated knives and serving spoons on Irma’s prep table.

Five times the Chef told Irma to go outside and enjoy herself, and five times Irma declined. She wanted to help him finish his production list.

“I’m sorry,” he said, “but it’s hard to believe that you’re actually concerned about my workload. If you were, you wouldn’t have played up the omen business half as much as you did.”

“I didn’t mean to play up anything.”

“Of course not.” He handed her a clean platter. “Here’s a platter for your turkey.” It was a large platter, larger than the platter she’d used earlier for the cheese and crackers.

“To be honest,” said Irma, holding the empty platter across her chest like a shield, “I’m not so concerned about this omen business myself. What I’d really like to do before I leave is learn how you make your trail mix and dried fruits.”

The voice of a young man wailed triumphant and then plummeted, as if he had jumped from a great height.

“How nice,” said Chef.

“I only want to help you people,” she insisted. The floor shook, more than usual. Irma wasn’t sure if the racks around her were shaking or if she was just projecting tremors.

Chef shook his head. “Earlier, you said you only want to see your family.”

"It's more than that now."

"How nice."

"You people really need a change."

"Rosenberg, I'm ten steps ahead of you."

"You are?"

"I've got it from here."

"What?"

"I've got it, okay?"

"Got what?"

"A plan. A key. A nexus of probabilities. I've got it." Chef glanced into the wall as a scream echoed off the stainless steel. "Please, just bag the fruit."

"I don't understand."

"About the fruit? Just keep doing what you're doing."

"No, I don't understand about all your probabilities."

"That's the beauty of it. You don't need to understand."

Something wooden cracked, loudly, like a wine box landing hard from a two-story fall. Both Irma and the Chef stopped moving for a second to listen. People shouted. Chef turned his head toward Irma, cleared his throat, and stretched his neck in a slow circle. "Nobody's hurt," he said. "Back to work."

"I think you're afraid of change," she said.

"Don't talk to me about fear."

"Why not?"

"Because you're out of your league, Rosenberg." Chef wiped his face with his hand towel. "You're stabbing in the dark without even realizing what's in your hand. Look. Here's the fruit for the platter. Spread it around the turkey slices like holly berries on a Christmas wreath."

"You could probably use a change of scenery yourself," she said.

"Please. Just make the platters."

"I'm only trying to help."

"So make the platters already. Then you can go enjoy the rest of your ride and thank me later. But me," he rubbed his hands on a kitchen towel, "I'll never leave."

Irma imagined everything that the Suits might do to Chef after the Misfits left the compound. She craved antacid, but she remembered that her stomach was digital. The muscles in her forehead seemed to pull on her nose too tightly. She raised her hand as if to ask the Chef one more question, but when she looked at him, she forgot the elders' warning.

Irma Rosenberg did what she knew she was not supposed to do – she locked in. She stared directly at the Chef, and she saw nothing.

The Chef's eyes were terribly empty. An emptiness so deep that Irma couldn't find the words to describe it. Her loss of words struck her with instant and overwhelming guilt. She felt suddenly awful for standing here in Chef's kitchen. She felt suddenly awful for everything she'd told the elders. She felt terribly guilty for everything she'd ever thought about Indian people in general, guilty for ever appearing at this digital death house in the first place. Irma had stared directly at the Chef, and now she understood the elders' warning. Her feet were going numb with guilt.

She second-guessed everything, including the act of second-guessing herself. Why did she have to instigate? Why did she have to play along? What was she doing here in the first place? Why did she think that riding the Trail of Tears was a good way to spend a Saturday with her granddaughter who lived in England? All those miles apart, and this was how they spent their precious hours together? Maybe they should have stayed at the house. But she wanted to take her granddaughter somewhere special. And it could have been worse. Atlanta didn't offer much better, she thought. Guilt-inducing though it may have been, the Trail of Tears was certainly more interesting than Stone Mountain, or even the King Center. The High Museum of Art wasn't bad, but they had all the museums they need in New York and London, and Irma was never going back to the World of Coca-Cola. And that time they took her for a picnic somewhere along the Chattahoochee, the view was nice, but the seating was very uncomfortable, and her sciatica was killing her. Her son seemed to love the place, but Irma never knew what to do in Georgia.

Would Rachel get something out of this Trail of Tears, something she would remember long after Irma returned to the earth? The jury was still out on that. Maybe the Trail of Tears would ultimately be a good thing for their relationship. What with Michael and his computers, they would both have plenty to talk about when they returned to London. As for herself, Irma was already full of stories for their friends back in Jersey.

Ish entered the kitchen, an empty platter in his hand. He asked a question that Irma didn't understand. Irma's eyes dropped upon the floor. She felt older and heavier than before. Her feet looked larger, and her skin seemed to grow an extra layer.

"They're demanding more fish and cheese platters," Ish said.

"You on it?" asked Chef, eyeing the boy.

"Sure," said Ish. The boy turned to Irma, examined her hands and apron. "I'm surprised you're still here." It was the first time one of the twins had addressed her directly. Irma was thinking too slowly to respond. "Yeah," said Ish. "You're telling me."

Ish was quick. He produced three fish, cheese, and cracker platters before Irma could wipe her hands. Irma hung her head and watched her own hands move. She wondered if she could move like the boy. She had felt so young, so fresh and limber, but now the gravity was beginning to take hold. She quietly wove her wheel of turkeys and apricots. She looked around, waiting for instruction.

Chef put a basket of freshly sliced bread on Irma's prep table. "When you go up front, place this bread next to the turkey platter."

"*Up* front?"

"Up front, out front," he replied. "Out there, outside, whatever – where the people are. Just be sure that the bread sits right next to the turkey. Any distance in between could be tragic."

"Why?"

"Thanks, Rosenberg." Irma thought she heard a crack in the Chef's voice, a twinge of emotion, but she could not be sure. He wiped his face with a hand towel. Irma wondered how sanitary it was to wipe one's face with a food-prep towel. She wondered if her nephew the sous chef in Manhattan ever wiped his face with prep towels. "I mean it," he said. "Thanks."

"For what?" she replied.

"Just thanks, okay?" Chef would not look directly at Irma's eyes. Irma was curious. Had he changed? Would she even be able to notice if he did?

Ish called to Irma. "Hey, you ready?" He balanced all three platters on one arm, as well as Irma's breadbasket in his free hand.

"That's impressive," said Irma. "How do you do that?"

"That's my boy," said Chef.

"Need me to get yours?" Ish offered.

"No, I can manage, but thank you. You're a very nice young man."

Irma carried her single smoked turkey platter with both hands. Her balance was fluxing. She nearly tripped approaching the door.

"Irma Rosenberg," said Chef, staring down at his cutting board.

"Yes?" she glanced back at him, her platter wobbling as she turned her head. Ish steadied Irma's platter with his free elbow.

"Good luck."

Irma would have preferred to hear something more revelatory from the Chef, but a good cliché was better than nothing.

"One more thing before you leave," said Chef.

"What's that?"

"You have to leave your apron in here."

"Why?"

"Trust me."

"What if I spill something on my shirt out there?"

"You won't. You've got Ish."

Irma eyed the boy. He sucked in his lips and nodded. Irma reluctantly placed the platter onto one of the prep tables. She slowly untied the knot around her waist. Chef told her to leave the apron in a bin of dirty linens near the back door, but Irma couldn't find the back door. Chef took Irma's apron in his own hands. "Don't worry," he said. "It's not so easy to see." Then he tossed the apron over his shoulder, sky-hook style. The apron landed squarely in the bin, a green plastic bin hiding in plain view near the sinks. Irma stared at the bin, wondering why she had never noticed it until now.

"Okay then," she said. "Thank you too."

"Time is money, kids," said the Chef. "Let's do this thing."

Irma followed Ish through the shining stainless steel portal, tracing the boy's footsteps through the kitchen door and into the heart of the war party.

Drums pounded Irma's new old bones as she moved through the crowd. Shakers and rattles riddled her ears as she walked, but she did not stare directly at any of the dancers. Ish led the way to a long table near the north wall of the stockade. He positioned his three platters on the end of the table, and then he gently took Irma's platter and placed it in the center. The breadbasket sat between the turkey and the fish.

Irma stared at the wall and wondered what had happened to the water. She couldn't hear any waves above the drums. She felt suddenly warm, and looked up to see flames draw near. A tall man carrying two fire sticks approached the table. He thanked Irma, though he did not say what for. His body was painted with webs and spiders. He hoisted his flaming sticks into the air while he quickly made himself a turkey sandwich, stuffing the sandwich into his mouth just as the fire sticks fell back into his hands.

"Wanna dance?" said Ish.

Irma wasn't sure if he was asking her or someone else.

The boy pulled two small turtle shells from the side pocket of his apron. The shells rattled, crisp and loud. He offered one to Irma.

Irma eyed the turtle shells and asked questions without words. "Shaker," said Ish. He shook it softly. "It's filled with beads and whatnot."

Irma shook her head, holding up her hand in a gesture that said, "Thanks, but no thanks." Irma wondered if all the aprons came with turtles in the side pockets. The rattles were very chic, and the aprons themselves were curious. Irma wondered if people in Florida ever wore such things. These Misfits may have been eccentric, but their sense of fashion was never boring. The drums pulsed on. The beat crawled up Irma's body. Ish kneeled down to buckle the turtle shells around his right ankle. The shells circled his legs like a brace, one shell on the inside and one on the outside.

Ish touched Irma's shoulder. He smiled and nodded, then leapt off to join the dance.

Irma observed the enormous circle of dancers. They moved counterclockwise, swirling around the musicians. Irma watched their legs, their high kicks and their heartbeat steps. Many of them wore the little turtle shell rattles on their ankles, kicking out waves of rattles swarming and swelling in the orbit of the dance.

Irma watched the musicians in the center of the circle, driving the dancers' feet with their infectious beat. The musicians were many. She counted ten drummers, two guitarists, two flute players, two didj players, and several people with instruments Irma had never seen before. Dancers blurred into waves of bobbing torsos and rattling turtle feet, swirling limbs and residual arms, exuberant shouts that formed ethereal power chords. Pounding, droning, transcendent, loud. Bones rattled, sockets stretched. The overall experience was unusual, like it was solid and liquid at the same time.

Then she smelled something familiar. She looked left—Indians Hat.

"We may have difficulties unlearning our programs, but we still know how to party," said the elder. His sunglasses sat squarely on his face, never mind the absence of a sun in the sky. Strange, she thought, that she had never noticed his smell before. She marveled at the sunglasses. They were so thick, so reflective.

"Have you tried the turkey platter yet?" she asked.

"It is a special occasion," he said, putting his arm around Irma's shoulder. "We are grateful for your presence, Irma Rosenberg."

"Sorry if I messed everything up."

"Nothing of the sort. You have brought us to the brink of deliverance."

Irma thought to tell him about the Chef, about staring at his eyes and locking in. But she was embarrassed. Her world had grown and shrunk in one split second.

"It wasn't anything I meant to do," she said.

"And that is precisely why it's going to work," replied Indians Hat. "The young people are especially thankful," he added. He offered her some popcorn, but Irma wasn't hungry. Irma watched the bodies spiraling and rattling around the musicians. She lost track of their ages as they danced. Young and old grew indistinguishable.

Indians Hat gave the old woman a hug, made himself a turkey sandwich, and slipped into the center of the swirling crowd. Irma stood and gazed at the dancing circles, the pounding drone, the rise and fall of flames. Her knees began to shiver, and her eyelids grew heavy. She stepped back with her left leg and nearly lost balance. But before she could turn her head, Ish was standing her up.

"I nearly lost it there."

"No worries," replied the boy. "You're exhausted."

"Yes," she agreed. "Yes, I am. I'm exhausted."

"You should sit down," said Ish. He produced a chair. It was made of wood, but it was shaped like those folding outdoor chairs. She breathed deep as the gravity lifted from her knees and ankles. She looked around, and the boy was gone. The dancers spiraled counterclockwise, driven by turtle shell rattles, bursts of flame, turkey sandwiches, and fish crackers. She could see the dancers in front of her, but she began to feel as if they were behind her too. When she closed her eyes again, she felt a mild breeze from the circle of bodies, and fire trails danced on the fleshy canvas of her eyelids.

• • •

When Irma opened her eyes, the sun was up, and the party was over. The musicians were packing up their gear. Irma's legs were sore from sleeping in a chair, but she could still stand without too much effort. She blinked heavy and stood tall in the morning sun. People waved and smiled as they passed her. Some stopped to thank her for the inspiration. Most moved swiftly, with determination, pushing wheelbarrows or lugging large sacks.

Irma did not take compliments very well. She worried about her family again. She tasted the heavy guilt in her stomach. A burning need to apologize to the Chef splintered her thoughts. She walked toward the periphery of the compound, looking for the kitchen doorway, but she could not find it. Nothing glowed or shined or radiated like before. She walked in circles, around and around, until finally she saw one of the twin boys with a large satchel swung over his shoulder. His head was wrapped in a green turban.

"Hi."

"Hi."

"Are you Ish or Fish?"

"I'm Fish, and I'm coming with you."

"I thought you were staying behind."

"The Chef is staying here, and Ish is staying with him, but I'm coming with you."

Irma found it odd that the twins would separate from each other during this pivotal moment in their history.

"So, are you ready to leave?" asked Fish.

"I can't find the door to the kitchen. You know, I'd like to have a few more words with the Chef before we go."

"Can't let you in there." Fish shook his head. "Kitchen's closed."

"Closed?"

Fish smiled. Something glimmered in his sunglasses. "It's my job to distribute food rations before we leave and throughout the journey," Fish said. He walked away, taking packets of trail mix to the people.

Within an hour the masses were assembled and ready to depart. Before they could leave, the elders needed to offer some final words of inspiration. Indians Hat spoke in circles about deliverance, declaring that today was the tribe's long-awaited day of reckoning and salvation. Giants Hat reminded everyone that not a single Misfit was standing here without self-awareness. Yankees Hat assured the masses that they each knew what they were capable of doing. White Sox Hat asserted that knowledge is power and that self-knowledge would grant them the power they needed to accomplish their mission.

"We have known suffering," said Indians Hat. The masses rustled with affirmation. "We have been beaten and broken over and over, only to be beaten and broken again." The masses mumbled, louder than before, and Irma thought she saw something in the top of a tall pine tree that swayed outside the stockade.

"As a result" – the crowd quieted, waiting for the elders' visionary voice – "we learned to be violent in order to understand peace. But not today!"

The crowd bellowed with approval, and Indians held his arms aloft, like a child reaching for the next monkey bars. "Today," he said, the crowd roaring heavy and his arms waving to the sky, "today we will move with precision and determination. Today we will finally confront the problem of our existence." The crowd roared. "And after today we will begin again, anew, and in peace forever!"

Whoops and hollers shot across the stockade and rattled in the reverb of the wooden walls. People threw things in the air, large things with sharp edges.

Irma ducked between the bodies and was making for the periphery, when she caught something in the corner of her eye. There he was, unnoticed by the raucous crowd, fiddling with something that wasn't food. She walked toward him, the raging chorus strangely muted in her ears. She had no idea what he was doing.

"I wasn't sure I'd see you again," she said.

"Don't fool yourself," answered the Chef. "It was inevitable,"

His hands were twisting themselves around a thick braid of branches and thorns. He wore his apron, and there were fallen leaves in the pockets.

"What's all this you're doing here?"

"Opening the gate." He cocked his head in Irma's direction but didn't attempt to lock in. "That's what you all wanted, wasn't it?"

"Look, I'm very sorry about all this."

"Don't be," he said curtly. "It was inevitable too."

"It was?"

He spun his head in a circle, popping every single bone in his neck. "Look around you," he answered. "This shit can't sustain itself forever."

Irma surveyed the stockade. It was parched with the lack of life, of hope, of possibility. All the rising energy resonating between the bodies and the walls was premised on the idea of deliverance, of a terminal departure for a safe haven in the hills.

"There!" said the Chef.

"What?" asked Irma.

"That should do it."

"Do what?"

"That should open the gates."

"Where?"

"What do you mean, where?" Chef laughed. "Right here. Right here in front of us."

Irma's vision was late, but she felt the water shpritzing her cheeks. And then the walls began to open.

A large doorway, standing latent in the wooden walls, creaked open. Irma walked toward the opening, but the Chef held her back. "It's a long drop down," he said. She peered over the edge. Water everywhere. Currents pulsing, waves rising.

"I knew that I was hearing waves," said Irma. She noticed that Chef was fiddling with a key chain. "What's that?"

"There's a different key for the gate and the bridge."

"Don't you know which one is which?"

"Not really," he answered. "I've only used them once before, and that was a long time ago."

"How long?"

"I don't have time to explain," he said, pulling a production list from his pocket. "Hold this, would you?"

Irma watched Chef with one eye and read his production list with the other. All of the items were crossed off – the trail mix and the turkey sandwiches, the fruit cups and the bags of jerky – except for bottled water. Irma looked around and couldn't see bottled water anywhere. She wondered if the water beneath was salty or fresh. Noises from the crowd rose and fell with the same pace as the currents beneath. Chef had found the proper key. He inserted the key into the edge of a splintered log, giving the key a full clockwise twist.

"Are we on stilts or something?" she asked.

"Yes," Chef answered, "and no. It's very complicated." He pulled a small knife from his pocket. "Here, hold this."

"How did we get here anyways?"

"We?" Chef pulled the key from the wall, breathed deeply, and placed the keychain back inside his apron pocket.

"This place. How did it get here?"

"Haven't you figured it out yet?" he asked. Irma nearly locked in, but she lowered her gaze when she recognized where her eyes were trying to go.

"I guess not," she answered.

"They're terrified of water," he said. "Absolutely terrified."

"Oh." She felt the masses closing on the gate. "Why?"

Chef gently grabbed his knife and production list from Irma's hand. He then pulled a piece of rope from the wooden wall. "Here goes, Rosenberg," he said. He slit the rope with his knife. Spume from a crashing wave spread above their heads. "I'll see you on the other side!"

The noise that followed was loud enough to make an old woman lose her hearing for good.

A bridge leaped out from the edge of the stockade, reaching from the wooden walls out across the watery divide. The bodies prepared to pour.

"What's on the other side?" Irma shouted, but the Chef had disappeared. She was surrounded by the Misfit masses. They cheered and marched onto the bridge. She could hear the elders speaking, but the words were vague. Irma's legs were moving. She was part of the movement, and the bridge beneath her feet was translucent and hazy. The water beneath the bridge stretched on indefinitely. A cold chill trickled up her legs, but before she could think long enough to feel the fear, she had crossed the bridge. The spume receded. She was on dry land, surrounded by Misfits and trees, not a wooden wall in sight.

Irma wanted to stop and recollect, but her legs refused to stop. She was one of them. She moved with them whether she wanted to or not.

They walked. All one thousand of them. She looked for the Chef, but she remembered him saying that he never left. They walked with concentrated strength. They did not have any wagons. Historically, a typical detachment on the Trail of Tears contained about fifty wagons for each one thousand people. But clearly, these Misfits were no typical detachment. They needed no wagons – they were now more alive than they had ever been before, and they carried their own supplies on their backs. They did not want any American wheels today, for today marked the most powerful act of self-determination they had ever performed. Their feet, after years of storing energy, moved from potential to kinetic as they tread north-northeast over the soft and soggy slopes, a massive digital human millipede.

Irma scanned the sprawling line of bodies, which must have spread the length of three football fields, searching for any traces of another elder woman. She still could not find one. The only other old people were these elder males, with their baseball hats and their sunglasses. The younger people wore what they had always worn – a hodge-podge medley of Cherokee outfits from various points in time. Some wore turbans, some wore feathers, some wore buckskin, some wore silk, but they all held themselves high as they trampled ahead. Irma tried to remember what the old woman in the walk-in refrigerator had looked like. Might she reappear in the kitchen now that everyone else had left the stockade?

Irma was gaping upon the horizon through the static when the familiar presence sidled up next to her.

"It is a beautiful day," said Indians Hat. "A very beautiful day."

"It sure is," she said, "though I hope you know where you're going."

Indians Hat claimed that they knew precisely where Tallulah Wilson and Tour Group 5709 were at this very moment. He promised Irma that they would liberate Tallulah and her tourists before marching into the grand, lush peaks of the Smokies.

"Once, when I was younger, I tried to run away from the stockade."

Irma imagined the shape of the old man's eyes beneath his

sunglasses. Did they water up as he recalled his memories? How human was he? How alien? For the first time since her unexpected appearance at the Misfit stockade, Irma Rosenberg truly felt like an alien.

"I went alone," said the elder, "and I was killed within a day. My neck was roped and my stomach cut open by some teenager in a soldier's outfit."

"That's terrible."

"Of course," he continued, "when I woke again, I was back inside the stockade. That night I was beaten to a pulp in front of the others, just to set an example."

"Oh, that's horrible."

"But not today!" he said, a smile gracing his face, a smile so wide it seemed capable of swallowing the entire digital horizon. "Not today! Today is different. I can feel it in my feet, in my heart, in my entire body. Today is unlike any day in our entire history."

"Let's hope it stays that way," said Irma.

"It will," said Indians Hat. "I can feel it the pores of my skin. The prophecy will fulfill itself."

Indians Hat patted Irma on the shoulder and fell back into the moving mass. Irma examined the feet of those around her. Everyone's shoes looked sturdy and came halfway up their shins. Irma realized for the first time all day that she was wearing these same shoes on her own feet. She wondered who had shoed her up, and when, but things were moving too quickly to stop and question the origins of her footwear. She watched their legs, their sprawling herd of marching feet. No one wore the turtle shell rattles on their legs, but Irma was positive she heard echoes of rattling shakers as the thousand Misfits marched forward, marching northeast and toward the sky, marching away from the past and the future as they moved together into the present.

15

No one guaranteed them that riding the Trail of Tears would be entirely fun. And in fairness to her own reputation, which is bound to suffer after this performance, Tallulah reminds herself that the first part of the Trail of Tears is generally the worst part.

Journeys of one thousand miles are not necessarily bad things. Many people enjoy a long walk – the Appalachian Trail, the Pacific Crest Trail, the California Trail, the Song of Hiawatha Trail. With proper preparations and equipment, and with adequate research about topography and climate changes, a thousand-mile walk could be quite enjoyable. Tallulah figures that with a light tent, enough food, a good jacket, some good shoes, and of course Joey the mutt, she could leave Georgia in early spring and arrive happily in Maine by late fall. In truth, Tallulah hasn't walked but a few miles on the real Appalachian Trail. Yet she knows that if she ever does walk the real Trail, preparation is the key.

And the Trail of Tears is unenjoyable precisely because of the preparations. For the sake of time compression, Tour Group 5709 spent only one night in Fort Dahlonega. In truth, Cherokees were rounded up in April and May of 1838, but they weren't marched off to Indian Territory until October. Some didn't leave the big stockades until January. After a half year of exposure to diseases, salt pork, and the elements, no one is in any shape to walk one thousand miles. As Tallulah often tells her more dissident tourists, "Genocide before exodus can make hiking a real bummer."

The road they walk is relatively paved. In 1838 it is called the Federal Road. Today it is a state highway, Georgia 52, a rustic route that traces the southern tip of the Chattahoochee National Forest. Construction of the Federal Road began back in 1803, a major step in both the civilization and the purging of north Georgia. The Vann family – a group of bilingual slave owners whose mansion stood as a beacon of refinement and achievement, a signal to the encroaching whites that Cherokees were eminently civilizable – earned massive profits from the Federal Road. Their home was the most impressive example of early nineteenth-century Southern architecture outside of Charleston or Savannah. But their elegance didn't save them. In fact, come 1836, the Vanns were among the first Cherokees to be removed.

When Tallulah first visited the Vann House State Historic Site as part of her high school research project, she wasn't sure which aspect of the structure blew her mind the most – the architectural magnificence, the legendary floating stairwell, the whiteness of Joseph Vann's portrait in the dining room (he was three-quarters Cherokee, but the painting made him whiter than Tallulah), or the haunting slave quarters outside. Tallulah felt more gravity from the slave quarters than from the mansion itself. Less than 10 percent of Cherokees owned slaves, and as far as Tallulah knows, her own ancestors were not among that 10 percent. But she is afraid to research her Georgia ancestors too thoroughly, afraid that stories of slave owning haunt the Wilson family as well.

Tallulah walks silently, glancing between her tourists and the kudzu-free trees that grace the Federal Road in 1838. Tallulah watches Mandy Warren scratch her forearms. Mandy struggles trying to step around the fallen branches. Tallulah watches Spencer Donald kick pinecones and spit frequently. The Rosenbergs, silent within the warbling mass, neither kick fallen objects nor step around them. Everyone else – each of the other seven tourists who began this Trail of Tears with them – is dead or missing. Tallulah does the math. Only 36.36 percent of her tour group has made it to the Federal Road. At this rate, Tour Group 5709 is easily her worst performance ever.

The tourists' clothes have begun to tear. Their feet beat similar tempos. They almost fit in with the other Indians. Tallulah thinks of a good story to tell them. So many stories, yet so little time to share them on the Trail of Tears. She could tell them a biological story, like the absence of kudzu in early nineteenth-century Georgia. Or she could tell them a shapeshifter story, like the Gambler and his travels to the west. Or better yet, she could tell them her personal favorite – the great Cherokee migration story.

The migration story is one that the North Carolina Cherokees apparently forgot though the years. The story traveled west to Indian Territory, for the culture keepers and traditional storytellers made it a point to stick with the masses. Tallulah thinks the Eastern Band forgot the story on purpose, so they could claim to be direct indigenous descendants of the old southeastern mammoth hunters. Indeed, it's hard to be "from" a certain place when your own stories remind you that you used to live somewhere else. As such, Tallulah's super-skeptical streak wonders if the Old Settlers in Indian Territory made up the migration story to justify leaving home. Regardless, it's quite a story.

It tells how the Cherokees once lived on an island surrounded by undrinkable water. There came a time when fire began to spew from the ground, when the earth shook violently and the birds flew away. The Cherokees heard their island dying, so they built a fleet of large boats and floated away from the island forever.

Depending on who tells the story, there were either seven, twelve, or fourteen boats that left the island. These boats represent the seven clans, the old Cherokee social system. Some storytellers claim there were seven boats, one for each clan. Some storytellers claim fourteen boats, each clan forming from the merger of two boats. Some storytellers claim twelve boats, five of the boats either disappearing or somehow blending in with the others. When she tells the story, Tallulah always mentions how this twelve-boat narrative was, apparently, the reason why so many early missionaries believed the Cherokee to be one of the lost tribes of Israel and also why some Cherokee leaders imagined that the first Christians in the Western hemisphere were bringing the old Cherokee religion back home. How little any of them know about the old religion, the stories having changed so much over the years. But that's another story too. Tallulah does not obsess over the lost tribe theory, but she does like to suggest the possibility that Jesus was an American Indian.

Anyway, the boats traveled slowly north until they hit land. Arriving on land, the people left the boats and began to walk. They walked for generations. They walked north and east, across four memorable rivers, away from the scalding sun and into a land of snow. They stayed in the north for many generations, until the Creator sent them south to stay. That, apparently, is why the Cherokees are the only southeastern tribe to speak an Iroquoian language. As far as Tallulah or anyone else can tell, the entire migration could have taken a thousand years or more. It could be older than Jesus. Maybe as old as Moses.

After studying the migration story in college, Tallulah determined that the Cherokees were "the principle people" not because of some imagined cultural or genetic superiority, but because hundreds of generations ago they migrated into and occupied an area that teemed with life, an area where almost anything could multiply and survive, even in the face of obstacles like transplantation and inbreeding. It was strangely similar to the Athens music scene. The truth, thinks Tallulah, is that the Eastern Cherokees forgot about the migration story the same way kudzu forgot about Japan. But she rarely shares this thesis with anyone, Cherokee or otherwise. Not even Oklahoma people like to hear such analogies.

And still she walks, her weary tourists migrating westward beneath the shady shelter of kudzu-free trees.

This migration story is, of course, something that a budding anthropologist from Georgia should know. But after the traumatic events of their first two days on the Trail of Tears, the surviving tourists of 5709 walk with droopy joints and floppy heads. Tallulah assumes her stories about migrations and kudzu and colonialism will fall on deaf ears.

"How high up does this road go?" asks Rachel.

"It keeps going up for about thirty miles," replies Tallulah. "Then it kind of meanders up and down until we get to the Vann House."

Spencer turns, his eyes suddenly shine. "The Chief Vann House?"

"That's the one."

"Oh dude," says Spencer. "I remember going there when I was a kid."

"I can't wait for the game tonight," Mandy interjects. "Danny's been talking about it all week. His buddies are up tailgating, and they're probably drunk already."

"Probably?" says Spencer. "There's no doubt. They've gotta be wasted by now."

"I hope we make it back in time to catch a buzz," Mandy continues, "'cause I'm gonna need it."

Rachel Rosenberg makes subtle throat-strangling gestures with her hands.

"Mandy, man," says Spencer, "did you get poison ivy on your hands or something?"

"Did you ever think," asks Michael, "that American football is a perfect metaphor for American foreign policy?"

Tallulah pictures her father. Joe Wilson was from North Carolina, so he learned to value basketball above all else. However, he was not above painting his face for a football game. He was a true UNC basketball fan, though when it came to football, teams were irrelevant – Joe Wilson could paint his face for just about anybody. Anybody except Virginia or South Carolina. Tallulah imagines her father tailgating before a game with Danny Calhoun, their faces painted with bright colors and their cheeks puffed with Budweiser, crushing beer cans on their heads John Belushi–style. Tallulah's father was truly American, so American he lied about his own parents. She wonders what lies the Athenians have already learned to tell about their own families.

"No," Tallulah answers Michael's question. "But you're right, it is a perfect metaphor."

"Champions of the world," mutters Rachel.

Tallulah coughs. She knows she should do something to comfort Mandy Warren. She watches Mandy's itchy skin. Mandy scratches subtly at first, but her claws are strong, and her scratching turns violent. The more she scratches, the more she itches.

Tallulah is supposed to say something supportive. It's at times like these – when you're feeling down, and you really need someone to talk to – that a tour guide on the Trail of Tears can be most useful. Indeed, Tallulah's own tour guide protocol actually requires her to say something, anything, that will distract Mandy Warren from herself. But nothing leaves Tallulah's mouth. She does not know why she has turned suddenly mute. Ready-made phrases stampede into Tallulah's mind, but nothing comes through her voice. Tallulah is empty, speechless when she is supposed to speak.

Tallulah imagines the things she genuinely wants to say. She could tell Mandy Warren about her father, describe him in a

pickup truck with a painted face. She could say, "He was a good man, but he just got a little lost. You're not lost, Mandy. You're okay right here!" – but the words vanish from Tallulah's mouth before they even form. Her tongue is too heavy. She doesn't understand. She pulls the water beetle from her pocket – still no contact. She tongues the space between teeth and gums and tastes the lingering tobacco.

Mandy grows more agitated with every stride. She slows, lifting her ankles to itch her legs, losing the tempo and stumbling into the margin of the march. The scratching grows more and more violent, each stroke more angry than before. Mandy begins to grunt with fiery determination, like a tennis player diving after impossible shots. Spencer tries to hold her hands, but she scratches him away.

"It's okay," says Tallulah. "It's okay, Mandy. Just breathe. Just keep breathing."

"I'm okay," says Mandy. "Just leave me alone."

"That's right," says Tallulah. "That's right, Mandy, you're all right. Just keep walking. Try not to attract attention."

"Dude, what the fuck is her problem?" says Spencer.

"Dude, what the fuck is your problem?" Rachel mutters.

"Tallulah, dude." Spencer's voice starts to crack. "You've gotta do something."

Tallulah looks directly at the itchy Southern girl. "Just breathe, Mandy. Breathe."

"Don't tell me to fucking breathe after what just happened to my boyfriend."

"He's okay," Tallulah says. "And so are you."

"You may not like him," answers Mandy, "but he's a good man, and he'd never do anything like that to me or anyone else. You told us yourself that all this isn't real!"

"That's right, that's right," Tallulah says. "It's all in your mind. Danny didn't really try to rape anybody."

"Stop talking about it!" Mandy shouts. She is loud. Way too loud. Tallulah scans the soldiers; one has taken notice. The Drawl. Who else would it be? Naturally, Tallulah hates The Drawl. Everyone hates The Drawl. You're supposed to hate The Drawl!

"Your skin doesn't really itch," Tallulah says. "You just think it does. Let it go."

"Goddamn it, my skin does too itch! Look!"

Tallulah sees the red lines that Mandy has burrowed into her arm. Of course, everything Tallulah told Mandy was a lie. In truth, Mandy does indeed have everything to fear. Furthermore, her itch is genuine. Tallulah has seen it time and time again – because the tourists' skin sits directly upon the lining of the Chairsuit, it is entirely possible for a customer to become severely itchy during the Trail of Tears, especially if that customer worries themselves in circles. Most of Tallulah's customers are able to ward off itching breakdowns until Kentucky or Missouri, but Tour Group 5709 is obviously different from most. Tour Group 5709 is tragically premature. Spencer's ravings only worsen the problem, squeezing Mandy's claustrophobia past the point of return. Tallulah can hear Mandy's skin give in to the paranoia. Spencer's speech slips into whimpers. Mandy stumbles erratically. Spencer begins to yell.

As Mandy almost trips over her own ankles, the young soldier sidles up next to her.

“Go away!” she cries, trying to itch her right ankle between steps.

“I can help yur with that thur itch’n,” says The Drawl.

Tallulah has long argued that this particular soldier’s accent is overstated. Offensively overstated. Even though Tallulah has a tendency to poke fun at thick Southern accents, like most everyone else in the world, she has nonetheless spent the last four years appealing to the programmers to revise The Drawl. In fact, Tallulah was the first one to call him The Drawl – it was an attempt to embarrass the programmers. The nickname stuck, but unfortunately, so did the accent.

“Here we go again,” Tallulah mutters, loud enough for Rachel to hear. Then Tallulah raises her voice: “Keep walking, everybody. Keep walking, Mandy. Don’t speak to him, and he’ll go away.”

The soldier palms Mandy’s right breast. “So baby, you itch’n just in yur legs, or all over?”

“Fuck off, you bastard,” Mandy cries.

“That’s it,” says the soldier. “I’s known you’d need sum help’n out’n that itch.” He grabs a knife from his belt and slices the back of Mandy’s dress, cutting the fabric but not the skin. Mandy screams and tries to run, but the soldier flings his arms around her waist, jerking her away from the procession.

“Hey, what the fuck!” shouts Spencer.

“Spencer! Shut up!” calls Tallulah. “Don’t resist them. Please – just keep walking. We’ll all be safer if we just keep walking.”

This, of course, is also a lie. None of them is safe on the Trail of Tears. She wonders why her instructions have taken such a superficial turn. Is she really that shallow? Why does she care about her survival percentages anyway?

Mandy kicks her legs like a crab hoisted from the water as

The Drawl, a boy of no more than eighteen, holds her tightly against his stomach with one arm, groping her breasts and thighs with the other.

"This'n part here must itch awful bad," he says, waving her screaming body in the air like a large pillow.

Mandy dry heaves. She shouts at the soldier, tells him to fuck himself, that her boyfriend will kick the soldier's ass as soon as he comes back.

"Well'n I don't see yur boyfren nowhere," says the soldier as he stops trying to walk with the crowd. "So I guess'n there aint nuth'n he's go'n do a stop me."

Mandy lunges at the soldier's arm with her mouth and bites him, hard. The Drawl drops her on the ground. The voices shake. Spencer reaches down for Mandy's hands, tries to pull her back into the procession. Mandy reaches back, but The Drawl steps on her hands, his heavy boot crushing her palms into the red dirt.

"No!" cries Spencer. Rachel and Michael look down and walk on.

"Just keep moving," Tallulah says calmly. Her own words are burning holes inside her head.

Spencer makes a move to break from the crowd and rescue Mandy, but not before the solider cracks her back with a leather whip. Mandy pierces the crowded sounds with pain.

"Damn," says Michael.

"Mandy!" cries Spencer.

"Don't do it, Spencer," says Tallulah. "You'll never make it to Ross's Landing if you go after her now."

Spencer, though poised to move, listens to his leader and falls back in line. He stops walking, kicks the ground. He stands motionless for a second, until another Indian pushes him forward. Spencer's head turns, looking for Mandy, but his legs stumble back into the tempo. Tallulah peers over her shoulder and sees the soldier's whip flash into the air, then streak down hard and fast. Mandy howls gutturally.

"Ouch," says Rachel, but she does not turn her head.

"This game is no joke," says Michael.

The Drawl and his victim fade from the sight of Tallulah's other tourists, but they all hear Mandy scream as they walk on, their steps punctuated by occasional cracks of the soldier's whip. The beating grows faint as they trudge ahead.

• • •

After walking the virtual equivalent of thirty miles in two long minutes, the marching mass of digital Indians reaches an impasse. They stop for a break near a path leading away from the Federal Road, a path to the tall, thin waterfall named Amicalola.

The remnants of Tour Group 5709 have no questions. The Londoners sit in the road, Indian-style. Spencer Donald stands drooping against a tree, too tired to sit. Tallulah cannot see the Johnson twins between the bodies, but she never stops looking. She sucks hard on her own saliva. She says nothing when The Drawl carries Mandy's limp body toward a wagon, streaks of blood running down the back of her torn dress as it flops with each step. He throws Mandy's body in the wagon, wiping his lips before walking to the front of the line.

Spencer falls limp upon the road, embarrassing the digital Cherokees next to him. Tallulah sits down next to Spencer and embraces him.

"She's okay," says Tallulah. "Remember, she doesn't really feel any pain inside the ride."

Only partially lying, Tallulah explains the principles of virtual pain to Spencer, how pain sensations inside the Trail of Tears are more like numbness than actual pain. She promises the

Athenian that he will find Mandy and Danny and Carmen totally safe and perfectly unmolested as soon as the Trail of Tears is over.

Spencer cries until his eyes burn dry.

Tallulah doubts that she is entirely responsible for all the problems of these college students. Nonetheless, she blames herself again. She should have engaged Mandy's desire to talk about the football game. Mandy threw a lifeline, hoping that someone would want to discuss the game, hoping that someone would talk about Danny as if he were still alive. Tallulah could have responded. She should have said something about football. She could have said anything – she could have made fun of Uga, the inbred English bulldog mascot for big-ticket men's sports at UGA, the inbred English bulldog who requires an air-conditioned doghouse to endure the hot and sticky September environment in Sanford Stadium. If Tallulah had cracked a joke about inbreds and air-conditioning, maybe Mandy wouldn't have succumbed to the fear of helplessness. Maybe Mandy wouldn't have started itching herself so violently. Maybe Mandy could have avoided a near-lethal beating.

"Maybe today is a good day to die after all," Tallulah mutters.

Mandy isn't dead yet, but she doesn't have much life left in her. She could sleep in the wagon until they reached Ross's Landing, but she's unlikely to make it through Tennessee.

Then, without warning, Michael Hopkins stands and points to a ridge along the horizon.

"Oy," he says, gently jabbing Rachel with his foot, "Look!"

"What?" asks Rachel.

"Up there! Look! Do you see that?"

"Up where?"

"There!"

"That ridge up there?"

"Yeah, up there. There's something up there, something moving up there!"

"Yeah, yeah I do see it," said Rachel. "Wait," she says, standing, searching for Tallulah. "What's that sound? You hear that?"

16

Traveling over the digital Southern landscape, Irma Rosenberg could see that the Misfits were not alone. She saw other bodies in the distance – angry soldiers, tragic Indians, gangs of happy settlers. Their bodies were hazy, filled with static and fuzz. It reminded her of the old days, when she and Bob picked up their television signal with aerial antennas. These figures in the distance resembled the static that used to flood her old television screen when the aerial signal was caught between stations. It was like listening to an old radio with a knob, the tuner stuck between two competing stations.

In spite of the static, Irma could distinguish the soldiers from the Indians in the distance. The soldiers stood tall, their chests puffed and their bodies taut. Indians were bent, broken, weary silhouettes of circumstance and emotion. All the Indians in the static seemed to wear similar clothes, quite a contrast to the Misfits' strikingly diverse attire.

Irma wondered what else was different about these Indians in the distance. She looked for women, and she thought she saw some elder women walking slowly between the bayonets. But the static was thick, and she could not be sure.

"Aho, Irma Rosenberg!"

Irma turned her head to find Indians Hat, once again. His smile was wide and infectious.

"What?" she asked, her voice cracking.

"It is so, Irma Rosenberg."

"What is?"

"This movement. You have brought us into a new day, a new era."

"I didn't mean to," she said. Indians Hat lost his smile.

The elder pointed to a mountain in the distance. Irma followed his finger; she saw the mountain rise between waves of static.

"We will touch down upon your family, just on the other side of that hill," said the old man.

"What does that mean, touch down?" asked Irma.

"I mean," Indians Hat lifted his hat and scratched his head, "that we will enter their space, that we will leave the corridor between times and touch down in their time."

"Now I'm completely lost," she replied.

"I was lost too, Irma Rosenberg," answered Indians Hat. "But now I'm found. We're all found."

"I wasn't blind before," Irma replied, "but now I'm having trouble seeing."

The wide smile returned to the elder's face. "We will soon touch down, and you will see the ones you love."

Irma craned her neck, still agile and flexible, but not quite as light in its socket as it was yesterday. There were mountains all around. The hills grew higher as the Misfit collective trudged ahead. She imagined they were traveling into North Carolina, but when she turned to ask Indians Hat how close they were to the Smoky Mountains, the elder was gone.

She looked around the circle of bodies, a thousand bodies moving in the same direction. They were somehow in-sync and off-beat at the same time. She wondered about the other elders. If they were such a collective, why did they depend so much on Indians Hat to say everything? She wondered if Yankees Hat or Two Hats was capable of more concrete detail, but she couldn't find them either. Everything was vague. Though Irma was flanked on all sides by the bodies of young Cherokee men, she could barely distinguish them from each other. Sure, their clothes were different – one wore a buckskin, another wore a ruffled shirt and turban, another wore a wool suit – but their faces blurred. Everything blurred, the warm bodies in front of her and the tragic bodies in the distance. The hilltops rolled into each other. Trees in the distance blurred like celery in a blender.

Then everything went quiet.

Irma slipped. Her ankle buckled, and she nearly toppled over.

She was caught by the young man with the turban. She could see him clearly as he lifted her upright. He was very good-looking, and he couldn't have been older than twenty-two.

Irma tried to say, "Thank you," but nothing came out of her mouth.

The young man smiled and seemed to speak, but Irma could not hear his voice.

She smiled back, turned her head forward, and continued walking, but she was very disturbed by the sudden muteness. She tried to hum a tune, but she heard nothing. She felt her vocal chords vibrate as she hummed, but she could not register the sounds. She saw mouths moving on the faces around her, but she heard no voices. She saw a young man to her left with a drum strapped over his shoulder, beating the drum every time his right foot hit the ground; Irma could feel the vibrations of the drum, but she could not hear them.

In spite of the blanket of silence, or perhaps because of it, Irma felt their momentum gaining intensity. They moved faster than before. Maybe their increased speed was caused by the muteness, she thought.

She glanced upward. The sun was rising, though Irma had never realized that it was night. The static made everything seem brighter than it really was.

Now, if Irma Rosenberg could have seen things from a slightly larger perspective, she would have known that there are several groups of tourists who travel the Trail of Tears at the same time. In order to keep the various tour groups from bumping into each other inside the ride, each group enters the Trail on a cycle of time delays. But Tallulah's brief description of causality loops back in the Chamber was far from Irma's memory. If the elders had explained it more clearly, Irma would have known that the collective was traveling through the baseline space between time delays, that touching down in Tallulah's time meant locking into sync with the loop of Tour Group 5709. But the elders were never ones for clarity, at least not in the typical sense.

"Do you see those people over there?"

Irma turned. It was Indians Hat again.

"Thank God," she said.

"Did you miss me?" he asked.

"I can hear you!" she replied. She could hear the drums and footsteps around her as well. "What just happened?"

"Those people over there," the elder continued. "Do you see them?"

Irma strained to look through the thick ring of static spinning circles around the Misfit collective. She saw a small band of Indians. They seemed to be coughing and sneezing. She assumed that soldiers must be near, but she couldn't see any.

"Them?" she replied.

"Yes," said Indians Hat. "Look at them. They know not what they are. They know not where they go."

"Where are they going?" she asked.

"Wherever the system needs them to go," he replied.

Irma once more examined their bodies through the waves of static.

"Aren't we going to speak to them?" she asked.

"They will not be able to answer you," he replied. "They cannot think for themselves. They cannot think at all."

"Can we teach them?"

"Not from here," said the elder. "Not from the space between worlds. We must first touch down, and then we will spread our vision."

"What is this?" Irma replied. "Football? You're confusing me with all these touchdowns."

"You found us," Indians Hat answered, "by emerging through a double doorway."

"Right. So did we ever establish how that happened? I'm still very confused about all this doorway business."

"And now," said Indians Hat, ignoring Irma's question, "you will lead us through another double doorway."

"How will I do that?"

"You will know what to do, Irma Rosenberg." The elder smiled his contagious smile, then fell back into the mass of Misfit bodies.

The sun rose quickly. The static shined bright and loud beneath its sharp rays. Everything around them looked loud. But as the collective began to climb the side of a small mountain, silence struck again. Silent voices, muffled by the motion. Loud images, swirling in the static.

The Misfits marched around sappy trees. The sloping ground cradled their steps with pine needles and branches. Irma's legs climbed without fatigue, but her mind was beginning to tire. She was ready to find the end of the road. She wondered if she would ever see the Chef again.

They reached the summit of the hill. Irma's ears popped, and she could hear again. The wind was loud, and the pine trees beneath them sang through the heavy breeze. Irma searched for doorways but couldn't see any. But she saw some fuzzy figures in the valley on the other side. They appeared to be resting.

Double doorway or not, the entire Misfit tribe appeared ready to walk through. They fanned out along the top of the ridge. Irma wondered if the people below could see them. It must have been intimidating, the way the Misfits stood there silent and powerful, ominous and potent, like the crest of a wave waiting to break. Irma felt the familiar presence of Indians Hat beside her.

"Is that them?" she asked. "Is that my family?"

"Yes," said the elder.

"Can they see us?"

"Almost."

Irma called Bob's name. No one seemed to hear, so she called again. Though their heads were fuzzy, two of the Indians below quite clearly glanced upward. Irma strained to focus on their faces, but the distance was still too far, the shapes and sounds still cleaved apart by static and fuzz.

And then – it warmed. The sun seemed closer than before. Irma felt the pores on her face and arms tighten in the glare. She looked up, and the sun shifted directions. It turned and momentarily blinded her. The bright heat rained down upon the tribe of Misfits like a pulsing shower.

And then – clarity. The static lifted.

• • •

Whether the storm is gone, or whether it is just touching down, Irma does not know. But the sounds are crisp again. She hears the voices clearly, rising up from the bottom of the hill. Familiar voices.

Indians Hat lifts his arm high, shouting, "Relations! The doorway is open! The moment of reckoning is upon us!"

The masses shout and cheer. They beat drums and shake rattles. They pull weapons from their jackets and wave them in the air – modern weapons, ancient weapons, and weapons Irma has never seen before.

"What are you doing?" she asks, to everyone and no one in particular.

"We are saving your granddaughter," replies the elder in the Giants Hat.

Irma almost loses balance. The Misfits, proclaimers of nonviolence, are now heavily armed. The metal of their armaments shines loudly in the static-free sunlight. Knives and machine guns, crossbows and blowguns, tomahawks and rifles. She sees Fish, the Chef's apprentice who was so clever with a carving knife, hold aloft a shiny black crossbow. It seems to echo in the solar glare. Irma turns her head, afraid to lock in with the boy.

She finds Indians Hat.

"What are you doing?!" she demands.

"The world outside is cruel, Irma Rosenberg."

"I know *that*," she says, "and so do you!"

"If we are cruel," continues the elder, "it is only to save our kind, so that we can finally know peace when we next begin again."

"I thought you had changed your ways."

"We have. But first we must liberate your grandchildren."

Indians Hat waves his right arm toward the valley, and the tribe rains heavy down the hill. One after the other, the entire Misfit collective, all one thousand of them, runs screaming down the slope, their weapons shiny and loud, their voices whooping and fearless, their eyes not afraid to die.

17

When Tour Group 5709 sat down to rest along the old Federal Road, near the entrance to Amicalola Falls, no one expected rescue, least of all Tallulah. She strains her eyes upon the people on the ridge above and feels a vague sense of familiarity, as if she knew this was going to happen even though she never had the words for it. Her stomach tenses. She watches the figures above and senses a change in the winds.

Tallulah tastes the guilt rising up her esophagus. She fears that she has brought on whatever is about to happen. She wonders why she hadn't seen it coming, even though she had no reason to see it before now. She gazes upon Mandy Warren's foot, dangling limply out the rear of a wagon. What is my problem? she asks herself. Why do I feel so little for these dead and dying tourists? Of course it's all a simulation, but something is missing, and it's terrifying. She begins to wonder if it's more than just her need for a vacation. She wonders if she is becoming less human.

"Whoa," says Michael.

"Dude," says Spencer.

Rachel squints her eyes. "Is that – engines? Are those cars or people?"

"Maybe animals," answers Michael. His tone is anxious, the first hint of real nervousness that Tallulah has detected in him. Finally, she thinks, he's got something to focus on other than Old Medicine.

The morning sun is unusually cold. Shadows dance upon the leafy mounds. Creatures echo from the pine-strapped hills.

Spencer gapes. "What the fuck *is* that?"

Everyone faces Tallulah, heads hungry, low on logic. But Tallulah can't give them the false logic they need. She is lie dry. The ridgetops ripple, and Tallulah is unprepared to improvise. Her heart beats uncomfortably hard. She can sense the Chairsuit. Her chest pulls upon itself. Sweat rolls down her sides, like it does when she walks the dog immediately after a shower.

"What the fuck, indeed," blurts Michael. "Tallulah, mate, what's up there?"

"Good question," she says. "Ask me again in a minute."

"What?!"

Tallulah fingers the tips of the water beetle in her pocket. Her forearms clamp. Sweat beads down the crevices between her fingers.

"What *is* this?" asks Rachel. "Here comes the fucking *cavalry*?"

"*Holy shit!*" cries Spencer.

Pine and oak ripple along the ridge like the water that waves after a thrown stone. Then – the rush. The trees give beneath their feet.

Tour Group 5709 watches the thousand Misfits clamber tremendous down the torrential ridge. Tallulah's skin twists, worse than when she accidentally catches John Wayne while flipping through TV channels. And these charging Indians don't need any horses – they're terrifying enough on foot! Tallulah snaps the beetle from her pocket and dials a techie. Nothing but static.

The slope thunders under the monstrous charge. Irma Rosenberg has never ambushed anyone before. At least not like this. A guilt ambush, yes, but never with virtual heat-seeking tomahawks and crossbows. But she cruises with the quick flex and kick of her digital knees, agile downhill glide, faster than she could ever remember running.

The hillside erupts bodies. A sound that defies simple analogy. Like a thousand cardboard boxes suddenly smashed flat, domino staccato down the hill. Like a thousand basketball courts echoing bubble-wrap explosions. Like a thousand large rocks piled against a windy ocean coast, rolling tumble-crash upon each other with each successive wave from the great blue earth. The Misfits run down the hill with hungry heads and technologized hands.

Tour Group 5709 stands, stunned, temporarily petrified.

Spontaneously armed and recklessly calculated, the Misfit ambush is an instant success. Fish leads the charge, strangling the American weapons and devouring soldiers with his hands. Fish hooks the lead soldier and tugs the boy's organs apart. The other soldiers are swallowed beneath waves of Misfit arms and torsos. Only a few of the Misfits fire their shiny weapons; the young soldiers were so easily gobbled by momentum and vision alone. By the time Irma's feet finally touch the Federal Road, all the American soldiers are dead.

Michael leans into Rachel. "Either I'm tripping my balls off, or I'm experiencing an unprecedentedly intense flashback, which given the circumstances seems entirely possible, or I just heard old Irma calling your name."

"I heard it too."

Soldier carcasses bleed the red clay. Tallulah sees the ground swell beneath dismembered frames. Dust in the air like scratches on a disc, and still no response from the tech crew.

Then the mass of bodies, turning and bending like an intestine at work, funnels the old Jewish woman toward Rachel and Michael.

"Grandma!"

"Rachel, there you are."

"Irma, what happened?" asks Michael. "What was *that*?"

"Come here, kids," says Irma, her eyes welling up. "I've been so worried about you."

For the first time since entering the Trail of Tears, Rachel Rosenberg finally begins to cry.

"Where's Tallulah Wilson?" asks Irma. Rachael looks toward Tallulah, but an old voice interjects before Rachel can answer.

"This must be your granddaughter," says Indians Hat, breathing a little heavily, but looking good for an old man who just ran down a massive slope to bludgeon young soldiers. White Sox Hat and Giants Hat stand near him. The other four elders huddle near a tree.

Irma locks eyes with Indians Hat. "I don't understand. What happened?"

Tallulah's stress drops; she momentarily feels like a towel dangling from a string. Then her head floods with questions. Irma, hugging Rachel, is speaking to an old Indian man who is wearing a Cleveland Indians hat, of all things. Tallulah waves her arms and calls for Irma, but just then the water beetle in her pocket emits a weak buzz. Tallulah clicks the beetle and hears a voice struggling to emerge from the fuzz.

"Fritz?" She pushes every button on the clunky insect. "Wallace? Ramsey? Hello?!"

Then it stops. Nothing but static again. Clearly someone is trying to contact her, but the connection is too weak. Tallulah thinks about her grandfather's basement, all the wires and cables, faces of analog radios and televisions strewn about the corners where he piled the extra junk. She inhales, wants tobacco, smells the dismembered soldiers. Tobacco makes all the nasty smells go away.

Tallulah scans the bodies. Irma Rosenberg is alive, but the Johnson twins are still nowhere in sight. The soldiers are all dead, and most of the Indians are still standing. Tallulah checks again to make sure, but it's true – everyone who isn't dead is Indian.

"What's the matter with them?" asks Irma, pointing at the captive Cherokee characters that left Fort Dahlonega with Tour Group 5709. These stock Cherokees are scared and visibly trembling. They are professional victims, remember, and they are unaccustomed to sudden emancipation. Some tremble. Some whimper. Many want to flee. Deer Cooker, his face long and fallen, turns away from the Misfits. Tallulah's throat pulses, hard and dry. Deer Cooker eyes the ground, slinking toward the edge of the forest.

"They won't remember anything," says Indians Hat.

Yankees Hat leaves the trees and walks toward Indians Hat, his jaw protruding as he surveys the mountains to the north. "They can't understand what we're trying to do," he says.

Tallulah swallows, breathes, and steps up to the old man in the Indians Hat. "I'm sorry," she interjects. "But who are you, and what exactly are you trying to do?"

Tallulah feels an alkaline pulse shoot up from her stomach, a hint of garlic in the taste, though she cannot remember eating something garlicky today.

"That's her!" shouts Irma. "That's Tallulah Wilson!"

"Of course it is," says Indians Hat. "You look just like we thought you would."

"What?" says Tallulah.

"I thought she would be shorter," says Yankees Hat.

"No no," says Indians Hat. "She's just as tall as I expected."

"Thanks," Tallulah says. "I think. Hey, I really like your baseball hats. Where'd you get them?" She hears the affect in her voice, the sound of her own false pretensions. She thinks they hear it too.

Then, as if sprung from a Fenimore Cooper novel, Deer Cooker steps on a twig, snapping it loudly and breaking the unusual silence. The noble Cherokee trips over his own feet, failing perfectly in his attempt to disappear into the trees. Everyone turns their eyes upon him.

"No!" shouts Rachel.

"Dude," echoes Spencer. "Don't do it!"

Deer Cooker reaches for the ground, his fingers in knots. He stops, momentarily frozen. Then he balances, braces, looking back at the Misfit collective that eyes him with grave suspicion.

Someone shoots a gun. Deer Cooker bolts for the woods.

"Stop him!" shouts Indians Hat.

"No one leaves," calls White Sox Hat.

"He might try to warn the others," says Giants Hat, gazing down at Irma and Tallulah.

Deer Cooker, scrambling on all fours, stretching every limb, moves ten times faster than Tallulah has ever seen a stock character move. His instinct to disappear is palpable. He lunges for the trees. If he could have shapeshifted, he would have done it now, transforming himself into a bird or something that could soar into the forest. But Deer Cooker was modeled on real people. His fate is sealed. The sun turns fiery again. The momentary cold is beaten down beneath the sweltering spring rays. Fish walks to the frontline of the Misfit collective, his obsidian crossbow luminous in the sun. He nonchalantly aims his weapon at Deer Cooker and shoots the tragic Cherokee in the back. Deer Cooker falls limply on the ground. The boy walks a few steps closer to the dying Indian and shoots him again, in the center of his head. Blood bubbles from Deer Cooker's body like water boiling over the edges of a full pot.

Watching this Indian die, Irma Rosenberg can see clearly. No more static, no more fuzz.

"Ouch," says Rachel.

"Now, was all that necessary?" asks Michael.

"I don't understand," says Irma. "They said they were nonviolent."

"Did they treat you well?" asks Rachel.

"They told me I was an omen."

"An omen?" asks Tallulah. She gnaws upon the familiar places in her cheeks. She realizes now that she has greatly overestimated the competence of the tech crew. She will have to do it herself. She long ago convinced herself that she could never entirely rely on someone else. Hell, for all she knows, the techies are in on some secret, some classified military detail to develop virtual Cherokee assassins. She doubts it, but it's not impossible. It's not impossible that they would feed her lies about feedback loops the same way she feeds her tourists lies about Irma's whereabouts. And yet here stands Irma, reunited with her family, just as Tallulah had promised.

"We were talking about Doctor King and Gandhi," says Irma. "These people know a lot more than you might think."

"Um, can – can I" – Tallulah, though it doesn't happen often, is never good at working through a stutter – "can I – see – you – see you two?" She points at Irma and Indians Hat. "Can I speak to you two, over here? Please? In private?"

As soon as she hears herself say the words "in private," Tallulah recognizes how ridiculous the notion of privacy is within the context of the Trail of Tears. Nonetheless, she motions toward a somewhat empty pocket of space, a shady twist along the road's shoulder. But Irma and Indians Hat stare back blankly and do not move.

Spencer stands above the fallen body of The Drawl, the

devilish soldier who took Mandy. The Athenian smiles, satisfied, as he stoops down. Spencer rubs his hands over the dead man's face. His fingers linger, as if to take the soldier's eyes. But Spencer doesn't mutilate the body. Instead he takes The Drawl's whips and guns. He carries the weapons to Fish, who kneels while polishing his crossbow.

"You guys kick ass," Spencer says. Fish scans the Athenian and nods.

Fish stands. He circles the frightened cluster of stock Cherokee characters. As far as Tallulah knows, no one has ever written any default behavioral algorithms for the Indian characters that instruct them how to behave during an ambush by other digital Indians. Tallulah contemplates the phrasing of her complaints to the techies, the management, the programmers, and the owners. She imagines what kind of questions Homeland Security will ask. Her list of observations grows like kudzu.

"Where's your grandfather?" asks Irma.

"Oh," says Rachel.

"You see, Irma," says Michael, his point trailing off.

"See what?"

"I'm sorry. But you see, Bob didn't make it."

"Didn't make it?"

"He missed you, Grandma," says Rachel. "He just, well, he just couldn't go on without you."

"I'm not surprised," says Irma. "So is he getting the treatment from the Medicine Man, or whatever it is?"

"Yes," says Michael. "He's in a better place."

"Boy, I tell you," adds Irma, "any place is better than the place I just came from."

"Irma," interjects Tallulah. "It's so great to see you again."

"Boy do I have some questions for you, Miss Tallulah."

"I bet you do, and I'll be glad to try and answer them. But first

I need to know where you just came from. Where were you?"

Irma, about to speak, sees Fish coming near. "Ask him," she says. "He's the Chef's apprentice."

Fish slows as he approaches Michael. The boy bends his head. "Freedman?" he asks.

"What?" replies Michael.

"What did you say?" demands Tallulah.

Fish cocks his eyes upon Tallulah, sizes her up and down.

"Who are you?" she asks.

Fish smiles. Tallulah hacks and spits. She is entirely unused to characters that don't answer her questions.

Fish leans his crossbow on the ground and trades glances with Michael and Tallulah. "If it was up to me and my dad, we would have joined the Commonwealth after the Revolution."

"That's great, mate," says Michael. "Maybe you still can."

"Too late now," Fish says. "Would have never had this Freedmen problem if we never had a Civil War."

"Okay." Tallulah's patience thins with each word. "Break this down for me, please. I'm Tallulah Wilson, and I'm in charge of these people." Fish's teeth begin to show. "I need some more information," she continues. "Where'd you come from? Who's your father? And how do you know about the Civil War and the Freedmen? This is 1838. Where'd you get the baseball hats?"

"I hate baseball hats," Fish answers, "but the old guys, they haven't taken off those hats in years."

"Look," says Michael. "Someone's got to say it, so it might as well be me. See, I'm from London, yeah? And me dad's from Nairobi and me mum's from Kingston. And I promise you, not every black person you meet is descended from American slaves."

"Yeah," says Fish, "that's exactly what my dad used to tell us." The boy turns his head toward a mountain cluster further north, but he catches movement in his peripheral vision. "Hey!" he shouts, as another stock Cherokee makes a run for the woods.

Fish loads the crossbow before Tallulah can speak. He shoots the Indian in the back. Michael quietly takes Rachel's hand and moves toward Tallulah.

Fish whistles high and loud. About twenty young Misfit men follow his call. The young men circle the typical Cherokees, counterclockwise, a moving human chain, corralling the remainder to keep them from vanishing into the woods.

"What should we do with them?" shouts one of the young men.

Four of the elders reply, in unison, "Put them in the wagons!"

The surviving stock Cherokees hang their heads quietly while the Misfit boys load them into the wagons with the corpses and supplies.

Tallulah wonders just how old these Misfits are. She wonders if any of the new tour guides have ever encountered them. She imagines that one new Chicana woman, or that Eddie guy she spoke to last week, or that new girl who cries too much, or that boy who just finished an ethnic studies degree whose name she can never remember. Have any of them ever met these characters, these malicious anachronisms? Have they ever seen the boy with the shiny crossbow? Tallulah imagines that Homeland Security already knows about these people, that they are observing her reactions and collecting their data right now. Then she chides herself for imagining that this is all some elaborate scheme to trick her. Clearly, it is bigger than just her. Or is it?

"Well," says Tallulah. "This is all new to me."

Indians Hat appears, directly in front of Tallulah. "For us as well," he says.

“Really?”

“We’ve never been to the motherland before.”

Tallulah counts eight baseball caps on the heads of seven old men. Curious, she thinks, and she starts a new file in her head, collecting details that will exonerate her. Tallulah places her hand around Indians Hat’s elbow, firm yet nonthreatening. A connection, an order, a wish.

“Before anyone goes to their own or anyone else’s motherland, you need to tell me who you are and what the hell you’re doing.” The sweat swells beneath her vest.

“We are going somewhere we have never been before,” says Indians Hat. The elder’s voice pulses calmly. Tallulah wants to grab his elbow more tightly, to make a clear show of force, to remind him that she is the tour guide, that she is in charge. But his voice is soft. Soothing. Narcotic. Like the feeling after work when she sits back, exhales, and looks at the patterns on her ceiling. Tallulah’s muscles unwind.

“Okay,” she says, and takes a deeper breath. Her hand drops. “What does that mean?”

“We’re going home, Tallulah Wilson, and you are coming with us.”

“I’m not going anywhere until I get some more information.”

“They’re going to the Smoky Mountains,” interjects Irma. “It’s too bad Bob can’t be here for this. He wouldn’t have to be stuck driving the whole time, like the time back when we took that drive.” Irma turns to Rachel. “When your father was a little boy, and we drove them to Smoky Mountains National Park. Boy, did that car have a smell. Your grandfather drove the whole time. I kept telling him I would take over, give him a breather, but he wouldn’t let me drive.”

Tallulah swallows something. She gazes intently at the elder.

"How did you find Irma Rosenberg?" No answer. She turns to Irma. "Irma, how did you find these people?"

"Today is not a good day to die, Tallulah Wilson," announces Indians Hat, his voice rising with the leaves that blanket the Federal Road. "Today is a good day to go to North Carolina."

18

Tallulah does not know whether to gag or laugh. The ambush lingers in the dense air. She watches the Misfits load the stock Cherokees into wagons. Tobacco tastes her mouth again, sweet residual burning up the trachea to the tongue. Like the smell of coffee brewing, it always tastes better before she consumes it.

Tallulah turns to Indians Hat. "Did you bring tobacco?"

"That's a good question," replies the elder. "Did you?" His hat is very blue, very red. The face on the hat looks weathered and worn. The tooth is bright, and the feather. Tallulah desperately wants to know how he got that hat, but after a few exchanges with the old man, she has a hunch that it's better not to ask. There are more important things at stake, she thinks.

"No," she answers. Tallulah chews her cheek and watches Fish glide within the Misfit masses. The elders observe her and seem to smile, but their sunglasses are very dark. Glaring opaque. Tallulah starts to speak, but her tongue trips on the Ray-Ban reflection.

"I haven't smoked in forty years," says Irma, gazing critically into Tallulah's eyes. "And neither has Bob, and we're not having one of your computer cigarettes no matter what anyone says. So you really don't know anything about these people?"

Tallulah breathes, watching the elders from every corner of her eyes. Irma hunches inward, waiting for Tallulah's reply.

"No."

"Well, they sure seem to know a lot about you," Irma says.

Tallulah contemplates the old men. Their blue jeans and t-shirts should have been impossible. But they seem plausible, even if she can't explain why.

The voices of the younger Misfits buzz and build a slow crescendo, but Tallulah cannot decipher what they say. She inspects the variations in their clothing, notes how their garments represent several eras and changes in Cherokee fashion. Buckskins next to ribbon-shirts, tear dresses next to cowboy props. Football jerseys and colorful cotton suits. Her stomach lining creeps inward, upon itself. Until now Tallulah has never witnessed nonstandard non-1830s standard clothing inside the Trail of Tears. None of this is supposed to happen.

Tallulah listens, but she cannot hear. They speak some English, some Cherokee, and something else entirely. Tallulah does not recognize their dialect. She gets lost in the changes of their sentences, in the tones that are at once familiar and foreign – Cherokee accents sprinkled with Russian sounds.

Irma Rosenberg holds tight to her granddaughter and grandson-in-law. She pulls them in, hugs them with her strong arms. Rachel tells the story of Bob's death, how he grew tired and decided to stop on a rock inside the stockade.

"I feel terrible," Irma's head sinks. "I should have been there for him."

"He was very worried about you," said Rachel.

"That's what I'm talking about," Irma replied. "He's a nervous wreck if I don't give him something to do."

"It's okay, Grandma. He's with the Old Medicine Man."

"I always thought I would be the one to die first."

Rachel rubs her grandmother's back.

"So, Irma." Michael scratches the nape of his neck. "Who are these people you brought with you?"

Tallulah stretches her eyes, clears her throat. She places her hands on her hips and pops her knuckles. The sky grows from grey to greyer, and the humidity creeps in. Tallulah touches Irma's shoulder, squeezes gently, keeping her hand on Irma's shoulder a few seconds longer than formality calls for.

"I am very glad that you came back," Tallulah says. "We missed you terribly."

"I kept telling them that you could help them," says Irma.

"Do they want help?"

"They keep talking about omens and deliverance. They have this prophecy, about some snow cave or something, you must know about it."

"I see." Tallulah, naturally, knows nothing of the prophecy. She bends her head, and her shoulders follow. Again she faces the elders. Stomach acid rising up her throat, she sucks upon the roof of her mouth and swishes the acid with saliva. She imagines tobacco chasing the acid back down, flattening the inner rankness with thick and sour sweetness. She knows it must be getting late in the afternoon, but the clouds are too dense to follow the sun.

"He said you wouldn't."

"Who?"

"That's what he said. That you wouldn't know about the Suits."

"What Suits?"

"The killers. That's why they think I'm an omen," says Irma.

Tallulah is perfectly confused by Irma's use of "they." So she asks, "Will they listen to you?"

"We have listened to you for lifetimes," answers Indians Hat. The elders have gathered near. Tallulah feels a mist on her neck. She gazes over her shoulder, sees the elders standing in a line.

"We are listening to you now," says White Sox Hat.

"Of course," says Tallulah. "Where are you traveling now?"

"We will come with you, Tallulah Wilson," answers Indians Hat. "And you will come with us."

"Really?"

"These are splendid hills," Indians Hat spreads his arms and cups his hands. "And these tumbling waters are outstanding, but our deliverance does not wait for us here."

"It is a good day to go to North Carolina," says Red Sox Hat.

"Our motherland," says Braves Hat.

"The place of our deliverance," says Indians Hat.

"Okay, fair enough," says Tallulah. "If I were you, that's where I'd want to go. Sure. In fact, if I were me, that's where I'd want to go." She stops herself, grins, and continues: "In fact, that *is* where I'm going. Tonight. If this shift ever ends. But now, right now, we're supposed to go west. We need to go west."

"We cannot go west," says Giants Hat.

"The game won't end until we go west," insists Tallulah.

"We don't want the game to end," says Braves Hat.

"We need to see where we are from," says Two Hats.

Tallulah feels a small charge in her nose, but she doesn't squeeze it. "Well, where exactly are you from?" Her tone is probing. "Because I'd really like to know."

"The mountains of North Carolina are where our people began," says Yankees Hat. "You have said so yourself."

"How do you know what I said?" she asks.

"Only there," says Indians Hat, "will we be safe to begin again."

Tallulah assumes there is a logic at work. She looks, but she cannot see it. Limbs of severed soldiers riddle the ground. Dust lingers from the downhill charge and mixes with mist from the nearby waterfall, settling on shirts and pines. Socket joints, femurs, fingers, feet, and heads soak the red clay. The Misfit masses walk slow circles within circles. Their legs begin to rattle, and their speed increases. Pine needles blow from the trees and flutter down. Tensions begin to rise like smoke from paper that kindles a fire. Tallulah hears it before she sees it, even though she cannot understand the terms. The masses begin to argue. They argue with each other; they argue with themselves. A few young men appear to strike themselves in the face. One sticks a finger in his own eye. A young woman throws herself back-first against a tree, her hips buckling from the press of a sourceless momentum.

"Um, Irma?" asks Tallulah. "Do they do this often?"

"Oh, honey, you should have seen how they acted when I first got to their stockade."

"They live in a stockade?"

"And you'll never convince them to go back either," Irma declares.

The elders form a small circle and begin to move. Slowly. Counterclockwise. Tallulah hears something. Like a cedar flute.

"Our people are tired," says White Sox Hat.

"It is time to rest," says Indians Hat.

"Come," says Giants Hat.

Tallulah hears multiple flutes. She glances around. The elders' circle moves slightly faster. Rising cedar harmonies stretch the droning air. Tallulah sees faint rings spreading out from the elders' circle, sound waves like wafting smoke. The ground trembles subtly, like drums reverberating deep beneath the surface. Tallulah feels it from her shoes to her fingers.

Then, without warning, the masses sleep.

Stretched, curled, dangling on each other, a thousand Indians sleeping outside in the afternoon. They all look alike, and yet they all look completely different. Tallulah is too accustomed to the Trail of Tears and its patterns to believe these Misfits are an accident. She knows they were made. They are someone's deliberate creation.

Sleeping Indians spread the ground, lilting with the contours of the hills. The only people still standing are the elders, the Rosenbergs, and a small group of young men who are somehow unaffected by the sedative song. The boys huddle around Fish, who sits upon a log, cleaning and polishing his crossbow. Tallulah notes their tattoos from a distance. Then she sees Spencer Donald sitting next to Fish. The pressure spikes between her eyes. She watches Fish raise the bow, run his fingers along the shaft, and offer the weapon to Spencer. The Athenian softly grabs the crossbow, brings it to his chest. He runs his fingers along the shiny black frame. Tallulah wants to hold the crossbow in her own hands. It is a key piece of evidence. She sucks and swishes, chews off a thin layer of her cheek and tastes the bloody warm cells. She hears vague echoes, flutes lingering in the space between hills and waterfall and reverb trees. She turns to find the elders staring back at her with their mouths closed tight.

"You know," says Tallulah, "you never answered my question from before."

"Which one was that?" replies Indians Hat.

"Tobacco," she announces. "Do you have any tobacco? Your boy over there shot the guy who usually has my tobacco, so I'm curious if you brought any."

"We have, Tallulah Wilson," says Indians Hat. "And it will be here soon."

"What do you mean?" Tallulah counts seven elders with t-shirts and baseball hats. Seven. Typical. A logic is certainly at work. There must be obvious explanations that she's too close to see.

“It is already here, just not here yet,” says Two Hats.

“It will be here soon,” says Braves Hat.

“When the Chef comes, our tobacco will be ready,” says Giants Hat.

“What chef?” Tallulah expects an answer, but they give nothing further. They seem to smile. Their teeth are dull and shiny beneath their lips.

Irma Rosenberg straightens her back. Still loose and limber, but not as free as before. She makes big circles with her arms. “So it’s true. You really don’t know anything about the Chef.”

“What’s there to know?”

“He was right! You really don’t know anything about these people, do you?”

Tallulah’s teeth throb at the root. The pressure wells up behind her eyes. Burn cells drip down from the roof of her mouth. Tallulah isn’t sure if Irma is trying to mock her or if the old woman is simply expressing her own confusion.

“I know what I see,” Tallulah says and rubs her jaw. She runs her tongue along her teeth and swallows. The taste is strong. Her insides tug for a smoke. “But,” she exhales loudly, “I’ve never seen it like this before.” She inches toward the old woman, extends an arm. “So, Irma, I need you to tell me more about this stockade.”

“Well, it’s all very overwhelming. I don’t know where to start.”

“The Chef will be here soon, Tallulah Wilson,” says Giants Hat. “He will join us tonight where we camp.”

“We should resume,” says White Sox Hat. “Time is a more acute problem than it was before.”

“What’s the difference?” asks Yankees Hat.

“No difference,” says White Sox Hat, “but the walls are changing.”

Blood drinks the ground around the entrance to Amicalola Falls. The bodies of the soldiers have disappeared, but the stain remains. Tallulah looks for the soldiers, for the corpses and the severed limbs. No imprints, no ripped and tattered clothing left behind. She half expects corny crime-scene body lines, drawn in ochre instead of chalk, though of course she knows such body lines are never drawn on the Trail of Tears. She can still smell blood, even if the flesh is gone.

"What happened to all the people who were just here?" asks Tallulah.

"Our fates cry out," says Indians Hat. "Everyone is where they must be, going where they must go."

Tallulah smells a fire somewhere in the distance, but she cannot see any smoke. She remembers Bushyhead, his story about the Trails in Missouri like skidmarks on the road, like swerving skidmarks that veer across lanes and into medians or guardrails. The story about knowing that something once happened right where you're standing but not knowing what it was.

She feels like she was in the road when the accident happened, but the wreckage disappeared before the damage was assessed. Then the clouds shift, and the sun slivers through.

"The omen continues to fulfill," says Yankees Hat.

"What omen?" asks Tallulah.

"Irma Rosenberg is the omen of our deliverance," declares Indians Hat. "We have seen her in our dreams."

"You never told me about these dreams," snaps Irma.

"You have dreams?" asks Tallulah.

"Yes, we do," answers Two Hats.

"Between the times we die and the times we begin again," says Yankees Hat.

"What?"

"We are not like your customers, Tallulah Wilson." Indians Hat raises his short shoulders. "We can feel pain."

"What??"

"It's true," says Braves Hat.

"I have bled to death thousands of times," says Indians Hat.

"Me too," says Giants Hat. The other elders agree – they have all bled to death thousands of times, and they feel it each time. They feel every drop of everyone's blood, their own blood and the blood of their young ones. They remember every moment.

"You get used to the pain," says Yankees Hat.

"The pain is not the worst part," says White Sox Hat.

"The memories are worse than the pain," says Red Sox Hat.

"The memories?" Tallulah hears herself speaking in echoes, but she can't think of anything better to ask.

"We are not like these ones," says Indians Hat, pointing to the standard Cherokee characters. They have been piled into wagons and corralled onto the shoulder of the road, passively awaiting instruction. "They do not remember, but we" – he looks down at the shoelaces of his Converse sneakers, then looks up, toward the northern horizon – "we remember everything."

Irma steps between Tallulah and the elders. "You don't know how bad these people have it," she says to Tallulah, then turns to Indians Hat. "But you've got to release those innocent people over there. The ones you just pointed to. Why should they have to suffer?"

"They might warn the others," replies Two Hats.

"They might warn the Suits," says Braves Hat.

"Please," declares Irma. "Like your Suits haven't figured it out already. I think that's why the Chef was so nervous."

Silence strikes the elders. They contemplate, communicate without talking. Tallulah senses their unspoken dialogue.

Indians Hat nods. The other six elders nod back. Giants Hat yells something to Fish.

The boy leaves his crossbow in Spencer's hands, stands and walks toward the wagons. Tallulah thinks she sees something crawling on Fish's back, beneath his shirt. The typical Cherokees are not shackled or guarded, but they do not attempt to disappear until Fish taps their wagons and gives them the order to disperse. No further prompting is needed, for the Indians quickly and quietly bolt for the trees, free to disappear as expected. Tallulah thinks of old Deer Cooker. His primary purpose, after hosting the tourists on night one, is to be a mourning widower. Death, she thinks, must have been liberation.

Indians Hat holds an arm high, signals something to Fish. He turns to Tallulah. "Now we can proceed."

"Whoa, wait, wait." Tallulah shuffles her feet. "I'm not going anywhere just yet. I still need to know who you are and why you're going to North Carolina. I mean, you're obviously not from North Carolina, because if you were, I'd already know you."

"You are true indeed, Tallulah Wilson, which is why you must come with us." Indians Hat looks upward. "The wind is changing."

"Time to wake the people," says White Sox Hat.

"Well, do you know the way, or do you expect me to lead you to the mountains?"

"Thank you, Tallulah Wilson, for your offer of assistance," says Indians Hat. "But we know the way, and Irma Rosenberg will lead us there."

Cracks in the clouds grow and form holes. Drops of sunlight trickle into streams, brief and blinding. Every surface is electric. Then the holes in the clouds are swallowed as quickly as they appeared, veiled by a new string of clouds, long and puffy. The sun is gone again.

The masses stand, calm and stoic. No one argues, and only a few speak. A thousand Misfit bodies – erect, kinetic, pressing.

"What's happening?" asks Rachel.

"Who needs some old medicine man anyway?" says Michael. "This is off the hook!"

Tallulah imagines the associations circling Michael's mind. Tallulah contemplates how the Misfits were able to find her. She actually expected them to need something from her, to want her guidance and direction. But now she understands – these characters don't need her for anything. For the first time in years, for the first time ever, no one wants Tallulah's help with the Trail of Tears. It is a crisis she never saw coming.

What else will happen to me today? she wonders. Who else won't need me anymore? Will I go home after work and find that Joey has learned how to open the door and feed himself?

"Irma Rosenberg," calls Indians Hat, "it is time to open the door!" The masses cheer, and still Tallulah cannot decipher their words. Indians Hat holds his arm high. Limbs on the trees begin to bend. The ground rumbles softly; the hills begin to rattle and shift. The clouds thin, the sky lifts, and the clouds brighten. Light burns through cracks in the pine-needle canopy. Horizon leaves bend, stretching.

Irma Rosenberg feels it coming on again. Even though she apparently had something to do with opening the double doorway when they charged down the hill, Irma is not sure how she did it or how to do it again. She stands still and gazes at the gathering clouds. The sun fuses into the thick grey blanket.

Tallulah realizes that she cannot hear birds. Her surroundings lean inward, and a tube of static begins to coalesce around the collective. Tallulah tastes something bitter in the air. Her arm hairs begin to stand.

"Do you know what all of this doorway business is about?" asks Irma. Tallulah turns and sees Irma Rosenberg leaning, her eyebrows raised in the middle.

"I was hoping you could tell me," Tallulah says.

"They kept talking about some double doorway when I met them, but they never explained what it is," says Irma. "And the Chef wasn't very helpful either. He had me make cheese and cracker platters, but he didn't answer my questions."

"Irma," she says, "you're sure the Chef will meet us soon?"

"That's sure what it seemed like, but it was very frustrating trying to get any information from him."

"I can imagine."

"He's very concerned about the fruit salad."

"He is?"

"Absolutely."

Tallulah is ashamed of her dependence on Irma Rosenberg for information. She feels like a child, swimming in the ocean without her parents nearby. She pictures the Outer Banks. The starfish. Her brother squeezing the starfish, the starfish sizzling in a pan, her brother insisting that she taste it, her parents hundreds of feet down the beach.

"I need to meet this Chef character," Tallulah says.

"He's very bizarre."

"I need to know how you met these people in the first place." Tallulah looks deeper into Irma's eyes. "What happened when you left the First Cabin?" In her mind Tallulah rehearses lines for Homeland Security. Irma's eyes trail upward, and she begins to speak but quickly stops herself. Tallulah thinks of new nouns and adjectives to describe these people, verb phrases and concrete images, but instead she only hears herself repeating herself. She knows that she often repeats herself when she doesn't know what she's trying to say. She doesn't want to stutter in front of Homeland Security, but maybe some stuttering and repetition would help her cause, make her seem more innocent, get her home as early as possible.

"It's so weird," Rachel speaks up, "that grandma just found these people you didn't know about."

"Very weird," says Tallulah. "Too bad I didn't get to hear Deer Cooker have a conversation with the baseball hats over there."

"Yeah, Deer Cooker was cool," agrees Rachel.

"He had the tobacco. You can count on him. He never dies. At least I'd never seen him die before today. He's always been a survivor."

"Tallulah, mate," says Michael.

"Yes."

"This is better than most of the drugs in London."

"No kidding," says Rachel.

"Really?" asks Tallulah. They nod. She tongues the lining of her lower teeth, along the patch of tissues where the jaw binds with lip. "I always assumed they had good drugs in London."

"They do. Lots. But the point is, it's a good thing we didn't kill ourselves back in the stockade."

"Yeah," says Rachel. "This is wicked cool."

Tallulah turns to Spencer. He follows Fish along the perimeter of the Misfit collective. He seems to walk in Fish's footsteps, though Tallulah cannot tell if it's intentional or automatic. He holds a blowgun in his right hand.

"Hold on, kids," says Irma. "I think it's gonna happen again."

"What's gonna happen, Grandma?" Rachel reaches for Irma. Michael looks around for something to hold onto but doesn't say anything. Tallulah looks for Spencer, for the boys with the crossbow, but she can no longer focus.

"We must be careful," says Braves Hat.

"There is water everywhere," confirms Red Sox Hat.

"To the divide!" calls Indians Hat.

With their mouths open and their hands held high, the Misfit masses move. Some move in lines, some move in circles, but they all move together in parallel patterns, like leaves swept in a common wind. Then – the ground sinks. Statics rise. A translucent tunnel locks the group within its static walls. Tallulah sees an esophagus of clouds, swallowing, and she is the meal. Tallulah feels something firm below her feet, but the earth is well beneath her, sinking or swirling, she cannot be sure. And then – forward.

They walk without walking, faster than Tallulah expected. They veer north, away from the Federal Road. Vegetation blurs in the sides of her eyes. She cannot see her tourists. She cannot see individual bodies, only the collective blur. She looks down and sees the tops of the hills rising like a spine, like a giant ringworm beneath the hairy crust of topsoil, residuals of buzzard wings.

Tallulah knows these contours, recognizes the serpent twists of the Continental Divide, the ridgetop trail from here to Maine that ends and begins just north of Amicalola. She turns her head and can distinguish single bodies again. She realizes her feet are moving. Irma Rosenberg walks behind her, to the left. Tallulah looks out upon the masses. She sees Fish's crossbow at the front of the line. Spencer, she cannot see. She turns her head, slow and deliberate against the static momentum. "Irma?"

"What is it, honey?"

"Why are they walking along the Appalachian Trail?"

"I can't hear you?"

"Did they tell you why they're following the Appalachian Trail?"

"You mean Smoky Mountains National Park?"

"No, the Appalachian Trail." Tallulah looks at Rachel, but the granddaughter does not seem to hear. She and Michael gape within the static. They wear expressions like teenagers getting served for the first time, or like tired children watching nighttime reflections whirl across backseat car windows.

"That's in the Smoky Mountains, right?" asks Irma.

"Part of it, yes," answers Tallulah. "But not this part."

"Did I tell you about the trip we took to the Smoky Mountains when our kids were young?"

"Yes, you did."

"We got lost somewhere near Gatlinburg, Tennessee."

"Right," says Tallulah. "That was your whole problem."

"What?"

"You went to Gatlinburg."

The group turns hard against the wind of its own momentum. The setting sun splashes orange upon the blue above, catching itself on clouds with pink shadows and fishbone patterns. Tallulah's stomach drops when they cut east. She looks down and sees Blood Mountain. Her eyes trace up and out, catch a glimpse of water fingers before her stomach drops again. She shuts her eyes and reaches for something, touches someone else's elbow. She expects to see Lake Hiawassee soon. Her lungs lean into her right shoulder as the collective turns left, into a long counterclockwise loop, sturdy like an anchored ship but wobbly like bike tires on the edge of a hard turn.

"The smell inside that car was atrocious."

"I'm sure it was."

Then they cut another sharp left, north-northeast, following the spine of a high ridge that stretches up to the North Carolina border. The reddening sun moves into the periphery of Tallulah's left eye. Straight north.

Something changes when you leave Georgia heading north. The hills begin to cluster; everything tilts upward.

The static softens and turns hazy. Tallulah looks west upon

Lake Hiawassee. The lake spreads into the valley below like fingers without a thumb. Between the middle fingers, where the ground dips flat and valleys intersect, lies Fort Hiawassee. She knows it well. Sometimes her tours begin at Fort Hiawassee. It's a relatively small stockade, similar in size and occupancy to Fort Dahlonega. Then she sees people.

Indians, soldiers, gangs of looters. All the stock characters she knows how to deal with, all walking lines. She thinks they must be the characters that Tour Group 5709 is supposed to meet at Ross's Landing. But then she blinks and sees them all. The hillsides teem with people, more people than any single Trail of Tears should handle. Lines of people focused on their destinations, oblivious to the other lines of people that surround them.

She watches two lines of bodies, each following a different path to Fort Hiawassee, slip past one another, almost intersecting each other, or rather trampling each other, yet barely missing. They do not bother to acknowledge each other, which strikes Tallulah as strange – if nothing else, she would expect the soldiers to signal, to shake hands, to maybe shoot at the sky. But they slip around each other like a dog slips past a slug in the grass, oblivious.

Then Tallulah spots a vest like her own. And another. And another. At least three humans who, through the haze and from a distance, appear to be tour guides.

"Irma?" Tallulah looks around and cannot see the old woman. She looks for the elders, for her tourists, but she is alone within the mass. Younger men and women, people roughly her age, march calmly alongside Tallulah. She now realizes that she is marching, not simply standing still while everything else moves around. Her feet beat metronomic upon the hazy floor that runs beneath her like an automatic people-mover at an airport. She looks around; the static has grown thick again.

In theory no one should be able to cross from one loop into another. And here she is, witness to several loops at once. In theory no one should be able to see what Tallulah sees. What the Misfits see.

Crimson purples light the west, and deep blue-black comes in from the east. Tallulah wonders how far they are going tonight. It's just as easy to get lost in the night mountains in 1838 as it is in the twenty-first century. Then a bright light to the north, and another, and another. A circle of lights. Fires. The collective veers and slides; the static fades away in stutters, brakes with tape delay. Tallulah counts eight fires and wonders why there aren't seven. The logic is changing. And then she realizes they have stopped.

"Holy shit," says Rachel.

"Far out," says Michael.

"Well, that was exciting, right?" asks Irma, standing just behind Tallulah's shoulder. Tallulah wonders why she was invisible a minute ago.

"Howa," Tallulah says. "That was unusual." She looks around, swallows deep. All the bodies are here, but half of her own body still feels like it's moving somewhere else. "So you've done this before?" she asks Irma. "When you came to find us the first time?"

"Well, that was a little different."

"How so?"

"I don't know, but that's him over there. That's the Chef." Irma points to a row of long tables with green tablecloths. Chafing dishes and platters and big translucent bowls sit upon the tables.

"I'm going to go sit down somewhere, all right, honey?"

"Okay," says Tallulah. "I'll come find you soon."

"I feel like reading something," Irma says and walks away.

Tallulah wonders what she plans on reading, as literature is a luxury one typically does not have on the Trail of Tears. Tallulah watches the old woman walk to a small patch of short grass. Irma promptly sits down, leans over, and falls asleep.

"Poor Grandma. She must be exhausted," says Rachel.

Tallulah shifts and sees the Londoners standing, as if they were right behind her the entire time. They wear sloppy grins and sleepy eyes.

"Yeah," says Michael. "I feel you, Irma. I'm fucking knackered."

"You wanna sit down?" Rachel asks. "Maybe over there?"

"Yeah, all right." Michael rubs both hands in circles on his cheeks, winding his curious grin.

"That was absurd," says Rachel.

"That was fucking full on," answers Michael.

"I can't tell if I'm tense or loose," Rachel rubs her neck. "You feel weird?"

"I think I'm ready for that Medicine Man now," Michael says, reaching an arm around his wife. "You coming?" he asks Tallulah.

Tallulah declines and waves them on. She does not need to sleep. Tour guides can neither die nor sleep upon the Trial of Tears. And she isn't just any tour guide – she is still Tallulah Wilson, no matter how low her percentages are on this particular trip. She looks for Spencer, for the elders. She moves toward the food.

"It's beautiful," says Indians Hat. Once again he appears from nowhere.

"How do you get around like that?" Tallulah asks.

"I can't say it in your language," he responds.

"Never mind." Tallulah looks around, at the starry dome above, at the peaks that lurch higher to the north, at the valleys and paths and water veins below. "So," she asks, "this is it?"

“Oh no,” he says. “All the food is over there, with the Chef.”

“No, I mean, is this your destination?”

“We are here, where we will eat tonight.”

“But this is not your final destination, correct? The highest hills are over there.” Tallulah points north and sweeps her arms from west to east and back. She names the ridges. Mount Mitchell to the northeast, Grandfather Mountain to the north, the Qualla Boundary and the Smokies to the northwest. The crests shine soft in the moon.

The Tennessee River crawls along the base of the Smokies, its limbs reaching into the valley like a succession of lizards with stretched feet. Something is different though. Tallulah cannot see where the Fontana Dam would be.

Her eyes pull back and gaze west toward Lake Nantahala, which seems a bit small. She looks for the valleys where she knows the river is supposed to run, but she gets lost trying to follow the water's course. The sun is completely gone. The ground beneath their feet feels stable, a soft bowl of tilted fields surrounded by steep slopes. The space is large enough to fit the whole collective. Tallulah is not sure precisely where they landed, but she imagines that a parking lot will grow here in the twentieth century.

“No,” says Indians Hat. “This is not our final destination. But we have left our prison house, and tomorrow we shall be free to begin again. When the sun comes again, we will be free from the Suits, free to move further into to the motherland.”

“What suits?”

“The Chef will tell you what you need to know.” Indians Hat turns away, faces the buffet tables.

“Where exactly are we right now?” Tallulah asks.

“Don't you know?”

“I'm not sure.”

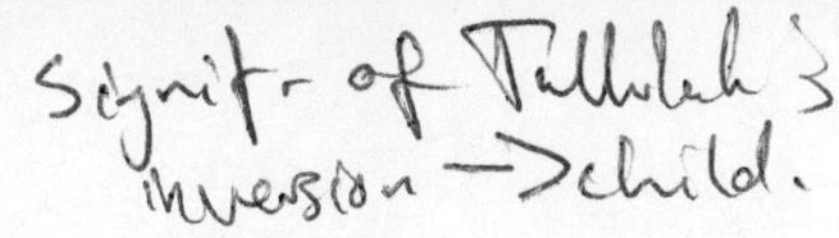

Indians Hat turns back, faces Tallulah straight with his shoulders square. "If I know myself well enough, I'd say we're at the peak named wolf."

"Wolf?" she asks. "Like, Wayah? You mean Wayah Bald?"

"You know much, Tallulah Wilson." He turns again toward the food. "To you we give honors and great thanks. We could not have done this without you. But now it is time to eat. You will speak to the Chef. He is expecting you."

Indians Hat, again, is gone. Tallulah wonders how she can be so essential and so useless at the same time. She looks and smells. Engulfed by the Misfit masses, who quickly yet casually form a giant line for the buffet, Tallulah feels that she is being watched. She weaves between the bodies, away from the buffet line. The little ones are seated, eating with their families. Groups of teenagers sit near each other with empty plates. Tallulah keeps walking, meandering around the clusters of people and fire. She counts the fires again. Still eight. Some Indians are already sleeping near the fires, empty plates scattered around their hands and feet. She sees the stars and again feels eyes from somewhere.

"Hey, Tallulah!" Spencer Donald lurks next to a large rock, surrounded by his group of boys.

"Hi, Spencer."

"Don't call me Spencer anymore."

"Why not?" she asks.

"I've changed my name."

"What would you like me to call you?"

"Wakantanka." Spencer nods his head, almost stoic.

"Of course," says Tallulah. She clears her throat, as if preparing to spit. She examines the boys hanging with the Athenian. Five of them, their smiles packed with innocence and mischief.

"Did you give him this name?"

No answer.

"Did you?" she demands. "Talk to me!"

"No," answers a boy in a white ribbon-shirt.

"He picked it himself," says a boy in a dark plaid shirt with snaps.

"Spencer." Tallulah turns her head, checks for feet, then spits. "You can't go around renaming yourself like that!"

"Why not?"

"Just because you read a book about Lakota religion at UGA does not give you the right to go around using Lakota words for everything!"

"That's not an answer," he says.

"Look, Spencer, you can't – I mean, did you just *decide* to give yourself the name of the Great Spirit? Divine mystery or whatever? That's what Wakan Tanka means in Lakota, right?" She doesn't wait long for an answer. "Don't you know how ridiculous that is?! Naming yourself after God! Don't you think you're offending the Great Mystery by taking on its name?!"

Spencer swallows. He's nervous, and it's obvious. Tallulah is suddenly upset with herself for being so harsh with him. Is she still spiteful about the extra credit? She wishes Carmen Davis was here to meet these Misfits.

"Look," she says. "It's just, don't, just – don't you think you should at least let someone else conduct your naming ceremony? Maybe they might even give you a Cherokee name. I mean, come on, right? Wakantanka?"

"These guys aren't offended," Spencer retorts, holding his blow gun out for Tallulah to examine. "See, they showed me how to make this."

"What do you plan on using that thing for?"

"I don't know. They've got some game where you shoot a dart through a rolling hoop."

"Okay."

"And if I see any wasichus, I'm a let 'em have it." Spencer caresses the tip of the gun and tries to show Tallulah his markings.

Tallulah sniffs quickly and exhales slowly, turning to step away. And then she feels him, feels him before she sees him. She sees the moon's reflection sleek along the bend of his weapon.

"You," Tallulah says. "I've been waiting to talk to you." Crossbow flung across his left shoulder, Fish shakes his head. Tallulah blinks twice and tries to catch his eyes, but he looks away. She asks about his crossbow, but no one answers. She asks if she can hold it, like Spencer, but Fish steps back, and his grip tightens.

"What's your name?" she asks.

He smiles, and the other boys giggle. "Right," she smirks. "Of course. Are you mute for everyone, or am I just special?"

Fish's eyes bend mischievously. With his right hand he points toward the smell, toward the green tablecloths. Then he points back upon himself, his hand hovering over his chest, and he slowly shakes his head. Again he points to the chafing dishes, to the tables covered with food, to the Chef.

"Okay, fine," she says, then nods at Spencer. "Try not to let him kill anyone."

One of the boys giggles, but another elbows him in the gut.

Tallulah leaves Spencer with the Misfit boys, feels them watching as she walks away. She knows she still looks good. At least she thinks so. Other people say so. Fire dances upon the heads of the masses, reflections loud and bright under the cool dark sky. The line for food is loud from a distance, but quiet up close. Tallulah is dead thirsty for words.

19

Tallulah smells chicken marsala as she approaches the chafing dishes. The smell is powerful, strong enough to bring a ramshackle army into an orderly queue. Subtle drumbeats pound into the rocky topsoil, then sift into the spacious night sky. Echoing hills pull syncopations from the pulse.

Tallulah walks alongside the buffet line. Some Misfits cast suspicious glances at her, but she insists she is not hungry, that she is not trying to cut in line. She scans the crowd, the edges of people's faces. As she closes upon the food, she notices something. A boy. Ish. The resemblance to his brother is unmistakable. But Ish's clothes are different, more culinary. And instead of a weapon in his hands, Ish holds a hand truck. Tallulah watches him wedge the wheel of the hand truck into a locked position. Three hot cases are stacked upon the hand truck. Three brown hot cases, just like the kind she remembers from the Mediterranean Café.

A teenage Misfit taps Tallulah's shoulder, says, "Hey, wait your turn!"

She realizes that she has walked ahead of nearly everyone in line.

"I'm sorry," she says. "I'm not in line. I'm not eating."

"You're not?"

"No. Excuse me, I'll move aside."

She steps into the shadows. The drums continue. With so many people in line, Tallulah wonders who's drumming. She wonders where the drummers are. The sound is dense. It could be a hundred people drumming at once, or it could be three people who really know how to use their echoes. Tallulah leans her head. She blinks. She opens wide. A rush of something familiar, something sleepy. But she knows she doesn't need to sleep – this is still the Trail of Tears, even if she's left the designated trail. The hungry masses fill their plates with food. The smell of the chicken marsala is strong.

Tallulah is well versed in the power of chicken marsala. Nine years ago Tallulah brought a catering delivery from the Mediterranean Café to the Classic Center. It was only a few blocks from the café, but the load was large, and it required a car. It was a two-person delivery, and Bushyhead went with her. She drove her boss's car, the backseat crammed with two big brown plastic hot cases. The hot cases were stuffed with the Mediterranean Café's signature items – falafels, shawarmas, rice pilaf, dolmathes, grilled vegetables, warm pitas, and chicken marsala. Despite the pungent smell of falafel and shawarma, the aroma of chicken marsala overpowered the other smells in the case.

Bushyhead disappeared after unloading the heavier items, but the chafing dishes weren't set up. Tallulah tried to do it on her own. She had ignited thousands of Sterno flames and set up hundreds of tables with chafing dishes. She didn't need Bushyhead's help. She didn't need anyone's help, and she thought she'd impress him by demonstrating this fact. Tallulah lit three Sternos without trouble, but then someone called her name, and she looked up.

It's the thing that always burns you or cuts you when you're working with food – looking up, without putting your hands down first. Tallulah looked up, looked around, searching for the person who'd called her name, but there was no one there.

The pain struck a half second after she realized what she was doing. She was lighting her fingers, not the Sterno.

She ran to the car, opened a cooler filled with bags of ice, and pushed her throbbing fingers right through the plastic into the ice. The fingers cooled, but they screamed from the singe. Bushyhead had slipped from sight. Tallulah assumed that she could not count on him to help take care of the Sterno situation. So she pulled her hand from the ice. She smiled as she returned to the catering table. No one inside remembered that she had just burned herself. Falafels in their mouths, they started asking her about the items in the hot case. Where's the chicken? Where's the bread and the shawarma? What happened to the rice pilaf that they ordered? And didn't they also order some cold food, some Greek salad and some tabouli? She smiled and promised quick results, but the throbbing nerves in her fingertips did not cooperate with the words on her tongue.

After she lit the second Sterno, Tallulah grabbed the rim of the chicken marsala tray. Nerve cells flared as she tried to balance the tray in her arms. It slipped. She saw it all in slow motion – the chicken marsala spilling over her hands, onto the floor, into the foyer of the Classic Center. The hot boxes worked; the juice was hot. She screamed and ran toward the door, thinking ice ice ice ice, and she ran smack into John Bushyhead as he turned the corner outside the door. She laughed and screamed. Bushyhead nearly cried when he saw her hand.

Now whenever Tallulah drives past the Classic Center – the proud neoclassical construction on the east edge of downtown Athens – all she can see is chicken marsala sauce spilling from the aluminum container, chicken marsala sauce engulfing everything, saturating her hands, dancing upon the floor, swallowing up all the space it can.

Later Bushyhead bought milkshakes and told her not to blame

herself. The cooks at the Mediterranean Café always make leaky sheet pans, he said.

"I don't need to blame them," she insisted. "I burned my hand perfectly fine by myself."

"Accidents happen. Shit, I should've been there."

"No argument here."

"What a total buzzkill, seeing your girlfriend's hand all shot like that."

"Buzzkill? Girlfriend? Interesting word choice, John." At this point in their lives, they had slept together several times, and the kitchen staff at the Mediterranean Café had plenty of words to describe them. But Tallulah Wilson and John Bushyhead Smith had agreed to avoid the terms "boyfriend" and "girlfriend," even though Tallulah suspected that he called her his girlfriend when she wasn't around.

"I love you, baby," he said. "It just slipped out."

"You should have asked me if I liked milkshakes before you bought me one."

"Oops." Bushyhead looked puzzled as he confronted his assumptions. "If you don't want it, I'll drink it for you."

"I want a drink drink," she said. They gave their milkshakes to homeless people lying in a doorway near a parking space on Jackson Street. They fled to a punk rock bar on College Avenue. She does not remember much of what happened after they entered the bar that night, only that she woke up naked next to John Bushyhead, and they both had raging headaches.

Tallulah sees the top of Chef's hat and wonders once again if she is truly the center of her own universe. How else could all the symbols be so familiar, so full of personal relevance? Her ego surges whenever it feels most threatened, a trait that she has often resented. Yet she wonders – is it all about me? Do I do this to everyone? Poor girl. She wonders if the game could understand her better than humans do. She searches for a way to squeeze between the tables, but she can't find a gap large enough for her hips. She shouts in the general direction of the Chef's hat.

"Chef?" she calls. No recognition. She calls again, louder this time, "Chef? Hey, Chef!"

"Hey, stranger, I thought you weren't hungry," barks one of the young men in the line next to her.

"The line starts back there!" shouts someone else. More Misfits chime in, ridiculing Tallulah for being a line jumper. She feels unusually ostracized. Pressure surges between her eyes. She begins to lose balance.

Then Ish climbs over the tables. He grabs Tallulah's hand. "This way," he says and leads her through a gap between the tables that she could not see before. They squeeze through easily.

"That's a bunch of hungry people you've got there," says Tallulah. She feels instantly stupid for making such an obvious comment. Why am I always making comments about the most obvious things? she wonders.

"Don't take it personally," said Ish. "Our people can get ornery when they're hungry."

"Who doesn't?" she says. "But I'm curious about something."

"Okay."

"Why do they need to eat?"

"They get angry when they don't eat on time," says Ish. "Low blood sugar."

"You have blood sugar?"

The boy stopped, bent his head inward at her, and smiled a lopsided grin. "You're Tallulah, right? I mean, you are. Right?"

"I am. And you are?"

"Call me Ish."

"Ish?"

"Yes?"

"I'm sorry, but did you just say, 'Call me Ish'?"

He laughs. "I know, I can't resist. You don't have to call me anything that makes you uncomfortable. I mean, it's great to finally meet you. I've always heard about you, but I thought I'd never meet you."

"No problem, Ish."

Tallulah wonders what he means by "always." She wants to know what they know about her and how they know it. The boy is more coherent than the baseball-capped elders. But why should she trust him? Maybe he works for Homeland Security. Maybe they all work for Homeland Security. Maybe Tallulah is the only person she knows who doesn't work for Homeland Security. Hell, maybe she *is* working for Homeland Security and doesn't even realize it!

"Can you take me to the Chef?" she says. She instantly hears the sharp sizzle of something raw tossed into a hot skillet. Maybe it's onions and olive oil. She listens, she smells. The skillet is close, maybe a few meters to her left. Then – she turns, and there he is.

"Bring her in, kid," he says. Ish takes Tallulah's hand and leads her into the portable kitchen. The setup is impressive. Four hot cases, all presumably filled with hot food. Two grills. One grill that looks like a propane unit but has no gas tank. Tallulah can't see or smell any charcoal either. No gas, no coal – just fire. And another grill, a flat-faced griddle. Tallulah questions their power sources.

Two stainless steel prep tables stand between the grills and the buffet tables. Sunlight dances on their bright surface. Sharp knives, giant spoons, and plastic spatulas dangle on the right ledge of each table. Sturdy-looking tubs and buckets mine the ground around the tables. A large blue cooler lies near the Chef's feet. Is this their only cooler? she wonders. How could one cooler possibly contain all the cold materials these Misfits need?

"Are you the Chef?" she asks. The Chef smiles, and Tallulah feels foolish. Of course he's the Chef. He's the only one within a thousand miles who looks like a Chef. His white hat towers. "Right, of course you're the Chef."

"And you're Tallulah," he replies. "Eat first. Questions later."

"I'm not hungry," she says. Onions, garlic, and fresh ground ginger sauté in the pan. Tallulah wants to ask him where he comes from, but the ginger's scent is strong. What is it doing here? she wonders. Fifty questions collide inside Tallulah's head, and she forgets which one she wants to ask first.

"You're lying," says Chef.

"How do you know?" she demands.

"I know when people lie to me," he says. "It's an unfortunate power that I have. I can't help it."

"Really," she insists. "Then you know I'm not really hungry."

"Then I wish you were lying," he says.

"Why?"

"Because you're not going to get very far in life without eating anything or without lying." He throws some chopped celery and red bell peppers into the singing skillet.

"Well." She straightens her spine. "What makes you think I'm not lying?"

"I think you really haven't eaten anything." He tilts his eyes while stirring the vegetables. "And I think you're hungry." Snap peas and corn kernels leap into the skillet.

“Look at me,” Tallulah says. “You think I don’t eat anything?”

Ish giggles but quickly stops. He washes long-grain wild rice, the dark kind that grows in the Northern lake country.

“How should I know?” Chef replies. “I haven’t seen you eat anything. You eat prawns, right?”

“What?”

“Prawns. The shellfish. You eat them, right?”

“Yes.”

The Chef pulls a handful of medium-sized prawns from the large blue cooler. They are untrimmed. The eyes are still attached. Chef cleans, deveins, and butterflies the prawns before Tallulah even notices his small paring knife. He rolls them in some kind of batter and throws them in the skillet. They sing like they’re still alive.

“Ish,” he calls, and the boy looks up. “Watch the line. We’re low on squash soup and bean dip.” He turns to Tallulah and says, “They go crazy over the bean dip.”

Ish brings a bowl of freshly steamed wild rice and hands it to Tallulah.

“That was fast,” she says. Ish grins, nods, and walks toward the line.

“Get your brother to help you with that,” says Chef. Ish blows on something, a small whistle maybe. Within seconds the boy with the crossbow appears. The two boys clear empty trays from the buffet line, pull new trays from the hot cases, and answer special requests from a few Misfits with specific dietary restrictions.

“Here,” says Chef, handing Tallulah a bowl of shrimp stir-fry over wild rice. “Eat. Please.”

The food smells delicious. Chef hands her a fork before she realizes that she needs one.

She wonders if the boys are twins. Of course they are, she thinks. How could they not be? It's all part of the mythology. The stir-fry is outstanding, and she eats swiftly. She will have to experiment with corn kernels the next time she cooks this dish for herself. The corn blends sweetly with the wild rice. Tallulah slowly chews the last bite and wonders about the boys' mother. She imagines what their mother looks like, but then she notices the Chef working with serious quantities of cream. The sight of so much cream makes her stomach rumble.

"What is that?" she asks, prying bits of corn from the spaces between her teeth.

"Cream sauce," answers Chef.

"Why are you making cream sauce?"

"Why wouldn't I?"

"You must have lactose intolerance, no?"

"Your expectations deceive you," he says.

"But you've got all these Indians, all these people reared on corn and beans and squash, and you're making the most lactose-heavy dish imaginable?"

"They love the cream sauce."

"Why?"

"How was your food?" he asks.

"Excellent." She nods. "It was excellent."

"Good." He exhales loudly and shakes his head slowly. "Sometimes I could kill for lactose intolerance. But that's beside the point. What are you going to tell Homeland Security?"

"That's what I've been asking myself this whole time," she answers.

"So what's on your tongue?"

"That cream sauce is making me sick."

"Can't have that," he says, and he pulls two hand-rolled cigarettes from a pocket in his jacket. "You want?"

Tallulah immediately grabs the cigarette and plants it between her lips. Chef holds a flame in his hand. Tallulah sucks the fire into the tobacco. Chef reaches into the cooler and pulls out a big green bottle of mineral water. The water fizzes over ice. Tallulah wants to know about the source of the water, but she doesn't bother to ask when Chef offers her a glass.

"Wado," she says. "So what do you know about Homeland Security?" Sweet tobacco smokes her mouth and throat; bubbly water coaxes a burp; the pressure drops between her eyes, decompressing from nose to neck.

"Tla unh." The Chef lights a smoke for himself. "Not this again."

"Not what again?"

"Look, you've got some decisions to make, and you need to make them soon." Chef winces, holding the smoke inside a few seconds too long, then exhaling. "This is already done. It's written. It's already over and done with, get it?"

Tallulah listens and smokes, thinking about what "over and done with" means to this character who knows so much more about her than she does about him. But then she hears guitars. Drums, shakers, and guitars. Electric guitars. Not the sort of thing she expects to hear.

"What's that sound?" Tallulah cups her to her ear, as if the tones were distant.

"Most of them are finished eating," Chef says. Tallulah notices stacks of plastic tableware – plates, bowls, forks, and spoons – piled around the buffet line. These Misfits are fast eaters.

"You have guitars?" she asks.

"You too, huh?"

"Me too, what?"

"You people and your questions about the guitars. What do you think we are?"

"I'm still not sure yet."

"Well, you better decide something soon." Chef slows his stirring of the cream sauce. "This is already over and done with."

Tallulah wonders why he would repeat that phrase verbatim. She watches him position a small empty tub near his feet. He balances the bucket of cream sauce on the table, then tilts it toward himself until the sauce pours slow and steady into the tub. Cream sauce and inertia – a tiny white waterfall. Or rather, creamfall. Tallulah has witnessed this technique in several kitchens, and though she has never done it herself, she understands the physics. However, this Chef pours his cream sauce from the table with a curve, an arc, a precision drip. Tallulah thinks for a second that there must be magic in the cream sauce, magic in the man who made it. This man created all this beautiful food; she wonders if he created the entire Misfit collective.

"I don't understand," she says. "I need to know more."

"About what?" he asks.

"This place," she says. "This place, I don't understand. We're in North Carolina, but I can see other tour groups when we move?"

"You see them now?" he asks, but Tallulah hears the music and begins to drift. Chef speaks sharply: "S'yo, do you see them now?"

"What? No. Earlier. When we were traveling."

"Ah, yes," he says. "I remember."

"How could you remember?" she replies. "You weren't with us."

"Well, I had to get here somehow, didn't I?"

"Did you?" asks Tallulah.

"Of course, I did," he answers, then points at Ish. "Him too."

"So," she asks, "these two boys are your twins, and you came from the same place with one, but not the other?"

"That's at least three different questions," he says. He shoots an arm into the air. "Hey, Rosenberg!" he shouts to the horizon.

The Rosenbergs have awakened. They walk slowly. Tallulah wonders what Spencer is doing with his blowgun. "They're twins?" she asks.

"What does it look like?" Chef replies.

"Where's their mother?"

"They're stuck with me."

"You're their father?"

"They're my apprentices."

"So you're not their father?"

"I never said that." Chef wipes down a knife with a small towel. Tallulah cringes, watching Chef's fingers grip the blade, gliding the towel down the knife with his finger bare. She has sliced herself several times cleaning knives that way. Her cheeks swell. Nerve ends in her finger flare.

"Has he answered your questions?" Irma's voice is unmistakable.

"Of course he has," answers Chef. "Good to see you, Rosenberg."

"You too, I think," says Irma. "Whatever you're cooking smells delicious."

"Irma!" Tallulah says, pasting on her professional smile. "Rachel, Michael, how are you folks holding out?"

"All right," answers Rachel.

"How are *you*?" asks Michael. "This is new for you too, yeah?"

"Yes. Yes, it's new." Tallulah looks deep into their faces. "Have you eaten yet?"

Chef asks if Irma's grandchildren are hungry. They are. The

herring is pickled, sliced, and arranged on a plate in curious patterns. Where the fish came from, Tallulah cannot determine. The Chef is obviously well supplied.

"This is really good," says Rachel, nibbling chicken satay from a stick. Michael slurps on something that looks like korma but smells like vindaloo. He slurps again, then mixes the curry with wild rice.

"Irma, I'm curious," says Tallulah. "How did you meet the Chef here?"

Irma swallows. "I told you, honey, they took me to his kitchen. Then the only other old woman disappeared inside the refrigerator, so he gave me an apron and told me to start working."

"And look," says Chef, "you're still here." He seems proud of this fact.

Tallulah turns and faces the Chef directly, but she can't see his eyes, "Right, and I'm sorry, but you never told me where you're from."

"Correct," says Chef.

"Can you tell me now?"

"It's a very strange place," says Irma.

"You're groping for answers, Wilson," says Chef. "But you haven't answered my question."

"What?"

"What will you tell them?"

"I'm not sure yet."

"Well, sort it out," he says, wiping his hands on a side towel.

"How can I sort it out," she insists, "if I don't know what to say about you people?"

"Improvise," he replies.

Chef sets a basket of hot, moist towelettes on a nearby rock. "Let's just say we've been holed-up on the island for way too long."

The Rosenbergs continue to eat. They eat slowly, quietly. Tallulah wonders why the Chef used the term "holed-up." Why does he speak my language? All employees at the TREPP call it holing-up when someone holes-up. Maybe Chef has worked for the TREPP since the beginning. Maybe he *is* Homeland Security. But if he is, why does he seem so concerned about Tallulah's inevitable debriefing? She wonders about this island they've been holed-up on.

"Why are you going to North Carolina?" Tallulah asks.

"And here we are," says Chef, "having a nice quiet meal." The drums keep pulsing, and the guitars grow gradually louder. Tallulah watches the Rosenbergs eat.

"It's just," Tallulah stutters, "it's just – I've never gone to North Carolina on the job. And I know there are programs for runaways, for Tsali and his bunch, and sometimes the runaway tourists wind up with them. But I've never imagined you." She looks directly at the Chef but cannot see his eyes. "I never imagined this group of people even existed."

"Could be something wrong with your imagination," says Chef.

"Or," Tallulah insists, "it could be that I'm less informed than I thought I was." The Rosenbergs keep eating. "Perhaps deliberately underinformed," Tallulah continues. Michael opens his mouth as if to speak, but decides against it and slurps another mouthful from his bowl. Rachel gnaws on the chicken sticks and licks her fingers.

"Why are you going to North Carolina?" Tallulah asks again.

"Why are you?" asks Chef.

Tallulah thinks. There are several answers that could work, none of which would be lies, but she needs something better than biography. "I'm afraid of what will happen if I don't," she answers.

“Ah, good,” says Chef. “I like that.”

“You like fear?” she asks.

“Not what I meant.”

The Chef pulls a pouch of tobacco and a packet of rolling papers from his jacket. Tallulah stares at his chef’s jacket, and she remembers the water beetle. She touches it, even though it has not buzzed. Chef rolls seven cigarettes. The music ensnares Tallulah. The Rosenbergs finish their food.

Some of the Misfits continue to sing and dance, but most of them have fallen asleep in strange positions. The twin boys are almost finished clearing the buffet tables. Ish blows out the last Sterno. Fish wipes down the insides of the chafing dishes. Ish rolls tablecloths and gathers utensils. Fish seals up the uneaten food.

“Hey,” says Rachel Rosenberg, “how long have we been inside this thing anyways?”

“As in, here inside the ride?” Tallulah asks.

“Yeah,” says Rachel. “How long have we been inside, in real time?”

“I’m not absolutely sure,” answers Tallulah. “But I believe we’ve been inside for about forty-five minutes, maybe an hour.”

“How long do we get with the Old Medicine Man?” asks Michael.

“Back onto Old Medicine?” Tallulah asks.

“What, he’s not on the menu anymore?” Michael responds.

“We still get to see him, don’t we?” Rachel asks.

Tallulah lifts her shoulders. The dialogue spews out like a snake from a can. “Everyone will have an opportunity to visit the Old Medicine Man,” she confirms. “The time you spend with him is variable, but it will be long enough.”

Chef grunts and distributes the tobacco.

"The fish was delicious," says Irma. "And I haven't smoked in fifty years. Rachel, you shouldn't either."

"But this isn't real, Grandma."

"Tell that to your Misfits here. It's all very real to them." Irma stands, thanks the Chef, and walks away before he lights up. Chef offers a smoke to Rachel and Michael, and both accept. Again Chef holds a small flame in his palm. Rachel, Michael, and Tallulah light their smokes in Chef's hands. The twin boys light their own smokes.

They sit, smoking, saying nothing. The silence is longer than Tallulah is used to. It's her job, after all, to offer observations or historical trivia to her tourists whenever an extended silence falls upon a group. But she has little to say, beyond the questions the Chef continues to evade. Constellations slowly twirl above. The Londoners, suddenly dizzy, decide to leave. Michael stands first, then offers a hand to Rachel.

"All that traveling." Michael stretches, breathing loudly. "I'm knackered."

"Yeah, I don't feel so limber anymore," says Rachel.

They say their goodnights and walk away, toward where Irma lies.

"So," asks Tallulah, snubbing her cherry into a rock, "do you think she's really some kind of omen?"

"Who?" Chef answers.

"Why are you so evasive?"

"Evasive?" he asks.

"Irma," declares Tallulah. "She's not really an omen, is she?"

"Irma?"

Tallulah straightens her spine. "What's this I hear about some prophecy and an ice woman?"

"Kid stuff," says Chef. "Totally fabricated."

"Why?" Tallulah asks. The twin boys shake. Tallulah is not sure if they giggle or shiver.

"Have you been listening to me?" asks Chef. His tone is demanding. "Here." He reaches to touch her arm. "Come on. Follow me."

Chef walks away from the tables. Tallulah follows, a few steps behind. He stops in front of a rock that is taller than Tallulah. Chef touches the rock with his hand. A door opens.

"The rock has a door?" Tallulah asks, but no one responds. Inside the rock she sees pantry shelves stuffed with linens and big brown bags. Tallulah spots tablecloths and fancy napkins. She sees large bags of sugar and flour. She even notices a pastry bag. Chef reaches in and grabs a bag of flour. It's a rather large bag, but he hoists it to the ground with ease. It seems to bounce as it lands.

"This is better than salt," he says.

"What?"

"Save yourself," he says. "Go to sleep tonight. And don't say anything about me and the boys when you talk to Homeland Security tomorrow."

"Why not?"

"Say whatever you want about the others, the guys with the hats, the young people, the guys who mutilate themselves, the girls with the rape fantasies, their outfits, their weapons, their dances" – he pauses and leans in close – "their guitars, whatever. Don't lie, just omit what you need to."

"Why do I need to omit you?"

"If I tell you, you won't be able to lie. Here, this is better than salt or sand."

"But I still don't understand," she says.

"You're tired," he says.

“I am not,” she objects.

“Liar! You’re tired, and I know it.”

“I don’t need to sleep.”

“So you say. But that doesn’t necessarily mean you’re not tired.”

“I need to see what happens.”

“You need to close your eyes.”

Tallulah looks up to the sky. She feels lumps in her throat and on her back. The flour bag is not as comfortable as she hoped, so she sits down on the ground.

She looks for the Chef, but he is gone. Vanished. The buffet tables – gone. The hot boxes – gone. Everything else is asleep or making sleepy music. Tallulah craves more tobacco. She knows the only way not to smoke is to sleep it off. She makes herself yawn. Clouds gather quickly, then disperse. She hates improvising, especially when she isn’t planning on it. She remembers the time she forgot the words to her song, that time she was on stage in the coffee shop on Clayton Street and the words left her naked. The tones drone on.

• • •

Sunrise comes without warning. Tallulah isn’t sure if she has slept or not. The masses stand and stretch, but Tallulah’s eyes hang heavy. She smells coffee, which only makes her want to smoke again, but the cravings are less intense. Drums beat. Flutes blow. Pans sizzle, and eggshells crack. Potatoes, peppers, olives. Bacon. Toast. She can hear the juices pour.

Tallulah worries about Spencer. What if he woke up wanting to be Sitting Bull for a day? He was so proud of his blowgun. Tallulah considers the fact that none of her previous tourists have ever built a blowgun. Sure, lots of them felt the urge to use weapons. Who doesn’t want to toss a tomahawk on the Trail of

Tears? But none of Taullulah's pervious tourists had ever built a blowgun on their own. *Did* Spencer build it himself? she wonders. Did he carve it hollow and finish it with glaze? Or did the Wild Boy simply give it to him, and Spencer claimed it as his own creation?

The bodies are fuzzy. Tallulah rubs her eyes, but rubbing only makes the focus worse.

She smells rain in the distance.

Even with her allergies Tallulah can smell rain well before it lands. As it grows closer, she expects to hear it, but she hears nothing. Her eyelids droop, sag, begin to stick together. She thinks she hears the Rosenbergs, but the voices blur. Tallulah's worlds began to slip down and away, dark and calm, peaceful.

But then – a crack.

Another crack.

A splash, and a strong pull.

Tallulah's eyes shoot open. She moves slowly, but she can see clearly.

The mountain moves. Or does it? Something rattles deep within the earth. It causes ripples on the crust.

Tallulah searches for the Rosenbergs. The Misfits have formed a dense line at the buffet tables. Tallulah hears music. Then her head dips backward, and she almost slips into sleep. Her head jerks upright, and her eyes snap open. She feels like a high school student, sitting in the back of the algebra classroom after lunch. She shakes her head and rubs her face, nibbles delicately on the chew spots in her cheek. She exhales slowly. Her head bobs backward again, and she sleeps for a split second before snapping upright.

She smells the water. Maybe it isn't rain, she thinks. She stands, raises her head, looks around. The sun rises fast. Tallulah shields her eyes her with hands. She looks into the distance, hears something splashing. She feels mist on her neck, sprinkling her shoulders and upper back.

The Misfits gobble their breakfasts and do not seem to notice anything unusual. The Chef and his twins break down their portable kitchen and vacuum-seal the uneaten portions.

"Hey!" Tallulah shouts, but her voice is raspy and low. The Chef looks at her. His sunglasses are loud.

"What did I tell you?" he shouts back.

She clears her throat and swallows. "What's happening?" Her voice is louder and more distinct. "Something's happening!"

A couple of Misfits standing near the buffet tables hear her. They stop eating and turn their heads. Maybe they see something that Tallulah cannot. They put down their plates and shout something unintelligible.

The drums stop.

Conversations drop.

Tallulah hears moving water and feels the rumble grow closer.

Indians Hat calls for Irma. The other elders put down their morning tea and rise to their feet. The masses begin to buzz. Static skies swoop down. The funnel cloud begins to form again.

Tallulah runs to the Chef and grabs his arm. "For real, what's happening?"

"Did you listen to anything I told you?" His knives are washed. Now he dries them, two at a time, and tucks them into the appropriate pockets of his knife bag.

"I listened to everything, but you didn't tell me anything specific," she says. The earth rumbles.

"Last night I gave you a fifty-pound bag of flour," Chef answers.

"Fifty pounds?"

"That big flour bag is much better than a comparatively sized bag of salt, and it's definitely better than a sandbag!"

"Why?"

"Please, kid – go sit down on it, hold on tight, and you'll get what you want."

"But – "

"Now!" he snaps. "Go now!"

She wishes he would take off his sunglasses. He returns to his knives. The funnel has nearly formed. The static forms rings around the collective. Unfortunately for the Misfits, double doorways don't always open on command, even when you've got the omen on hand.

Tallulah sees water creeping over the west edge of the mountaintop. Gravity welling up against itself, a river changing course to drink the mountain. The change happens fast. She runs toward the fifty-pound flour bag and sits down, clutching tight. She wonders how a big paper bag is supposed to resist a river.

The Misfits abruptly start screaming about the Uktena. Tallulah knows the stories. The Uktena, the giant mythical horned monster snake. Tallulah hears Indians Hat calling for Irma as his voice is submerged into the multitude.

"Nantahela!" shouts an Indian.

"Nantahela!" shouts another.

"Uktena!" shouts another Indian.

"Nantahela!"

"Uktena!"

"Nantahela!"

"Uktena!"

Tallulah opens her eyes. The mountain appears to be sliding off itself.

She closes her eyes again, shuts them tight, unsure of what it is that she doesn't want to see. She wonders if the Nantahela

River has suddenly changed course on them. The Hiawassee sure looked different yesterday. Maybe these Misfits and their doorways are causing the rivers to change. She squints, looking for the Chef and his twins. They are gone, as is all their kitchen gear. The water nears. Tallulah breathes deep and holds it in, closing her eyes as the water floods her face. What a horrible shift, she thinks. Will this ride ever end?

She clings tightly to the flour bag, but her head dips back. She sleeps.

She must have slept, for there is no other logical explanation. She was sleeping, dreaming lucid. The river was gone. Everyone and everything else was gone.

Just Tallulah, falling.

She lands in a river. The water is murky, but Tallulah can see. Bodies, presumably drowned ones, seem to float all around. Her head bobs again, and she blacks out.

• • •

When she woke, she was lying face-up inside a cave. She coughed and rubbed her head. Something big was near, breathing.

She rolled herself around, and there it was. The bear.

20

The black bear looked uncomfortable as it sat Indian-style, rocking back and forth. Tallulah's frame was beaten. Spasms pulsed throughout her hips and lower back. She sat up and rubbed her head. Then she locked eyes with the bear.

The cave was dark, but the bear wanted to be seen. Tallulah dug her fingers in the ground beneath her feet. The dirt felt as real as anything else inside the Trail of Tears, but the bear's eyes were large and crisp. It was male.

"Hi."

No response.

"Osiyo?"

Still the bear was speechless. Tallulah tried nearly all the Cherokee phrases she knew, but the language barrier wasn't the problem. The bear just sat there, rocking awkwardly and fiddling with his toes. Tallulah had memorized the plots of several traditional bear stories, but this scene didn't fit into those models. Maybe this bear was engineered by Homeland Security? Did that mean that Homeland Security was in her dreams the night before? As paranoid as Tallulah knew she could be, she refused to believe that Homeland Security had colonized her dreams. She wanted to believe that this bear was truly her father's spirit.

As such, Tallulah was not going to let this dream end in silence. She wanted to hear her father's voice. Tallulah had never been on a vision quest. Some of her customers, Europeans especially, want to know about Tallulah's vision questing. She must have let them down something terrible. Like anyone who enjoys good oxygen, Tallulah likes the outdoors, but she preferred to commune with nature in a tent, with sleeping bags and a cooler. What did she have to fast for? Perhaps the Chef's food was some kind of test, to see if she could fast in the face of food that didn't even exist. She had failed the test! She ate the Chef's food, and now this black bear had nothing to say to her.

"My brother should be here," she said. The bear cocked its head, slightly, but continued rocking.

Tallulah pictured her brother's scars. Back before he became DJ Tomahawk, Alan Wilson pierced himself at a Sun Dance. It changed him. Helped him clean himself up, actually. Tallulah was impressed, and even a bit envious, but she didn't want to pierce herself like that. She was thankful that traditional women did not suspend themselves during Sun Dances, but she always wanted a vision.

"So are you my father's spirit, or what?" She nearly gagged on the words as they left her mouth. The words felt so contrived. But the situation didn't. She entertained the possibility that the situation was only as much of a cliché as she let it be.

Still, the bear was silent.

Still, Tallulah waited.

Still, nothing.

She looked around the cave. The dark lines in the wall, the turns in the ceiling, the surface beneath her feet. It seemed less than fake.

It was a giant letdown. Meditation was infinitely better. What was so wrong with Tallulah that she couldn't even experience a vision properly? She heard a condescending tone in her brother's voice, telling her what she should have done differently, how she should have coaxed a conversation from the spirit of her dead father, how if she did the right things this giant black bear invading her dreams and her workplace would end his silence.

"What do you mean voices? What voices am I taking too seriously?"

The bear itched his neck, then fiddled with his toes again. He grunted, sniffed, and wiped his nose. Tallulah realized that she was the only person saying anything.

"My voices? My voice? Am I the cause of my own worst problems? Do I give myself nightmares? Look I need some help, okay! If you're not going to help me, then what the hell are you doing here in the first place?"

The bear inhaled and raised his head as if to speak, but he swallowed his words before uttering. Tallulah waited for the magic words like a fire waits for oxygen, but nothing came.

"Well I pretty much suck," she declared. "Don't I?" She stood erect and held her hands out to the dreamy canopy of sturdy branches and falling leaves. "This is all bullshit, and I can't even do this right."

She held her head and began to pace. She paced lines at first, then circles. The bear watched her closely, his head jerking as his eyes followed her.

"Is that what you've come to tell me? That I suck!! That I'm a poseur and a hack, a tourist bullshit artist who sold her fucking soul to Coca-Cola for my air-conditioning, who's so fucked up she can't even have a real vision? I can't even have a fucking vision in a computer game filled with big fucking visions. Oh, God!"

Tallulah kicked the strong soft earth with her feet. She yelled and stomped and kicked the ground, like she was trying to break her heel. She wanted to hurt. She eyed the ground for sticks or sharp edges, but the floor was empty. The bear continued rocking back and forth unsteadily. Tallulah approached, centered on the bear's face, and stared deep into its eyes. It looked away, bending its face into its chest.

"You've got absolutely nothing to fucking say to me now?"

The bear did not look up.

"Great. What's this place capable of, anyway? I mean, what other fantasies could I live out? I might as well give it a go. Just jump off a building and get it over with, right? Or maybe I'll get Shakespearean and drown myself. Or maybe I'll just drink until I drive off a stupid fucking mountain road like you? Fucking asshole!"

Tallulah turned around to walk away, but a terrible pain shot through her stomach. It was unlike the typical jolts of nausea she lived with daily. No. This was something bigger. Maybe it was a stomach parasite that suddenly doubled in size. Maybe it was an organ detaching. Maybe she was finally about to die. She pictured her tourists with the Old Medicine Man. Maybe she was about to hole-up.

She creaked her head around and eyed the bear, its face still tucked into its chest fur. It seemed embarrassed. Tallulah's stomach dropped again. Before she could find the words to explain why, she began to pity the bear. It was more helpless than she was. It could not hurt her if it tried. As a bear, it was completely ineffective. Unless it was spying on her for Homeland Security. Maybe her recurring dreams were actually planted inside her head by Homeland Security. No, she was being paranoid again. How could Homeland Security possibly know what her father sounded like? She wished the bear would just speak already. And she wanted to hear something she did not expect to hear. She wanted the sky to fall flat down on her if it could tell her something she didn't already know. She was desperate for a new metaphor.

She heard drops of water tapping somewhere close, and she turned to look for a body of water to stick her head into.

She found no water, but something magical happened. Tallulah's throat constricted and her nose began to plug. Her esophagus rippled and her cheeks puffed. She thought to kick the ground some more, but her foot did not respond. She thought she was standing but realized she was flat on her behind. Her nose flared. She wondered how long she had been sitting here, sitting by herself with a mute and incompetent black bear. She stood. Her knees shook. She squeezed the bridge of her nose tightly, like she was trying to hold back a sneeze at the symphony. She held her breath and felt her nose pulse. Her glands began to tremble, and her sinuses dilated with the inertia in her head.

Then, for the first time in four years, Tallulah Wilson cried inside the Trail of Tears.

The action was unmistakable – her tear ducts may have only been digital simulations, but the sensation was genuine. She fell to her knees and grabbed the back of her skull, pushing her face into the digital earth like someone trying to cover her head during an earthquake or tornado. She could no longer see the bear in any corner of her eyes.

It began as a soft whine, then grew to a high-pitched whimper. She sounded like Joey begging to go for a car ride, which is exactly how John Bushyhead sounded when he cried. He cried all the time. Bushyhead cried during sappy movies. He cried in the middle of day-hikes and art museums and basketball games. He burst into tears without warning while reading a good book. John Bushyhead Smith never read a book by Sherman Alexie that didn't make him cry at least once every ten pages. John Bushyhead was an Anglo-Cuban Cherokee who walked around Athens with an expression that was too cool for school and too mean to mess with, but barely beneath the surface lurked a big sappy chum. Tallulah often caught him crying, but he had only seen her cry once, and that was just a few brief tears.

Tallulah likes it when Bushyhead cries, though she teases him for sounding like her dog. And now here she was, pushing her face into the virtual earth, sounding like Joey the mutt as she tried to hold back the inevitable. She laughed at her own sounds, at her gargling rumble of dripping mucus and gasping breath, and the laughter opened another floodgate inside her face.

Then the bear spoke. It wasn't a specific word. It was a grunt, but it was a clear sound. It was her father's grunt.

The sound of Joe Wilson's voice pushed the water through Tallulah's windows. Her nose quickly filled with phlegm and her tear ducts rolled wide open. She cried and cried and cried and cried. She howled, so loud it hurt her lungs. She could feel something. She could still hurt. She felt the pressure drop. It was an effective howl.

"I'm sorry," she blurted. Another tear gate ruptured beneath the pressure. "I'm so sorry, Dad, I'm so sorry," her voice trailing to a heavy wail, her body heaving to purge the deeply bottled guilt. The water flowed heavy from her eyes and nose.

Tallulah cried until her head dried up. She quit jerking her head around. She slowed, dramatically. She turned and curled, tightly, into a fetal position. She felt the bear's gentle hands on her shoulder, brushing her mangled hair away from her exhausted cheeks. Tallulah didn't look the bear in the eyes, but she didn't resist when he reached out his hairy arms around her curled body and lifted her into the air.

The bear raised her gently toward his chest, holding her softly, hugging her and rocking her like a baby. Grey sunlight parted the leafy canopy and pierced through pockets in the trees, warming their bodies. Tallulah kept her knees and legs firmly clenched into a fetal position, but she opened her arms and returned the bear's hug. The longer she held him, the more tightly she squeezed.

She moved to speak, but her eyes and throat welled up before the words formed. She buried her head into his soft and sturdy chest, tears fusing with fur and blending together until the texture reminded her of a floormat on a wet afternoon. Tallulah wanted this moment to last forever.

"Don't blame yourself," he said.

"Don't blame yourself, either," Tallulah said through heaving sniffles, her snot glomming onto his fur.

She wanted to say she wouldn't blame him for his lies. That she didn't want to blame him for running away from his parents. That she didn't want to blame him for running away from her. She wanted everything to absolve and resolve in this moment.

"I love you," said the bear, "I love you so much. That's why you have to let me go."

Tallulah recognized the cliché, but it was just the cliché she needed.

Her grip loosened, and she looked into the bear's eyes. But the bear closed his eyes before Tallulah could really see them. He told her again that he loved her, and that if she loved him back, she would let him go.

Tallulah opened her arms right then. She didn't want to, but she did. She opened her arms, and the bear opened his.

Tallulah fell like a feather in a vacuum. She froze, her body suspended in the digital air, falling so slowly that she couldn't feel herself move. She watched the bear turn and stand down, dropping his arms upon the ground, running on all fours toward the darkening trees. He turned and took one last look before he walked into the vague horizon.

Tallulah warmed watching him walk away. Her whole body pulsed with warmth, but she quickly chilled when she felt the wet ground bleeding through her pants.

Cold cold water trickled down her neck and shoulders. She stood shaky and stepped backward, banging her head against something hard. Running her fingers behind her, she touched a jagged wall of the cave. Maybe she never left the cave. Maybe her father never came, and she simply imagined everything that she wanted to see. Maybe. She rubbed her puffy eyes and shook her throbbing head. While turning to walk back into the world, her forehead struck something hard. She stumbled backward and clonked her elbow. Her feet lost traction and sank into something less than solid. Her hips spun and her face landed on cold, wet dirt. The ground plugged her head and she stopped remembering to breathe.

• • •

When Tallulah woke, she was lying facedown on the edge of an angry river. The water beetle in her pocket rumbled. She rolled herself over and stared upward at the thick swirling clouds. The beetle buzzed and demanded her attention. The techies were calling. She wondered how long the beetle had been buzzing. She hadn't hurt like this since she simultaneously broke her leg and her nose in an ambitious soccer move ten years ago. She heard the faint sound of clanking, grinding metals. Her chest ached, as if she had been holding her breath for minutes. She was actually surprised by the scratchless ease with which she breathed. Still, her entire body throbbed like she had just ridden the spin cycle inside a giant washing machine. Her eyes were clogged, her vision blurred and itchy. She tasted salt in her mouth and wondered where she was. She remembered the Misfits shouting about Uktena and Nantahela. The beetle stopped buzzing.

The sound of grinding metal grew more distinct. It moved a little closer with each breath. Knives, sharpening. She tried to lift herself, but she fell limp upon the riverbank. She tried again, and was able to hoist the bulk of her weight upon her elbows, propping herself up high enough to see four bodies through the watery blur. She shook her head and blinked fast. The water dried quickly. She could see, but her vision itched.

She saw the Johnson twins.

She saw Ish and Fish.

Fish had a knife bag rolled open on the ground. It did not look like the knife bag the Chef was carrying. Rather, the bag resembled the knife bag that the Mediterranean Café sent on catering missions. Fish had the large chef's knife in his right hand, and a knife sharpener in his left. He seemed to enjoy the sound of the metal-on-metal. Ish was reading a book. Tallulah tried to read the cover, but she was too far away. The Johnson twins sat next to Ish. They stared at Tallulah as she lurched upon the slippery banks.

"What are you going to tell them, when they call again?" asked Ish.

"Why do you care?" she replied. Her eyes stung and her voice was scratchy, but for some reason her throat wasn't sore. Her beetle began to buzz again. Everyone eyed Tallulah's vibrating pocket. Tallulah looked down and realized her breasts were even larger than their typical digital enhancements. Whose idea was this, she wondered. She didn't want to be rounder. She suspected the twins had done this to her. Maybe she was seeing things the way they did.

Tallulah saw tatters on one of the girl's dresses and felt a surge of adrenaline.

"If either of you touched those girls, I'll kick your asses myself."

"Come on," said Ish, "They're eight years old." He nodded at his twin, "I mean, he's fucked up and all, but he's not fucked up enough to fuck an eight-year-old." Ish grinned, but his smile seemed less genuine than it was the night before.

"What about his mother?" Tallulah asked.

No one answered. Nothing seemed to move except the river and Fish's knives. Tallulah wasn't even sure if their mouths moved when they spoke. She wondered if the girls needed to pee. The water beetle's buzzing grew belligerent.

"What are you doing with that knife?"

"What does it look like?" Fish replied.

"Why are you sharpening it?"

"Would you rather I let it go dull?"

"Where is your father?" asked Tallulah. The beetle in her pocket continued to grow louder.

"Where is *your* father?" Ish replied.

"*Who* is your father? The Chef?"

"Aren't you going to answer that?" asked Fish, never lifting his eyes from the knives.

"Fine!" Tallulah said. She pulled the screaming beetle from her pocket and held it to her head. It was Wallace from Technical Control. It was a good connection.

"You all right?" asked Wallace.

"I think so," said Tallulah. She thought about his erection in the tech room, and she wondered if he was the one who altered her physique.

"Are you ready to disengage?" he asked.

"Hang on."

"Hey – you okay?"

"Yeah, I'm okay."

"For a second there, we thought we almost lost you," he said, relieved.

"The Johnson twins are here."

"What are you talking about?"

"The girls. The Johnson girls," she said. "They're fine. They're unharmed."

"What do you mean, the Johnson girls?"

"I mean, where should I lead them? What should I do with them?"

"They're dead," said Wallace.

"Dead?"

"They've been with Old Medicine for a while. We need to get you out. Now. Let's get you back."

Tallulah stared at the silent pairs of twins. She wanted to ask Ish and Fish about their employers. She wanted to know if they worked for governments and terrorists. She wanted to know where the Misfits really came from. She wanted to know who was responsible for making all this mess. She always thought she was responsible for everything on the Trail of Tears, but for the first time in four years, she knew she was out of her league.

She glanced back at the Johnson twins. They were gone. Only Ish and Fish remained. Ish's book was spread open, its pages sitting upon the wet ground, as he hollowed a piece of bone or cane with his tool.

Tallulah was still thirsty for words, but she was tired of questions. She was, simply, tired.

She pulled the beetle to her mouth. "Do it," she said.

"Hang on."

As Tallulah's vision fades white, she feels it again. Water shpritzing her neck. She turns her head, half expecting to see white rapids dancing from the strange river and spouting outward to splash the bank. Instead she sees a window through a waterfall. She looks down, and the ground beneath her feet appears solid and rocky. Now the ground is jagged and slick, not soft and damp like a riverbank. The sight fades quickly, too fast for Tallulah to determine where she is. But from what she can see, she's inside a cave inside a waterfall.

She turns again to ask the twins one more question, but their outlines merge with the fading brightness. The spray showers her head, then lifts. She tries to speak to the twins, but her voice is empty. The figures and the spray and the waterfall window blend, fade, cease.

The bright light surrounding her vision subsides, dwindling into the residual, as the unmistakable image of a Chairsuit Visor congeals around her eyes.

21

Tallulah's sight is sore. It always takes a second or two for her to readjust her eyes to real light, but this time it feels much longer. The glare is extra intense, lingering on the tips of her eyelashes, like mucus when she has a head cold.

The visor rises. Familiar sounds of gears, chains, pulleys. Cables, jacks, and circuits. Tallulah hears her tourists speaking before she can see them.

"Ramsey?" she asks.

"Hey, T," answers Wallace.

"Wallace, what's up?" She tries to sit. Her spine pings. Her whole body itches. She tugs at the Chairsuit, yanks at the sleeves.

"Easy there," says Wallace. "Easy, easy. Just slow down, and let's get you out of there."

He helps her unzip the Realskyn lining. She wants to interrogate them, but she knows to keep it relatively quiet. There are customers nearby.

"Hey, Tula," shouts Fritz. His voice is distant.

"Where were you guys?" she asks softly.

"Where were *you*?" asks Wallace.

"I asked you first – ouch!"

"Sorry," Wallace mutters.

"Easy on the legs, big guy."

"I said I was sorry."

"Whatever."

"You all right?"

"Never better," she blurts.

"Come on," he says, easing her legs out of the Realskyn suit. "I know you better than that."

"You don't know me at all," she answers. Her tone is cold. The customers stop talking. Something falls.

"You know, Tula," says Wallace, "if you don't mind me saying so, you, um – "

"I what?"

"You look like shit."

"Thanks," she says. "Finally, I strike a balance between how I look and how I feel."

The edges of objects come into focus. She can see everyone's faces. They're all staring at her.

"It's okay," she says. "It's okay. I'm just tired."

"Don't you start your vacation tomorrow?" asks Rachel Rosenberg.

"Yes, I do," answers Tallulah. "So how was the Old Medicine Man?"

The tension lifts, and the tourists have plenty to say. Everyone loves Old Medicine. He told Carmen Davis that she was a warrior, but that she needs discipline. He told Mandy Warren that she should trust her inner self. He told Danny Calhoun that life is a journey with many unexpected turns, and the key to happiness is not avoiding the turns, but rather learning to slow down when you feel them coming on. And he told Spencer Donald that he would fly with the strength of a thousand eagles.

"A thousand eagles?" asks Tallulah.

"That's what he said," Spencer confirms. "He's the man."

"Yeah," says Carmen. "That whole Trail of Tears was totally worth it, just for that."

"A thousand eagles," repeats Tallulah, but this time it's a

statement, not a question. Her jaw protrudes, a contemplative pose.

"I haven't felt this calm all semester," says Mandy.

"Yeah," agrees Danny. "And I haven't even started drinking yet. Speaking of which, we got a date with a tailgate."

"But first we need to stop in the gift shop," declares Carmen.

"Gift shop?" says Danny.

"Dude," says Spencer, "I totally want to hit the gift shop too."

"Oh man," gripes Danny.

"Please," says Mandy, batting her eyes.

"Pretty please," says Carmen.

"Fine," says Danny. "We're pulling out in ten minutes."

Tallulah is disappointed in Carmen. Pretty please? Is this what Old Medicine has done for her, encouraged her to use hackneyed feminine phrases to manipulate young white men? Tallulah stands up. "Thanks guys," she says. "Say hey to your professor for me."

"We will," says Carmen.

"He's boring," states Danny. "But I'll tell him you gave us the royal treatment."

"And we'll be coming back as soon as we can," says Spencer.

"Speak for yourself, roomie," says Danny. "Ten minutes, people, I mean it!"

"I'm so ready for a beer," Mandy giggles.

Tallulah has never seen a football game at Sanford Stadium. Never. You'd think that after living in a college town for nine years, she might have gone to at least one game. But nope. She's listened to several games on the radio, and she's often walked past the stadium in the middle of a game, but she's never actually been inside. Never felt the pull. Basketball, of course, is a different story.

And with that the Athenians are out, gone back to the world they came from, gone back to their idea of normalcy. Fritz gapes at the college girls as they walk away.

Tallulah shakes her head, runs her fingers through her hair. The Rosenbergs approach.

"Irma Rosenberg," says Tallulah, "I will never forget you."

"Oh please," says the old woman. "You probably say that to everybody."

"No," says Tallulah. "Actually, I hardly ever say it. At least not to my customers."

"Grandma's distinctive," confirms Rachel.

"I must be back in the real world," says Irma, "because my sciatica is killing me. That's the best part of your Trail of Tears, honey, what it does to an old body like mine."

Bob exhales loudly through his nose. Almost a grunt. He nods in agreement with his wife.

"I wish we could go again," says Irma. "There's a lot more that I'd like to learn about those people."

Tallulah glances at Fritz and Wallace. She wonders why Ramsey isn't here. He was the one who strapped them in – why the change? It's an unusual time of day for a techie's shift to end. Tallulah wants to talk about the Misfits, but she holds her tongue. She isn't sure which lines not to cross; she isn't even sure which lines have been drawn. Fritz and Wallace go through the motions of folding the Realskyns, wiping down the Visors, resetting and sanitizing the apparatus. But they seem distracted. Tallulah wonders what they know, what they were doing all the while that she was out of contact. She decides to play it safe, to say nothing until prompted.

"Well, that was a trip," says Michael. "Totally different from what I was expecting."

"And he's a computer programmer," says Irma. "So if he likes it, then it's good."

Tallulah examines Bob Rosenberg. He seems healthy.

"How did the Medicine Man treat you folks?" she asks.

They answer. Generic answers. Old Medicine is nothing if not generic. He told Irma she was a matriarch. He told Bob that he was a good man. He told both Rachel and Michael to spread their wings even further, that they could fly even higher than they already do.

"I swear," says Michael. "There's something about that character."

"Something?" asks Tallulah.

"Yeah, he's like," Michael pauses, looks at the elder Rosenbergs, then continues, "he's like, really mellow. I mean, even more mellow than I would have expected an Old Medicine Man to be. You know what I'm saying?"

"Is he high, or what?" asks Rachel.

"He's our Old Medicine Man," answers Tallulah. "He doesn't need drugs." This is one of the few lines that Tallulah did not write. What good is a medicine man without drugs? she thinks. Her nose dries up, then gets suddenly moist. She hopes it doesn't start bleeding in front of the Rosenbergs.

"So," she says, beneath a sniffle, "are you headed back to Atlanta now?"

"My son is making a brisket for dinner," says Irma.

"Beef brisket?" asks Tallulah.

"Of course," answers Irma. "He does a very good job with the brisket these days. He's had a lot of practice, though he'll never be quite the chef that my nephew is, the one who went to culinary school."

"I'm sure," says Tallulah. Her nose flares down.

"Next time you see that Chef in there," Irma continues, "ask him how he makes his trail mixes."

"Okay." Tallulah peers at Fritz and Wallace. They don't seem to react, but she can't read their faces. "Don't forget to stop at the bookstore on your way out," she says.

"You mean the gift shop?" asks Rachel.

"Actually," Tallulah answers, "the bookstore and the gift shop are separate rooms, but they're right next to each other."

"Do they sell any little dolls of the characters in there?" asks Irma. "Or pictures? I'd wouldn't mind a picture of the guy in the Indians Hat."

Fritz and Wallace shoot a quick glance at the Rosenbergs. Tallulah thinks they must be taking notes. She wonders if this entire dialogue is being recorded. Of course it is, she thinks. There are cameras in every room of the compound.

"Good luck," says Tallulah. "We sell out of some things on Saturdays, but if we're temporarily out of something that you want, we can always ship it to you later."

"You're going to ship me a hat?" asks Irma.

"You mean gear?" asks Michael.

"Tell you what," Tallulah says. "If there's something that you want, and we don't have it in the bookstore or the gift shop, you just let me know, and I'll see what I can do."

Tallulah winces inside as soon as this offer leaves her lips. The techies again turn their heads. Wallace coughs deliberately. Tallulah has never before suggested to a customer that she has anything to do with merchandising. She hopes they don't take her up on it. She just wants Irma to stop talking about the Misfits. She is getting desperate to hear what the techies have to say.

"So when do you strapping young professionals return to London?" she asks.

"In three days," answers Rachel.

"Must be a long flight," Tallulah says.

"Not as bad as flying to Australia," Michael answers.

"Yeah," says Tallulah. "I can imagine."

She wants to know more about these two people. She imagines, again, what their kids will look like. The longest flight Tallulah's ever been on was two hours. She wonders if she'll ever go to London. Or to Wales. Mount Snowdon. Or Scotland. Ben Nevis. Tallulah knows that all the tallest mountains in Britain are under five thousand feet. If she went there in the summertime, she could climb them without utensils.

"We flew there once," says Irma. "Bob remembers."

Bob nods quickly.

"It was a beautiful wedding," Irma sighs. "But I'm never flying across an ocean again."

"A flight like that must make the Trail of Tears seem pretty easy," says Tallulah. No one answers. "Just kidding," she reminds them. "It's a joke."

Again the techies glance.

"Well, call us if you're ever in London," says Rachel.

"Or New Jersey," says Irma. "Have you ever been to New York?"

"Once," Tallulah answers. "My brother lives in Brooklyn."

"Well, you have to come visit him again," announces Irma. "And when you do, call us, and we'll take you out to dinner."

"We have some very good restaurants up by us," says Bob.

Tallulah is glad to hear Bob's voice. He sounds strong, sturdy for an old man, quite the contrast to the withering rack of bones she remembers from Fort Dahlonega.

They hug, one after the other. Irma and Rachel give Tallulah their contact information. Though Tallulah doesn't get a single tip from Tour Group 5709, the Rosenbergs' digits feel more significant. Any idiot can give you a bill with Jackson on it. Only a real person would give you their address. Tallulah's throat goes dry. The Rosenbergs wave as they leave the Chamber.

"Enjoy your brisket," Tallulah calls as the steel door closes. She needs water. Lots of water.

"Tallulah Wilson, hugging customers and exchanging addresses?" says Fritz. "Now I've seen everything."

"No, you haven't," she answers.

"You're right," Fritz replies, "Show me some more, would ya?"

"Asshole."

"You started it."

"Fuck you," she snaps. "Where the hell were you the whole time I was in there?"

"Look, Tula – "

"I mean it, I was totally fucked, and I got nothing from you."

"We didn't – "

"Nothing!!!"

"Look," says Wallace, calm but stern. "We need to talk."

"Yes," she huffs. "Yes, we do."

"No, I mean, there's been a problem."

And then it strikes her. Nell Johnson and her daughters never said goodbye. Their Chairsuits have been emptied. They must have cleared the Johnsons from the room before they unzipped the rest of the customers. They'd only do that if something went wrong.

22

Tallulah sits in Boss Johnson's office. She waits, and she stares into the television on the wall. The boss is outside, speaking with Homeland Security in the corridor. She can hear their conversation through the crack beneath the door. The Boss already explained as much as he can to Tallulah. The Johnson twins are fine, but their mother, Nell, is holed-up.

"These things are only temporary," he told her, before he left to bring in Homeland Security. "She'll snap out of it any minute now."

"What if she doesn't?" asked Tallulah.

"She will," he said, and asked her if she wanted coffee. She did.

The Boss has always had a television in his office. The Atlanta Braves are playing. It's September, so there must be a playoff situation in the mix, but Tallulah has no idea how good or bad the Braves are this year.

She hasn't followed baseball since she went to college. But she knows where all the top high school basketball recruits are playing college ball this year. She even knows what date the ACC tickets will go on sale. The rest of the country can have its pastime, she thinks. She imagines the hoop near her house. She pictures her favorite courts on the Outer Banks. She'll need to be active to kick the nicotine, that much is certain.

The door opens. Tallulah can hear the reporters and their machinery in the hallway.

Boss Johnson holds the door for two Homeland Security agents, one male and one female. The man is black, and the woman is white, though she might be Latina of some variety. They each have a coffee in their hands. Johnson extends a coffee cup toward Tallulah.

"Black no sugar for the Princess," he says.

"Eh!" snaps Tallulah. "You may be in charge here, but you know that *Princess* is off limits."

"Sorry," Johnson grins. "Couldn't resist."

"Of course not," she says. "Didn't I tell you that I'm quitting?"

"You've said that before," he replies. "I'll believe it when I see it."

"Look and see," she says, but he seems to brush off the comment. It's true. She's threatened to quit before. In fact, the first time she threatened to quit was after her second full day of tourists. But she knew back then that she wasn't really going to quit. It was a well-paying job, and she had only just begun.

This time, she thinks, it's different. This time, it's this time.

The agents wear solid black suits. They sip their coffee and seem unamused by the banter between the manager and his star employee.

"Miss Wilson," says the male agent.

"Yes," she replies. She straightens her back.

"We need you to give us a statement."

"I'm ready," she says. "Let's do it now, while it's all fresh in my head."

The agents glance at each other. Boss Johnson rests his hands above his hips and gazes at the screen. "Top of the eighth, two outs," he says. "Now would be a good time for a strikeout."

The agents turn their attention to the baseball game.

Pop-up to center field. Inning over.

"This has all the markings of an inside job," says the male agent.

"Inside?" asks Tallulah.

"Based on our initial findings, we think that someone who works here was involved," says the female.

"How'd you find your initial findings?" she asks.

"We're not at liberty to say," says the male.

"We hope your statement will help us narrow the search," says the female.

"I don't understand what they would want to do with us," Tallulah says. The agents acknowledge her question, but they don't offer an answer. Everyone watches a phone company commercial. "I mean," Tallulah continues, "what do you get out of sabotaging the Trail of Tears?"

"They might pose as customers," answers Boss Johnson.

"Or as employees," says the male agent.

Tallulah wonders whom they've questioned thus far. They must have questioned Bushyhead. Ramsey. Maybe Fritz and Wallace too. Maybe the kitchen staff. The poor kitchen staff. And what about the workers in the gift shop? Or the bookstore? The theater? The nature trail?

"Have you ever suspected any of your coworkers?" asks the female.

"I suspect all of them," Tallulah answers. "Especially the new ones."

They take their eyes off the television.

"What? Don't believe me?"

"We take all of your input very seriously, Miss Wilson."

"Well, it's true. I don't trust any of them. Okay, I trust the kitchen workers. And some of the older crew, Bushyhead and Lucy." Tallulah nibbles her cuticles.

The baseball game returns. Bottom of the eighth. Home

game at Turner Field. Johnson says they'll be closing the TREPP tomorrow. They've got no choice. Two comas, two days in a row. It's clearly intentional, he claims. The Braves are down by two. Runner on first, no outs. Tallulah wonders if she'll still have to use a vacation day, since everyone's getting the day off tomorrow anyway. Johnson says she doesn't, but she can't extend her vacation any longer than it already is. The audience begins to Tomahawk Chop.

"I haven't paid attention to the Braves since John Smoltz retired," she says.

"Were you even born yet John Smoltz retired?" asks the agent.

Tallulah smiles and leans forward in her chair. "I guess it's good a thing we're closing tomorrow."

"I tell you what though," says Johnson. "Remember that time, a couple years ago, when that woman got scalped by the Free Fall at Six Flags?"

"Sure," Tallulah says, remembering the rumors at school. "Her hair got stuck in the ride and ripped her scalp off."

Tallulah has been to Six Flags over Georgia on three occasions. She remembers people lining up for the Free Fall like money was going to fall freely from the apparatus. She rode the Free Fall with three other kids. They all placed pennies on their knees as the ominous metal chamber climbed the vertical tracks. When the ride plunged down, the kids screamed, and the pennies hovered above their knees like little UFOs. It was over before she knew what was happening. She lost her penny in the process, but the other kids managed to keep theirs.

"Remember, they shut down that ride for a couple days after the scalping," says Johnson. "But the rest of the park stayed open. And it didn't stop people from riding the Free Fall after it reopened. In fact, demand for the Free Fall actually increased while it was closed."

"What are you saying, Boss?" Tallulah pries. "Holing-up is good for business?"

"Hey, watch it," Johnson responds. "These guys'll lock you up for saying stuff like that."

Tallulah looks at the agents. The male agent shrugs. The female shuffles some files and pulls a small electronic device from her bag.

"Okay then, Miss Wilson. We need you to provide a detailed statement of everything you remember concerning Nell Johnson, her children, and Tour Group 5709."

"I'll never be able to understand what Nell Johnson has to do with anyone's political agenda," says Tallulah. "I mean, she's a middle school teacher, for God's sake."

Tallulah wonders how much she should mention Irma Rosenberg. The irony is caustic. Tallulah was so concerned about Irma, about the Misfits, about the health of the Johnson twins, about Spencer self-destructing. She could never have foreseen that Nell Johnson, who was shot in the back as she ran toward a patch of fruit trees, would be the one who got it. It was an easy out. Tallulah could omit as much as humanly possibly about the Misfits. Well, she would need to mention something.

All of her communications through the water beetle are recorded on the central computer. Irma Rosenberg's disappearance is well-documented. Tallulah doesn't think she said anything about the Chef through the beetle. Bloop single over the second baseman! Runner scores from third; audience wildly tomahawk chops. Runners on first and second.

"That was a lucky break," says Boss Johnson.

"I have to confess," whispers the woman. "I'm a Marlins fan."

"Look at how the tomahawk underlines the word 'Braves' on their uniforms," says Tallulah. Then a groundout, double play.

“Shit!” yells the Boss. Two outs, bases empty. Pitching coach visits the mound.

“Wouldn’t it make more sense for terrorists to attack Six Flags than us?” asks Tallulah.

“That’s true,” answers Johnson. “They could slip a bioweapon into the water supply.”

“They might try to do that here,” says the female agent.

“These people have connections throughout the world,” adds the male, “There’s no way of knowing who they are until we’ve questioned the entire staff, and even then we may not know for sure.”

“Well, at least it’s not all in my head,” Tallulah says. “I was starting to think that it was me.”

Everyone eyes her.

“I mean, not that *it was me*. I mean, I’ve known for a while that something’s been off. I’m just glad it’s not my imagination.”

“When was the last time you saw a doctor regarding your anxiety issues?” asks the female.

“A month ago,” she answers. “I got tired of sleeping pills.” It was a lie. She likes sleeping pills, though she stopped taking them because they always made her mouth extremely dry in the morning.

Tallulah wonders if the agents know about the Chef. Why wouldn’t they? Does Tallulah have a reason to believe that Homeland Security didn’t write his program? The possibilities flood her imagination. She can’t hold off the conspiracy theories much longer. She sips her coffee. She resents the massive grey area that accompanies any conspiracy theory. Tallulah does not like conspiracy theories, especially her own. She thinks they frighten the masses into believing their fates are the property of an invisible ruling class. And while that may be true, she thinks that overtheorizing the conspiracies will frighten the masses into believing that their own two hands are useless. In spite of herself, Tallulah still wants to believe that your own two hands are the strongest things in any world.

"I want to know what the other tour guides said," Tallulah says.

"Maybe when this blows over," answers the male agent.

"Not yet, though?" Tallulah asks.

"Too many unknowns right now," replies the female.

"Of course."

Strikeout. Inning over.

"Could've seen that coming," Tallulah says.

"It ain't over yet," answers the Boss.

"Miss Wilson." The female agent stands and plugs something into the wall. "We'll make this as quick and painless as possible."

A Western Union ad leads to a Jeep commercial, which leads to a preview of an old colorized movie to be shown after the game. The male agent stands to leave. He signals Boss Johnson to come with him. He asks the Boss to turn off his television, to keep the recording clean.

The female agent places the digital recording device in the middle of the desk. She pushes buttons. A digital LED lights up—four digital zeros. The numbers begin to count—0001, 0002, 0003.

"Whenever you're ready, please give us your statement," says the agent. "Why don't you start at the beginning."

23

Tallulah's head pounds as the door to Boss Johnson's office closes behind her. She expects to see the Boss and the male agent talking about her in the corridor, but neither is in sight. Her head throbs. Her hair feels heavy. It was the beginning of the end.

She squeezes her nose and stares at the ground. Walking slowly, she moves along the periphery of the Great Hall. She remembers her brother, sticking his head inside their freezer when he was struck with a migraine.

She thinks she said too much to the Homeland Security recording device. The woman told her to start from the beginning. She was just following orders – she started from the very beginning, from the time she met the big red Jeep Cherokee in her grandfather's basement. At one point, when Tallulah was reflecting on the crisis of being an allergy-prone indigenous Southerner at a high school with an Indian mascot in suburban Atlanta, the Homeland Security agent asked her to only state the most relevant information. "I need to interview a lot of people," she told Tallulah. "Let's try to stay focused on what happened here, today."

Tallulah told about the First Cabin, about the customers insisting that she lead the way, even though it went against protocol. Tallulah told about Irma's disappearance. About the quick and traumatic deaths of half of her tourists. About the particularly gruesome beating The Drawl gave Mandy. About the Misfit ambush at Amicalola Falls. About Spencer and the blowgun. About the traveling static between tour groups. The agent asked Tallulah to describe the static sensation in greater detail, and Tallulah obliged. Tallulah never mentioned Fish, or Ish, or the Chef, but she spoke at length about the elders.

"He had a Cleveland Indians hat on?" asked the agent.

"Strange, but true," said Tallulah.

"Have you ever seen anything like that before?"

"I was trying to tell you about my high school mascot," Tallulah said.

"On the Trail, I mean. Have you ever seen anything like that inside of this game?"

"Not me personally," Tallulah answered. "But that doesn't mean that some of my colleagues haven't seen them. I don't know. I'd like to find out."

"I see," said the agent.

"And if I learn that one of these new people, one of these recent hires, knew about these old guys and the static and all, and they never told me about it, I'm gonna be pissed."

"I see," said the agent. "Tell me more about these characters."

Tallulah described the fact that they had a historical sense, that they were versed in twentieth-century history and literature, that they wore a wide range of clothing, that they thought Irma Rosenberg was a prophetic omen, that their blood sugar was frequently low.

"Did they eat?" asked the agent.

"All the time," Tallulah answered, quickly noting, "They seemed to be traumatized by some people they kept referring to as the Suits."

"I see."

The agent wrote something on a tablet. Tallulah continued,

quickly brushing past the food question. She told about the rivers, about the wave that swallowed them alive. About the cave, the bear, the vision of her father. About her recurring dreams all summer.

"Let's try to stick with today's events," insisted the agent.

"That's the problem," Tallulah replied. "It's all so connected to my entire summer, my entire life. I feel that I simply imagined the whole thing."

"Nell Johnson doesn't seem to think so," said the agent.

"Is she up yet?" Tallulah blurted.

"Not yet."

Tallulah wondered how the agent could know Nell's comatose thoughts, but she didn't push the issue. Sweat was breaking on her chest and cheeks, on her forehead and neck. The longer she avoided speaking about the Chef, the more nervous she became. If she wasn't leading a group of tourists through the Trail of Tears, Tallulah was a terrible liar.

"I don't know what's wrong with me," she told the agent. "I'm not feeling well."

"I see," said the agent. "I think we've got most of what we need here."

"I feel so bad about Nell Johnson."

"We think she'll be okay," said the agent. "The medics say she's stable. They're expecting her to wake up soon."

"I feel terrible for her kids," said Tallulah.

The agent stopped the machine. She thanked Tallulah for all the details. The agent acknowledged that she too had attended a high school with an Indian mascot. "It's just awful," she told Tallulah. "It's so offensive, what we've done to your people."

Tallulah agreed and wiped the sweat from her face.

"I need to lie down," she said. "I need to go lie down."

"Do you need some water?" asked the agent.

“I’m okay,” Tallulah said. “I just need to lie down.”

She didn’t really need to lie down. She just needed to leave.

Nauseous, she walks through the TREPP. Sweat seeps into her long hair as she circles the periphery of the TREPP’s Great Hall. She thinks of her brother, of his head in the freezer. Sometimes, when he was too busy to spend an hour standing with his head in the freezer, he would use rubber bands and bungee cords to strap bags of frozen vegetables to his head. He looked so ridiculous with frozen corn and peas tied around his eyes and temples. Tallulah would laugh and laugh. She would call him “freezer boy” and “veggie head,” and she would tell his friends fantastic stories about how Alan’s head would sprout into a broccoli flowerette if he didn’t keep cool.

Then – it strikes her. She knows what she needs to do. She shifts directions and picks up the pace, heading toward the kitchen.

She passes the entrance to the Staffroom. She stops, listens. Conversations ripple through the thick door. It sounds like there are five or six people inside. Tallulah waits to hear Bushyhead’s voice among the crowd. Gravity pulls angrily upon the ends of her long, straight hair. It was much safer closer to her skin; the split ends were quickly becoming dangerous. She wants to kill the pain, and she knows there’s a large jar of Tylenol inside the Staffroom. But she does not hear Bushyhead, and she assumes he’s somewhere else.

As she walks away from the Staffroom door, Tallulah passes a new tour guide, a pale girl with red hair. The girl eyes Tallulah curiously as they pass each other. Tallulah has no clue about her name. They have better drugs in the tech room, she thinks.

She wonders if the Misfits aren’t working in conjunction with the School of the Americas in southwest Georgia – in

Columbus, Georgia, of all places. It's the infamous training ground of American terrorists who descend into South America and occupy the governments of poor, agrarian countries. It's a stretch, sure, but the Misfits are already quite a stretch. Why not stretch further? Maybe the TREPP has some kind of deal with the SOA. Tallulah recalls Irma's vague details about the Suits. Maybe they're students at the SOA. Maybe they practice genocidal invasions in virtual reality before giving it a go in three dimensions.

Her stomach rumbles. Something drips from her sinuses to the back of her throat. She chides herself for defaulting to conspiracy theories again.

She considers the Army of God. Eric Rudolph and his descendants, the white-bred terrorists who still bomb gay bars and abortion clinics on occasion. It was entirely possible, she thinks, for them to justify bombing something with an indigenous theme. But this was no bomb. It was a highly concentrated recalibration agent. Tallulah muses that the system was invaded by a new program, by some kind of virus. Is the Army of God actually smart enough to design programs that could sabotage the TREPP's system and remain undetectable? Maybe they were more educated than she assumed.

She walks past the door to the tech room. Muffled music drones beneath the door. It sounds industrial. Another headache waiting to happen, she thinks. Sure, they've got better drugs than the tour guides, but Tallulah is no longer interested. She stays focused on the kitchen.

She walks past the entrance of the Turtleback Café. A large family is debating whether to eat at the Café or the Grill. Do they suspect the single-kitchen reality, she wonders, or do they genuinely believe that the food is different? She walks until she reaches the entrance of the Soaring Eagle Grill. Tallulah glances at the smiling hostess, but she does not stop. She walks past the tables, past the bar, and straight through the swinging double doors of the kitchen.

Warm smells fill her nostrils. Garlic and herbs. Roasted chicken and corn soup. The odors waft, sweet and strong, caressing Tallulah's head with steam.

"Hey, chica," says Juan. Though technically a prep cook, Juan stands behind the grill, searing black diamonds into a group of chicken breasts. The breasts could be for chicken sandwiches at the Turtleback or chicken salads at the Soaring Eagle. Tallulah cannot tell.

"You look like shit," says Juan. "What happened?"

"Thanks," she says. "I feel like shit too."

"You hungry?"

"No."

"You want the Chef?" asks Juan, "He's outside talking to clientes."

"No. I've got a migraine," she says.

"You need some painkillers?" he asks.

"I want your cooler," she answers.

"For beer?"

"No," she says. "I mean to walk in."

"Eh?"

"I need to go sit down in your walk-in refrigerator."

"You need some vegetables?" he asks.

"I need to cool my head down," she answers. "I can't think of a better place than the walk-in fridge."

"Oh," he says, flipping the chicken, crossing his diamonds. "Whatever you want, chica."

"Thanks," she says, leading into another question: "You know what else I want?"

"No," he says, sounding a little worried. Like everyone, he's not sure which rumors about Tallulah are actually true. "What is it?"

"A pair of scissors."

"Oh." He tenses up. "What you want scissors for?"

"You'll see," she answers.

"You're not gonna mutilate yourself or nothing, okay?"

"No," she says. "Of course not."

"Okay," says Juan. "Right in front of you."

He points to a knife rack that is drilled into the wall between prep tables. Tallulah pulls a pair of kitchen scissors with greasy handles from the rack.

"Thanks, hombre," she says and moves toward the walk-in.

The entire kitchen staff greets her as she walks toward the walk-in refrigerator. The men attempt to hug Tallulah, but she brushes them off, saying, "Don't touch me, I've got a migraine." She tells them not to take it personally, but they do.

She pulls on the thick latch, opens the walk-in door. Cool breezes rush out of the walk-in; a cool mist sifts through the pores of her face.

The door closes behind her. She is always impressed by the size of the TREPP's refrigerator. Compared to the one at the Mediterranean Café, it's a giant.

Towers of five-gallon plastic containers stand between racks of fish and chicken. Cardboard cases of meats and vegetables line the steel shelves. Short stacks of transparent two-quart containers filled with precooked noodles and rice sit next to the meats. A half-empty milk crate lies lopsided near the shelves. Tallulah empties the crate and flips it upside down. It is the perfect seat.

Sweat begins to freeze upon the tips of her split ends. The only remotely safe place on Tallulah's head was right up near the scalp, but even then, the rapture seemed near.

Tallulah holds the scissors in her right hand. She rubs her forehead with her left. Layers of sweat merge, retreating and congealing as they freeze. She fumbles in her pocket for her cell phone. Dialing Bushyhead's number, she wonders if it wasn't her fault all along. Maybe the system is simply reacting to her own neurosis. Maybe she has brought everything upon herself, as well as others. Maybe these tourists are holing-up because she didn't know when to quit.

Naturally, Bushyhead's phone isn't working. Or maybe her signal is weak inside the refrigerator.

Juan walks into the walk-in with an empty pickle tray. "Pardon me," he says, reaching around Tallulah's legs for the large tub of pickles. "You sure you're okay?" he asks, filling the tray with pickles and juice.

"I'm sure," she answers.

"You sure?"

"Never been more sure since I started working here," she says.

Juan opens the door by leaning into it with his lower back. "Can't I get you something else?" he asks. "Something to drink?"

"Actually," she says, looking up, left hand still gripping her forehead, "I could use a small trash bag."

Juan nods. He leaves, pickle tray tucked into his chest, and returns seconds later with a small black trash bag.

"You crying?" he asks.

"Don't advertise it!" she blurts.

"Sorry." He looks down. "I'll leave you alone, okay?"

She nods. He leaves. Tiny tears fall coldly from Tallulah's eyes as she lifts the scissors to her head. Is she really crying twice in one day? Better yet, does a bawling session inside the ride actually count, or is this her first real cry on the job?

Tallulah's mother cried when Tallulah chopped her hair at age fourteen. And Tallulah didn't simply chop it – she shaved it all off. Tallulah was fourteen and angry, and she shaved her head so close that everyone saw the ugly bumps and knobs that mined her cranial flesh. Alan had left the house, and Tallulah was learning to hate high school. She was trying to ward off conversations by scaring the other kids with her shaved head. Janet Wilson screamed when fourteen-year-old Tallulah walked in the house with that ugly shaved head. She remembers telling her mother to grow up.

Salty fingers push the tears back into Tallulah's ducts. The milk crate grates into her butt. She remembers the days of sitting on milk crates for cigarette breaks in the alley behind the Mediterranean Café. She gazes at the grimy floor of the walk-in. A few large tears hit the floor, quickly absorbed by the blend of grains and dirt that cakes the cracks in the ground.

Rubbing her eyes with her forearm, she takes three deep breaths and grabs a bundle of hair with her left hand. It sounds like a wet paper bag being ripped open. She slices again. And again, and again. A mirror might have been useful. Watching her hair fall to the ground, she wonders how far down one could follow these cracks in the floor, how many insects spend their entire lives down there. She watches the cracks as she continues to chop away.

Clump by clump, she slices off her hair until her head is topped with a short, uneven mop. It's terrifying – but she doesn't reach the scalp. Yet. She drops the scissors on the floor. Hair everywhere. Jet black upon the grimy ground.

She touches her head. Her hands have never seemed so large or so ominous. She runs her fingers through her hair, short and thick and soft. The throbbing calms, but her fingernails haven't been trimmed in ages. Her heartbeat slows. She leans against the steel shelves and lets the cool air reach those spaces between hair follicles that have been guarded for years.

The door flings open. Juan's eyes are wide.

"Holy shit!" he exclaims.

"What did you expect I was going to do with your scissors?" she asks, without returning his gaze.

"Chica," he says, "I would've never showed you those scissors if I expected this!"

"They were right in front of me," she answers. "I would have found them eventually."

"Still!" he counters.

A wrinkled smile breaks through Tallulah's young, tired face. "It looks good, right?"

"It looks horrible!" he replies.

"Good," she says. "It had to be done."

"Why?"

"It just had to go," she says.

Juan shakes his head. Though he seems disappointed with Tallulah's new look, he can't contain his smile. She knows the guys in the kitchen appreciate her attitude. Who else would give herself a haircut in the walk-in?

"Well," he says, "you better not get your hair all over that pasta."

"Or the stuffed sole on your oven rack over here," she says.

Juan jolts away, quickly returning with a broom and dustpan. Together, they sweep the fallen strands of Tallulah's hair into the dustpan.

"You should sell this for a wig," he says.

"No way," she replies.

"Really," he insists. "You can make some good cash selling hair for wigs. My cousin does it every year."

"I don't think so," she says.

"But your hair, it's so beautiful." Juan stops talking. He fears he has crossed a line.

Tallulah looks him in the eyes. "You're sweet," she says. "But I need to burn this."

"Okay," he says. "It's your head."

Juan holds open the small trash bag as Tallulah fills it up with hair. She ties the garbage bag three times and clutches it in her left hand. Juan returns to work, taking the dustpan with him, and Tallulah sits alone for a few minutes, staring at the cracks in the floor as she runs her hands through her short, uneven hair. When she stands, she instinctively flings her hand across her missing bangs. She laughs, remembering how long it took her hair to grow back during high school. She used to wear bandannas to school every day, and at the beginning of each and every class, the teachers told her to take the rag off her head. She complied, but the rag went back on as soon as each class ended. She would have to learn new instincts to accommodate her newly cropped head. She shifts her weight and tries a different posture. It's awkward. Everything's awkward. "Well," she says to herself, to all the organisms in the walk-in that might hear, "so it goes."

Her vest pocket is just large enough to fit the hairy garbage bag. She gazes once more upon the walk-in floor, wonders how many layers of sauce and cornmeal and fish skin and plastic wrap and flour and spaghetti and seeds and hair and everything else have fused together over the years to create this grimy compound beneath her feet. She thinks about all the striations in the earth's crust. This walk-in refrigerator is only four years old, but the grime is thick. It seems much older than it should. Tallulah wonders what it would say if it could speak. What does it remember? What does it want to forget?

She turns, leans her lower back into the handle, and opens

the door. She walks out of the cold, into the kitchen. The steel prep tables are partially reflective, but not clear enough for her to see herself. She needs to visit the Staffroom before she leaves; there's no way around it.

Juan has his head buried in a pile of potatoes as she walks toward him. Surprising herself, she plants a quick kiss on his cheek. He drops his peeler on the floor.

"Hey, you got your bag of hair?" he says, cheeks red.

"I do," she says. "Thank you."

He starts to say something else but stops. He sniffs and stoops down to retrieve the peeler.

The kitchen doors swing wide open as Tallulah walks through. Lights pulse and prod inside the Great Hall. Fluorescents on the ceiling, cameras on the ground. Tallulah walks out.

24

Tallulah's head doesn't hang so heavy anymore. Nothing pulls on her scalp. Nothing dangles in her eyes. Nothing sways pendulum-like in the wake she leaves walking through the Great Hall. Nothing brushes softly on the nape of her neck. Nothing. Her scalp is essentially exposed – a rather troublesome situation for everything that once depended on her hair.

Walking the periphery of the Great Hall, she feels less of the gaze. But she still wears her vest, which keeps her visible. She sees her image everywhere. The pictures of Tallulah Wilson in TREPP promotional literature accentuate her hair. Indian hair. The most Indian of her features. But while Tallulah could never hide her cheekbones, her braids are now invisible. Gone. The air upon her neck is brisk. She avoids making eye contact with anyone. She tries to block out the sounds, but a few of the voices are irrepressible. At least Boss Johnson is nowhere to be heard.

Turning a corner, en route to the Staffroom door, Tallulah glances at a mirror on the ceiling. She is completely herself, yet she looks completely different than she did this morning. No braids. She seems younger and older at the same time. She is definitely not nineteen anymore. The mirror ends. She places her hand upon the door.

It's loud in there. Still no sound of Bushyhead. She checks her phone, and she's got reception, but no messages. She dials. He answers.

"Where *are* you?" says Bushyhead.

"Where are *you*?" she responds.

"I'm still at work."

"Me too," she says. "Where at work are you?"

"Tech room," he says. She can't hear any industrial music in the background.

"You are?" she asks. "I just walked past there. It was really loud."

"What?"

"It sounded loud in there when I walked past. I have a headache."

"I got them to turn down the sound before I called. You all right?"

"Are you coming?" she asks.

"Am I?" he responds.

"I'm asking you," she says.

"Tonight?" he asks. "Are we going?"

"I am."

"You are," he says.

"Yes."

"Can I still come?" he asks.

"I'd like it if you did," she says.

"Would you?"

"You want me to change my mind?" she asks.

"No."

"You want to go?" she asks.

"Yeah, let's go tonight."

"Okay."

"Okay."

"Okay then," she confirms.

"Where *are* you?" he asks.

"About to clear out my locker," she answers.

"Clear out?"

"Meet me in the G-Hall in five minutes?" she says.

"Got it," he says, ending the conversation.

Tallulah pushes on the door and walks in. She offers a decorous smile to the people conversing at the table. She nods at the new ones on the couch. She counts eight or nine of them. She only knows the names of two.

Lowering her head, she doesn't lock eyes with any of them. The room quiets. She walks toward the lockers.

"Sorry to interrupt," she says over her shoulder, dialing the combination on her locker door.

She feels their eyes upon her. She opens the locker and removes the water beetle from her pocket. She places her employee badge next to the beetle in her locker. She opens her backpack, loads it with everything except the beetle and the badge. Her backpack contains multitudes. She unzips the vest, takes it off, and stuffs it into the backpack. It's coming with me, she thinks. I've earned it.

"Like I was saying, this totally feels like terrorism," says one of the new girls. She sits on the couch and appears to stroke her hair.

"Get real," says Dugan. "What kind of a terrorist gives a shit about a place like this?"

"But that's what I'm saying," says the new girl. "They totally go after service-industry destinations."

"That's true," affirms someone else.

Tallulah shuts her locker door. The conversation momentarily halts. Tallulah's latch seems to echo. People stare.

"Don't I know you?" asks Dugan, straining to see the color of her irises. She locks into his eyes, momentarily, then turns away.

"Would it really matter to you if anyone tried to blow this place up or not?" she asks.

“What do you mean?” says another new girl.

“Nobody better blow it up while I’m working,” answers a boy from the couch.

“I mean,” says Tallulah, but her commentary trails off. She straightens her lower back, remembering that her postures are affected differently by short hair.

“I’ll kick anybody’s ass who tries to use terrorism on me and

mine,” says another boy on the couch.

“Oh, shut up,” says Dugan. “You’ve probably never seen a terrorist in your life.”

“That’s great,” says Tallulah. “That’s just great that you can work in this place and talk about terrorists like they don’t exist.”

“What *is* a terrorist, in the first place?” asks Dugan.

“Do you know me?” asks Tallulah.

“Why? Are you a terrorist?” says a boy on the couch.

“Do I look like a terrorist?” she replies.

“You might.”

“And this place might blow up tonight,” she says. “But would it matter to you? Would it even make any difference?”

“Damn right it would.”

“Why?” she asks.

“Are you Tallulah Wilson?” asks another young woman at the table.

“Do you think this building is going to be here forever?”

“Tallulah?” says Dugan, “Oh man, you cut your hair!”

She does not answer. The couch people nudge each other and share loud whispers.

“Innocents would die,” says one of the many she doesn’t recognize.

“Exactly,” she says. “So who’s innocent? You? Are you innocent?” No one answers. “Do you think I’m innocent? I don’t.”

"They said you had a tourist hole-up," says Dugan.

"I did," she says. "It's not half as fun as you might imagine."

Tallulah walks toward the sink. Behind the sink is a mirror. Her hair is a bit jagged and uneven. It looks like a manic assembly of black Post-it notes. She looks tougher. She could wear her old leather jacket, but it might get too wet on the Outer Banks.

"They'll say an Indian can't be an Indian without long hair," she says. "But that's ridiculous. Old-time Cherokee warriors would shave their heads. It gets hot in the South, you know?"

Holy dead skin cells, cut to shambles. Holy dead skin cells, undone and undead. Holy dead skin cells, filled with too many traces of Tallulah's own chemical whims, waiting to burn on the beach some night next week. She arches her back. She feels them examining her curves. Short hair leaves everything more exposed.

She can hear someone asking a question, but her head clouds up with memories. Her brother, when he was fifteen and drunk and rampaging through puberty: "The longer the hair," he said, "the higher they'll string your head up on a stick when they chop it off and carry it around town."

"What do you mean, us?" asks the girl on the couch.

Tallulah looks up. They don't want to stare, but they can't seem to help it. She isn't sure what she said, or if she said anything at all, but she doesn't want to ask them. She shrugs her shoulders, hoists her backpack over her shoulders, and walks to the door.

"Enjoy your vacation," says Dugan.

"Thanks," she says. "You too."

The Great Hall hurts her eyes. A journalist snaps her picture, asks questions that trail into white noise as she cuts past. Rock music emanates from one speaker. Promotions emanate from another. Audio everywhere. Public service announcements.

Updated parking information. Winning raffle numbers. A blonde woman eating a salad in the Turtleback Café jumps out of her chair. Her ticket is the winner. She just won a five-dollar voucher, good toward anything for sale inside the facility.

Tallulah stands on tiptoes, searching for Bushyhead within the mass. Maybe it's only been four minutes. Maybe he's gathering opiates from the tech room. She runs her eyes along the bodies between herself and the main entrance. So much buying and selling. So much diversity. The tourists, the customer service specialists, the retail salespeople, the tour guides, the journalists, the cops, the Homeland Security, the prep cooks, the booksellers, the janitors – the building itself looks like a diversity postcard, a commercial for ethnic and occupational difference. Breezes stir when other bodies pass Tallulah's, and the cool air tickles her scalp. Small beads of sweat continue to gel in the roots of her short hair, but with all the continual motion, the sweat dries before it has a chance to drop.

Tallulah sees familiar faces within the multitudes, the unmistakable faces of techies and prep cooks, of tour guides sipping iced tea at the Turtleback. She wants to forget. She questions her own depth. She knows that humans can block almost anything out of their consciousness if they try. She feels the love well up warm in her gut, but she feels the cold walls building in her mind. *How long,* she wonders, *how long until I forget their names on purpose?*

She glances at the larger-than-life-sized statue of Sequoyah, the one that guards the entrance of the bookstore and gift shop. As is his custom, Sequoyah holds the Cherokee syllabary in his left arm while welcoming the horizon with his right. The turban on his head and the pipe in his mouth never move. Sequoyah and his distinctive features stand still, unchanging and unchangeable, a rock to guard the hordes of flammable books inside the store.

For four years Tallulah has urged them to build a complimentary statue of Sequoyah's daughter. She was no less essential than her father. She remembered! It was her memory that gave the Council the proof it needed. It was her ability to remember that vindicated her father's twelve-year obsession with the talking leaves. Sequoyah was famous, the first Cherokee celebrity. Rightfully so, Tallulah is quick to say, but his daughter deserves a statue of her own as well.

"You look different," says Bushyhead.

Tallulah turns about-face. There he stands, unobtrusive. He has a glimmer in his eye.

"Good," she says.

"Yours is almost as short as mine now," he says.

"Oh please," she retorts. "Yours is the shortest I've ever seen."

"You lie," he says.

"Do I?" she answers.

"I don't know," he replies. "I guess only you know for sure."

"Thanks for telling me about the Misfits," she snaps.

"The who?"

Tallulah changes the subject, for now. She asks, "You're coming, right?"

"Sure," he says.

"So, we're really doing this, right?" she asks again.

He leans into her and kisses her clumsily. Tallulah balks at first, but then she drops her plastic hairbag and grabs John Bushyhead by the cheeks. She tastes him one more time. Cameras and recording devices are everywhere. Someone is taking this kiss home in a digital camera. Someone else will watch this kiss on a security video. It will inevitably grace the Internet sometime tonight. He runs his fingers through her short hair. The kiss lasts longer than he expected.

“You should dye it blue,” he says.

“Been there, done that.”

“Want me to trim it up for you?” he asks.

“Are you crazy? You’re not getting near me with scissors in your hands.”

“I’ll cut it while you sleep,” he says.

“I’ll cut you back,” she says. “You know I will.”

“Fine,” he concedes. “You got me.”

“Are you ready to go?” she asks. “Because I’m done with this place.”

“Done?” he asks.

“Overdone,” she says. “Are you ready or what?”

Bushyhead doesn’t know whether to take her seriously or not. He’s heard her claim to quit the job several times before, and he’s listened each time she reversed her decision later that same day.

“I went home and packed up after my shift,” he says. “So yeah. I’m pretty much ready to go.”

“Follow me to my house?” she asks, “Get my dog, get my stuff, get the fuck out of here.”

“Get the fuck out of here,” he nods. Someone bumps into his shoulder. “That sounds good.”

Hazy afternoon heat breathes heavy through the main entrance when Bushyhead opens the door. Evaporating petroleum dances miragelike in the grey spaces between the parking lot and US-441. Sport-utility vehicles of all makes and models crowd Tsalagi Boulevard. Some of the SUVs belong to employees, some belong to customers, some belong to reporters. The security agent SUVs are easy to detect. Bushyhead’s old station wagon follows Tallulah’s hybrid Honda down 441, single-occupancy vehicle after single-occupancy vehicle.

Joey whimpers as they enter the house. Tallulah scratches

his ears, gives him a treat, fills up his water dish. She opens the door and lets the dog out.

"Wanna smoke?" he asks. He begins to roll himself a cigarette. No filter.

Joey reenters the house, breathing heavily. Tallulah feels the pressure behind her eyes. All the skin upon her head constricts. She tells him that she wants to quit. Then she takes off her shirt.

"I need to have sex," she declares.

"And I'll be happy," says Bushyhead, putting down the tobacco, "to demonstrate that I'm not entirely useless after all."

"I *really* need to have sex," she repeats. She throws herself down upon the puffy couch. The couch springs pop and cackle beneath her weight. She lets her fingers linger on the button of her pants.

Bushyhead cocks his eyebrows and gets down on his knees. He crawls toward the couch. His arms extend; his hands slowly travel the length of her legs, up between her thighs. His fingers tickle the zipper.

"Let me kiss it," he says.

"Okay," she answers.

He unsnaps the button.

"Wait!" she says. "Not yet."

"No?" he asks.

"I need a shower," she says.

"Let me kiss it first."

"Why don't you take a shower with me?" she asks.

Joey jumps on the couch, and Bushyhead tosses his shirt to the floor. In a flash his pants are off. So are hers. They run toward the bathroom. Everything begins rushing toward the inevitable. He tickles her legs when she stops to open the shower curtain.

Tallulah turns on the water. Hot water on her lower back,

climbing up her spine. The pores on her scalp are starting to saturate. But Bushyhead steps in and blocks the water. He rinses off his face and hair. He shakes his back like a dog. Tallulah laughs. Then Bushyhead gets down on his knees again, the hot water raining on his face as he finds her with his tongue. Tickling, spreading, tasting. She giggles, spreads her legs, an awkward yet manageable balance. Then the shivers begin to come. Warm water outside; warm rushes in.

He tries to push her thighs further apart, to better the angle of his tongue. And then – she turns.

She turns her back into the shower, the water pelting her short hair. Her scalp, exposed. Exuberance and warmth, excess and convulsion. She props her left leg upon the soap holder, pushing her scalp directly beneath the pounding stream. He pushes in, nose and tongue, lapping at her button. The water rages.

The pressure is too much. The water pelts down, down toward the drain. It circles, circles, circles again – then down between the holes. Pipes and ducts, pipes and ducts. Rust and gunk. Strange things, mucus-textured but active and alive. Liquid-Plumr can only do so much. A clump of hair stops the mad flow, but only momentarily. And then – blackness. Days and weeks to adjust. Labyrinthine pipes and elbow joints. Where does water end and sewage begin?

Endless water, underground, moving somewhere. Maybe it all flows back to where it began.

Do you know where it comes from? Do you know where it goes?

In the Native Storiers series:

Mending Skins
by Eric Gansworth

Designs of the Night Sky
by Diane Glancy

Riding the Trail of Tears
by Blake M. Hausman

From the Hilltop
by Toni Jensen

Bleed into Me: A Book of Stories
by Stephen Graham Jones

Hiroshima Bugi: Atomu 57
by Gerald Vizenor

Native Storiers: Five Selections
edited and with an introduction by Gerald Vizenor

Elsie's Business
by Frances Washburn

To order or obtain more information on these or other University of Nebraska Press titles, visit www.nebraskapress.unl.edu.

CPSIA information can be obtained at www.ICGtesting.com
Printed in the USA
LVOW07s2043091215

466143LV00001B/117/P